R. D. Shah spent his formative years in the north-west of England before attending Rugby School in Warwickshire. At seventeen, he attained his private pilot's licence in Florida and, shortly after, attended the University of Miami where he studied motion picture and psychology before returning to the UK to work in television and leisure. He has travelled extensively throughout Europe, Russia, and the Americas. R. D. holds a scuba diving licence which he gained along the shores of the Hawaiian island of Kauai. All this experience has prepared him for a career in writing. He lives in Wiltshire with his girlfriend and is currently working on his second book.

Relics

R.D. Shah

Library of Congress Control Number:		2013912144
ISBN:	Hardcover	978-1-4836-6465-1
	Softcover	978-1-4836-6464-4
	Ebook	978-1-4836-6466-8

This book was printed in the United States of America.

Rev. date: 07/18/2013

To order additional copies of this book, contact:
Xlibris Corporation
0-800-056-3182
www.xlibrispublishing.co.uk
Orders@xlibrispublishing.co.uk
307028

Dedication

To Alison for everything

'I love you more than yesterday but less than tomorrow.'

Chapter 1

'And that was Fiona Morris with a round-up of today's headlines here on the BBC World Service. We now return you to our religious correspondent, David Bernstein, for coverage of events live from Rome.'

'Welcome back to the 267th papal inauguration here in Vatican City, hub of the Roman Catholic faith and focus for over one billion of its followers, on this beautiful January afternoon. I'm reporting to you now from the specially constructed BBC pavilion overlooking St Peter's Basilica, giving us a bird's eye view of today's proceedings. And, as you'd expect, the turnout is immense with an estimated twenty thousand people, all crammed into St Peter's Square, waiting to get their first glimpse of the new Pope. For those listeners who have just joined us, let me bring you up to speed. It's been two weeks since the passing of the much beloved Pope Leo XIV, causing wide speculation regarding who will now take up the reins of spiritual power within the Catholic Church. Some have rallied around Cardinal Anitak Onawati of Angola, whose work in Africa has received universal praise from religious and world leaders alike. Another candidate Cardinal Rocca of Germany, described in the media as the "priest's priest", has been commended for his good work in the Middle East. It's, therefore, virtually impossible to predict who will have the number of nominations needed to become Pope, but the cardinals have been in secret enclave behind closed doors for almost forty-eight hours now, deciding who will become the next supreme pontiff. Not an easy job, but about forty-five minutes ago we saw smoke billowing from the famous chimney on top of St Peter's Basilica, as the cardinals' votes were burnt, signalling the end of enclave and the dawn of a new spiritual era. And just a minute ago, we received official word that the decision has indeed been made. And the newly elected Pope is none other than our own British cardinal John Wilcox. What unbelievable news!

'We've had our researchers do a spot of fact checking, and, back in the twelfth century, the first, and the only British pope, was Adrian IV, whose reign lasted just four years, and since then none has followed. Now this, as I'm sure many viewers will already know, was due largely in part to King Henry VIII, who split the Church of England away from mainstream Catholicism, thus causing a spiritual rift between the old and the new ideologies. But it now seems, after eight hundred years, we've finally been forgiven for the disagreements of the past, with today's elevation of Cardinal John Wilcox to the highest position in Christendom, namely pontiff of Rome.

History has been made here today, with the first British Pope in centuries, and this is truly a proud day for . . . Hold on, I'm getting word that the new Pope is about to make his way on to the famous balcony for his first official address. The doors are still closed, but I'm being told he'll appear on the balcony any second now. Whilst we're waiting, I should mention that, because of his liberal thinking, Cardinal Wilcox had been viewed up until now as a long shot. Many churchmen were surprised that he was even promoted to cardinal in the first place, and I'm sure they must be stunned by today's decision.

And back to the action in St Peter's square, and, do you know, I can't see a single Union Jack in sight. It seems the decision has caught British Catholics by surprise, too. No, there we go, a few Union flags are now being raised and . . . I'm getting a message in my earpiece. One of our correspondents on the ground informs me that Cardinal Wilcox has chosen the title of Adrian VII. No doubt a diplomatic choice to appᶜ many within the Church who voiced concerns at an English cardinal becoming Pope, and . . . Yes, yes, here we go. The balcony doors are opening, and . . . There he is, our first glimpse of Pope Adrian VII wearing his white inaugural garments and, of course, the unmistakable papal tiara. I don't know how well you can hear me over the roar of the crowd, but they're going absolutely wild, and I can see flags of every nation flying high and the cheers. Oh my! I don't know how well you can make it out at home, but the noise here is deafening. Unbelievable! I must say, it's hard not to get swept up in the enthusiasm of this event. And I'm not even Catholic!

Pope Adrian VII is waving to the crowd with both hands, and they are just as enthusiastic. It seems the politics of his selection is of little importance to this crowd, for they have a new Pope and that's all that matters. Wonderful! The pontiff is again raising his hands to quieten the people below, but they're having none of it. I could really do with some earplugs. Wait a minute! That's odd. Someone has walked on to the adjacent balcony . . . a man, also wearing a bright white robe. Now he's pulling himself up on to the parapet and is waving frantically to the crowd. It seems we have an overenthusiastic fan. I reckon someone's going to get fired for this lapse in security.

Oh my God, he jumped! No, he's still . . . Oh, this is just horrible. That same man has just hanged himself from the balcony. Everyone's gone silent, and the security men are bundling the Pope back inside St Peter's. Please bear with us as we try to find out exactly what's going on.

Hold on, I'm getting word from our man on the ground. Apparently pieces of metal fell from the man's hands as he jumped. No, wait, I'm being told they're pieces of silver! Ladies and gentlemen, we're now going to hand you back to our London studio whilst we try to make some sense of this tragedy. This is David Bernstein reporting live from Rome.

Jesus Christ! Paul, that's fucking horrib . . . Huh . . . ? Well, then cut to a break. Will someone please cut to a break?'

Chapter 2

'And so it gives me great pleasure to introduce to you the man who made this evening's event possible. His dedication to this area of archaeology is unquestionable, and his knowledge of the subject undeniable.' Archaeology dean, Thomas Lercher, gripped the sides of the lectern firmly as he addressed the rows of Cambridge Alumni sitting attentively before him. The audience consisted of a hand-picked mix of academics and patrons whose pockets were deep enough to make a difference.

The dean took a step backwards, rearranging his arms comfortably behind him.

'Allow me to welcome to the stage an outstanding archaeologist, an even better friend, and, most importantly, a member of the Cambridge Alumni'—he craned his head playfully—'which means we get him on the cheap.'

Laughter rippled through the auditorium, and, satisfied his joke had gone down well, he threw a hand in the air and gestured to his left.

'Ladies and gentlemen, I give you Professor Alex Harker.'

Standing at around five foot ten inches, Alex Harker had the slender build of a sportsman. His thick jet-black hair, peppered with grey, was a testament to his years as at thirty-eight, he was about to cross the line into middle age. Dressed in a black tuxedo with polished brogues, he strode confidently over to the speakers lectern, where the dean greeted him with a smile from ear to ear. He took Lercher's hand and shook it enthusiastically, it was obvious the good dean wanted to milk this moment for all its worth, refusing to loosen his grip until the clapping had completely subsided.

Harker turned back to face the crowd gathered in the auditorium of Trinity College and waited for the applause to fizzle out. 'Distinguished patrons, associates, ladies, and gentlemen,' he started, 'history is a fickle and biased creature. It is written largely by the victorious and then reinterpreted by the generations that follow. As we all know, written history is ambiguous at best, depending on the mindset of the writer at the time and then upon the interpretation we make of it. But I'm willing to wager that, in most cases, it's never very far from the truth. Of course, embellishment is inherent in human nature, and we know of many monarchs, countries, and battles whose history has been . . . 'He looked over the audience with a knowing smile. 'Well, let's say infiltrated by a few white lies. For decades, archaeologists have worked tirelessly to piece together the histories of separate countries and their inhabitants, but in recent years, they have attempted to produce a seamless history of the world at large, and in these efforts, they have done a sterling job. But as archaeology discovers new sites and ever more important evidence, we find ourselves continually rewriting or amending what we already know, and, as we do so, our understanding of the past becomes that much clearer.'

The audience continued to sit patiently, some still as stone, others shuffling in their seats, but it was clear that everyone's attention was firmly focused on the Cambridge professor as he drew them in further.

'This is the reason I got into archaeology: to know that your next dig, the next artefact you pull from the ground, could completely rewrite what we know about our past and, in doing so, change our conception of world history.' Harker paused and smiled at the sea of nodding heads before him. 'And, more importantly for me, if nothing is found, then you good people wouldn't be inclined to fund another dig and I'm out of a job.'

Laughter erupted, and he finally felt at ease. Apart from falling off the stage, what could go wrong now, but then a lone voice resonated from deep inside him: *Don't get cocky. It's not over yet.*

'The truth of our past is something I believe everyone is entitled to share in and to view the objects and texts that make it so. I feel this is a universal birthright, not to be restricted to a select few. So allow me to now introduce you to a remarkable piece of history.'

Raising his arm, Harker gestured to the large oak doors on one side of the auditorium. With a creak, they slowly opened and clicked into place, revealing a large rectangular room beyond. Mahogany-panelled walls rose majestically over the black-granite tiles covering the floor, and, as two burly security guards made sure the doors were in place, halogen lights brightly lit up an array of glass-fronted exhibits lining the perimeter.

Dominating the centre of this room was a large display case illuminated from beneath and already flanked by another couple of guards dressed in navy blue uniforms.

'Ladies and gentlemen, I give you here the largest collection of Dead Sea Scrolls ever to be exhibited in the UK and transported direct from the shrine of the book at the Israel Museum in Jerusalem.'

Within moments, the crowd was being ushered into the exhibition room. Whispers of excitement passed back and forth as Harker made his way down from the podium and joined the end of the queue. He was confident the speech had gone well, and the audience seemed genuinely engaged. Anyway, he was an archaeologist, not an after-dinner speaker, and the scrolls would now speak for themselves.

The tabloids had jumped on the story of the British textual archaeologist who had found a collection of rare scrolls in a cave near Damascus, which chronicled daily life around the time of Christ. They included numerous references to the crucifixion and to Jesus's apostles, which inevitably magnified their significance amongst religious leaders.

The press had labelled Harker as Christ's text keeper, much to his own annoyance, but such exposure had been warmly welcomed by Dean Lercher and his colleagues, even though the majority of his students now referred to him irritatingly as the Text Master.

At the time of this discovery, the Syrian department of antiquities had swooped in on the site and taken the documents off to their own labs for investigation, making it near impossible for Harker to gain access. It had taken over a year to get himself invited to their laboratory, and, after a further six months of testing and restoration, the writings were finally made public and accredited to one Professor Alex Harker.

The writings were not that different in content from the legendary Dead Sea Scrolls, for similar inks and papyrus had been used. The author, presumed to be Jewish, had produced eleven scrolls, written in ancient Hebrew, which described the aspects of daily life in the years immediately before and after the death of Jesus Christ. Harker could still remember the chill of awe that had coursed through his veins on reading those first references to the crucifixion and the beginnings of the Christian religion. These discoveries were hailed by the media as a fantastic insight into the evolution of the Christian faith, but, to Harker, they were primarily another source of knowledge and understanding of what had really happened two thousand years ago. These ancient writings had now given society something factual to depend on in a world rife with religious scepticism. Many of the people who would come flocking to see these texts wanted to find their faith substantiated in writings that had not been diluted and altered over the past two millennia. In an age of science, and freedom of speech, Catholicism had taken a considerable battering. Where faith was once enough, people now demanded fact, and artefacts such as the Damascus texts, as they became known, would give them what they needed—hard evidence.

During one of their first excavations in Jerusalem, the Cambridge team had uncovered a thousand-year-old well. The water itself was long dried up, but the artefacts and clothing surrounding it dated back to around AD 1190. After a year of digging and dusting, they had established conclusively that not only had this well been a major watering hole but it had also been used by Richard the Lion Heart and his invading forces during the Third Crusade. Harker had personally found a huge cache of weapons and four iron breastplates bearing the king's insignia.

He had already begun negotiations with the Israel Antiquities Authority to bring these artefacts back to Great Britain, when a young boy, no older than ten, had walked on to the dig site and asked for the man in charge. When the site manager appeared, the youngster had closed his eyes, murmured a short prayer, and then detonated a half pound of plastic explosive strapped to his chest. The blast was so great the boy's severed head was later found on a rooftop over a hundred metres away.

Harker had been off site at the time, having spent hours in the Foreign Affairs offices, trying to obtain shipping permits from the commissioner who, frustratingly, had been unavailable most of the day. In fact, it was only when Harker returned to the site in the late afternoon that he became aware of the day's terrible events.

Twenty people had received moderate injuries, a further five were in a critical condition, and three people were dead. The tragic loss of life was worsened by the death of his site manager, for Harker's right-hand man and personal friend, Richard Hydes, had been vaporised instantly. The two men met whilst studying archaeology at Cambridge and had become good friends. When Harker secured his grant for the dig, Hydes was the first person he had called upon for the position of site manager. His old friend jumped at the opportunity, and they had immediately flown together to Tel Aviv to begin applying for visas, work permits, excavation permits, and, of course, religious consent.

The whole process had taken six months, during which time Hydes had fallen in love with a beautiful Israeli interpreter called Mia. The pair had been married just months before the bombing, and it later turned out that the young suicide bomber had been a recruited by Hamas's military branch. Later, there was talk that the attack had been in retaliation for allowing a Jew to work on site, namely Richard Hydes himself.

Unfortunately, the implications had not registered with Harker when he had offered his old friend the position. Archaeologists, like doctors, were usually respected on both sides of the fence and left alone by the extremists. Or so he had thought. Mia had subsequently blamed him entirely for the lack of security surrounding her husband's death. He had tried to explain that her own government had refused to provide any further protection, but this fell upon deaf ears. Her eyes streaming with tears, the recently married Mrs Hydes had thrown him out of the house and even cursed his name. At that moment, he made himself a promise and stuck to it like gospel: always hire locals and never hire a Jew when operating in the Muslim world.

Present in the room this evening was the man who had helped see him through the crisis and who had been site manager on every dig he had undertaken since. Hussain Attasi, or Huss as he liked to be called, had been working as a digger at the ancient well site in Damascus and was injured in the same explosion that had killed Richard Hydes. It was Huss that had taken charge of the site within minutes of the blast and had organised the initial clean-up. Harker could still see the image of Huss clearly in his mind—the nineteen-year-old's white shirt sprayed red with blood and his face smeared black with bomb residue as he stood arguing with the Israeli military.

Huss had taken it upon himself to organise an ambulance for the injured and had then stopped the military from entering so as not to disturb the site further. The young apprentice had held his ground against four armed soldiers, despite receiving deep shrapnel wounds to his left arm, and he had even used duct tape to hold the edges of the wound together so he wouldn't have to leave the dig. If that wasn't impressive enough, the tenacious teenager had convinced the soldiers that there had been threats of a second bomber, thus dissuading the soldiers from entering until Harker himself could finally arrive. He had hired the boy full-time the very next day.

At first, Huss had accepted and then felt guilty about taking the job so soon after Richard Hydes's death, but Harker had soothed his worries, and the young Palestinian was back on site within a day. Huss had remained with him ever since, participating in every dig over the past five years. Even though the blast had left him with a total of only six fingers, a thumb, and an ever-stiff biceps, he had always carried his injuries proudly as a badge of war. It also gave him, he believed, the right to be as sarcastic as he liked.

The exhibition room was now alive with movement as the guests milled their way around the seven smaller exhibits, each one flanked by a smartly dressed security guard. The large glass case standing in the middle contained the scrolls themselves, each securely perched on an oyster-blue perspex stand and protected by three additional security guards keeping an ever-vigilant eye on the well-dressed attendees.

Harker allowed himself to relax for a few moments and just soak up the atmosphere. He had encountered so many problems, and even dangers, whilst trying to bring these scrolls to Cambridge, and now here they were, nicely packaged and sat on display in one of the oldest universities in the world, surrounded by some of the wealthiest people in Great Britain.

'You know, Alex, I've heard you talk often about Hussain Attasi, but I could never believe he was quite the pain in the arse you described. Well, you were right,' Dean Lercher said in a genuinely surprised tone.

Harker glanced over at his assistant, who was now showing an elderly couple an exhibit at the far end of the room whilst berating the dutiful guard for not standing up straight.

'Yep, he really is, but he's also one hell of an organiser. He'll always bitch and moan about it, but whenever you've got a problem, he'll find an answer.'

The dean nodded, courteously, before licking his lips in a manner Harker was all too familiar with. The twitch drew a smile from him as he waited for his friend to pluck up the courage and ask whatever was on his mind.

'Alex, when you've got the time, I'd love to know the real story behind your acquisition of the Dead Sea Scrolls. So go on, how did you pull it off?'

He could see the dean now going from playful to pushy. 'Tom, you know everything I've ever learnt on all my other digs, but, without sounding too cryptic, I'm taking this one to the grave.'

His old friend didn't look surprised. 'Well, whatever you did, I'm glad you did it. Or maybe *he* did it,' he added, motioning towards Huss. 'Maybe he's the lead the media have so far missed. You haven't been resting on his laurels, have you, Alex?'

Harker almost tut-tted out loud at the suggestion. 'Stop trying to goad me into telling you, because it's not going to happen. Besides, Huss isn't the negotiating type.' The image of Huss, who was now reprimanding one of the security guards over a blemish on the man's tie, instantly stressed Harker's point.

'OK, you win, Professor,' Lercher frowned, 'but the board of trustees has been riding my back about it for months now, and I don't fancy the wigging they'll give me for not finding out.'

'So what will you tell them?' Harker asked.

'Oh, I don't know. Basically something like you're a bit of an arsehole who won't tell me.'

Both men chuckled and then stood silently, enjoying the spectacle of so many eager and excited-looking expressions all around. It was a short-lived pleasure, though, before a young man wearing a black suit burst into the room, looking breathless and flustered.

'Dean Lercher, can I speak with you?' the young man puffed, whilst straining for his next breath.

'It looks like you already are, my boy.' The head of archaeology raised his eyebrows. 'For goodness's sake, compose yourself, Jenkins.'

The student took a few deep, calming breaths before continuing. 'Thank you, sir. But there's another guest just arrived, and he's looking for Professor Harker.'

The dean looked confused. 'Well, then, why not show him up here?'

'He's not here for the event, sir.' Jenkins looked a little embarrassed. 'He says he's a lawyer, and he insists on speaking with Professor Harker in private.'

Dean Lercher again raised his eyebrows skyward. 'Not in any trouble, are you, Alex?'

'Not that I'm aware of.' Harker shrugged. 'What's his name?'

'It's a Mr Caster, but he didn't give me a company name. Shall I bring him up, then, sir?'

Harker shook his head, feeling he could do with some fresh air. 'No, I'll come down to him. Thanks.'

'Oh and, sir, some urgent post arrived for you.' The undergraduate handed over a special-delivery letter, and Harker slipped it straight into his pocket, not wanting to discover at that moment if another debt collector was after him.

Jenkins nodded politely and headed back the way he had come, bumping into a security guard as he went.

'That boy's got no sense of balance. You should see him on the Rugby pitch. Bloody useless.'

Harker tapped Lercher on the shoulder. 'Hold the fort. I'll be right back.'

Chapter 3

Harker's footsteps echoed around the empty cobblestone quad as he briskly began to make his way to the visitors' waiting room. Suddenly, the 8 p.m. bell rang to signal the end of another day's lectures, and with it emerged wave after wave of hungry students, all pushing their way forwards to the front gates. Many recognised him from his public lectures, and with a smile and a nod, they respectfully moved aside to let him easily slip through the swelling crowd. Most of them were in their early twenties, the age when teachers stopped being seen as the enemy and became potential equals—most of the time anyway.

The mild night air carried the sweet smell of pollen, which seemed odd in late January but had been noticeable for the previous two weeks. *Bloody global warming*, Harker reflected as he pulled a small foil packet from his trouser pocket, popped out an antihistamine, and gulped it down. Regardless of his hay fever, it was still a pleasant change from the usual cold, wet weather that British winters were famous for.

Harker reached the waiting-room door and paused momentarily as a twinge of apprehension caused his chest to tighten. *Please don't let this be about something negative, not tonight.* He had racked up ten parking tickets in the last two months and hadn't paid any of them off. Parking in Cambridge was a nightmare, and he had planned to question the council on every single ticket but hadn't yet got around to it. Months spent preparing for the arrival of the Dead Sea Scrolls had thrown him out of organisational kilter, much to the detriment of his bank balance. He turned the cold metal doorknob and made his way inside.

At a table on the far side of the room sat a well-dressed man in a pinstripe suit, with a purple tie neatly tucked in beneath his buttoned waistcoat. He immediately jumped to his feet and pushed back his thinning, almost nonexistent, blond hair as if keen to make a good first impression.

'Professor Harker?'

Harker nodded in response. 'Mr Caster?'

'Yes, that's me. Many thanks for giving me some of your valuable time on such an important day.'

'Not at all, but I can only spare you a few minutes. Please take a seat.' Harker pulled up a chair on the opposite side of the table and sat down. 'I haven't seen a hat like that for a while.' He motioned towards the distinctively domed black bowler nestled in the man's lap.

'Ah, yes, they're an acquired taste, but I wouldn't be seen dead without it.' The lawyer chuckled and carefully placed it down on the table. 'Congratulations on your Dead Sea Scrolls exhibition, by the way. It's quite a coup for the university.'

Harker politely nodded and then gestured to his black tuxedo. 'As you can see, I'm right in the middle of it.'

Mr Caster clasped his hands apologetically. 'Yes, I am sorry for the timing of my arrival, but it is of upmost importance that we speak.'

Harker waved his hand to cut off the older man mid-sentence. 'This isn't anything to do with parking tickets by any chance?'

The lawyer looked confused. 'Er . . . no, Professor, I'm not from the parking authorities.'

'In that case, please continue,' Harker said with a feeling of relief.

The visitor reached into his top pocket and produced a business card, which he passed over. Its white surface was blank except for just two silver embossed words in the centre: Maptrel Associates.

The name wasn't familiar, but the puzzled look on Harker's face was ignored by the lawyer as he continued enthusiastically.

'I'm here on behalf of a client of mine who wishes to acquire your services.'

Harker placed the card on the table and slid it back across. 'I'm afraid you've a wasted trip, Mr Caster, because I only work for the university.'

The lawyer nodded understandingly. 'Yes, I'm aware of that.' He once again reached into his pocket but, this time, pulled out a slip of paper, and placed it in the centre of the table. 'But I'm hoping this might change your mind.'

Harker cautiously peered down at what appeared to be a company cheque and read the print: '£250,000 payable to Mr Alexander Harker.'

The sheer amount made him jolt upwards in shock, smacking his knee painfully against the table leg.

'A quarter of a million pounds! For what?'

Caster settled back comfortably in his chair. 'For a meeting with my client later tonight.'

Harker had momentarily zoned out as he envisaged the pile of bills he could pay off with that much sterling, not to mention his mortgage.

'I'm flattered by this offer but . . . Who did you say your client was, again?'

'I didn't, and I'm afraid I'm not at liberty to say, Professor. But I can assure you that if you're not interested in what my employer has to say after you meet him, then I have been instructed to tell you that the money is still yours to keep.'

There were three things that Alex Harker would never say no to: one was a friend in need, the second was a mystery to unravel, and thirdly, a cheque for £250 grand, no questions asked.

'Mr Caster, I think I would be happy to take your client up on his offer.'

'Excellent.' Mr Caster clapped his hands together like an excited child. 'I'll have a driver pick you up at the front gate in an hour.'

In only one hour! The dean would be furious with him if he left the exhibition early, but that kind of money bought a lot of excuses.

'I'll be ready and waiting.'

The two men shook hands and stepped outside. At which point, an unpleasant thought entered Harker's head, stopping him dead in his tracks.

'Mr Caster, forgive me for asking but . . .' He glanced around the now-empty courtyard to make sure they were alone. 'This meeting isn't of a sexual nature, is it?'

He felt an idiot for asking: after all, who'd pay that kind of money for a thirty-eight-year-old archaeologist? Unless it was something kinky! His heart began to sink.

'I can assure you, Professor, it's strictly your expertise that is required. But please feel free to bring a friend along if you wish. Goodbye for now.'

With that, the mysterious lawyer let out a chuckle of amusement and disappeared through the front gate. Harker found himself alone in the courtyard with nothing but his own embarrassment and the cheque to keep him company. He carefully slid it into the top pocket of his tuxedo and tapped it lovingly, his mind suddenly flooding with images of a new car and sun-soaked holidays. This was honestly turning into the best day of his life.

Chapter 4

'Honestly, Alex, you're a bloody mercenary. You've got absolutely no soul whatsoever.'

Harker gazed out of the limousine's tinted windows and across the moon-lit woods surrounding them as the car continued up a dark, foreboding driveway. The black Mercedes had pulled up outside the college gate exactly on the hour and then had driven them out of London towards Milton Keynes, just off the M1. Dean Lercher had insisted on accompanying him as soon as Harker had shown him the cheque, even if it had meant leaving the exhibition rather early. The only problem was that during the hour-and-a-half long drive, he hadn't shut up once.

'You know, I bet this is drug related.'

Harker scoffed at the suggestion. 'I hardly think a drug cartel would have need of an archaeologist. Besides, they could have just kidnapped me and saved themselves the money.'

The dean wagged a knowing finger. 'Not if they wanted you complicit and agreeable. Anyway, you've not had time to cash their cheque yet. Do you know I once heard of an Iranian archaeologist being forced to smuggle LSD into Britain, using hollowed-out religious statues?'

Harker rolled his eyes in frustration, refusing to even consider the dean's newest theory. His old friend was understandably suspicious of the mystery invitation, but he was also probably a little jealous of the huge sum of money involved.

'Give it a rest, Doggie. If someone had offered you that amount, you'd have sold your own mother to pay for the taxi ride, so how about you cut me some slack?'

Lercher started flicking his top lip back and forth with the tip of his index finger, a twitch telling Harker that his comment had touched a nerve. It was a twitch that made Dean Lercher, or Doggie to his friends, so easy to read and even easier to beat at poker. In fact, his nickname had been coined during one of their monthly poker sessions when someone remarked how the good dean possessed facial features resembling those of a pedigree Lurcher and how similar both their names were. Doggie, for his part, hated the nickname vehemently.

'Yes, you're right, I probably would have. But the thing you have to remember about me is that I'm a total sell-out when it comes to money, and everyone knows it. You, on the other hand, are not, and don't call me Doggie. You know I hate it.'

Harker returned his gaze to the dark expanse of woodland outside the window. 'Let's just hear them out and see what they have to say, OK?'

Lercher sat back in silence and continued to flick his top lip ferociously. 'All right, fine. Bloody merc.'

The jibe didn't even register as Harker now fixed his eyes on the dimly lit mansion looming out of the darkness in front of them.

Situated in five hundred acres of Buckinghamshire countryside, Bletchley Park, which their driver had now identified, was a unique mixture of Victorian, Gothic, Tudor, and Dutch Baroque design, eliciting the marmite reaction from all who saw it for the first time. You either loved it or hated it, and Harker absolutely loved it, but less for the place's architecture and more for what had been achieved within its walls. The original building dated back to the eleventh century, but it wasn't until the 1930s that it became truly interesting. In 1938, the site was due to be demolished to create space for a housing estate, but, before demolition commenced, Admiral Sir Hugh Sinclair (director of Naval Intelligence and head of MI6) bought the site on behalf of the government. During the next seven years, Bletchley Park became home to some of the greatest code breakers in the world, who assembled there to crack the Nazis' military code during World War II.

It was also the birthplace of Colossus, the world's first computer, which was instrumental in breaking the Nazis' enigma machine and thus allowing the allies to eavesdrop on German intelligence and help win the war. For, had it not been for the events unfolding in Bletchley Park, there would have been a very real possibility that the Nazis could have triumphed.

The limousine's tyres crunched as they moved off the smooth tarmac driveway and on to the gravel parking area, finally coming to a halt outside the main entrance. Waiting for them was a stocky blond-haired man, dressed neatly in a plaid jacket and grey slacks, who promptly opened the passenger door.

'Good evening, Professor Harker . . .' He then turned to glare unwelcomingly at Doggie. ' . . . and Mr Lercher. Welcome to Bletchley Park, gentlemen. My name is Lusic Bekhit, and I'll be your guide. Please, follow me.'

They were led briskly through the entrance hall and then immediately guided to a side door, opening into a long, white-painted corridor.

'Just down here, gentlemen,' said Lusic, ushering them along.

Their guide's accent was familiar to Harker, who had visited that country many times and even assisted at digs conducted in the Valley of the Kings, the final resting place of the ancient pharaohs.

'That's quite an unusual accent, but I recognise it. Southern Egypt, the Aswan region, isn't it?'

Their bulky guide smiled. 'Impressive, sir. You've spent time there, then?'

Harker nodded. 'Yes, over the years. I have a friend there, a translator, who was born near Lake Kassar. But I think you're the first person I've ever met from there who had blond hair.'

The Egyptian proudly ran a hand through his the dense golden locks. 'My mother was German,' he explained.

Doggie, perhaps feeling like third leg in this exchange, immediately jumped on the comment. 'Ah, interesting heritage, I think I can detect the German twinge ever so slightly, and I'd say you spent your early years growing up just outside Munich.' He finished this announcement with a smugly confident smile.

'Actually my mother died at birth, so I was never exposed to that language, nor have I ever had the pleasure of visiting Germany.' Lusic's tone was patronising, not attempting to hide his obvious dislike of the dean.

Harker stared down at the floor, not wanting to succumb to the laughter welling up inside him as Doggie pursed his lips uncomfortably, struggling to contain his embarrassment.

'My mistake. I'm just getting over a bout of flu. It affects the ears, you know.'

Lusic nodded politely, ignoring the obvious gaffe. 'Mr Lercher, if you would care to wait here . . .' He pointed to a solitary leather-seated dining chair pushed up against the wall.

'What? You mean I can't come in?'

A stern shake of the head sufficed to answer the dean's question.

'Well, I'll be here if you need me, Alex,' Doggie offered, before taking his seat.

'This way, Professor,' Lusic instructed cordially and directed his visitor into the adjoining room.

Harker found himself in an ornate medieval-looking hall with thick oak beams running across the width of its twenty-foot-high ceiling. The white walls were liberally adorned with pictures, but it was too dim to make any of them out in detail. To his left, a semicircular stone fireplace jutted from the wall and was surrounded by two comfortable-looking armchairs.

'Please take a seat, Professor,' Lusic gestured before disappearing through a connecting door.

Harker sat down on one of the plush chairs and seized the moment not only to appreciate the warmth of the fire but also to enjoy the silence Doggie had denied him over the past couple of hours.

His mind began raking through the mountain of unanswered questions this mysterious meeting had raised. The most prominent one being, why here? Was he in trouble? Bletchley Park was a government building, after all, but the size of the cheque had suggested otherwise. There was no way any minister worth his salt would palm off £250 grand of the taxpayers' money just like that, at least not now that New Labour was out of power.

Harker gradually succumbed to the hypnotic flickering of the flames. Apart from the spitting embers, the silence around him was almost deafening. It was only after five or so minutes of waiting that he heard a voice sound out.

'Professor.'

Harker spun around to see the source of the voice which had caught him off guard. In the gloom of the connecting doorway stood the tall silhouette of a man. The eeriness of his sudden appearance caused Harker's heart to skip a beat, and he leapt to his feet.

'I do apologise. I didn't mean to startle you. Please be seated again and allow me to answer some of the questions you undoubtedly have.'

Harker dutifully sat back down and watched as the newcomer seemed to glide unnaturally towards the armchair opposite, before sinking into it and crossing his legs all in one fluid motion. In the darkness of the room, it was only the fire's glowing light that allowed Harker his first proper look at the man seated in front of him.

He was dressed totally in black, including his brogues and leather gloves, so that the mane of pure white hair cascading over the back of the armchair was in startling contrast. His appearance was unsettling enough, but what really stood out were the black-lensed aviator's glasses resting on his nose.

'Professor Alex Harker, thirty-eight years old and born in Belfast. Your father died in an IRA bombing, and you were brought up by your mother until you left home to become a priest in the Roman Catholic Church, aged eighteen.' He inhaled deeply and straightened his glasses before continuing. 'You remained in the service of the Church for eight years until leaving to become a textual archaeologist, a career that you have followed ever since. For some years now, you have been teaching archaeology and religious philosophy at Cambridge University, and your credits include discovery of the Damascus texts and, most recently, an acquisition to display a number of Dead Sea Scrolls, including the famed Isaiah scrolls for the first time in the UK. Quite an achievement, considering all the political implications.'

Harker smiled politely but remained silent. There was obviously a point to this sinister and rather invasive introduction, and the sooner this fellow got to the point, the better.

'Your main personal interest now lies in religious texts and relics, and it is that which has brought you here to me tonight.' The man nestled both hands in his lap, his sunglasses reflecting flickers from the hearth.

Harker had struggled to curb the sudden anger he had felt at hearing the death of his father mentioned in such a cavalier manner, but his irritation was soon replaced by a growing curiosity at this man's strange appearance. In the dim light, his skin appeared to be a very dark grey and his lips either light black or even blue! The accent was also unusually cultured—English but with a Middle Eastern inflection to it that he had not encountered before.

'Well, you've certainly got me there. Now, how about you tell me who you are. And, for the record, it was only the generous size of the cheque that brought me here.'

'Of course.' The mysterious donor emitted a deep gravelly laugh, revealing bleached white teeth that almost glowed in the murkiness of the hall. 'Money makes the world go round, does it not? Allow me to introduce myself. My name is Sebastian Brulet, and I am the CEO of

Maptel, the company behind the cheque that I suspect you are keeping safe in one of your jacket pockets.'

Harker, without any change of expression, pointed to the pocket in question. 'Good guess,' he replied, obviously unimpressed.

Brulet now continued swiftly. 'Professor Harker, let me get straight to the point. Having been lucky enough to be born into a wealthy and influential family, I have never wanted for anything, and I received the best education money could buy. My father wished me to continue in the family business, accumulating yet more wealth as many generations of Brulets had done before me. But when he himself passed away, leaving me everything, I found myself at a crossroads.' Brulet got up and casually made his way over to the fireplace, resting his elbow on the marble mantle shelf. 'At that stage, I could either continue to amass another fortune or I could do something else with it, and I finally decided that my path would lie in helping people less fortunate than myself. By that, I mean people who didn't enjoy a first-class education or the kind of loving childhood that would allow them an unprejudiced view of the world.'

Brulet pushed back the lock of white hair that had fallen across his gaunt features before continuing. 'Since then, Maptel has become one of the prime supporters of charity organisations around the globe. From new school buildings throughout Africa to poverty programmes right here in the UK, we are involved in them all.'

As the CEO continued to speak, Harker found himself increasingly distracted by the fine white hair hanging down to the man's waist. The heat from the fire caused individual strands of it to rise and fall as if caught in a mild breeze, giving him the look of someone being filmed in slow motion. This image was so hypnotic that Harker had to shift in his seat to stop himself from nodding off right in the middle of Mr Brulet's ongoing disclosure.

'Our efforts have had real impact, and, as a result, we've gained many friends and allies throughout the world's religious communities. It is these such contacts that have opened our eyes to certain events occurring outside the realm of public knowledge. And that is why I have asked you here tonight.'

Harker's interest perked up at the last comment, and he smiled politely. Finally, it seemed the fellow was getting somewhere. 'How can I help?' he asked bluntly.

Brulet pushed his sunglasses back into place, as they had been slowly sliding forward. 'Some of these contacts have warned us about a secret organisation known to us only as the Magi, which, in some form or another, has strong ties with the Roman Catholic Church. I'm embarrassed to say that we don't even know how this organisation is structured, let alone what it is they're working on. But what we do know is that a partnership was formed over forty years ago, back in the '70s, and it is funded even to this day by Church money.'

Brulet raised a theatrical finger to his lips. 'Its activities are all very hush-hush and conducted behind closed doors. Falling into the Church equivalent of a black ops file, we believe. Nonetheless, it is an operation we are keen to learn more about.'

There was seriousness in Brulet's tone that stopped Harker from making light of the 'black ops' reference.

'Mr Brulet, I'm sure the Church does engage in many under-the-table dealings, but I doubt that any of them are illegal or as mysterious as you make out.'

The white-haired man sat back in his chair and gently smoothed the creases in his trousers. 'You could be right, Professor, but considering the numbers involved . . .'

'What numbers?'

'In recent years, the Catholic Church has seen numbers drop and, with that, its incoming donations. Did you know that over the past few decades, the Church has had little option but to reel in its spending because of this? Almost all its expenditure has been cut except in one case.'

Harker made the obvious connection for himself. 'The Magi?'

Brulet nodded thoughtfully. 'Yes, the Magi have been receiving in the region of fifteen million pounds every year since '78.'

Harker let out a gasp at the huge sum of money just mentioned. 'Every year? That's almost . . .' He quickly summed it up in his head. 'Half a billion pounds! That's a lot of cash.'

Brulet smiled at Harker's astonishment. 'It certainly is, but that's only the half of the story. Over the past few years, we've managed to source the names of only four individuals connected with this organisation, but, in each case, and before we've been able to make contact with them, they've turned up dead. Victims of apparent accidents except one who just died recently in what can only be described as a bizarre suicide. The individual in question was contacted by us shortly before his death, and he was someone, as it happens, I believe, you knew well.'

That statement hung in the air as Harker realised the connection. For only one of his friends had ever committed suicide.

'You're talking about Archie Dwyer?'

Brulet sat back in his chair and nodded. 'Father Archibald Dwyer, the man who hanged himself on the balcony of St Peter's Basilica on the day of the Pope's inauguration two weeks ago. It appears that whatever information he wanted us to have has now been taken with him to the grave.'

Harker felt numbed by the last comment. He had known Archie since childhood, and both of them entered the church at the same time. But sadly the two men hadn't spoken since Harker relinquished his dog collar in search of the new life he had found for himself in archaeology. He knew the funeral would take place soon in Italy where Archie had been living, but, what with the Dead Sea Scrolls event and all that had come with it, Harker had not planned on attending. Considering the state of their friendship—or lack of it—in recent years, he'd not wanted to cause embarrassment by just turning up but had promised himself that at some point he'd visit the grave to pay his last respects.

'Professor, we would like you . . . No, I would like you to attend the funeral and find out whatever you can.'

Harker shook his head apologetically. 'Mr Brulet, it sounds like you need a private investigator, and that's not what I do.'

Brulet leant in closer. 'Anyone attending from my company would attract too much attention, as would an ordinary gumshoe, but you'd have a genuine reason for being there.'

The look of hesitation on Harker's face encouraged Brulet to offer more information. 'Professor, the fact is Father Dwyer wanted to tell us everything about the Magi and their activities, but he suspected he was being closely watched, which means there's a good chance he left that information somewhere for us to find. If he did, I want you to bring it to me so we can hold these Magi people to account.'

Harker rubbed his hands together in frustration. 'Mr Brulet, I wouldn't even know where to start.'

The white-haired man leant in closer still and placed a hand on Harker's forearm. 'Why don't you begin by opening that letter you received this evening? I believe it was special delivery.'

Brulet's remark caught Harker by surprise, as he had totally forgotten about the letter Jenkins had handed to him back at Trinity College before the meeting with Caster had further distracted his thoughts. Reaching into his pocket, he pulled out the white envelope and examined the stamp indicating the country of origin. 'It's from Italy. Archie's handwriting?'

'How did you know?' Harker asked uncomfortably.

Brulet waved a hand dismissively. 'Don't read too much into that. Father Dwyer already mentioned that he might be sending you a letter.'

This answer did not exactly put his mind at rest, but for the moment, he was prepared to let the matter go. Harker carefully slid his finger into the flap before gently tearing it open and retrieving a sheet of handwritten paper from inside. He held it up to the firelight and began reading the contents out loud.

'Alex, my time is short. Follow the path of the old world. Follow the path of the master's name from A–J. Maddocks 23-45-64. "Trust your logic and not your faith". What the hell does all that mean?'

With a blank expression, Sebastian Brulet shook his head. 'I really don't know, but I would beg you to attend his funeral. Speak to his family and friends there, as it's possible he confided in them. Then go and check his residence. It has yet to be cleared out, and that won't happen until after his burial, so he may have left something there for you to find.'

'That's a lot of possibilities, Mr Brulet.'

'Well, there's also a lot of zeros on our cheque, Mr Harker.'

Harker momentarily glanced down at Brulet's hand and suddenly realised just how grey the man's skin was. In the dim light of the fire, it reflected almost silver, matched by his facial complexion, which appeared the same tone. Brulet pulled back awkwardly, noticing Harker's interest.

'It's a skin condition I have, which dulls the natural colour, I'm afraid.' He removed his hand speedily. 'But don't worry, it's not infectious.'

Harker restrained the urge to brush the area of his forearm that Brulet had touched, not wanting to make the man uneasy. 'OK, I'll do it. You sort out the travel arrangements, and I'll see what I can find out but no promises.'

Brulet was clearly pleased by this decision, and once again his dazzling white teeth were on full display. 'Excellent! Excellent!' He reached into his jacket pocket and produced a business card. 'You can contact John Caster on this number for him to answer any queries you might have.'

Harker pulled out the card he'd been handed back in Cambridge. 'I've already got one.'

Brulet effortlessly popped the second card into Harker's top pocket. 'Well, now you have two.'

He offered a handshake, which was snatched by Harker unflinchingly as if to prove that Brulet's unfortunate skin colour had never been an issue.

'You won't be expected to contact me directly, but, should it become absolutely necessary, then Mr Caster can arrange it. Meanwhile, Lusic will have all your travel details ready for you on the way out.' Sebastian Brulet gave his visitor's hand one last shake before letting go. 'It's now in your hands, so good luck. I know you won't let us down.'

There was only one question Harker needed to ask, and he'd almost forgotten it. 'What day is the funeral because there are some university matters I need to take care of before I leave?'

Brulet sat back comfortably in his chair and tapped his fingers together. 'Well, you better get them sorted quickly, Professor Harker, because your plane leaves at 6.30 a.m. tomorrow morning. Oh, and try to keep a low profile, if you can, as we don't won't want to cause any undue panic. Meanwhile, Godspeed.'

Chapter 5

Vito Malpuso grabbed the heavy blue duffel bag and hastily made his way down the creaking wooden stairs of the run-down Italian farmhouse. He snatched his car keys off the kitchen table and headed out to the red Citroen parked outside.

The rustic farmhouse had seen better days and situated south of Rome in the Villa Doria Pamphili region; it was well off the beaten track. The building stood on an incline, overlooking the surrounding vineyards that chequered the area, offering a view any local would be proud to call his own.

Vito dumped the oversized holdall into the back seat and slammed the door shut with a thud. All this cloak-and-dagger stuff was not for him, and his nerves just weren't built for it. He'd been fretting about moving on to another location for the last two days, but the phone call he'd received only minutes earlier had made the decision for him. 'Get out now. It's not safe. Go to the Hotel Del Papa, room 322, and wait for my call.' The urgency in the contact's voice had made Malpuso's stomach churn, and, within minutes, he had slung all his possessions into the cheap duffel bag and was on his way out the door.

He heard a scuffling sound behind him and spun around to find a large grey rabbit in the centre of the dusty drive, looking as nervous as he was. Vito let out a relieved sigh and clapped his hands, sending the animal scampering off into the dark.

No, his nerves were definitely not designed for this.

He scanned the rest of the forecourt, holding his breath as he listened for any sounds of movement. Satisfied, there was nothing of concern, he wiped his sweaty hands across the thighs of his blue denim jeans and made his way back inside. The brown-plastered walls of the bare living room were cracked and peeling, giving it more of a condemned than a rustic feel, and Vito took one last look around the place that had been his home over the past two weeks. His decision to hide out in this farmhouse had seemed like a good idea at the time, but, on arriving and taking stock of the cobwebs and lack of fresh water, he realised what a mistake it had been. It wasn't only his idea to go into hiding, as both of them had agreed on that, but his decision had been the poor choice of location. *Bright idea, Vito*, he thought, but none of that was important now. It only mattered that he got himself out of this place as soon as possible.

Content that he had remembered everything, he pulled the Citroen's keys from his back pocket and was making his way back towards the front door when an unsettlingly deep voice boomed out.

'Going somewhere, Mr Malpuso?'

Vito stiffened instinctively and slowly turned around. Standing calmly in the doorway stood the most gigantic man he had ever seen, with the piercing eyes of a predator and a deeply malevolent smile. Towering almost seven feet tall, the giant was dressed in a grey boiler suit with both sleeves rolled up to reveal bulging forearms.

Vito froze on the spot, his hands now shaking uncontrollably.

'I thought I would miss you,' said the hulking colossus, his deep monotone voice sending a cold chill through the other man's body. 'Lucky me.'

The lumbering giant then covered the three-metre gap between them in two strides and grasped Vito by the throat, his oversized fingers squeezing tighter and tighter.

'Where is it?' The brute's accent sounded Eastern European, overlaid with the huskiness of a sixty-a-day smoker. 'It's simple. You tell me, and I let you go.'

Vito clawed at the man's fingers as they fondled with his windpipe, the pressure causing his eyes to fill with tears. 'I . . . I . . . don't know what you're talking about.'

The leviathan suddenly released his grip, sending him sprawling on to the hard terracotta floor with a thud. 'Do you know who I am, Vito?'

The small Italian coughed up spittle as he struggled to recover his breath. 'I know what you are.' He spluttered again as a wave of new-found confidence gushed through him. 'But that matters not, because I don't know what you want, and neither would I tell you anything even if I did.'

The huge man shook his head in disappointment. 'Well, my name is Drazia Heldon, and I'm positive that I can change your mind.' The giant noticed the Italian, eyeing the plastic coverings on his shoes, and he smiled with a shrug. 'That's so I don't get any blood on them. Now, let's begin, shall we?'

Chapter 6

The late Rev Archibald Dwyer was one of those people Harker had counted as an old friend but not a close friend. Both of them born in Belfast, Northern Ireland, the two boys had grown up in the same suburb and attended the same Catholic school.

The death of his father when Harker was only eight had, of course, changed the whole family dynamic. Liam Harker had been caught in a bomb whilst making his way home after a long day at the Bird's Eye chicken factory where he worked as a quality-testing manager. At the age of forty-five, and after twenty years watching chickens being slaughtered, he had decided to turn vegetarian, although his family were less than enthusiastic. That fateful evening, he had popped into the Celery Stick for a vegetarian takeaway and had just made it outside when a car bomb exploded. In fact, it turned out that the IRA had been targeting the busy pub next door.

At the age of eighteen, Harker had been accepted into a Catholic priest's internship at the Vatican. Within three months, he was almost fluent in Italian, and, by the end of the first year, his ability to pick up new languages and texts had not gone unnoticed by his supervisors. For a period of two years, his time was spent under the guidance of Cardinal Priest Salvatore Vincenzo, head of the Vatican's Pontifical Commission for sacred archaeology. The department dealt mainly with the preservation of ancient Christian cemeteries and mementos, but Vincenzo was also a keen linguist, and the young Harker had enthusiastically spent time assimilating as many new languages as he could. His mentor had secured him access to the textual division of the Vatican and the young priest had set about familiarising himself with the great number of texts that had passed into the Church's hands over the last couple of millennia. By the end of his time at the Vatican, he was permitted to browse through the famous and heavily guarded main library, where the most important treasures were to be found, and Harker had been stunned at the sheer volume of works still needing to be properly catalogued. Many of them had apparently sat, locked away in storerooms for hundreds of years without being inspected. Even then it had seemed almost criminal to him that so many texts written throughout history were left unread and unstudied when they could surely offer new insights into the very religious figures the Church now revered. Applauding his application to the cause, the library's curator, Cardinal Entonian, had two words for it: due diligence.

That evidence of institutional lethargy had caused Harker's first pang of concern about his chosen way of life as a priest within the Catholic Church. Nevertheless, he had persevered, and, by the end of his three-year training, Harker had been assigned to the parish of East Harling in the country suburbs of Norwich. Archie Dwyer, on the other hand, had been given a parish in Belfast, where sectarian violence had intensified, and the community needed spiritual guidance more than ever.

The two friends had kept in regular touch since their induction into the priesthood, but that had all stopped when Harker hung up his collar. The fact was that he'd barely spoken a word to Archie Dwyer since quitting the priesthood. Archie had never forgiven him for what he saw as abandonment of his faith, and he deeply resented Harker's lack of clarity over the reasons for his leaving. Harker consequently suspected Archie had seen his resignation as a personal failure as if Dwyer's own faith and commitment to the Church hadn't been strong enough to save his closest friend. Harker's explanation that he felt that he could serve Christianity better if he was outside the priesthood had not gone down well in their last face-to-face conversation, and Archie had completely failed to see the logic in his argument. Deep down, Harker had always hoped that the two of them would make up again at some point, but that wasn't to be. Certainly not now.

Such were the thoughts that occupied him during the flight to Da Vinci airport and the subsequent taxi drive to the church of San Lorenzo Fuorile Murahis in the centre of Rome, where Archie's funeral was taking place. After his mysterious meeting with Sebastian Brulet, he had gone home, packed an overnight bag, and, after a few hours, wrapping up some urgent business, he had headed straight to Heathrow. The two-and-a-half-hour flight had been bearable, and even having two screaming children sitting nearby hadn't been too much bother, but to find, on arrival at Da Vinci, that his bag had taken an alternative flight to Belgrade . . . well, that had been the final straw. By the time he had established its whereabouts, Harker was really running late, and although relieved to climb into a taxi, the drive had proved a further nightmare. For getting out of the airport later than he'd expected had meant getting caught up in Rome's rush-hour traffic. By this time, he was an hour and forty-five minutes behind schedule, not to mention sweaty as hell, by the time his cab finally reached the destination. The vehicle's air-conditioner was not working, and he was just tucking another serviette, provided by the driver, under his armpit as they arrived.

'This is it, signor. The church of San Lorenzo is just over there.'

Harker gazed through the window at a plain-looking edifice across the way. Its facade was lined with six free-standing, medium-sized iconic pillars with ornate metal bars in between them and a grand doorway in the middle. Harker got out of the taxi and stretched, his sweat-soaked shirt feeling suddenly chilly as a gentle breeze blew over him. *What a ride!*

'That will be eighty euros,' the driver demanded impatiently, wanting to get back on to the main road before he was collared by a passing traffic warden.

Harker pulled out a wad of notes and began counting them off.

'And ten for the serviettes,' added the grinning driver. Annoyed at the con he had fallen for, Harker shook his head and added the extra before passing it over.

'Maybe next time you'll get your a/c working,' he grumbled.

The man rolled up the notes and shoved them into a small wooden change box resting on the passenger seat. 'If I did that, my friend, I'd make nothing on the serviettes.' He laughed sarcastically and drove off into the crowded street.

Harker shrugged off his annoyance and made his way through the gates into the nave of the church. At least, he had made it here in one piece.

The inside was truly magnificent with a white marble floor under six grey pillars rising to a coffered golden ceiling. The huge altar sat in front of a twelve-foot oil painting of Christ suffering on the cross, behind which a spectrum of colours shone through beautifully crafted, stained-glass windows. Four smaller chapels led off the main axis, each with exquisite busts of angels and saints, some of which Harker recognised as being carved by the master sculptor Bernini himself. On either side of the nave, a row of wooden pews ran towards the altar, and a tiny congregation sat listening patiently to the priest deliver his blessings from the pulpit, in front of which was a light pinewood coffin supported on two metal trestles.

Being over an hour late, Harker had hoped to slip into the crowd unnoticed, but as there were only four mourners, and the priest conducting the service, the subtle option seemed impossible. He walked as casually as possible down the aisle and took a seat. Three of the others present were dressed in full Catholic clerical dress, and two of them gave him an unemotional nod. He didn't recognise either of them, but a fourth person was smiling at him curiously.

Claire Dwyer looked as good as ever, dressed in a respectfully low-cut black dress and a trim black hat that was tipped slightly on to one side. She gave Harker a small wave before turning her attention back to the priest.

'In the name of the Holy Father, we commend his spirit to heaven. May he find the peace in death that eluded him in life, amen.' The priest gestured the sign of the cross, and the congregation all bowed their heads one last time. Then the other men stood up and began offering Claire their condolences. Harker waited for the priest to finish his bit before heading over to her.

'Alex, it's so good to see you. Thanks for coming.' Claire threw her arms around him, as fresh tears began to well. 'I didn't think you were going to make it.'

Despite his relationship with Archie being on the rocks, Claire had never held that against Harker, as sisters sometimes do. The two of them had been close during their earlier years but had hardly spoken over the past five. She pulled back from their embrace, and, despite her running mascara and puffy eyes, Harker felt a surge of attraction. She had definitely improved with age, shedding the puppy fat that had clung to her throughout her twenties, and the long red hair was no longer greasy with split ends. All in all, she looked pretty good.

'Sorry, I'm late, but taxi ride here was a nightmare.'

She stopped him with a vigorous shake of her head. 'You're here, and that's good enough.'

The two smiled at each other fondly as old friends do.

'I should have contacted you as soon as I found out. It's not an excuse, but things have been a bit crazy for me lately,' Harker offered, feeling a little embarrassed.

'Don't worry, Alex, I understand—what with the scrolls and everything. We're all very proud of you.' She glanced towards the pine coffin. 'So was Archie, although he never would have told you himself.'

That thought comforted Harker. Even before their bust-up, Archie had never been one for complements. Whether it was odd or an apt characteristic for a Catholic priest, it was difficult to say.

'Still I should have phoned. I apologise.'

Claire smiled. 'Apology accepted.'

Thankfully, the awkward silence that ensued was interrupted by one of the other attendees.

'Miss Dwyer, please accept my deepest condolences for your brother. He was a good man, who will be missed.'

The man's voice was unusually high pitched, and his accent sounded German, although Harker couldn't place the region, but his clerical garments signified he was a cardinal.

'Cardinal Rocca, thank you for coming. Your presence would have meant a lot to Archie.'

'It was the least I could do, and I only wish more people could have turned up. But considering the circumstances of his death, I just hope others may find room in their hearts for forgiveness.'

The last comment made Claire wobble slightly, and Harker quickly steadied her with a supportive hand. Seeing she was about to well up again, he stepped forward.

'Cardinal Rocca, I'm Alex Harker, an old friend of Archie.'

The cardinal shook his hand limply. 'Yes, Professor Harker, I know who you are, I've seen your face on the news many times. It's a pleasure, and thank you for coming.' He turned his attention back to Claire. 'Miss Dwyer, I am at your service, so please do not hesitate to call me if the need arises.'

With a gentle nod, the cardinal headed back into the church, followed by the other priests, leaving the pair of them alone.

Claire had always been bit of a tomboy—a toughie by nature—but Harker could see all that strength had now deserted her and understandably so. She looked so fragile and delicate, and it took all his self-control not to throw his arms around her and start getting wet-eyed himself. But that would have really set her off, so he resisted.

'So what now?'

Claire gazed up at him and rested a gentle hand on his shoulder. '*Now* I need a drink.'

Chapter 7

'I thought more people would have shown up. He always seemed popular within the church.'

Harker settled back into the tanned, wicker chair and took a sip of his frothy cappuccino. The Portofino cafe was just around the corner from the basilica of San Lorenzo so had only taken a few minutes to reach. Situated on the bank of the River Tiber, the cafe's terrace overlooked the cramped expanse of Rome's old quarter. Harker had been a regular customer of this little coffee shop during his time studying to become a priest, and he was surprised to find it still in operation.

Opposite him, Claire Dwyer was polishing off her second Stella Artois and already loosening up. 'It's because he committed suicide, isn't it? Still considered a cardinal sin in the eyes of the church.'

Harker shrugged sadly, struggling to put a positive spin on her answer. 'It's still a crappy reason for his friends not to come and show their last respects. It surprises me, Claire, it really does.'

She stared at him thoughtfully and picked at the label on her beer bottle. 'He wasn't the same man you remember, Alex. He'd changed so much that even I found it difficult to talk to him, and you know how close we were.' She gazed out across the piazza towards a group of teenagers who were jostling for a seat on one of the stone benches that surrounded the square. 'Of course, everything changes. It always does.'

Tears once again appeared in the corner of her eyes, and Harker reached over and placed his hand on hers.

'You want to talk about it?'

She pulled away coldly. 'I don't think it would make any difference. Not now, anyway.'

For the second time that morning, Harker felt a surge of guilt. He had always felt a certain kinship with Claire and now hated playing with her emotions to obtain answers. Should he tell her his true reason for being here in Rome, he couldn't be sure of her reaction. He was tempted all the same, but *why deliver more pain over Archie when it could all be a wild-goose chase?*

He inhaled a deep breath and gave himself time to ponder the thought before deciding, for the moment, to keep it to himself. 'It would make a difference to me.'

The comment stirred Claire from her thoughts, and she turned to him, smiling. 'He was his old cheery self, an eternal optimist, up until about six months ago.'

'And then?'

'And then he just changed. He became withdrawn . . . depressed. It wasn't long before he stopped returning my calls, and, when I did get to speak with him, he would ask me the oddest things like "You think I'm a good man, don't you, Claire?" and "I've always tried to do the right thing, haven't I?" He was suddenly looking for constant reassurance.'

The idea of his old friend seeking guidance perked Harker's interest because anyone who had known Archie also knew that it was he who offered reassurance, not the other way around. It had been that way since Harker could remember, and it was an incredibly superior, if not downright annoying, characteristic.

Claire sighed and gazed up at the hot midday sun, enjoying the warmth on her face before turning back to him. 'I keep thinking that if only I'd flown out earlier and cornered him, you know, throttled some sense into him, he'd still be with us.'

Harker sat back in his seat, unwilling to let Claire reprimand herself. 'There's no way you could have known, so don't do that to yourself.'

She sagged back into her chair with a groan. 'Maybe, maybe not, but what you don't know is that I spoke to him just a few days before he died. He was mostly babbling something about a meeting and about putting things right. I don't know about what, though. Truth is, I wasn't really paying much attention because, the way he was acting, I thought he was just going off on one, you know how he could be . . . God, was I wrong.'

At that moment, the waiter appeared to remove her empty beer bottle, and they waited silently for the young man to wander off to the next table before continuing.

'Do you know whom he was meeting?' Harker enquired.

'Some man . . . I can't remember his name. It was something like Medic or Maddy.'

It sounded similar to Maddocks, the name in Archie's note, but Harker didn't want to mention that now, not yet. 'Doesn't sound familiar. Have you told anyone else?'

Claire looked up at the sun again and laughed. 'God, Alex, you know both our parents aren't here any more. I'm the last in our family now. Who would I tell, and why? It was suicide case closed.' She took a swig from her bottle. 'I just wish I knew why.'

Brulet's warning echoed through his mind, *Do not trust anyone, Mr Harker. Anyone.* The words were lost on him as he watched his old friend begin to crumble under the weight of it all. She was just as confused as he was about this whole damn affair.

'Claire, there's something you need to know.' His firm tone made her lean towards him, her face alight with curiosity. 'I was approached by someone who seems to think Archie may have been in some trouble before he died. So I offered to look into it.' He even considered telling her about the huge cheque that had sealed the deal but wasn't sure how she would take that. 'The thing is, together we may be able to find an answer.'

Claire sat in silence, just staring at him blankly. He couldn't tell now if she was mulling the news over or about to go ballistic, so he readied his hands underneath the table to catch any object hurled his way when, much to his relief, she calmly sat back in her seat. 'Who asked you?'

'A company . . . well, more like a charity, I think,' Harker said, nervously playing with his coffee mug. 'But they genuinely believe there's more to Archie's death than meets the eye.' He could tell she wasn't convinced, so there was only one way to get her on board: by telling the truth. He cleared his throat with an uncomfortable cough. 'They also offered me money, which is the reason I know they're serious.'

'How much?' There was no resentment in her voice.

'Just a small fee,' he lied. 'And that was for attending the meeting, regardless of whether I looked into it further.'

Claire's jaw fell open. 'So you're getting a pay cheque out of this! Jesus, Alex, what did they want you to do?'

She seemed genuinely shocked now and was staring at him mistrustfully. He was losing her.

'They wanted me to find out what happened to Archie, and the truth is I'd been feeling pretty shitty about everything since he died. I'd always thought our friendship would pick up where it left off, at some point, but . . . well, that's not going to happen now, is it?' His throat started to dry up and he took a moment to take a quick sip of his cappuccino before continuing. 'So, when these people contacted me, it seemed a great way to do our friendship some justice as well as make amends. Besides, if Archie was in trouble, I want to know why, and I knew you'd feel the same way.'

He sat back confidently into his chair, aware of the gurgling in his stomach that was beginning to subside. He felt relieved at coming clean because everything he had said was true, and just saying it out loud seemed to absolve the burden of his guilt.

'It's all right, Alex, I'm not annoyed. I'm too sad to be annoyed but . . .' She ran a hand through her long red hair and sighed. 'I don't think Archie was involved in anything. It was more a case of him having a personal crisis, a . . .' she searched for the words, '. . . a falling out with his faith.'

Harker gently leant towards her. 'How can you be so sure?'

'Because I'm his sister, for one, and I knew him better than anyone. Besides, considering what they found on him, it makes sense.'

The confused look on Harker's face prompted her to continue.

'You know about the silver pieces they found on him. It was mentioned in all the news reports.'

Harker felt like an idiot, as he'd not heard anything about pieces of silver. 'I was only aware of the suicide and where it had happened, that's it.' He had seen a photograph of Archie's limp body hanging from the balcony at St Peter's in one of the British tabloids but had chickened out when it came to watching the YouTube clip. His usual curiosity had been surpassed by his wish not to see the tragic last moments of his former best friend's life.

'No, it's what they found on him,' Claire explained. 'In the pocket of his robe was a bag of thirty pieces of silver.'

The symbolism was instantaneously obvious. 'Like Judas Iscariot . . .'

Claire nodded sadly. 'The apostle who betrayed Jesus for the princely sum of thirty silver pieces and then hanged himself. That's how I know Archie must have had a religious crisis: a loss of faith that made him feel like he had betrayed the Church, and that's why he did what he did.' She glanced across at him, raising both palms upwards. 'Christ, Alex, you know how devout he was and how unstable he could be when he was growing up.' She rubbed at her temple as she struggled to convey the difficult truth. 'It was his faith that gave him his strength, but he was always just one step away from cracking up. Always.'

As her eyes began to fill up once more, she poked around in her handbag for a handkerchief. Harker pulled one of the taxi driver's serviettes from his pocket and passed it over. At least, those things had not been a total waste of money.

'Archie was a lot stronger than that, Claire,' he said it gently so as not to push her into a full-blown sobbing session. 'I know he had his own demons, but to kill himself in such a way . . . Well, there must have been a more serious reason than just a lapse in his personal faith. There has to have been more to it than that for him to commit suicide, which is a cardinal sin. That means going straight to hell . . .'

Harker watched her wince at the thought, revealing that Claire was more religious than she let on. 'And the silver coins sounds like he was trying to make amends for something a lot more serious.'

Claire crumpled up the tear-sodden serviette and threw it into the empty ashtray. She now glared at Harker as anger replaced her sadness. 'I'm sure, for whatever money you're getting, you'd like there to be more to it, wouldn't you?'

This comment caught Harker off guard, and not wanting to cause a scene, he waited patiently for Claire to vent her frustrations.

'If you hadn't been offered a fee, I wonder if you'd have even bothered turning up here at all. So much for you being his best friend.'

Harker once again felt his stomach begin to churn furiously as he tried to remain calm but failed miserably in the attempt. Not causing a scene suddenly seemed unimportant. 'Easy, Claire, I loved Archie like a brother despite any problems we may have had. If I'd known he was about to top himself, I'd have come running . . .'

Claire raised an eyebrow at his casual directness.

'That's right, I said *top* himself. And, if he'd had any fucking sense left, he would have called and let me help. As for the money, it was nothing more than a positive incentive in a situation that's totally negative. Now, I may not have been there in his hour of need, but you can bet your arse I'm going to find out what really happened to him, with or without your help.'

It was at about this point that they both realised the small cafe had fallen silent, and all the customers were now riveted by the argument unfolding right in front of their noses. A waiter heading towards their table was distracted by a portly Italian waving a finger, obviously keen to see how the heated discussion would end. Harker's indignation melted away just as quickly as it had arisen, and embarrassment began to take hold.

'I should go now before I say something I really regret.'

Claire, her eyebrows still raised in shock, let slip the beginnings of a smile. 'I'd say it's a little late for that.'

Harker stood up and rummaged through his wallet before dropping ten euros on the table. 'It was good to see you again, Claire.'

And with that, he was striding across the piazza, heading to where he had no idea, but he needed to cool down and regroup; that at least he did know.

He had only made it ten metres when he heard a voice call out to him from behind, and he turned to see Claire following hot on his heels.

'You're not getting away that easily, Alex Harker.' She grabbed his hand and held on to it tightly with the tenacity of a young child. Her smile was growing by the second. 'I'm sorry, I didn't mean to ...'

He cut her off and took her in his arms, hugging her tightly. 'No, I'm the one who's sorry. I'm angry. You're angry, and we've got no one to blame.'

Claire looked up towards the sky and gave a little shake of her fist. 'I do love you, Archie, but damn you can be a pain in the arse.'

They both laughed and then pulled apart from their clinch.

'So where do we go now?'

Harker looked puzzled. 'We?'

She gave him a determined look. 'If there's any possibility that Archie was involved in something that led to his death, then I want to know about it.'

'OK, Ms Dwyer, where first?'

She grabbed his hand and pulled him towards a light-blue taxi stand situated just off the piazza. 'I'm meant to pick up Archie's belongings from his house this afternoon. That's as good a place to start as any.'

He allowed her to pull him along. 'OK, I'm in your hands then.'

The two of them headed towards the taxi rank blissfully unaware of the grey fiat Uno parked up at the far corner of the square. Inside it, Drazia Heldon mopped his gigantic forehead with a handkerchief. It was a hot day, and the weatherman on the radio had warned that it could get hotter, rising well into the '90s. Heldon hoped not because the air conditioning in the Uno was useless.

On the passenger seat, his iPhone began to vibrate, and he let slip a moan. He knew who it was, and they weren't happy after all the trouble his boss had gone to in tracking down Vito Malpuso, and then Heldon had not managed to get a single word out of him despite the pain he put the small man through. The priest had been a lot tougher than he looked.

'Hello . . . Yes, they were right where you said they would be . . . No, No, I understand . . . Merely follow them and report back . . . Again, sir, I'm sorry about the priest . . . I won't fail you again, and I will find the items.'

The line went dead before he could say anything else, and he slammed the phone down on the dashboard. The digital clock above the steering wheel read 11.30 a.m., and he now promised himself he would have all the objects required by that same evening. Drazia Heldon pressed his huge palms together and said a quick prayer, before starting up the Uno's engine.

He waited for the white taxi with its two passengers to pass him before following it at a safe distance, snorting in disgust at the thought of the ex-priest in the vehicle. Was there anything worse than a man of the Church who had lost his faith? When this was all over, he planned to dispatch the low life with far more pain than he had dished out to Vito Malpuso. The good professor would feel the full force of his expertise. He smiled because he would have a lot of fun in applying it too.

Chapter 8

'Cardinal Rocca, let me be blunt and get straight to the point. An administrative error from time to time is understandable. It is almost to be expected, considering the vast extent of the Church's activities. But a twenty-five-million dollar black hole within the Academy of Sciences' budget is something else entirely. Two weeks ago, you assured me that I would have the accounts in full, and last week, you confirmed that once again, yet I've still received nothing. Please accept my apologies for having to concoct a story, but, given your recent actions, it seemed the only way to achieve this meeting. So now I am asking you for a third time, where are those accounts I requested?'

Cardinal Salvatore Vincenzo let his question hang in the air. He had already spent half the morning luring his clerical colleague into the Governorate offices to talk about these urgent matters, and he certainly wasn't in the mood to waste any more time or tolerate any further delay.

'Well?'

Cardinal Karl Rocca sat coolly on the opposite side of Vincenzo's grand mahogany work desk, looking remarkably unconcerned. 'As I told you at our last meeting, we are still accumulating the necessary accounts, and, once that task has been completed, I will hand them directly over to you. It should take us no longer than forty-eight hours.'

Vincenzo took both elbows off his glinting lacquered desk and placed them in his lap, concealing his increasingly clenched fists. 'That's exactly what you told me last week, and they never materialised.'

A smirk crept across Rocca's face. 'I'm not a miracle worker, Cardinal.'

Vincenzo's eyes began to widen in frustration as his guest calmly continued.

'But you have my word those accounts will be with you by tomorrow evening.'

This assurance lessened some of the tension between the two men, but Vincenzo was still far from satisfied. He sat back in his seat and eyed the younger cardinal with mistrust. 'Cardinal Rocca, I appreciate you've only been in your current position for a few months, but I feel the need to explain for a second time what our overall responsibilities are.' Vincenzo rose to his feet and surveyed the impressive marble-lined walls of his office, ignoring his visitor's rolling eyes. 'I am the president of the Governorate, the group of Vatican departments that exercises executive power, including the Papal State's accounting and administrative departments.' Vincenzo smiled sarcastically. 'And you, Cardinal Rocca, are the recently appointed president of the Administration of the Patrimony of the Apostolic See, and your role, amongst other things, is to oversee all the properties and academies belonging to the Church. You are there to ensure that all the incomes of these properties are properly accounted for and the results passed over to us for assessing. It is this income, in part, that allows the Church to stay financially secure and to operate effectively around the world.'

Vincenzo rubbed the base of his spine and lowered himself on to one corner of his desk, silently cursing the sciatica that was playing merry hell with his legs. 'Now, Cardinal, I know you must be still getting used to the extended duties of your appointment and additional responsibilities for other departments, but . . .' He leant forwards, ignoring the spreading pain in his thigh. 'I am only concerned now with one thing, and that is the twenty-five million dollars missing from the Academy of Sciences' budget!'

Rocca sat quietly as Vincenzo hoisted himself off the desk and settled back into his more comfortable armchair.

'If I do not have that report here on my desk by tomorrow afternoon, Cardinal, I will have no other option but to go directly to the Pope himself and ask for a formal investigation to be carried out.'

If Karl Rocca was concerned by this threat, he showed no sign of it. Instead, he simply stood up and made his way to the door before stopping briefly to face Vincenzo directly, his expression impenetrable. 'There will be no need for an investigation, Cardinal Vincenzo. I guarantee it. You will have those accounts on your desk by tomorrow evening.'

With that, he was gone, leaving the door wide open, and Vincenzo was still shaking his head in frustration when a priest appeared there, looking somewhat embarrassed. 'Shall I close the door, Your Eminence?'

Vincenzo nodded solemnly. 'Yes, but first I need you to do something for me.'

The priest ventured a few steps further into the room. 'Of course. What may I do for you?'

The Governorate president pondered the question for a few seconds before making up his mind. 'Can you ask Father Reed to come up here as I'd like a word with him?'

The priest looked unsure, whereupon Vincenzo pre-empted his next question.

'Like yourself, he's a recent addition to the department. But you'll find him on the ground floor section B, I think. Send him up here quickly, please. Actually, don't bother. I'll call him myself.'

The priest nodded dutifully before gently closing the door behind him with a click. Vincenzo picked up the receiver of his desk phone and tapped in an extension number.

'Father Reed, it's Cardinal Vincenzo. Could you please come up to my office? There's something I would like you to do for me.'

Vincenzo gently returned the receiver to its cradle and gazed out of the double-paned windows just in time to see a carefree-looking Cardinal Rocca strolling towards the Academy of Science building beyond. 'Cardinal Rocca,' he murmured, 'what exactly are you up to?'

Chapter 9

The blazing midday sun glinted off the taxi's silver roof as it once again renegotiated the cobblestone road it had driven down moments earlier. Harker watched in relief as it turned a corner and vanished from sight. The journey had been a fifteen-minute drive through a myriad of tight winding streets, which Claire was just as certain they wouldn't fit in to as the driver was sure they would. The local had been right, of course, even if they had come close to scraping a few stonewalls and even closer to running down an elderly street vendor. The remainder of their trip had been engulfed in an uneasy silence, and Harker felt relieved to be a pedestrian once more.

Archie Dwyer's home was located in the centre of Rome, less than a mile away from Vatican City and just a few minutes' walk from the famous Piazza del Popolo. The apartment was on the top floor, and the dome of St Peter's Basilica was easily visible on the other side of the River Tiber. The property itself was owned by the Vatican, and both Harker and Archie had been allowed to live there for the duration of their three-year training.

The dusty, humid air and the sight of the city now teased at Harker's memory, and he found himself reminiscing back to the times he and Archie had spent in that very neighbourhood. The lessons and learning were the most prevalent memories, but the hot weather and the experience of a new environment, especially one as beautiful and alluring as Rome, were not easily forgotten. Harker had found ignoring the local nightlife a lot harder than his friend had and, on a few rare occasions, had ended up passed out on the front step of their doorway. Not good behaviour for a priest in training, and Archie had been furious, severely reprimanding him before dragging him inside through the same door that Claire was now busily trying to unlock.

'I think the lock's broken,' she declared, taking a step back to survey the stone-built facade of the narrow house. 'And I'm not surprised either. Look at the state of this place. I don't know why you two would ever live here, or why he came back to it.' She gave the door a single thump in frustration. 'It's a total tip.'

Harker pulled his eyes away from the beautiful vista. 'He stayed here for the sake of the view. It's one of the best in Rome, certainly the best of the Vatican.'

Gently he extracted the set of keys from Claire's hand and carefully worked one into the rusty lock.

'All you need is the right touch.' He grinned cheekily. 'A man's touch.'

Claire immediately reached over and rested a hand on his shoulder. 'Of course, it also helps if you used to live here too.'

Harker jolted the key once more, gave the door a thump, and it swung back to reveal a wooden staircase beyond. 'Yeah, that helps as well.'

They headed up to the landing at the top of the stairs, which opened into a small lounge with a tidy kitchen off to one side. The entire space was now empty except for six large cardboard boxes stacked against the far wall with ARCHIE DWYER scrawled on them in black felt-tip. Claire moved over to the first box, opened out its flaps, and lightly browsed the top layer. 'This is it . . . everything Archie owned. It's not a lot, but he never was much interested in material goods.'

Harker shot her a wistful smile and tapped his collar. 'It's the lifestyle, goes with the job.'

She let out a frustrated sigh and closed the lid. 'OK, what now?'

'Now, we have a look at Archie's PC and check his emails.'

'I never even knew Archie used a computer. I thought he was afflicted by a continual bout of techno-fear.'

Harker found it odd that Archie's own flesh and blood seemed to know less about the man than he did—but wasn't that usually the way. 'Yeah, he used to be quite a whiz with Microsoft Office and used to regularly email me with his day-to-day thoughts.'

Claire pulled her head out of the box she was investigating and flicked a loose strand of hair from her face. 'Did he keep a diary by any chance?'

Harker shook his head firmly. 'No, he didn't believe in diaries, as you surely know. He always maintained that you change as you get older and that diaries from earlier years make you sound different from the man you've since become. It only confirms a sad human truth we're all aware of but are unwilling to openly acknowledge: that we're all hypocrites in one way or another.'

Claire smiled as she remembered her brother's tendency towards eccentric points of view. 'But he did write down his thoughts on philosophy and spiritualism,' Harker continued, 'he used to email me these, and we'd debate them. But that stopped when I left the Church. Not a bad thing, really. They could be pretty boring discussions.'

The affectionate expression on Harker's face drew another smile from Claire Dwyer.

'So where's your PC, Archie?' he exclaimed in frustration. 'Claire, why don't you finish checking these?' He pointed to the three unopened boxes next to her, and she immediately began delving into the first one. 'Meanwhile, I'll have a look upstairs.'

Claire didn't look up but only raised one hand in a thumbs-up gesture before continuing to rummage around.

'I'll be right back,' he added before disappearing up to the second-floor landing and heading through the doorway of his old bedroom. It was empty except for the metal frame and a couple of pillows. He then checked the nearby toilet and bathroom before stepping across the landing to his former friend's room. It was equally barren, and he strode across to the window and gazed out in the direction of the Vatican. It provided a good vantage point, and, from this high position, he could clearly make out the balcony of St Peter's Basilica where Archie had hanged himself. Suddenly the thought of his old friend standing exactly where he was now and contemplating how to end his life made him feel queasy.

It was as he lowered his eyes towards the floor, not wanting to continue gazing at his friend's favourite view, that he saw it. In the corner of the window pane, there was an engraving, maybe representing a word. Craning his head closer, Harker realised it wasn't a word at all but a mark scratched into the glass, no more than a centimetre in width and height.

Harker rubbed at a layer of grime on the surface, allowing him to inspect the image more closely. The mark was a symbol he recognised but hadn't seen in a very long time. The image consisted of an oval, which contained two figures riding a single horse, and, although crudely cut, there was no doubt in his mind what it represented. But what it was doing here in a priest's house was anyone's guess.

'I can't see it anywhere,' a voice sounded out from behind him. 'Did you find anything up here?'

Harker swung around to see Claire standing in the doorway, the neckline of her dress now covered in a fine layer of dust. He was about to motion towards the etched symbol when the outline of another image caught his attention. A distinct projection of the marking had been cast by the sun on to the opposite wall of the room but magnified to about a foot in height. It was hazy at first, but within seconds, a brighter ray of sunlight shone in through the pane, bringing the other shadow in to focus.

'Yes, I think I have.' Harker could feel the bubbling of excitement in his chest as he took her by the shoulder and pointed out the small symbol on the window. 'Claire, do you know what that signifies?'

Claire focused in on the icon before she shrugged and made a wild guess. 'The logo of whichever company made the glass pane?'

He shook his head. 'It's a pictogram, an ancient mark. That, Ms Dwyer, is the emblem of the Knights Templar.'

Claire stood back and shrugged again. 'Who?'

Harker stared at her in disbelief. 'You've never heard of the Knights Templar, the defenders of the Holy Grail? Been featured in scores of books and films.'

The mention of movies finally coaxed a glimmer of realisation from her. 'What . . . you mean from medieval times?'

Harker almost laughed at her knowledge or, rather, lack of it. 'The only way you wouldn't have heard about them in recent years is if you'd been living under a rock.'

Her look of growing annoyance quashed any further sarcasm in his voice as he cleared his throat to continue.

'Yes, from medieval times, you know, Knights and horses.' He pointed again to the insignia cast on the wall. 'And look where it's shining.'

She studied the enlarged representation and nodded. 'Ahh, yes, it's very nice. It really is.'

Harker shook his head in frustration. 'Claire, I love you, I really do, but you would have made a terrible detective.' He strode over to the projected image and lightly felt his way around the edges of the same wall. 'Many of the buildings around here date back hundreds of years, and I will bet some still hold a few secrets, but I can't believe I lived here all that time and never realised it.'

He pushed at the centre of the now dulling image, and instantly an entire section of the wall retracted inwards and slid neatly to one side, revealing a doorway. He then shot Claire a triumphant smile, his stomach now tingling with butterflies.

'It's a secret chamber,' he explained.

'For what?'

Harker grinned like an excited schoolboy and then pushed the wooden door ajar. 'Don't know, but let's find out, shall we?'

The musty damp smell from within made him wrinkle his nose as he peered into the pitch-blackness. He automatically brushed his hand up the inside wall in search of a light switch.

'Here we go.'

With a click, the light bulb directly above illuminated, initially blinding him, but, as his vision adjusted, he could soon make out a flight of stone stairs leading downwards to a rusty metal door ten feet below. The stairway looked worn, and the moss-lined walls with a patchwork of glistening damp gave a clue to its age.

'What's in there?' Claire had raised her head over Harker's shoulder, strands of her silky red hair tickling his cheek.

'It's a staircase,' he responded, rubbing at the itch on his face unconsciously. 'Let's see where it leads.'

Fragments of grit and loose plaster crackled beneath Harker's feet as he carefully made his way down towards the discoloured entrance, visible at the bottom. Close behind him, Claire had a hand firmly clamped on his shoulder as her high heels began to teeter on the hard stonework.

'Not a great day for these fancy shoes,' she remarked with a laugh.

Harker's curiosity at what lay below was becoming overpowering. He placed one hand firmly on the ice-cold metal handle and gave it a pull. It fell aside with ease, the hinges well oiled, revealing only darkness. He scanned the pitch-blackness beyond, shapes emerging into view only as his eyes adjusted. His entire body tensed apprehensively, not knowing what lay ahead. A few feet to his right, a small red light blinked at him through the dimness.

'Hold on.' He gently took Claire's hand off his shoulder and placed it securely on to the frame of the open door before cautiously entering.

Harker had only made it a few steps inside when something solid smacked against his shin, and he leapt backwards as his nerves got the better of him.

'Alex!' she cried out in alarm.

He reached down and repositioned the offending obstacle. 'It's just a chair . . .'

Claire allowed herself to take a deep breath, now embarrassed by her skittishness.

'. . . and a table.'

Harker proceeded carefully towards the blinking light, his vision now adjusting to the dimness. He could make out the dull images of the chair and the desk, with a side lamp positioned on top of it. After fumbling around for a few moments, he managed to switch it on. Again, the sudden brightness made him curse, and it took a few seconds for his vision to return to normal. Finally, the entire room came into view. In truth, it wasn't so much a room as a converted basement, with a circular red carpet covering most of the stone-flagged floor. Standing upon it was a plain wooden writing desk and a chair. In the centre of the desk was a PC, its red power button flashing.

'What is all this stuff about?'

Harker turned back to see Claire checking out a variety of posters covering the whitewashed brick walls.

'Well, that's a Salvador Dali painting called the Disintegration of the Persistence of Memory.' He was pointing to a poster displayed nearest the door. 'The one next to it seems to be a portrait of Sir Isaac Newton . . .' Harker glanced back to the desk '. . . and this hidden room must be your brother's private study.'

He slid into the chair and pressed the power button, the monitor immediately flashing into life. Claire joined him as the Hewlett Packard ran through its start-up procedures.

'This is all very secretive, Alex. Hidden doors, concealed rooms . . . what was he hiding?' Her voice had acquired a shrill of excitement to it. 'Either he was some kind of secret agent . . .' she forced a smile through quivering lips '. . . or he's been hiding something he was ashamed of.'

Harker reached up and patted her shoulder. 'If you're talking about anything nefarious, I don't believe it for a second.'

Claire nodded woefully; her eyes began to mist, and she pointed to the flashing monitor. 'Well, there has to be some reason he committed suicide. If there are pictures of naked children on that computer, I want you to destroy it.'

Her words caught Harker by surprise; after his meeting with Brulet, he'd not even entertained the possibility that Archie was a paedophile, even if Claire had considered it.

'Archie was no child molester, and I know that for a fact,' he said firmly. 'No, this is something else altogether.'

Claire dabbed beneath her eyes with a fingertip so as not to ruin her make-up in an effort to compose herself.

'And as for the secret agent part, you may be closer to the truth there than you think.'

Claire was now kneeling beside him, her eyes fixed firmly on the screen. 'What do you mean closer than I think?' She grabbed Harker's face and turned it towards her. 'Alex, what aren't you telling me?'

The incipient tears were now gone, quickly replaced with anger as she tightened her hold on his cheek.

'You'd better tell me what's going on, Alex Harker. I'm his sister, so I have a right to know.' Her grip was becoming uncomfortable, so he gently pulled away her hand and placed it in her lap. He knew he was going to have to come clean eventually.

'OK, you know the charity I told you about—the people who paid me to snoop around?'

Claire gave a grim nod.

'Well, I didn't contact them initially. Archie did that because he had information about another group he'd had dealings with. It's a group connected with the Vatican.' Harker pulled out Archie Dwyer's hand-written letter and handed it to her. 'He sent me this.'

Claire delicately opened the envelope and read the contents out loud, 'Alex, my time remaining is short. Follow the path of the old world. Follow the path of the master's name from J–A. Maddocks 23-45-64. Trust your logic, not your faith.' She paused at the end of the last sentence. 'What the hell does that mean?'

Harker watched the muscles in her face morph from frustration to curiosity, and he almost gasped in relief. He pointed back towards the staircase and tapped the first line of the note.

'Follow the path of the old world . . . the shadow image on the wall that led us down here. The Templars were of the old world, and they no longer exist. Don't you see it's a trail for me to follow? Archie's laid out a trail.'

Claire stared at him, her expression full of doubt. 'And the numbers?'

At that exact moment, the monitor finally burst into life, displaying a page that was blank except for a log-in window in the middle. Harker gently retrieved the note from her and turned to concentrate on the screen.

'I think it may be a password for use on this computer.' He pulled the keyboard closer, tapped in the seven digits, and pressed Enter. The screen went black, and a message in large italics appeared.

'Incorrect answer: 2 attempts remaining before deletion.'

The monitor then reverted back to the log-in window.

Harker sat back and let out a disgruntled sigh. 'Your brother's put an encryption lock on it. Two more tries, and we'll lose all the information it contains for good.' He shot Claire a glance. 'Not bad for someone with techno-fear.'

She shook her head as if shocked at how little she knew about her own brother. 'So what now?'

Harker turned back to the screen. 'I'm not sure.' He looked down at Archie's note and read out the second part again. 'Follow the path of the master's name from J–A . . .'

As he mulled over this sentence, Claire stood up with a jerk and clicked her fingers.

'I've got it. One of Archie's friends here in Rome is an expat he mentioned a couple of times. His name is Justine Ashhule.' She pointed to the note. 'Look J–A, Justine Ashhule. I remember the name because it sounded so comical: Ashhule . . . Asshole. That has to be it?'

Harker shook his head. 'No, that's fourteen letters, and the password only has six.'

Claire, looking defeated, resumed her kneeling position, just as Harker let out a snort of amusement.

'Asshole! No, I don't think so. He'd hardly choose that.'

He had just finished saying this when a fresh idea popped into his head. 'Hold on! Follow the name of the master? What if the master represents God?'

Claire butted in, eager to prove herself useful. 'But that's only three letters, and it starts with a *G* not a *J*.'

Harker raised his eyebrows in excitement. 'You're right, of course, but in the Old Testament, the master isn't known as God. He's called Jehova.'

Claire tapped her forehead. 'The amount of Sunday-school classes I went to, I should have twigged that.'

Harker smiled. 'Yes, indeed you should have, but, if I remember rightly, you spent most of your time playing doctors and nurses with the boys, much to your brother's horror.'

Claire rubbed the side of her neck in embarrassment. 'Yeah, there was that.' She looked over at the note still in Harker's hand, with a renewed sadness in her eyes. 'From my earliest memories, Archie was always very protective of me.'

Seeing where this conversation was going, Harker attempted to reverse it a notch. 'That's why I never asked you out. Because I know he would have killed me.'

This admission drew a smile from her, and she rubbed his arm appreciatively. 'OK, let's try it then.'

Harker turned back to the keyboard and typed in 'Jehova'. The screen again went blank, and again the warning in italics popped up.

'Incorrect answer: 1 attempt remaining before deletion.'

'Damn, I felt sure that was it.' Harker stood up and rubbed his temples in frustration. The answer had to be here somewhere. He began running the clue through his mind again and again as he got up from the chair and commenced pacing up and down the room. 'The master . . . The master . . . J to A . . .'

He was on his third lap of the room when a name on one of the wall posters caught his attention, and suddenly everything fell into place. 'Of course . . . That's so simple.'

Claire practically lunged forward, eager to see what had caught his eye. 'What . . . what have you seen?'

Harker returned the note to his inside pocket and moved over to a poster depicting the crucifixion of Christ. 'There!'

Above the poster, and imbedded in the stonewall, sat a small light-blue tile no more than an inch across, carrying the letter *A* in fine italic script.

He tried to contain his excitement but totally failed as his breathing began to quicken. 'There's an *A* and then tiles marked with a *C*, next an *E*, then *G*, *I* . . . 'Harker followed the wall posters around the room, settling on the last one. 'And finally, *J*.'

Claire moved in closer to that poster, and, sure enough, just above it hung another small light-blue tile with the letter *J* in italic script also. 'I see it, so does that mean there's another secret door?'

Shaking his head, Harker moved over to the poster below the *J* tile. 'The "master" in Archie's note doesn't refer to God. It refers to the creative masters like artists, inventors, and composers.' He directed her attention to each of the posters in turn. 'Look, Archie's note read J–A, so if we take the first poster, under the *J* tile, which is Salvador Dali, and the next is a portrait Sir Isaac Newton, and that one's by the French painter Nicholas Poussin, Fredrick Chopin the composer, Ulysses the famous

Greek warrior, and finally Leonardo Da Vinci's "John The Baptist" . . . Six posters, indicating six masters. Take the first letter from each name, and we've got a six-figure password.'

Claire squeezed his arm firmly. 'Hold on, is it their surnames or first names?'

Harker just smiled and sat himself down at the desk. 'Let's find out. OK, we start at *J* which is the Salvador Dali, so the first letter of the surname is *D*, followed by Issac Newton, which is *N*.' He followed the walls around him, his eyes piecing together the password. 'OK, then the password must be DNPCUP? Unless that's a bra size I'm unfamiliar with, I'd say we should go with the first names.'

Harker zipped through the letters in seconds. '*S-I-N-F-U-L*. That has to be it. Sinful.'

Without hesitation, he typed it in to the log-in window and pressed enter. The screen went blank again, and he heard Claire suck in a worried gasp, which only heightened the tension further. The screen stayed blank for what seemed an eternity before eventually buzzing into life with a series of clicks and a whirr from the hard drive.

'Welcome, old friend,' the message read.

Harker wiped his forehead with dramatic exaggeration. 'Phew, for a second there, I thought . . .'

Claire dutifully knelt back down beside him. 'I never had any doubt.'

He shot her a sarcastic grin before turning his attention back to the monitor. The screen was blank except for one unopened document. Harker double-clicked on the icon, and a news cutting appeared on the screen.

'See, no naked children. I told you.'

Claire let out a relieved sigh. 'Thank God.'

They both huddled in close, trying to read the news column.

'Claire, it's in Italian, and you don't speak Italian.' Harker nudged her aside, and she reluctantly resumed her earlier position as he scanned the article. 'It's a news report about a fire at an orphanage in Castel Madama on the first of September this year. Four children were caught in the blaze and died. Officials believe it started through an electrical fault.'

He tapped a photo at the foot of the report, which showed the charred fire damage to one of the orphanages' outer walls. In the forefront stood an elderly man with bright white hair, wearing a partially burnt blue jumper and faded jeans, with a look of shock spread across his face. The caption read:

'Tivoli's night of sorrow: Orphanage director Benito Giuseppe looks on in horror as fire fighters try to control the blaze which killed four of the young residents.'

Harker sat back allowing Claire to examine the photo.

'What else does it say?'

'That's it, nothing else significant.' Harker let his words trail off as he tried desperately to connect the dots. What did the deaths of four orphans in a fire have to do with Archie? Unless . . . ? An unpleasant feeling settled in the pit of his stomach. *Did those cracks about molesting children have some basis in fact?* He tried to push the vile idea from his mind. Archie wasn't the type, but, then again, what was the type? He was torn from such thoughts by Claire pulling at his arm.

'Alex, why is this timer running?' She drew his attention to the small digital timer located in the corner of the screen. The numbers were scrolling down in seconds. 'Is it a bomb?'

Harker took a closer look at the spinning numbers. 'No, it's not a bomb,' he said firmly.

'How do you know?'

He pointed to the first set of numerals. 'The countdown is measured in hours look, twenty-one hours, ten minutes, and still counting. No one would set an almost day long fuse, would they?'

Claire composed herself again. 'So what's this countdown for?'

Harker sat back thoughtfully. 'I'm not sure, but whatever your brother wanted us to uncover, it happens in just over twenty-one hours.'

She glanced down at her watch. 'That's nine o'clock tomorrow morning . . . What does it all mean?'

He gave a concerned nod. 'It means we need to get a move on. Claire, why don't you call for a taxi? I think we need to pay this Mr Benito Giuseppe a visit.'

Chapter 10

'Ah, Professor Harker.' Benito Giuseppe threw his arms wildly around Harker and gave him an over-friendly pat on the back. 'And you must be Claire Dwyer.' He clasped both her hands and delicately kissed her cheek. 'I am so sorry for your brother. He was a lovely, decent man, and you have my condolences. Had your call not been at such short notice, I could have arranged a full tour of the home, but, nonetheless, it is a pleasure to welcome you both here. Please take a seat.'

Benito gestured to the two small plastic children's chairs placed in front of his desk. 'Forgive me, but I don't have many adult guests. Most of the visitors to my office are a little bit smaller.' He made his way around to a comfortable-looking leather chair behind the desk and promptly sat himself down as both his guests shuffled about in their miniature seats. 'The kids call those the hot seats, but to me, they're just the naughty chairs. Now, please tell me, how may I be of help?'

Harker straightened out the crease in his trousers that was cutting off the circulation to his groin and tried to look as relaxed as he could whilst perched on a foot-high chair. 'Thank you for seeing us at such short notice, and I'm sorry we're late.'

The fifty-minute-long trip up to Castel Madama had been a challenge. The orphanage was situated far off the main roads, and even the taxi driver had trouble finding this isolated spot located outside of the main town. Claire had become convinced that the driver was deliberately trying to bump up the fare, but, not wanting to get dumped in the middle of nowhere, Harker had opted for the diplomatic option—keeping his mouth shut—and because Claire spoke no Italian, it was his vote that counted.

Benito Giuseppe smiled wildly, the veneers on his spectacles glinting in the bright sunlight that shone through the side window and on to the orphanage director's green leather-clad desktop. 'No trouble at all. Father Dwyer gave us so much of his time that it's the least I can do.'

Harker finally managed to position himself comfortably as Claire continued the struggle to figure out the best way to sit without revealing too much. 'Mr Giuseppe, we're trying to find out precisely what affiliation Archie Dwyer had with the orphanage?'

The director sat back in his chair and stroked his forehead thoughtfully. 'Is this to do with those rumours in the gutter press?' He glanced at Claire sympathetically. 'Because that's all lies. Your brother was no more a child molester than I am a brain surgeon. I'm afraid some journalists today don't have the honesty and integrity they once did. As long as it sells, they run with it and then worry about the consequences afterwards. I've already had the child-protection authorities crawling over this place for the past two weeks, and I can assure you that they left here quite satisfied.'

Suspecting that the conversation was about to plunge into the legalities of their visit, Harker butted in, 'No, Mr Giuseppe, I'm sure everything's above board, and that's not the reason we've come here today.' Lying was not one of Harker's strong points, and he'd been rehearsing this speech on the way over. 'The truth is that both Claire and I had lost touch with Archie, and, after his funeral this morning, we both realised how little we know about the last few years of his life.' The last part of the rehearsed speech now totally escaped him. *Damn!* 'So here we are.'

Benito rubbed his hands together vigorously, and, for a moment, Harker was sure this friendly Italian was about to lose his temper. A few seconds passed before a thin smile appeared on the director's face. 'I do understand. It's not until they leave us that we realise how short our time on this earth is.'

The remark received a depressed stare from Claire.

'I'm sorry, my dear, I don't mean to upset you.'

She smiled bravely and simply shook her head, much to the relief of the Italian.

'Well, what else can I tell you? Father Dwyer came up here to see us almost every weekend. He took the children on sightseeing tours of the city and also to the Vatican itself. He was always very giving of his time, and the kids loved him. He even had a great talent for making his sermons fun and exciting—something which is hard enough with adults, let alone when dealing with young children.'

This image conjured up pleasant memories in Harker's mind. Even as a young man, when most teenagers would rather die than take their siblings along with them, Archie Dwyer had never faltered in his protective attention to Claire and her younger classmates. It was a trait that Harker had always admired in his friend but never mastered for himself. That ability to engage always on the same level, regardless of the person's age, was one he'd obviously put to good use here at the orphanage.

'He was a great communicator . . . always was.'

'Yes, you're right, of course, Professor and he had a real talent for bringing people together.' Benito gave a short undignified sigh and looked out of the office window at a couple of the home's younger inmates playing with a frisbee on the grass lawn below, his mood suddenly darkening. 'But that all changed after the fire.'

'The fire?' Harker could feel Claire's eyes on him as he feigned ignorance of the disaster. No, he was not a good liar at all, but, thankfully, it was a fact that Benito seemed oblivious to.

'Yes, we had a fire break out here in September. It was a terrible accident, and we lost four of our children. It was the worst tragedy we've ever had at the orphanage, and, if I'm honest, we're still reeling from the loss.' The dark rings beneath the director's eyes told of the sleepless nights he had endured since. 'But no one took it harder than Father Dwyer. Like I said, it changed him—it really did.'

'In what way?'

It was the first time Claire had really spoken since the beginning of the meeting, and Benito shifted in his chair, turning his attention towards her.

'He took it very personally and simply stopped visiting us. I only saw him once again, shortly before he . . .' The Italian lowered his head slightly, though never taking his eyes off Claire. '. . . passed away, and that was it until I read of his demise in the newspapers.'

Harker leant forward inquisitively, wincing as the keys in his pocket dug painfully into his thigh. 'What did he want to see you for?'

'He wanted to apologise for his absence and to tell me that due to his new commitments, he would no longer be able to visit us here. He gave me a parting gift for the home, and that was it—he was gone.'

Harker was opening his mouth to speak when Claire beat him to it.

'What was this gift?'

Benito looked down at his squirming guests and smiled.

'Those seats can be torture. Please follow me, and I'll be happy to show you. I really ought to get some new chairs,' Benito added apologetically, 'but our budget is so tight. Please, this way.'

The curving corridor outside the director's office circled a grassy courtyard where two female carers were busily gathering the children for playtime.

They had only made it halfway round the walkway when something caught Benito's attention. He rapped on the corridor's glass window and pointed to a small boy who was down on his hands and knees, staring up the skirt of one of the supervisors. His knock on the window caused the woman to turn around, first to recognise Benito and then to see the pint-sized peeper almost beneath her. She shook her head disapprovingly and gave the child a light slap across the head before sending him over to confront the unhappy-looking director.

'I'm sorry, but I need to deal with this matter now,' Benito said wearily as the young boy yanked the corridor's glass door open with both hands and sheepishly ambled over towards them.

'Now, Gustavo . . .' The pudgy director bent down and spoke softly in Italian. 'We've spoken about this sort of behaviour before, haven't we?'

The boy nodded solemnly, barely making eye contact as he fidgeted with his hands. 'Yes, signor Mr Giuseppe.'

Benito knelt down to the child's level and placed a hand on the ten-year-old's shoulder. 'You know better than that, don't you, Gus?'

The boy nodded again, his face flushing as the embarrassment grew.

'Tell me, Gustavo, why is it wrong to look up ladies' skirts?'

'Because it's naughty?' the boy said, offering more a question than an answer.

'Yes, but why?'

Young Gustavo took a moment to think about it, his lips curling as he tried to remember the right answer. 'Because it's an infringement of their space.'

Benito tapped him gently on the shoulder, clearly pleased by this response. 'That's right, it's an infringement of someone's personal space.'

He allowed the youngster to think about that for a second before continuing.

'And what did we agree would happen if you did it again?'

The boy looked down at his feet and then up again with a cheeky grin on his face. 'I'd get second helpings at dinner.'

Harker came close to bursting into laughter at the boy's response, and he turned away to face Claire who, not speaking a word of Italian, was clueless to what was being said.

'No, Gustavo, don't be cheeky. There will be no frisbee playing with the other children until tomorrow. Now go back to the group and think about what you've done.'

The punishment didn't seem to have the desired effect, and Gus headed back to the group with a happy smile, already scoping out the other female carer whose skirt was even shorter.

Benito stood up straight again and continued with their tour, 'That boy suffers from an unhealthy obsession.'

'Didn't we all at that age?' Harker said as Benito exhaled a defeated sigh.

'In truth, yes, but that's the second time today I've had to reprimand him. Unfortunately, it's become more of a hobby with Gustavo. One I'm hoping he'll lose interest in over time.'

'Good luck.' The comment came out, sounding rather more sarcastic than Harker had intended, but Benito Giuseppe smiled at the truth in it before silently continuing down the corridor to enter a small classroom at the end.

The room was neatly lined with child-size desks and a world map hung on the wall behind the teacher's desk. Benito produced a silver key from his trouser pocket, unlocked the top drawer of the main desk, and then reached inside to pull out a framed picture, which he handed to Harker.

'From happier times.'

It was a group photograph of four brown-haired children with Mediterranean complexions, all sitting on the grass lawn at the orphanage's entrance. Standing directly behind them was Archie Dwyer with a satisfied smile across his face, and next to him stood two other priests, each with an arm resting on one of Archie's shoulders. Underneath the photo itself was a miniature map of the area surrounding the orphanage.

'Do you know who the other two priests are?' Harker asked.

'One's Father Maddocks and the other Father Malpuso. Father Malpuso only visited us a few times, but Father Maddocks came here almost as regularly as Archie. We considered both of them benefactors of the home, and he and Father Dwyer were close friends.'

The name resonated in Harker's mind as he remembered Archie's note: 'Maddocks 23-45-64.'

'They both gave much of their spare time to the orphanage and, of course, to the four angels.'

'Four angels?' It was Claire's curiosity that had now been aroused.

Benito pointed to the four children. 'Yes, that's what both the fathers called them.'

At first glance, the four children looked like . . . well, regular children. But, as Harker examined them more closely, he could see they were far from regular. At first, he thought they were all smiling, but they weren't. Each of the children had a look of sheer terror etched on his face, their mouths hung open as if shouting something, and their arms and legs were bent unnaturally. They were clearly disabled and severely so.

'Yes, it's the name that Father Dwyer—and then all of us—used. As you can see, they had serious physical problems, and when they first arrived here, we were unsure if we could offer the proper care they needed. But Father Dwyer convinced us otherwise, and he even secured a regular donation from the Church to pay for new wheelchairs and medication.'

Suddenly and abruptly, a plump Italian woman in a tight-fitting cream jumper and jeans appeared at the classroom's doorway, looking flustered. 'Mr Giuseppe, I apologise for interrupting, but I need you.'

Benito looked embarrassed by the intrusion of his blushing colleague. 'Can't it wait, Ms Malik?' He gestured to his guests. 'I'm a little busy.'

Ms Malik turned to Harker and nodded respectfully. 'I'm sorry, but it's Gustavo. He's doing it again, and he won't take any of us seriously. He needs to be properly disciplined, Mr Giuseppe. Would you talk to him, please?'

The director sighed despairingly. 'Don't work yourself up. I'll be right there.'

She nodded again and disappeared as quickly as she'd come. The grey-haired director turned back to his guests with sagging shoulders.

'You know, in the good old days, I'd have put him straight over my knee for a good spanking. Of course, nowadays, we can't even use harsh language. Would you excuse me for a moment?'

Benito marched out of the classroom, his posture stiffening already in anticipation of his little chat with the mischievous Gustavo.

Claire pulled the picture frame from Harker's hands and eyed it suspiciously. 'Maddocks . . . that's the same name as on Archie's note?'

Harker nodded silently and pulled the worn piece of paper from his pocket, passing it to Claire whilst taking the framed photograph back into his grasp. 'And I'm pretty sure I know what the numbers stand for.'

He placed the photo down flat on the desk in front of them and ran his fingers across the tiny map included below it. 'Those numbers aren't a code or password.' He drew her attention to the dark-blue digits ranged along the edges of it. 'They're map coordinates, look.'

Claire edged closer, holding Archie's crumpled note to one side of the frame as Harker traced the numbers to their point of convergence with two separate index fingers.

'23 by 45 by 64.'

His fingertips met near the northern edge of the map in a square that was empty of any additional marks except for a tiny hole where the map had been lightly punctured with a pin.

'What is it?' There was a tremble in her voice that he pretended not to notice as she bent down closer to inspect the tiny map.

'St Benedicts,' he explained. 'It's an old monastery about forty-five minutes' drive from here in the town of Subiaco.' Harker stood back, allowing Claire to get a closer look.

'So that's where this Maddocks person is, right?' She turned to face him, her expression full of questions, and, for an instant, he imagined himself staring into the eyes of his old friend Archie Dwyer. The two siblings physically had so much in common that now any attraction Harker had felt earlier that day instantly evaporated.

She noticed his discomfort, and a frown appeared on her forehead. 'Are you OK? You look like you've just seen a ghost.'

Harker gave a small shake of his head. 'I'm fine. It's just . . . It's just quite a trail Archie's left for us.'

Claire eyed him disbelievingly. 'I know, so I guess we go and track down Maddocks.'

Just then Benito Giuseppe bustled into the room, rubbihg his hands. 'I'm sorry about all this business, but the Gustavo situation is proving more time-consuming than I'd first expected. I see I'm going to have to spend some more time with the little pervert, teaching him the finer points of common decency. I'm afraid I'll have to cut this visit short.' He stretched a hand out towards the open doorway. 'Is there anything else you wanted to know?'

Harker passed him back the framed photograph. 'Just a couple of things before we leave. Firstly, is Father Maddocks here today by any chance?'

Benito slid the photo back in the desk drawer and locked it securely. 'No, I haven't seen him for a couple of weeks. He was meant to be here last weekend, but he didn't make it. I assumed he might be helping out with Father Dwyer's funeral arrangements, but he'll drop by soon, no doubt.' By now, the director was already ushering them back into the corridor.

'Just one other thing. Would it be possible to meet the children in that photo? The ones they call the Angels?'

Benito Giuseppe stopped dead in his tracks and slowly turned to face them, his eyes suddenly filling with sadness. 'I'm afraid that won't be possible. You see, they were the ones that died in the fire.'

Chapter 11

Father John Reed marched across the oval inner court of the Academy of Sciences with the brooding resolve of a bulldog. His meeting with Cardinal Vincenzo earlier that morning had left him with a great sense of unease. Being asked to spy on another cardinal was to his knowledge unheard of, and it made him extremely anxious. Vincenzo had labelled it a fact-finding exercise, but when Reed had asked the reason for such a drastic measure, the reply had been somewhat vague.

'John, the Lord God sees all and knows all, but, unfortunately, I do not.'

This answer had halted any further questions from Reed. After all, he trusted Vincenzo, and if the head of the Governorate requested that he dig deeper into Cardinal Rocca's affairs and the academy's accounts, then that was fine by him.

Reed calmly made his way up the steps and past the impressive stone columns of the academy's portico, after pausing a moment to enjoy the building's stunning architecture and sculptures. Originally built as a summer residence for Pope Pius IV in the fourteenth century, the villa resembled an ancient nymphaeum or grotto, its walls decorated with a multitude of intricate statues and reliefs. Reed had wanted to investigate this building further ever since his arrival at the Vatican, but he would have preferred to do so under different circumstances. The Academy of Science had existed in one form or another since the 1600s when the Roman Prince Federico Cesi, a keen botanist and naturalist, had set up what was named the Academia dei Lincei with the famous astronomer Galileo as its first president. This appointment was later considered an unfortunate choice after Galileo was charged by the Church with heresy for expressing his belief that the earth revolved around the sun, thus suggesting that our world was not the centre of the universe.

In the 1930s, it was rebranded as the Academy of Sciences, and its resources extended in six main areas of research devoted to continuing advancements in science and technology.

To be standing here made him almost feel giddy, for the academy had been home to some of the world's top scientists, an astonishing mixture of cultures, religions, and creeds all bound to one purpose. Its members included such notables as Niles Bohr, who had worked on the Manhattan project in developing the world's first atomic bomb, and Professor Stephen Hawking, who was arguably the greatest mind of the twentieth century, to name just a few.

Reed allowed himself to enjoy such thoughts a few moments longer before stiffening his resolve and heading inside.

'Good afternoon, Father. What may I do for you on this glorious day?' The smiling priest manning the reception desk enquired warmly.

Reed pulled out his ID card and passed it over. 'I'm hoping to speak with the academy's accountant, Father Roberto Sanchez. Could you point me in the right direction?'

The receptionist took note of the ID and then passed it back, his smile unwavering. 'I'm afraid he's not in the country right now. He's on leave, but he'll be back next week. Dr Heinz Marques is here, though, and he's one of the section heads. Could he be of help?'

It was Reed's turn to smile. 'Yes, thank you. Where can I find him?'

The receptionist pointed to a set of double doors on the far side of the room. 'There are four main departments in the academy, and those doors will take you into the first, which is the Social Sciences. To your left, you'll find a side corridor, so follow the signs for BIOETHICS, and Dr Marques is in the third section along. Listen out for his voice, you'll no doubt hear him before you see him.'

Reed nodded politely and made his way towards the beckoning double doors, unsure what he was now walking into. It wasn't to be long before he found out. He became aware of the high-pitched shouts and curses from halfway down the corridor. They provided an oddly unnerving combination of sounds which then went eerily quiet just as he approached the door marked DR MARQUES. He quietly twisted the handle and pushed the door open to reveal a corridor lined on either side by shelves housing display jars containing a variety of small creatures floating in clear liquid.

The smell of formaldehyde was permeated by a strong whiff of body odour, causing Reed's nostrils to flare. *What was it about scientists that tended to emit the oddest personal smells? Choice of diet? The chemicals they used? Or were they merely so fanatical about their work that occasional showering became more of an option than a necessity?*

The passage opened up into a square working area also surrounded by exhibits, in the middle of which stood a sturdy wooden table, supporting an open crate, measuring a couple of metres in length. The container shook violently as a middle-aged man wearing tan corduroy trousers and Hush Puppies struggled with something inside it. It looked like a tug of war was in process and the man was slowly being dragged into its depths, at one point coming close to being hauled off his feet entirely.

Reed cleared his throat a few times in an effort to gain attention before saying loudly, 'Excuse me. I'm looking for Dr Marques.'

Obviously surprised, the man swung around, glaring ferociously, and, in an upper-class English accent, replied, 'That's me. Who are you?'

He was wearing a white shirt, sleeveless plaid jumper, and a red bow tie that would have aroused the envy of many a university professor; but what made Reed step back nervously was the oversized pair of green rubber gloves he wore and possibly the largest pair of bottle-cap spectacles he had ever seen.

'Dr Marques, I'm Father Reed from the Governorate offices, and I was hoping to have a word with you.'

Marques raised his thick spectacles with one finger and squinted out from under them, tilting his head to the left as he measured up this unexpected visitor. 'I'm a little busy today. Can't this wait until tomorrow?'

'I'm afraid not, it won't wait that long.'

The scientist glanced around the room as if looking for any more uninvited guests and then beckoned him over with a grunt of resignation. 'Well, then, give me a hand, and I'm all yours.'

Reed made his way over to the wooden container and cautiously peered inside. Its edges were lined with a thick layer of polystyrene, enabling it to contain some twenty litres of frothy green water. At the bottom sat motionless a dark-coloured creature, about a metre in length, its long slim body twisted in the shape of an *S*.

'Say hello to Electrophorus Electricus, more commonly known as the electric eel.'

Reed automatically jerked his head back to a safe distance.

'Don't worry, he can't get out, Father,' Marques said with a dry smile. 'Now, if you wouldn't mind . . .' He produced a pair of oversized black rubber gloves and handed them over. 'You'd better put these on. That's a good chap. It won't take us long.'

Reed nodded reluctantly and slipped on the cumbersome mitts. 'OK, what's the problem?'

Marques gave the crate a vigorous slap, his bottle-cap lenses catching the light and illuminating his eyes so as to give him the unnerving look of a mad professor. 'We regularly receive cadavers of species from all around the world, whether from land or sea, and then store them in display jars containing various chemicals to stop them decomposing. I was trying to make a point of assuring my assistants that even the boss is not afraid of getting his hands dirty, but the problem is this one's still alive.'

Reed peered down at the furious eel, which still lay coiled up, its mouth sensors flaring in anticipation of its next move. 'Is that usual?'

'No, it is not,' huffed Dr Marques. 'But it does happen from time to time. So, if I get hold of it by the head, could you grab the tail?' The doctor steadied himself and prepared to pounce.

'Hey, wait a minute. What then?' Reed almost shouted the question as a surge of panic ran through his body.

Marques reached down to one side of the crate and produced a small wooden rod. 'And then, I'm going to bop him on the head with this.'

Reed smiled unbelievingly. 'That's not very scientific.'

Marques raised the rod upwards and gave it a practice swing. 'No, you're right, it's not, but it will work. The real key is to do as little damage as possible. Otherwise, it won't provide much of a specimen, will it? Right, let's go. I'll get hold of the head first.'

Reed made sure his gloves were on tightly as Dr Marques hovered above the open crate, swaying ever so slightly from left to right like some manic angler. Without a word of warning, he plunged his gloves into the froth and grabbed for the eel. Water flew everywhere, firstly dousing Marques himself, and then the eel sent a slimy offering right across Reed's chest, making him stumble back in disgust. Meanwhile, Marques jerked back from the crate, both gloves firmly clasped around the snout of the eel as it writhed wildly, spattering more of its ectoplasm over them both. 'Now grab the tail,' he yelled.

Reed paused momentarily as he tried to identify the tail amid the thrashing water. And, on seeing it flipping about, he moved forward, gloves extended at the ready. At exactly the same moment, the eel flicked its tail upwards only to tap Marques on the neck.

Reed watched aghast as the creature made contact with bare skin and unleashed its natural weapon of defence. A short fizzing sound could be heard as a few hundred volts of electricity surged through the now rigid Dr Marques. He flew back on to the floor with a thump, the eel dropping back into its crate with a splash.

Peeling off his gloves, Reed helped pull the wet and shaken scientist to his feet. 'Are you OK? I tried for the tail, but it got you first.'

Marques said nothing. He casually took off his now cracked glasses, revealing a pair of small beady eyes, and wiped the lenses with a dry corner of his jumper. He calmly popped his bottle-cap specs back on and then closed the lid of the crate with a bang, leaving the victorious eel thrashing around inside. The doctor sighed deeply and tapped the top of the container thoughtfully before returning Reed's concerned gaze. 'Now, exactly what do you want, Father Reed?' He growled, struggling to maintain his composure.

'I was hoping to speak with Father Roberto Sanchez, but I'm informed that he's on vacation.'

Marques nodded grimly, wiping some more of the eel's slime from his jumper. 'Yes, he seems to be on holiday nearly all the time lately, not that Cardinal Rocca notices.' He peered over the top of his glasses, raised an eyebrow, and smirked sarcastically. 'Not that I like to gossip, you understand.'

Reed nodded automatically, still feeling guilty for his lack of useful help in dealing with the electric eel. 'I understand completely, Dr Marques. There's not an area of the Vatican that hasn't received a new posting of some sort in recent weeks. It will take some adjusting for all of us.'

'True, true, but I dare say most of them don't keep themselves locked away out of sight most of the time'.

Reed had been given strict instructions not to impose on Cardinal Rocca at any time, but, seeing as the good doctor was so desperate to scratch an itch, he thought why not listen. After all, he wasn't actually interrogating the man. 'You're talking about Cardinal Rocca?'

'Well, now you mention him, yes. I mean he spends most of his time locked away in the northern corridor, demanding not to be disturbed, usually for hours at a time. Most irregular.'

The northern corridor that linked the third and fourth sections had been gutted by a fire three months earlier, leaving just a burnt-out husk.

The fire department had blamed a faulty electrical socket, but luckily no one had been hurt, and nothing of any great interest had been lost, so the mainstream media had shown little interest at the time.

'I thought it had already been refurbished?'

Marques nodded fervently. 'It has, but it's not furnished, yet still the good cardinal spends most of his days locked away in there.'

Father Reed heard the creak of a door behind him, and he spun around to come face-to-face with a startled-looking Italian boy in his early teens.

'I'm not finished yet, Elmo. Come back in ten minutes.'

The boy said nothing, simply offering a gracious nod before turning away and closing the door behind him with a clink.

'That's just one of the academy's assistants. He's meant to be picking up the eel for putting in storage.' Marques tapped the lid of the case again. 'Once it's dead, of course.' He shot Reed a resentful look.

'I really am sorry it was able to give you a shock, Doctor.'

The scientist grunted as he rubbed at the reddened sting mark on his neck. 'Not a problem. You're either a capable research assistant or you're not, and you, Father, are definitely not. Besides, it's my third shock of the morning. So I'm getting used to it.' He gave his neck one last gentle stroke before continuing. 'As I was saying, if the cardinal spent half as much time in the main academy as he does in the northern corridor, then we wouldn't be so far behind with our work schedule. Some of my colleagues even have a sweepstake going as to why he's closeted in there so much.' Dr Marques leant in towards Reed and tapped his nose. 'Personally, I think he's on the verge of a mental breakdown.'

Reed couldn't help but smile. Regardless of the gossiping and erratic behaviour, he liked Dr Marques. 'Is Cardinal Rocca in the corridor right now?'

The other man eyed him coyly. 'Ah, perked your interest, have I?'

'Not at all, Doctor, but I heard the fire was fierce, and I'm curious to see what state the place is now in.'

Marques studied him incredulously, and a big grin spread from ear to ear. 'Then, my dear Father, you're in luck because I believe the cardinal is off the premises, so follow me.'

He took Reed gently by the arm and ushered him out of the room, running in to a bored-looking Elmo, who immediately snapped to attention on seeing them both. 'Are you ready, signor?'

Marques dumped his rubber gloves into the hands of the teenager with a slap. 'You're always asking me to give you more responsibility, Elmo. Well, here's your chance.' He began leading Father Reed towards the northern corridor, stopping only to impart a few words of wisdom to his underling. 'Remember two things, and you'll be fine. Firstly, never take your gloves off, and secondly, make it a swift bop on the noggin.'

The two older men disappeared around the corner, leaving the young assistant alone with a pair of oversized rubber gloves. He headed into the research lab and over to the crate, which was already starting to wobble violently again, the eel no doubt preparing itself for round two, and, as Elmo slipped on the enormous black gloves, only one question was running through his mind, *What on earth was a bop on the noggin?*

Chapter 12

Harker slammed his fist against the solid oak door with a thud for the sixth time. After five minutes of waiting, he was beginning to think their journey here was in vain.

'I thought churches were never supposed to lock their doors,' said Claire, tapping her fingers together impatiently.

'Well, that's the general rule, but times have changed, what with all the art thieves about, and anyway this is a monastery, not a church.'

Claire raised both eyebrows at him. 'I feel I should know this. What's the difference?'

Harker stepped back from the entrance and surveyed the imposing stone complex built into the side of a cliff-face that constituted the monastery of St Benedict. The monastery was the first of its kind. Built by the Order's founder St Benedict whose own brand of Catholic ideology would eventually result in other Benedictine communes being constructed across the entire Western world. 'Churches are places of worship for the masses, but monasteries are communities for monks seeking religious enlightenment to strengthen their faith and better themselves.' He could tell from her vacant expression that she still didn't fully understand. 'Same faith but slightly different viewpoint. The monasteries of the Order extended all over Europe until the Reformation and founding of the Church of England, which largely destroyed it. Some monasteries survived, though they have hardly changed in hundreds of years. They take vows of silence to prove their faith, things like that.' He smiled at her. 'You'd hate it.'

Claire gave him a playful thump on the arm before returning her gaze to the large, stained-glass windows amid the brickwork above. 'Well, maybe they don't answer doors either.'

It was Harker's turn to raise an eyebrow sarcastically. 'Maybe.'

He was about to bang on the door one final time when the lock was released with a series of metallic clicks, and the door slowly creaked open. There in the doorway, like a ghost from the past, stood a Benedictine monk, wearing a floor-length brown robe. '*Come posso aiutarl*,' the monk enquired in Italian, his voice high-pitched and scratchy.

Harker could feel Claire closing up behind him, and he couldn't blame her because the monk looked pretty creepy. 'Do you speak English?' he asked for Claire's benefit. The doorman nodded with a grunt. 'Yes, I do. How can I help you?'

'We're looking for Father Maddocks. May we see him?'

The monk eyed them both up and down carefully before shaking his head. 'I'm afraid there is no one here by that name, my son. May I be of help in any other way?'

'I'm not sure. My name is Alex Harker, and I was asked to seek out Father Maddocks here at the monastery by a good friend of mine, Father Archibald Dwyer.'

If the monk did recognize Archie's name, he wasn't letting on.

'And this is his sister Ms Claire Dwyer.' As Harker glanced back at her, she extended a hand, and it was quickly snubbed by the monk who simply wrinkled his nose. 'Does that name mean anything to you at all?'

The holy man slowly shook his head. 'No, should it?'

'I'd hoped so. May we come in?'

The monk, whose hair resembled the traditional image of Friar Tuck, stepped back from the door and shut it partially in their faces. 'I'm sorry, but we are now in the middle of afternoon prayer. If you would like to come back another time, I'm sure we could accommodate you. Good day.'

As he began to close the door completely, Archie Dwyer's mysterious message flashed through Harker's mind, and he hastily thrust his foot into the remaining gap. 'Trust your logic, not your faith,' he blurted out. 'Does that mean anything to you?'

For a moment, the monk looked totally surprised, and then, a smile spread across his face. 'Indeed, it does, and in that case, you are welcome here. Please enter.' He opened the door wide again and beckoned them both into the main entrance of the monastery. After scanning the outside for any other visitors, and once satisfied they had come alone, he securely bolted the locks and turned back to them. 'My name is Father Valente. Please, follow me.'

Harker felt Claire's hand slip comfortably into his own, and he shot her a reassuring glance before trailing after their new-found friend. The monastery was impressive, but with none of the grandeur of adornment, one would usually find in a church. They proceeded through a warren of small bare rooms, leading ultimately to a narrow corridor. No one, meanwhile, spoke a word.

The narrow corridor opened up into a much larger inner sanctum, where they were greeted by the warmth of a huge log fire at one end of the room, beside which another Benedictine monk was stood, watching them suspiciously.

'Mr Harker, Ms Dwyer, please wait here. I will only be a moment.'

With that, their guide disappeared through a gloomy side door, leaving the two of them exchanging glances with the only remaining occupant. A few awkward minutes later, the first monk reappeared to usher them into a smaller adjacent room before carefully closing the door behind him.

An uncomfortable-looking bed nestled in the corner, and by the opposite wall stood a modest work desk, its surface littered with a variety of books. Perched on the edge of a wooden chair sat a wide-eyed Father

Maddocks, looking nervous. Harker recognised him instantly from the framed photograph at the orphanage.

'Father Maddocks, I'm Alex Harker. And this is . . .' As he turned to introduce Claire, Maddocks interrupted him.

'I know who you are, Professor, and you too, Ms Dwyer.' He got to his feet and shook Harker's hand before turning to Claire. 'I'm so sorry for your loss. Archie was a good man. Please, both of you, have a seat.'

Maddocks sat down again at his workstation and waited silently as his two guests made themselves as comfortable as possible. Harker's thigh was still aching from being squeezed into the small plastic chair back at the orphanage, and now this rough wooden bench wasn't helping.

'Archie said you would come, Professor Harker, although he didn't mention his sister. But you are welcome, nonetheless, Ms Dwyer.' He smiled at Claire before producing a packet of cigarettes and a Zippo from his desk drawer. He extracted one out and lit up with the shiny brass lighter before snapping it shut and inhaling deeply. 'You must have many questions for me?'

Harker almost choked at the last remark. 'Father, that's probably the biggest understatement I've ever heard. I'm not even sure why we're here, but Archie left me a cryptic note.' He slid Archie's message from his pocket and passed it over. 'It's this note which has led us here, and that's about all we know so far.'

The priest took another deep drag on his cigarette and then blew smoke towards a small vent set in the stonewall of his cell. He then glanced through the piece of paper before setting it alight with his Zippo, explaining, 'You won't need this any more.' He waited for the scrap to turn to ashes before returning his attention to the visitors. 'I am not sure how much you know about Archie's work at the Vatican's Academy of Sciences. Truth is, I'm not sure I even really know myself. But allow me explain to you some of the events of the last six months.'

Maddocks took yet another deep drag before continuing. 'You must understand, I'm only telling you this because of the faith I know Archie had in you, Professor.' He gave Claire an understanding nod. 'And, of course, you are his sister. But it is important you know that he told me to speak of this only with Professor Harker.' He turned aside to let out a short high-pitched whistle.

The door opened, and Maddocks gestured to Valente, who had been standing guard. 'Please wait outside, Ms Dwyer.'

She shot Harker an angry look. 'But I'm his sister, and I have a right to know!'

She sounded more embarrassed than angry, and Harker gently hugged her. 'Wait outside. You'll be safe.'

'But I . . . Look, I have a right to . . .'

Harker locked on to her green eyes and gave her his best 'it's not going to happen' look. 'Trust me, Claire.'

Her shoulders suddenly slumping, she nodded to acknowledge defeat. 'OK, I'll be outside.'

Maddocks smiled appreciatively as she closed the door behind her. 'I must apologise for that apparent rudeness, but Archie was adamant that I speak of this to no one but you.'

Harker could see the sincerity in the older man's eyes, and he gave a firm reassuring nod.

The priest smiled back before taking a final drag on his cigarette and stubbing it out in the ornate glass ashtray sitting on the desktop. 'This is rather silly. For the last two weeks, I've been running through my head what I'd say to you, and, now that you're finally here, I'm stuck. I'm not sure where to start.'

Harker tried to look at ease by settling back against the stonewall behind the bench, but it proved bloody uncomfortable although he refused to let it show. 'Let's just start at the beginning. How did you meet Archie?'

Father Maddocks shook his head, his face filling with a sense of realisation as if just remembering how he had intended to start his speech. 'Yes, OK, I met Archie about six months ago when I was asked to assist at the orphanage over in Castel Madama. Archie had made a request, through the Vatican, for anyone who could spare some time helping with the children. It seems more and more of them are simply left to the mercy of the welfare system these days, which is very sad, but that is the reality of it.'

Harker nodded in agreement, having learnt of the problems first-hand when he was training at the Vatican. The number of street kids was rising each year, despite what the Italian government preached to the contrary, and many fell prey to the sex traffickers. It was an ever-continuing tragedy, and Vatican officials were constantly attempting to turn the tide.

'I myself and another priest, Vito Malpuso, offered our services to Archie, and over the months, the three of us developed a strong bond. Six months may seem a short time for such a close bond to occur, but that was the way of it, nonetheless. Together we organised day trips and events for the children, all funded by the Vatican, and no expense spared. But there were four children in particular that we were drawn to, and we couldn't help but favour them with our attention above the others.'

Harker found himself interrupting without even consciously deciding to. 'You mean the four Angels?'

Father Maddocks smiled deeply, showing his yellowing nicotine-stained teeth. 'Ah, you know about them?'

Harker smiled back. 'Not much except what we learnt at the orphanage.'

'Then you know what happened. Well, allow me to explain. Archie was already very close to the Angels before we arrived, but it wasn't long before we too gravitated towards them as well. Even though they were horribly crippled, their minds were still intact, and each of them had his own unique personality and understanding of things. Vito felt the same as I did, and those six months were amongst the happiest of my life—truly serving some of God's most unfortunate.'

Harker himself was almost overcome by the obvious love Father Maddocks had for these Angels, and he smiled openly, happy for the priest to continue reminiscing.

'But that was before the fire. It blazed through a dormitory wing of the orphanage, killing all four of the Angels in one fell swoop. To be burnt alive is no way for anyone to die, let alone young children.' He scratched at his hand, obviously still disturbed by the very memory of it. 'The inferno was so hot, it fused their fragile little bodies to the steel frames of their wheelchairs. It was horrible. The accident was caused by a faulty electrical outlet, so the fire department told us afterwards, but it didn't make any difference because all of us felt guilty, especially Archie. He kept running the tragedy over and over in his mind as if he were looking for a missed clue, something he had seen but not recognised or properly assimilated. We could see it was tearing him apart, but he wouldn't discuss it with us. Not until he asked Vito and myself to meet him at his house in Popolo, and that's where this story really begins.'

Maddocks flicked open his pack of Marlboro and slid out another cigarette before even finishing the one still in his hand. He glanced at Harker. 'Do you mind if I have another?'

Harker stared at the packet hungrily. 'Only if I can join you.'

Maddocks offered him the pack.

'It's been two years since I last had a cigarette, but after today's events, I think I deserve it.'

The priest nodded understandingly and lit both cigarettes in turn.

Harker took a deep drag, admiring the smoke that he subsequently expelled from his lungs with a little cough, now relishing the sickening satisfaction that only a smoker can appreciate. *God, it tasted good.*

Maddocks allowed him to enjoy the sensation for a moment longer before continuing his story. 'You must remember, Professor, that Pope Leo XIV had just passed away, so it was our primary obligation to offer our prayers for him in St Peter's Basilica along with all our colleagues, but we didn't. Instead, we rallied around our friend, and that is a decision I will wrestle with for the rest of my days.'

Harker noticed the deep frown lines that appeared as Father Maddocks rubbed his temple. This was clearly a man who felt a heavy weight on his soul.

'Once we arrived at his house, Archie immediately swore us to secrecy and made us promise that whatever we were told must remain between us and revealed to no one else. I agreed straight away, but Vito took a little more convincing, and it was only after an hour of heated discussion that he finally agreed. Part of me wishes Vito had stuck to his guns and refused, but the other half thanks the Lord he didn't. It seems that Archie's work was highly secret, revolving around a hidden room situated somewhere in the northern corridor of the Academy of Sciences. He, along with a small group of other priests, was tasked with the study and restoration of certain relics. It was a task that had been going on for many decades. Now, Archie wouldn't tell us what this study involved, but he did say that he had been approached by a group of people who were intensely interested in this work and, more importantly, in the relics themselves. They managed to convince him that these items would be far safer in their custody than in the possession of the Vatican.' Maddocks shook his head despairingly. 'Don't ask me how they convinced him, but a week later, he did what they asked by taking the relics from the Academy of Science and hiding them safely somewhere else. A few days after that, the orphanage suffered the fire that killed the Angels, and Archie became convinced it was as a warning for what he had done.'

Harker stubbed his cigarette out on the sole of his shoe and placed it in the ashtray. 'Who was the warning from?'

Maddocks carefully stubbed out his own. 'He assumed it was from the same people who had initially approached him.'

'But you said he stole the relics on their behalf in the first place?'

Father Maddocks nodded. 'Yes, you're right, but Archie hadn't yet passed them on. He still had them hidden away somewhere, and he didn't say why. Maybe he had begun to have second thoughts. He said he had even considered returning the relics to the Vatican, but, as you can imagine, their theft had not gone unnoticed, and he felt trapped, to say the least. But now his guilt over the Angels was truly consuming him, and he finally decided to give the objects back to the Vatican but not before he had spoken to someone he totally trusted, someone high up in Church hierarchy. He then called upon Vito and myself to safeguard one of these relics until he returned, mentioning something about a necessary trip to London. We waited at his house for almost two days before receiving a special postal delivery: a letter from Archie, telling us that if anything happened to him, we were to stay well away from the Vatican. It explained we should retreat immediately to this monastery and wait there for his most trusted friend and that you would see to it that everything was put back in its proper place. That very afternoon, Archie hanged himself from the balcony of St Peter's Basilica during the papal inauguration. That was almost two weeks ago, and I don't mind admitting that I was beginning to doubt you'd ever turn up. In fact, Vito lost faith entirely, and he headed back to his family's farmhouse on the outskirts of Rome. But I got a call from him yesterday, telling me he was heading back to the monastery. We decided to request an audience with the new Pope and ask for his advice or forgiveness, whatever was needed, but . . . Well, I never made the initial call because Vito never arrived.'

Harker let out a small gasp, suddenly realising that he was supposed to know more than Father Maddocks did, but his disarray was overridden immediately by an acute curiosity. 'And what about the relic?'

Without a word, Father Maddocks opened a side drawer of his desk. He reached inside and gently brought out an almost foot-long oak casket, placing it delicately on the desktop. 'I promised Archie I'd keep it safe until he and I next met.' He gave an unhappy smile. 'Which made it a lifetime commitment until you appeared.'

Harker offered him a dry smile before examining the box's lid. The craftsmanship was of a classical Roman style, and the condition was pristine. In the centre was a symbol consisting of two crossed shepherd's staff. Harker knew it all too well as the ancient symbol for Christianity, having seen it so many times before, but what really caused a stir in him was the engraved image underneath of Tiberius Augustus Caesar, the second emperor of Rome. Harker felt his hands begin to tremble, and he wasn't sure if it was nerves, excitement, or a mixture of them both. The wood seemed to have hardly degraded, considering it must have been almost two thousand years old. Whatever was inside this aged box had probably been around since the life and times of Jesus Christ himself. His fingers gently traced the fine craftsmanship at the edges, down to a small metal key that jutted from the front panel of the box.

'May I?'

He was surprised at the high pitch of his own voice, and Father Maddocks, sensing the excitement in him, nodded approvingly. Harker carefully pressed his fingertips around the small iron key and delicately turned it until he heard the snap of the lock. He placed his hands either side of the lid and slowly opened it with his thumbs as would a child on Christmas morning, not wanting to tear the paper.

Both the top and bottom of the container had been lined with modern gel foam and then covered in a purple material that felt like silk. He could feel his heart begin to race as he identified the object inside, its slender stalks and protruding spikes composing two jagged semicircles. He pulled away a few inches from the open box, not wanting to even breathe on it for fear of damaging its precious contents. The item may have been in two pieces, but it was arranged in its original circular form and was now protected within a two-piece, transparent, hermetically sealed plastic case, allowing it to be folded together like a wallet. His mind was racing: *Was this real? The genuine article?* 'Is that what I think it is?' He couldn't take his eyes off it as if there was an invisible force trapping his gaze, banishing any semblance of free will.

Maddocks, meanwhile, was smiling innocently. 'Yes, my friend, that object is over two thousand years old and probably the Catholic Church's most prized and secretive possession. The crown of thorns that Jesus Christ was forced to wear on the day of his crucifixion.'

Chapter 13

Father Reed glanced up at the wall clock hanging above the doorway leading to the north corridor and let out an impatient sigh. He had spent over an hour watching this entrance and was beginning to feel foolish. In fact, this whole idea seemed more idiotic with every passing second. After all, he was meant to be discreet, and this was turning into an obvious stake-out. The thought made him smile, yet still he had to admit that Cardinal Rocca's odd behaviour was worth checking out.

Dr Marques had already given him a brief tour of the corridor, which turned out to contain a series of storage rooms for the entire academy before heading back to his lab, immensely keen to see if his assistant, Elmo, had managed to subdue the electric eel. Reed had been surprised to discover that all the refurbishment was indeed finished and, judging by the build-up of dust, it had been completed a while ago. Yet the rooms were still completely vacant with no furniture except some wall paintings.

So why was Cardinal Rocca spending most of his time there in the academy's empty storage facility?

The clock above him struck 4.15 p.m., and Reed let out a small yawn. He was getting tired of this, and in his frustration, he could only hope that the gossipy Dr Marques was in the process of getting another electric shock from his slippery nemesis.

With the last shred of his patience finally evaporating, and sick of this waiting game, Reed stood up, shaking off the stiffness in his muscles, and was about to leave when, up ahead, the sound of leather-soled shoes echoed down the corridor, coming towards him. Reed briskly stepped a few metres back and squeezed himself into the gap between a sagging potted fern plant and the wall. Within seconds, Cardinal Rocca appeared, rushing past him and continuing towards the same doors that Reed had been scrutinising for so long. Without so much as a pause, Rocca undid the lock and disappeared inside.

Reed immediately made his way to the closed door and placed his ear to its surface. There was nothing but silence. He paused for twenty tantalising seconds before deciding to take a chance and follow the cardinal inside.

Gently opening the door, he quietly made his way into the north corridor itself. The passageway was empty, and he instinctively stifled his breathing in an attempt to detect better any sounds. He half-expected to be suddenly confronted by a surprised and angry-looking Cardinal Rocca, but the corridor was empty and silent except for a faint buzzing from the overhead strip lights. Doors lined its fifty-metre length, providing access to numerous storerooms.

Where the heck had he gone to so quickly?

Without warning, fifty metres further along the passageway, the first strip light suddenly went out. Reed narrowed his eyes in an effort to detect any movement ahead, but there was none. Now the second light along went out, followed by the next and then the next. The approaching wall of darkness seemed to take on a life of its own, surging down the corridor towards him as if with purpose.

Reed could feel his palms begin to sweat as his fists clenched, and he was unable to move from the spot. This wasn't the first time he had been in such an unnerving situation, and he hoped it wasn't about to be his last.

The final strip light went out above him, and pitch-blackness enveloped him as if something tangible was trying to suffocate him. He was still fighting to control this irrational fear when he heard a scuffling sound from somewhere ahead.

'Hello, anyone there?'

His involuntary question bounced back at him through the gloom, the scuffling audible no more. Then, without warning, he felt a sharp pain at the base of his neck. Reed reacted just in time to feel a syringe needle withdrawing from his punctured flesh. He attempted to grasp for his attacker, but a cocktail of drugs hit his nervous system, and the priest's legs gave way. He sank heavily to his knees, both arms lolling helplessly at his sides, before finally slumping across the floor in a heap.

As Reed's mind began to cloud over, he heard a calm voice whispering to him from the pitch-blackness.

'Tsk, tsk, tsk, you know how rude it is to spy on people. Very rude indeed.'

The corridor lights flickered back on, and Reed's pupils struggled to contract themselves enough to allow him a somewhat blurry view of his attacker.

Standing directly over him, Cardinal Rocca was staring down with an expressionless face.

'I'm sorry, Father Reed, but you're going to have to take some time off. But don't worry, you're in safe hands.' A manic grin spread across the cardinal's face. 'Unfortunately, you chose the wrong side, my friend. That's a shame because you could have been useful.'

Chapter 19

'I don't believe it! It has to be a fake.' Harker peered closer, examining the crown of thorns from every possible angle. 'I don't suppose Archie carried out a carbon test, did he?' His question was half in jest, although he couldn't stop himself from glancing upwards in the hope of an answer.

'If he did, he didn't tell me. But it is genuine, of that I'm sure.'

'How can you be so certain?'

Maddocks raised his chin confidently. 'It is a matter of faith.'

'Isn't it always.' Harker had never been keen on blind faith, believing it caused as many problems as it solved.

The priest eyed him as teacher would a schoolboy. 'Ah, yes, Archie informed me of your own waning faith. Very sad.'

The last comment struck a nerve in Harker, and his face began to flush. 'It's not my faith in God that's waned, but my faith in the people that serve him.'

The comeback was deliberately cutting, and Maddocks raised his eyebrows in clear disappointment. 'I'm sorry you feel that way, Professor, but . . .'

Harker cut him off mid-sentence. 'Don't be. It's just the way it is. Now can we get back to this?' He pointed down at the engraved box containing the thorny crown. 'If this is genuine, it's the greatest Christian find . . . well, ever.'

Father Maddocks gave a sad nod of his head. 'Maybe yes, but I just don't understand how Archie could have been persuaded to steal it from the Vatican, where it rightfully belongs. And, more importantly, for whom?'

Harker carefully closed the wooden lid and sat back against the stone-built wall once again, his taut muscles now pain-free because of the adrenalin rush of excitement he was experiencing. He wasn't sure how trustworthy this Father Maddocks was, but Archie had gone to much trouble in bringing them both together, and that counted for a lot.

Within five minutes, he had told his new acquaintance everything about Mr Caster and the company called Maptel, his surreal meeting with Brulet and the man's bizarre appearance, the cheque for £250,000, the secret project the Vatican had been working on since the '70s, and the accidental deaths surrounding it. He told the old priest literally everything.

Maddocks said nothing throughout. He just sat there listening intently, his face totally unreadable, as Harker now moved on to his personal suspicions.

'And I now believe that Brulet's company, Maptel, is the same organisation that convinced Archie to steal this thing in the first place, but how or why is another thing altogether?'

As they both pondered the possibilities, a single thought cemented itself in the forefront of Harker's mind. In all the excitement of discovering this priceless artefact, he had managed to overlook one of the most important things Maddocks had said.

'Wait a minute, you said relics in the plural. What else did Archie take?'

The Father shook his head helplessly. 'I don't know exactly because he wouldn't show us, but he had another, similar box in his possession.'

Harker struggled to take in what he was hearing. 'Hold on a second, you're presented with possibly the greatest Christian relic of all time, and you weren't even a little curious about what the other box might contain?'

Maddocks gave an innocent shake of his head. 'I didn't even look in this box here until after Archie had committed suicide.' He pursed his lips disdainfully as if just saying the word was wrong. 'Archie merely said this box was of "great importance" and that was good enough for me.' The old priest straightened his posture, his expression defiant as Harker stared at him doubtfully. 'Trust in a friend is a virtue, Professor, not a sin. I trusted Archie more than I do you, that's for sure. At least *his* faith remained intact.'

The two men stared at each other for a few moments in an awkward silence, and Harker could see that priest was being totally honest. For some people, complete trust of a friend tends to dampen one's curiosity, and the old man was obviously one of those people. It was also becoming clear that Father Maddocks had no real idea what to do next and was actually looking to Harker for direction.

After a few more uncomfortable seconds, the priest finally opened his mouth, 'So, what next, Professor?'

Harker took a deep breath and rubbed the back of his neck. 'I'm not sure, but if Brulet and his cronies are behind all this, we don't have many choices. I'd like to take the crown back to England for safe keeping, but if they murdered four defenceless handicapped kids just to get Archie's attention, then they won't have any issues in killing me either.' Harker gently patted the wooden lid. 'So that leaves us with either the police or the Vatican, and if Brulet is half as wealthy and powerful as he claimed to be, then he could easily have informants within the department on the take. So that, as much as I hate to say it, leaves us with the Vatican itself.'

'Good, I think that's the right choice,' Maddocks agreed.

Harker nodded reluctantly. 'OK, let's get Claire and head there immediately. The sooner we get this on Vatican soil, the better.'

He turned the handle and swung open the door, only to be met by an eerie silence. 'Claire?' Harker called out as the two men made their way from the private chamber and into the now vacant room outside. They had only made it a few paces when they were hit by an odd yet familiar smell. Harker turned back to see Father Maddocks wrinkling his nose.

'What is that?'

The old priest lifted his nostrils to the ceiling and inhaled a deep breath. 'Smells like burnt chicken and wet dog? Yes, very disagreeable indeed.'

Harker was drawn towards the flickering glow of the open fire as he followed the stench to its point of origin. But what he saw there stopped him dead in his tracks. Amongst the bluish flames dancing upon the glowing embers rested the decapitated head of Father Valente, perched on two wooden logs, his hair melting into small beads of liquid that trickled in sticky trails down the now blackened skull. The man's lower jaw hung open unnaturally, and small holes had begun to appear in his cheeks where the flames had burnt through the thin flesh and were now licking intensely at the roof cavity of the priest's mouth.

Harker tried not to retch, his stomach turning, as he found himself staring into the dull, milky-white eyes of father Valente that were now cooking in their sockets like two boiled eggs.

'Oh, dear God!' Maddocks spluttered out the words as shock began to take hold, his hands trembling violently. A movement in the corner of Harker's eye made him swing around in time to see the door of the room slowly closing behind a large silhouette that became more distinct as light from the fire penetrated the darkness.

Drazia Heldon stood almost seven feet tall, wearing a long, dark overcoat that missed skimming the floor by only a few inches. Beside him lay Claire Dwyer, her eyes wide open in panic, her hands and feet bound with a plain nylon rope.

Harker tugged at Maddocks's black tunic, and the old priest turned around from witnessing one appalling image to the next. The shock caused him to freeze, his hands shaking with an even greater frenzy than before.

'Father Maddocks, you're a tough one to track . . .' Drazia bowed his gigantic head as if in acknowledgment of the fact, ' . . . but not impossible.' He turned his attention to Harker. 'And of course, many thanks to you, Professor. In truth, I don't know if I'd have found him if it weren't for you.'

The giant's voice was impossibly deep, and *his accent was European, maybe Serbian*, Harker thought. 'You and the lady . . .' Heldon pointed a thick oversized finger towards the writhing body on the floor that was Claire Dwyer. 'You were both easy to trail from that cafe to the residence, then to the orphanage, and finally here.' His large, piercing amber eyes now turned their interest back on to Father Maddocks. 'If you please . . . the item.' The assassin clicked his fingers towards the wooden box tucked underneath the priest's arm. 'Bring it to me.'

Harker glanced at Father Maddocks and shook his head. 'Don't do it, Father.'

'Be careful, Professor,' Heldon growled, placing the sole of his black leather brogue firmly on to Claire's neck. 'It would be a shame if you forced me to kill her and then take the box anyway. You can't win.'

The old priest nodded in acceptance, but, before he could take a step forward, Harker scooped the box out of his grasp and then, in one swift movement, held it directly over the flaming fire with its lid open.

'You let her go now, or I destroy what you want most. You can easily reach me but not before this crown goes up in flames. Now let her go.'

Heldon grinned from ear to ear, revealing an unsightly row of chipped, blackened teeth. 'So you know what it is,' he sniggered. 'You are Professor Alex Harker, once a wearer of the sacred cloth and a man with an unshakeable belief in right and wrong. You've spent most of your career searching for relics just like this. Do you really expect me to believe you would destroy it so easily? I think not. Now give it to me, and you may all keep your pathetic lives. But if you persist in this charade . . .'

The hulking leviathan gave a shake of his right arm, which had been hanging limply at his side, and in a split second, a foot-long razor-sharp sword sprung from further up his sleeve and snapped into place on the back of his hand.' . . . then everyone dies regardless, starting with her.' He gently stroked the tip of his blade menacingly against Claire's tear-soaked cheek. 'Just think that the entire filthy Dwyer bloodline could end right here, right now.' Drazia grinned once more, the pleasure he was taking from this situation palpable.

Before Harker could reply, Maddocks snapped into action. 'You son of a bitch,' he screamed, his face turning scarlet with anger. 'You murdering scum, you killed Father Valente, a good man, my friend, a man of God. How dare you desecrate this holy place with your evil!'

The towering assassin's mouth opened sarcastically. 'Your friend was no man of God. He was a fake just as are you with your corrupted beliefs. He deserves no respect, Maddocks, and neither do you. You are rotten to the core, like the rest of your kind, wrapped in a cloak of deceit and lies with only one wish: your own selfish preservation. You should know that before I killed your friend Malpuso, he only asked one thing of me: to spare his own life. Not to spare either of yours but just his own.' The monster smirked grimly. 'He died like he lived—as a coward.'

Without warning, Father Maddocks propelled himself towards the giant, screaming at the top of his voice, with his hands flailing wildly. He had barely taken a step forward when Heldon thrust his blade through the old priest's neck, impaling him on the razor-sharp weapon without a moment's hesitation.

Harker watched in horror as Maddocks shuddered, his hands slicing themselves on the blade as he tried to pull himself off the red-stained spike of metal protruding from his own throat. After one final quiver, his body went limp, and he expelled a gurgling sound as blood trickled from his gaping mouth.

Claire was already letting out a muffled scream, her eyes bulging above the piece of cloth tightly gagging her mouth. But she went quiet again on receiving a swift boot to the head from her captor.

Drazia Heldon stood motionless, his arm and blade still extended. Satisfied that Maddocks was dead, he gave another shake of his arm and the sullied blade retracted back into the sleeve as quickly as it had emerged, allowing its impaled victim to drop to the floor with a heavy thump.

'He didn't have to die today, but that was his choice. Do not make the same mistake, Professor. Now, before I lose my patience, give me the item.'

Harker could feel his veins pumping as his heart raced. This monster was going to kill them both; they'd witnessed too much. 'OK, OK, you can have the box. But first let the woman go.' He was surprised at how firm and confident his own voice sounded. 'Let her go, and it's yours.'

Drazia eyed Harker thoughtfully before finally nodding in agreement. 'OK, I'll accept that.' He hauled Claire up by the shoulders, undid the slip knot and gave her a little push towards Harker.

'Claire, you head for the front of the building and get the hell out of here.'

With merely a nod, she was taking off down the corridor, only glancing back at Drazia, who pursed his lips to blow her an intimidating kiss.

'Don't go too far now, little one. You and I have unfinished business.' The assassin returned his attention to Harker. 'Now, Professor, no more wasting time. Give me the relic.'

Harker raised the box away from the fire and closed the lid. 'You work for Brulet, don't you?'

The brute looked uninterested. 'It's not important who I work for or why.' A grimace spread across his face as he realised what was happening. 'This isn't a Bond film, Professor Harker, where I now reveal everything to you.' He began to move forward, both his arms outstretched to cut off any escape. 'This is real life, and the thing about real life is . . .' he stopped within reaching distance, his sword once more snapping into place '. . . it's not fair.'

No sooner had he finished the sentence than Harker threw the box towards the wall on his left, causing the giant to instinctively lunge after it with both hands. In the same instance, Harker launched himself through the gap between the assassin's long legs, sliding across the shiny, well-worn stone floor and out the other side. Within moments, Harker was on his feet and sprinting through the door and into the corridor, feeling a whoosh of air rush past his left ear as Drazia's arm-blade narrowly missed its target.

Harker smacked against the stonewall on the opposite side of the corridor, only glancing briefly behind him—something he immediately wished he hadn't done. The massive seven-foot frame of Drazia Heldon loomed only a couple of feet behind him, one hand outstretched towards Harker, the other tightly grasping the precious box.

The image sent a surge of adrenalin shooting through Harker's body, and suddenly he was running like hell. Within seconds, he had reached the main chapel and was heading towards the main entrance leading outside. Claire must have made it, he thought, as behind him the crashing of benches thundered in his ears. He jumped on to one of the pews and then hurled himself through the open doorway and out into the chilly early evening air.

Harker was already pulling himself up off the gravel when the sight in front of him caused him to freeze. Three police cars were waiting, their red and blue sirens flashing wildly, and in front of them stood five uniformed policemen, holding automatic handguns pointing directly at his chest. Harker raised his hands skywards automatically, and a suited man moved towards him, pulling out a set of handcuffs.

'Professor Alex Harker?'

Harker nodded his head, still dizzy from the wallop it had received against the corridor wall.

'You're in a lot of trouble, my British friend.'

Harker let out a deep sigh of relief. 'You have no idea.'

Chapter 15

Drazia Heldon flicked the Fiat Uno's gearstick into fourth and maintained a steady fifty down the dusty back road towards the main highway. In his wing mirror, he could just make out the flickering of red-and-blue flashing lights from the police cars outside the monastery.

Why had the law turned up? His breach of the building had been stealthy, just as he'd been taught, and had barely given those robed charlatans back there a chance to react, let alone make a call to the authorities. He wrapped his fists around the Fiat's narrow steering wheel and shook it with such ferocity that the entire car rocked back and forth. The assassin hated missing his prey, and that interfering professor was just that—prey to be dispatched. He massaged his aching temple, trying to disperse the pain accumulating in the front of his skull, but it would make little difference in the long run. He urgently needed his medicine.

Drazia reached into his pocket and retrieved a brown plastic pill case with a printed label that read: TAKE AS NEEDED >>>FOR THE CLASS 1 FORM OF CHIARI MALFORMATION.

He had been born with the condition, and, from what he understood, it was caused by his brain being too big for his skull. As a young boy, he thought it would mean growing up to be supersmart, but that idea had been quickly dashed by one of the orphanage directors, who had told him bluntly it would never improve his below-par mental abilities. In fact, the director had gone on to declare that it would cause him continual bouts of immense pain and even encourage psychopathic tendencies in later life. Drazia subsequently hated the man, but it seemed he had been right on both counts.

The doctor had called it 'a downward displacement of the cerebella tonsils through the foramen magnum', and quite how Drazia had been able to remember that complex explanation was beyond him because he had no idea what it meant. All he knew was that it caused the most blinding headaches imaginable, and without his medication, he simply couldn't function.

He tapped out a couple of pink pills into his giant palm and slipped them under his tongue. They began to work immediately, and within minutes, his head was beginning to clear enough to let him return to the problems at hand.

He'd not planned on letting the professor live but, for that matter, hadn't expected the authorities to turn up. He shook off his annoyance with a grunt. No matter, he would catch up with the Englishman in due course, and until then the police department would now focus on Harker as their prime suspect for the deaths of those two priests. A satisfying grin spread across the assassin's face as he recalled the look of terror on Harker's face as he had chased him through the monastery's corridors. He comfortingly stroked the wooden box resting on the passenger seat next to him. As long as he had the relic, his master would be satisfied, and that was all that mattered.

Heldon turned the metal key and raised the wooden lid. What he saw made him jam down hard on the brakes, bringing the Uno to a screeching halt and sending the box flying into the passenger foot space with a loud clunk. He hastily picked it up and took another look, just to make sure he wasn't imagining things. He wasn't.

A heavy, sickly feeling began to stir in the pit of his stomach. The box was empty. 'Shit!' He threw it to the floor in a rage and slammed his fists against the dashboard, cursing his own stupidity.

'Harker, you fucking bastard,' the assassin hissed through gritted teeth. At that exact moment, his mobile began to ring. *Un . . . fucking believable.* The master's timing, as always, was impeccable.

Heldon grabbed his metallic-coloured iPhone off the front seat and pressed the answer button.

'Do you have it?' the voice asked.

'I'm afraid there were complications, my master.'

This response was met by silence.

'But I'm in the process of rectifying it.'

'What exactly are the complications, Drazia?'

'Harker has the item.'

'He's still alive?'

'Yes, sir, I'm afraid so.'

A deep, unsettling breath resonated through the earpiece.

'My old friend, it's unlike you to make such a mess and at such a critical time. You know what's at stake, and we have less than twenty-four hours. We can ill afford these mistakes, not now!'

Heldon chewed his lip as the guilt he felt was quickly replaced by anger. He indeed knew the importance of it, and to be responsible for such a failure at this late stage was devastating. But he had not even mentioned the worst part yet.

'There is one other thing. He's just been taken into police custody.'

The sound of grinding teeth at the other end said more than any words could.

'But I do have some good news,' he continued, glancing behind him to the back seat and into the tear-soaked face of Claire Dwyer. Gagged and hog-tied, she continued to struggle against the nylon rope restraining her. 'I'm in possession of the Dwyer woman, and she may prove to be a useful bargaining chip.'

The silence continued unabated.

'Sir, do not worry. I will resolve this well before the deadline, I swear it.' The giant, irritated by the sound of desperation in his own voice, let that statement hang in the air until, after a few agonising moments of silence, the voice resumed, much calmer this time.

'No, leave this to me. I'll have the professor picked up by our men. It won't be difficult to find which police station they've taken him to.'

'And what are my orders now, Lord Balthasar?'

'I want you to go dark for a few hours and await my call. I'll need you to deliver the Dwyer woman at some point, but stay near the city and don't stray far. And, Drazia, we need her undamaged.'

Then the line went dead. Heldon slipped the mobile phone into his pocket and turned his attention to Claire Dwyer, who was still writhing on the back seat. He reached over and clamped one of his huge hands around her head, firmly forcing it upwards till her eyes met his. 'Did you know that in China they eat dog meat? It's true. You can buy the dogs whilst they're still alive from ordinary street vendors.'

Claire's confused expression drew a smile from the Serbian.

'But a dog is a dangerous animal, and, with its sharp teeth, it can really hurt someone. So you know what they do?' He raised his chin inviting a response and remained silent until she gave a shake of her head. 'They break the dog's legs, push them back over the animal's head, and hang it up by its feet. That way, the dog stays alive, but it can't cause any trouble.' A husky giggle emanated from the assassin's massive lungs as he loosened his grip on her skull. 'You're not going to be any trouble to me, are you now, little one?'

Fresh tears trickled down Claire Dwyer's cheeks. She shook her head submissively, the black streaks of her mascara absorbed by the tight cloth gag.

'Good! Now we're going to take a little trip.' He grabbed a dirty blanket from the floor and threw it over her. 'And if you need a bathroom break, forget it. Just piss in your pants.' He let out a deep bellow of laughter. 'And don't worry about making a mess because the car is stolen.'

Chapter 16

'So let me get this straight, Professor Harker. This is all some kind of elaborate treasure hunt laid out by your friend Archie Dwyer, the Catholic priest who hanged himself in St Peter's Square a few weeks ago?'

Superintendent Rino Perone eased himself down on to the edge of his desk. 'And now you're being chased by . . . and let's be clear about this.' The silver-haired detective picked up his leather notepad and flicked back a couple of pages. 'By a seven-foot giant with a sword for an arm, who's also kidnapped the priest's sister, your friend Claire Dwyer.' He slipped the pad into the breast pocket of his shirt and shook his head disbelievingly. 'And you seriously expect me to swallow this shit?'

Opposite him, Harker sat impatiently with his left wrist handcuffed to a wooden chair bolted to the floor. His jacket was covered in mud from having to lie on wet soil outside the monastery as the police arrested him. 'It's the truth. Everything I've told you is the truth.'

'Right.' The Superintendent nodded sarcastically. 'Yet there was absolutely no sign of this "giant" or your friend, even though we had the entire building already surrounded.'

Harker had to use every ounce of self-control to stop himself from shouting in frustration. 'Well, he must have escaped before your men totally surrounded it. I'm sure there's a back door. After all, it's a monastery, not a bloody jail cell!'

After being handcuffed and then thrown into the back of a blue Alfa Romeo, he had been transported back to the Questura in the heart of Rome. He had spent the entire trip trying to convince Perone to go back and search for Claire Dwyer, but the policeman had ignored his pleas, and, after discovering the corpses of Maddocks and the monk Valente, he could hardly blame him.

Since then, and for the past forty-five minutes, the interrogation had rolled on and on, and he had just finished telling his story for the ninth time, offering the truth, the whole truth and nothing but the truth. With one single exception, however. When he was initially being patted down by one of the officers, the man had missed the thin plastic case hidden under the lining of his capacious jacket. It had been the first time Harker was actually glad he had not gotten around to mending the gaping hole located inside his jacket pocket. He had made the rapid switch when the assassin's attention had been focused on running through Father Maddocks with his blade. Harker had never seen a person killed before, and even the bombings in Jerusalem had not prepared him for the sight of Father Maddocks being impaled right in front of his eyes: his body going limp except for a slight twitching as the priest's muscles spasmed, the life and then energy draining from the puncture wound in his neck before dripping on to the stone floor with a nauseating pitter-patter. It was a horrible experience; and Maddocks had deserved better.

'Hey! You better start paying attention,' shouted Perone, slamming his fist down hard on the scratched desktop and startling Harker from his thoughts. 'You've been a busy boy today, my friend, and you've left chaos in your wake.' Perone leant closer, a throbbing vein bulging from his forehead. 'In my fucking province alone, I make it a count of five. That's enough to brand you a serial killer, and I can guarantee you one thing—you are going to fucking burn for this.'

'Five? There were only two killings? Father Maddocks and the monk, Valente.'

The policemen pulled a slim stack of photographs from the top of his filing cabinet. 'Don't play dumb with me, boy. You think you can murder good people in cold blood and just get away with it?' He shoved the four colour photographs into Harker's hands. The first showed the orphanage director Benito Giuseppe lying on an ambulance gurney, his face completely charred on one side and his throat slit from ear to ear.

Harker struggled to hold down the bile collecting at the back of his mouth as he took in the next couple of images which showed Benito's two female assistants slaughtered in much the same manner. The fourth and final photograph was of the orphanage as it was, consumed by flames like some huge funeral pyre.

Perone stepped behind Harker and leant forward, viewing the death photos over his shoulder. 'It's a miracle none of the children were killed. Or maybe you feel squeamish about killing kids, eh?' He moved his mouth to within inches of Harker's ear. 'But, believe me, if you had, you'd be in a cell right now, having yourself a serious fucking accident.'

Harker lurched forward as far as his handcuffs would allow and threw up into the waste-paper basket next to him, the acrid smell of his own vomit causing him to expel a second load.

His lips curling in revulsion, Perone backed away to the other side of his desk. 'The aftermath is never pretty, huh?' He took a handkerchief out of his pocket and threw it into Harker's lap before opening the door and dumping the waste bin outside. 'Don't do that in my office again.'

Harker strained with the handcuffs to wipe the spittle from his lips, his mind racing for answers even as Perone continued his verbal assault, clearly encouraged by his chief suspect's discomfort.

'My God, you really are a sick fuck. Imagine if you hadn't hired a taxi to take you out to the monastery, we'd have never tracked you down so fast. Who knows how many more people you would have butchered, eh?'

Harker glanced over to the doorway as a hard-faced female cop with long black hair eyed the vomit-filled bucket with disgust before picking it up and disappearing into another office beyond.

Harker closed his eyes and tried to tune everything out. All that mattered was finding Claire, and every hour that passed was another nail hammered into her coffin.

The policeman finally slumped back in his chair and rubbed at his temple, the skin wrinkling upwards like a creased shirt. 'Now, why don't we go over all this again?'

Harker wiped his lips with the handkerchief one last time before gently placing the soiled piece of cloth on the desk. 'My name is Alex Harker, and I'm an archaeologist working for Cambridge University. I was employed to find out why Archie Dwyer killed himself—probably by the same group that I now believe murdered all these people you've mentioned.' He gestured towards the gruesome photos spread out across the table. 'I found a file on his computer which led us first to the orphanage in Tivoli and from there to the monastery in Subiaco, where we managed to escape the real killer of Father Maddocks, just before you found me.' Harker wrestled with his frustration. 'For Christ's sake, I've never killed anyone in my life. And the longer you waste your time finding that out, the longer they have to do God knows what to Claire Dwyer.'

Superintendent Perone reached over and tapped the death-filled photos. 'Never killed anyone until today, that is?'

His mind still reeling from the shocks of the last few hours, Harker put his head in his hands. This was going nowhere fast. 'I think I need to see a lawyer now.'

The police officer nodded solemnly. 'I'd say you're dead right.' Perone placed an old-style rotary telephone on to the desktop and left the room, deliberately slamming the door behind him.

Harker didn't actually have a lawyer since he had always relied on the university to sort out any personal entanglements, which had been far and few, but he had to call on someone to help him. During the superintendent's threatening analysis of the situation, only one number had sprung to mind, that of the only person he totally trusted with his well-being. Harker dragged the antiquated instrument towards him, dialled an international number, and waited. He was just about to hang up when the answering machine kicked in.

'Doggie, it's Alex. I'm in serious trouble. I need your help,' he paused for a moment and drew in a deep, steadying breath. How do you explain to a friend that you're in the process of being indicted for serial murder?

'It's a long story but, to put it bluntly, I'm being charged with murder by the Italian authorities. It's all a mistake, but, suffice to say, I'm in a lot of trouble, and I need all the help I can get. I'm currently being held at the central police station in Rome. I can explain everything, but I need your help, and quick.' He scanned the handwritten contact number printed on a slip of white paper glued to the base of the phone. 'It's Rome, 555-1246 . . . I'll be waiting.'

It wasn't until Harker had hung up that he became aware of the commotion unfolding outside the office. He turned around and glanced through the glass panel of the door to see Perone arguing intensely with three men dressed smartly in dark suits, white shirts, and black ties. Their alpha pulled out a double-panelled ID card and displayed it towards the small group of policemen that had now gathered behind the lead detective. Whatever he showed them instantly halted the discussion, and the officers moved aside, allowing the three men to make their way into the office with Perone following closely on their heels.

Great! What now? Harker thought.

'Professor Harker?' The man had a distinctly English accent.

'Yes.'

'My name is David Grant, and I'm from the British embassy. May we talk?' Grant immediately undid Harker's cuffs and threw them on to the superintendent's desk.

A wave of comforting relief descended upon Harker, and he stood up to shake the official's hand whilst simultaneously resisting the urge to hug the man. 'Damn glad to see you, I think.'

The man offered a polite nod. 'I have orders from the consulate to escort you to the British embassy here in Rome.'

Just over the civil servant's shoulder, Harker could see Perone eyeing him furiously like some mentally unhinged vulture.

'You've been issued with diplomatic immunity status by the Italian government.' David Grant pulled out a sealed, brown envelope and passed it over to Perone, who ripped it open to reveal a handwritten letter.

'That, Superintendent, is a signed directive from your chief of police and the minister of the interior, ordering you to place Professor Harker into our custody, effective immediately.'

It took Perone just a few seconds to read the letter before erupting in a fresh outburst. 'This is total fucking bullshit.'

'Then I suggest you speak with your own chief rather than vent your anger on me, Superintendent Perone.'

Grant's tone was final, and within seconds, Harker was being ushered past scores of fuming police officers by the other two servicemen. Within minutes, they were outside, and he was being bundled into a black X-type Jaguar with tinted windows, each one sporting the familiar bullet-proof symbol.

Behind them, Perone was unloading a choice selection of Italian insults that were obviously having little impact, but that wasn't about to stop him continuing. 'This is bullshit, total bullshit—that man's a suspect in almost five murders. You don't really think you're going to get away with this fucking outrage, do you?'

Opening the passenger door, David Grant paused momentarily. 'My dear Superintendent, I believe I just have.' As soon as the door was slammed shut, the Jaguar was on its way, leaving a furious Perone punching the air and continuing his torrent of abuse. The car turned a corner and began heading along the Via Nazionale, on a route leading out of the city.

Harker leant towards the gap between the two front seats, his head buzzing with questions. 'Who sent you?' was all he managed.

It was Grant who spoke, the other two men remaining silent. 'You've become quite a celebrity these days, and apparently you have friends in high places. Well, Professor, you've really managed to get yourself into a lot of trouble today, haven't you? I'd hate to think of the problems you would have caused us if you'd planned a longer visit. Now, there's something I need you to do for me.' He dipped into his pocket and pulled out something black. 'Would you put this on, please?'

He reached over and dropped the item into Harker's hand. At first, Harker thought it was a black tie, but a shiver ran through him as he realised what it was.

'A blindfold? Why do I . . . ?'

The pistol aimed directly at his face caused him to stop mid-sentence.

'You're not really from the British Consulate, are you?'

'No, we're not,' Grant replied, motioning towards the blindfold with the muzzle of his gun. 'Now, be a good man and put it on. That's if you want to live past tonight.'

Chapter 17

'You may now take off the blindfold, Professor.' The sombre tone of David Grant's voice caused Harker to hesitate for a moment as an image of the gun barrel still played through his mind.

Was this really how it ended?

He slid the blindfold off, automatically shielding both eyes as they adjusted to the light. He was in a garage, and a big one at that, housing six other cars, all top of the range. Next to the Jaguar he'd arrived in stood a metallic-grey Humvee, a blacked-out limousine, a light-blue Bentley Continental, a 750i BMW and, parked snugly at the end, a jet black Vogue Range Rover, completing the impressive row of cars.

'Civil servants are getting paid far too much these days,' Harker remarked, the joke drawing a vague smile from one of the men but ignored by the others.

'You see, that wasn't so bad, was it? Now if you'd like to follow me, Professor.'

Flanked either side, Harker was led down a short passageway that ended up in a six-feet by ten-feet granite-tiled room decorated with a luxurious red and gold wallpaper. The one called Grant made his way over to a small mirror hanging on the far side of the room. He pressed his hand against it, activating a glowing green light, which scanned the entire length of his palm. A moment later, the wall facing them began to pull apart, like a pair of curtains, and the low hum of hydraulics vibrating through the floor tiles could be felt and heard as the walls locked into place, revealing the interior of a lift.

'After you.'

Harker stepped inside and was promptly joined there by Grant himself who swiftly pressed an elevator button labelled *L*. Immediately the elevator jerked into motion as its wires took the weight, pulling them upwards. Half a minute of uncomfortable silence later, the doors slid open to reveal a red-carpeted hallway, and Grant ushered him out before escorting him down the corridor.

On the walnut-panelled walls hung a row of portraits of men dressed in the garments of different historical periods. Some of the images looked well worn, being sensibly protected behind glass, and although Harker didn't recognise the subjects, their styles of dress were unmistakable. The first was a stoic-looking man in traditional Roman uniform, armed with a gladius, or short sword, and grasping a legionary standard that displayed an eagle spreading its wings. The image was painted on a wooden panel as was popular during the first and second centuries AD, and, despite some telling signs of restoration, it looked totally original. The further along the hallway they proceeded, the more recent the style of dress became, ending up with someone wearing the uniform of a four-star general in the American Army. Harker recognised the medals from the first Gulf War and the war for Kuwait, but the man himself didn't look familiar.

Grant pushed open a solid wooden door next to the final portrait and forced a smile. 'After you, Professor.'

Harker could feel the inside of his mouth go dry again as his nerves intensified a notch. He took a deep gulp and determinedly made his way into the room.

The first thing that caught his attention was the smell of dust and old leather. The dim lights and the closed curtains blocking any natural light from getting in made it difficult to see clearly, but he could sense that the room was huge. It must have been over hundred metres in length by twenty metres wide, with thick wooden beams jutting out of the walls at different levels all along. As his eyes acclimatised to the low-level lighting, it suddenly dawned on him that he was in a library. Though it was only one room, there were four levels of walkway lining the perimeter so as to allow easy access to all areas. The room must have approached thirty metres in height, and the shelves of books ran all the way up to within a couple of feet of the ceiling.

Behind him, the door closed, but Harker barely noticed, his attention being consumed by the remarkable sight in front of him. He made his way over to the nearest tier of dark wooden shelves, running his finger across the bindings before stopping at a copy of Charles Dickens's *A Christmas Carol*. Harker pulled it off the shelf and gently opened it at the first page. On the flyleaf, a note in thick black ink had been neatly handwritten at the head of the page:

To my good friend Jacque de Montford, who taught me there is far more to one's spiritual life than simply that which lies on the surface. Your obedient servant and friend, Charles Dickens.

Harker recognised the signature as genuine. *Impressive.*

He carefully placed the volume back and continued to scan the shelves. The books were grouped by authors, starting with the works of Charles Dickens, and moving on to Mary Shelley, H. G. Wells, and so on. All of them signed first editions. There were novels, plays, poetry, and non-fictions, but what really made Harker's stomach churn in excitement was a shelf sign labelled RELIGIOUS TEXTS. Each volume here was carefully protected by a transparent case fastened to the wall by thick Teflon wire. Some still had their original bindings, whilst other older-looking documents had each individual page protected between two sturdy plastic sheets, which meant that some of the larger books took up an entire shelf. One caught Harker's eye, and he actually felt his legs wobble. The first page was written in ancient Hebrew script on what looked like age-old darkened papyrus. It contained a single word: Peter.

As Harker's mind was numbed by a sense of shock and awe, he was barely aware of the gawky childish grin he now sported, causing tears of sheer excitement to well up in the corners of his eyes. *Was this for real?* The response he received in a familiar voice startled him, and he jerked his hand away from the ancient text in shock.

'Yes, Professor, it's genuine. That's the lost gospel of the apostle St Peter himself, one of the most important accounts never to grace the pages of the most successful book ever printed: The King James Bible.'

On the other side of the room stood Sebastian Brulet, his featureless silhouette in stark contrast to the long white hair flowing over his shoulders and the sun glasses glinting in reflection of what little light there was in the room. 'No, I'm not a mind reader, Professor. The look on your face said it all.'

Harker moved a few steps closer in his effort to see better the man who had sent him on this nightmare journey in the first place. 'Brulet, what the fuck is going on, and where the hell is Claire Dwyer? I want some answers, or do you plan to have me murdered, like you had your henchman do to Father Maddocks?'

Brulet didn't move an inch. 'And what henchman would that be, Professor?'

'Don't screw around, Brulet. You know damn well whom I mean, about seven feet high and built like a brick wall.'

Brulet gave a curt nod. 'He's not one of mine, but, yes, I know the man you refer to—if you can call him a man.'

For some strange reason, Harker believed him, but he wasn't about to allow his supposed employer the satisfaction. 'Yeah, well, he's managed to follow me wherever I went, and since you and Mr Caster are the only people who knew I was going to be in Rome . . .'

From the darkened doorway directly behind Brulet, another familiar voice interrupted.

'I can assure you I've not told anyone of your location except for the police by alerting them to your whereabouts at the monastery.' The balding Mr Caster, the lawyer Harker had met back in Cambridge, stepped out of the shadows and into view. 'And I'm pretty sure I was doing you a favour by placing that anonymous call.'

Harker's head was spinning with questions whilst struggling not to lose his temper. 'Someone better tell me what the hell is going on right *now.*'

The last part of his sentence was delivered so aggressively that Caster actually took a step backwards. Brulet, on the other hand, took a step closer.

'The giant fellow you came in contact with is an assassin, Mr Harker. He's a professional killer by the name of Drazia Heldon, and he works for that same organisation I spoke of at our last meeting.'

Harker felt a release of frustration by expelling a deep sigh. Finally, he was getting somewhere, it seemed. 'What? You mean the ones associated with the Catholic Church who are receiving those huge sums of money?'

'One and the same organisation, Professor. It goes by the name of the Magi, and as you found out earlier today, they will stop at nothing to lay their hands on what I believe, and hope, you now have somewhere on your very person.'

Harker decided he was done playing games. He reached into his torn inside pocket and carefully pulled out the narrow, airtight plastic case containing the crown of thorns.

Brulet nodded respectfully. 'Yes, that's the item I mean.' He didn't take a step nearer but simply stretched out his hand. 'May I?'

The gesture was in no way threatening, but Harker hadn't endured today's dramatic events just to give it up now. And more importantly, if this Magi group wanted the relic so desperately, then it was the only bargaining chip he had for Claire's life. 'No, first you tell me everything, and then . . .' He placed the container back in his pocket. '. . . I'll think about it.'

Brulet lowered his arm, considering the suggestion. 'Fair enough. As you'll know the Magi was the name given to the three kings of undying fame.'

'You're referring to the three kings who made a pilgrimage to Bethlehem to witness Christ's birth?'

'That's exactly who I mean, of course.' Brulet began to pace slowly back and forth, all the time keeping his distance. 'The Magi consider themselves the true successors to these three kings.'

A tingling sensation stirred in Harker's flesh as a mixture of excitement and disbelief began to take hold of him. After this day's frenzied events, it was a feeling he was getting used to, but he still had to fight to control it as Brulet now continued.

'It is this organisation that claims to have been, though at a distance, connected with the Catholic Church since its very inception. Two of its leading dynasties have over time been terminated, through either assassination or accident, but the third and last remaining family . . . Well, Ms Dwyer and you had the misfortune of meeting one of their employees earlier today. That family is currently headed up by one of four brothers, namely Balthasar—or Lord Balthasar—as he prefers to be called.' Brulet rolled his eyes dismissively. 'Anyway, whatever you wish to call him, he seized the reins of power after their father died in a car-bomb incident some five years ago.' Brulet rubbed his hands together in seeming frustration. 'That was a death that, unfortunately, I myself have been blamed for.'

'Were you responsible?' Harker responded.

'No, but I wish I had been. That is what I find so unfortunate.'

The cold answer filled Harker with dread. He barely knew this strange man or what he stood for, but he allowed only one question to preoccupy his thoughts. 'Where is Claire Dwyer, and how do I get her back?'

Brulet's response came straight to the point. 'She is alive and now most likely in the hands of the Magi but only for as long as you still have possession of what they want.' He raised a long spindly finger in the direction of Harker's jacket. 'For the moment, she won't be harmed, but allow them to get their hands on that item, and they'll kill her without hesitation. Unfortunately for us, even this may not be enough to ensure her safety.'

'What do you mean?'

'I mean that there exists another item of equal value, and, if allowed to get their hands on it, they may decide they have no need of the one that is currently residing in your pocket.'

For the first time since this conversation began, Harker felt like he was being played. 'Why should I believe any of this or anything else you say for that matter?' It was now he allowed the barrage of questions flowing through his mind to erupt. 'And why get me out of that police station only to have your guys pull a gun on me?' He began.

That Brulet showed no sign of emotion at all began to enrage Harker even further. The strange man just seemed to absorb it all through those stupid sunglasses of his.

'And who the hell wears sunglasses at night? Well, Mr Brulet? And this had better be good because I've picked up enough horrific images and mental scars today to keep me in therapy for years!'

Brulet inhaled a deep calming breath, and from that moment on, he was all business. 'Professor, I've not lied to you since we met. All I have done is to omit certain truths. But I plan to rectify that right now if you'll allow me.'

Harker gave a simple nod.

'I would ask that you do not become alarmed at what I'm about to show you. My physical appearance can be somewhat overwhelming at first, so please don't . . . He paused and licked his lips, looking for the right phrase. ' . . . for lack of a better word, *freak out.*'

He placed a hand on each side of his sunglasses and slowly raised them.

At first, Harker thought he was seeing things due to the inadequate light, but, as Brulet raised his head towards him, his mouth began to dry up once more, and he struggled for his next breath.

For the first time, Harker could see how extraordinarily grey Brulet's skin was. It wasn't just grey; in fact, it looked almost silver. But it wasn't the colour that had goosebumps flaring up across his forearms. No, it was the man's eyes. The whites of Brulet's eyeballs looked perfectly normal, but the irises . . . they looked yellow. And his pupils weren't circular; they were almost cross-shaped!

On the outside, Harker managed to keep a calm demeanour, but Brulet had been right. Internally he was freaking out.

'What are you?' he gasped.

Even though Brulet's peculiar eyes gave away nothing, his facial expression proclaimed he felt insulted. 'Please, Professor, I can assure you that I'm just as human as you or anyone else.'

He paused as Harker took a few steps closer, his stare now merely curious. 'I never suggested otherwise.'

'No, but you were thinking it.'

Harker said nothing because the man was right. For a moment, the thought of alien species had briefly entered his mind but had been dismissed just as quickly. By now, he was standing within a few metres, still transfixed by Brulet's unique appearance.

'The misshaping of my pupils is a genetic condition passed from father to son. As you can see, it is a disorder that also affects the skin. Like a person with albinism, I cannot tolerate the sun for any prolonged length of time, and bright lights or direct sunlight would quite literally fry my retinas and cause permanent blindness.' He paused as Harker finally stopped moving closer. 'Which makes me something of a night person.'

This down-to-earth explanation merely intensified Harker's curiosity. 'What's the condition called?'

'It's a mixture of two.' Brulet actually sounded as if he were proud of it. 'The first is coloboma. That's a genetic disorder which affects the eyes, creating the yellow tinge of the irises and the ill-formed pupils which you are now staring at so intently.'

If this remark was meant to inform Harker that he was being rude, it didn't have the desired effect, and the professor stepped even closer. 'And your skin?'

'It's a form of Waardenburg syndrome that affects the pigments in the skin and can cause skin cancer in many cases. Apart from that, I am in perfect working order.'

Harker had heard of this condition before; years earlier, a young boy in his parish had been diagnosed with Waardenburg syndrome. But the effects had been nothing like the ones he was now staring at.

'Now you understand what I am, allow me to explain *who* I am and the situation you currently find yourself in.'

Harker finally snapped out of his trance-like state. 'An explanation? Yes, that would be a good start, Mr Brulet.'

'Then allow me to begin.'

Harker gave Brulet his personal space again back by stepping further away and nodded for him to go ahead.

'You believe you are working for a company—my company, Maptrel Associates. Well, Maptrel certainly exists, but if you looked it up, you'd not find my name mentioned anywhere. Maptrel is just one branch of many apparently independent businesses that are, in fact, all linked to a single organisation. It's an organisation that is never mentioned, and whose existence is known only to a select few. Almost all the employees of those companies have no idea of their connection to this central organisation. They've no idea that they provide financial stability to it, just as they've no idea that without this same organisation, they would not have a job to go to.'

Brulet motioned for Harker to walk beside him as he made his way towards the other end of the vast library. 'Professor, what I am about to tell you must never be repeated to another living soul as long as you live. If you do, then consider you life forfeit, for there are no half ways with a truth such as this.' Brulet's eyes glazed over as he waited for a reply.

'That's a difficult promise to make, Mr Brulet, especially when I don't know what you're intending to reveal.'

'Isn't it just.' Brulet smiled. 'Yet there it is.'

The next few seconds of silent internal deliberation by Harker were wholly unnecessary. Even before Brulet had finished his stipulation, he had known what his decision would be. Every fibre in his being was completely blocking out any thoughts of danger and screaming out loud:

Do it! Do it! Do it!

Nevertheless, he kept calmly silent for a few moments longer, not wanting to seem overly eager. 'OK, you have my solemn word.'

Brulet gently prodded his forefinger into Harker's chest. 'I'll hold you to that, Professor. Mr Caster, would you please allow us some space?'

John Caster offered him a polite nod and disappeared through one of the library's numerous side doors.

'Now walk with me, Professor, and allow me to explain exactly who we are.'

Brulet took Harker by the arm and began to lead him across the thick red carpet extending the entire length of the room. 'This library is a culmination of over two thousand years' worth of collecting knowledge, a collection that extends back to the first known origins of my family. We came from Egypt originally and a region bordering the Sudanese wastelands to the south. Ours was a nomadic tribe that lived a solitary existence, and for centuries, none ventured to the outside world. By choice, they stayed completely isolated.' He flicked away a strand of pure white hair that had fallen across his face before continuing.

'The Egyptians were the ultimate superpowers of the time, of course, and as they got stronger, they forced tribe after tribe into slavery so as to create an ever-growing workforce that could build ever larger monuments to their leaders and their gods. We know some of these today as the pyramids.' Brulet stretched out a finger towards an intricate scale model of the pyramids at Giza covered by a perspex dome perched securely on a stout wooden table between two book racks. 'My own tribe was ravaged by the Egyptian conquests, but they managed to resist and survive as free men and women simply because of their nomadic lifestyle which was ingrained at birth into every member of the tribe. Over time, the Egyptians empire bourgeoned as did the number of slaves subjugated in to lifelong bondage.'

Brulet gently pulled Harker away from the model and continued, leading him deeper into the massive library.

'You must understand that hundreds of thousands were thus born into slavery—an unfair, twisted birthright passed from one generation to the next. But it was not the only thing that was passed on, for the slaves too evolved their own religion, which eventually became the roots of . . .'

Harker couldn't resist jumping into this exposition. 'Judaism.'

Brulet gave a brief nod. 'Yes, the beginnings of it anyway. And, after many years, the belief in a certain prophecy came to pass. This prophecy told of a man who would deliver all those enslaved into a free and just world where a person's worth was linked to his ability instead of the rank inherited or bestowed upon him! Eventually, it was the Roman's turn to take power, but, in truth, they were far more interested in dominating the Egyptians themselves than the surrounding tribes, which they saw as lesser peoples with little to offer. This allowed a basic peace to reign on the fringes of the known world, and, for a few hundred years, nothing really changed—including the prophecy, which had continued to grow in strength and whose staunch believers included my own clan.'

Brulet stopped at a beautifully crafted African tribal table with two chairs alongside. He unhooked his arm from Harker's and sat down, encouraging his guest to do the same. 'Then, one day, word reached them that a man had been identified possessing all the hallmarks of the prophecy, which was by this point over five thousand years old. He had been born far from the heights of power and had not only preached the worth of every man, woman, and child but also possessed incredible powers of control over the natural world around him. A select few from my tribe were tasked with the journey to seek out this individual to find out if he truly was the one that the prophecy had foretold of. Those selected few included my direct ancestors, and their pilgrimage constituted the origins of our organisation. They did the unthinkable and made their way out of the desert and into civilisation. They travelled through Memphis and Alexandria, the two greatest cities of the Egyptians, and on through Gaza until finally they reached the town of Bethsaida where they became witness to the power and might of this extraordinary mortal. You may be familiar with the story as the Feeding of the Five Thousand.'

Harker struggled to take in what he was being told, his desire to believe conflicting with his academic sense of logic. If it had not been for the day's extraordinary events, and being surrounded here by so many ancient and significant texts, then he might have been less willing to succumb, but he felt himself being drawn inexorably into the fantastical story that Brulet was unfolding, the tone of conviction in the man's voice absolute.

'You're talking about Jesus Christ?'

A thin smile crossed Brulet's face, and he nodded gently.

'Yes, my family were traditionally amongst the first to acknowledge the man who was to become the son of God and bring true humanity to the world.' Brulet's voice was becoming hypnotic, and Harker found it increasingly difficult to summon up any of the questions that had previously occupied his thoughts. Before he could focus the will to do so, Brulet raised a hand towards him.

'Allow me to finish, Professor, and I will answer any questions you may have for me, but first a drink.'

He pushed a small button concealed underneath the table, and within seconds, Lusic appeared, the same man Harker had met back at Bletchley Park.

'Two coffees, please, and . . .' Brulet paused. 'Sorry, is coffee OK for you, or maybe a cup of tea?'

Harker, still giddy from his host's revelations, gave a weak thumbs up. 'Coffee is good.'

Brulet gave a contented smile at his guest's state of shock before returning his attention to the muscular German. 'Two coffees quick as you can please.' He waited until they were alone again before leaning in and whispering. 'Don't expect too much, however, Lusic is a top-notch fixer but an awful cook. His coffee-making skills leave much to be desired, I'm afraid.'

Harker's stunned look pressed Brulet to continue.

'I know it's hard to believe, how can anyone mess up a cup of coffee? I fear he's actually got quite a talent for it.'

Harker almost choked. 'That's not what's on my mind, Mr Brulet. Please, continue with your story.'

He couldn't tell if the laugh Brulet emitted was one of sarcasm, but the strange-looking man in front of him ploughed back into his account with the same zeal and enthusiasm with which he had begun it.

'Oh, yes, as I was saying, after seeing the Christ perform that miracle, they were captivated, believing that after so many years, the treasured prophecy had finally come to pass. So they joined his followers, slowly gaining trust amongst his apostles and disciples until they too were considered part of his flock. Unfortunately, during this time, there were storm clouds gathering over their native community in Egypt. Unbeknownst to them, a Roman legion had stumbled across their remote village, apparently by chance, and a fight had ensued. I'm afraid there are no records detailing anything except the bloody outcome. Men, women, and children were ritually slaughtered: all crucified as a warning to other tribes not to show disrespect to the might of the Roman Empire. When my ancestors later learnt of this disaster, and with no home to return to, the few remaining members of my people dedicated their lives to following Jesus. Thus, they were there when Jesus was arrested by the Romans, they were there when he was crucified, and they were there when he rose from the dead. They even say that this hereditary affliction first occurred around that time.' Brulet indicated his unusual cross-shaped pupils with a flick of his finger.

'It was declared that my family were thus blessed with the sign of the cross, and it has been passed down ever since from generation to generation.'

Brulet gave a humorous wink. 'But, of course, this claim is just an embellishment of the real truth. This condition of mine is—and always was—purely genetic, but, nonetheless, it did imbed them deeply within the framework of the early Church. In fact, when St Peter founded the first church of Christianity, my forbearers were part of his original flock. As the decades and centuries progressed, my family tree grew and then shrank. Persecution of the early Christians was rife, but still my family line survived until eventually the Roman Emperor Constantine declared on his deathbed in AD 336 that Christianity was to be the only religion of the empire. As you know, Professor, over the next 700 years, the Christian church and its diverse elements were moulded and sculpted by the most powerful into what became the Holy Roman Catholic Church. My forefathers, along with many others, thus helped to bring about the dark ages, a period when the entire western world was subjugated to conformity in the name of Catholicism, and anyone who resisted was burnt at the stake for heresy or drowned as a witch.'

Brulet took a moment to gaze thoughtfully at the library towering all around them, both his eyes suddenly looking weary. 'They say it takes only one generation to change the beliefs of men, but in truth, it takes longer than that, and with it come many deaths. In theory, it works, but, in the practice, it does not. Much like communism has shown.'

For a few seconds, they both sat quietly, not in an awkward silence but rather in a mutual understanding of the difficult history mankind had created for itself.

'By the eleventh century, the Church encompassed the hearts and minds of the known world, and, in that, my family were no different. During the dark ages, my ancestors were responsible for the trial and death of thousands of non-believers, becoming crusaders for Christianity and defenders of the faith. It was around this time that our organisation truly came into existence. It was originally constituted by a French nobleman called Hugues de Payens around AD 1121, but it wasn't until AD 1129, when recognised and blessed by the Catholic Church at the council of Troyes, that my family assumed a leading role in what was known as the Poor Knights of the Temple of King Solomon before changing the name some years later.'

Harker instantly recognised those dates. 'You mean the Knights Templars?'

Sebastian Brulet shot him a smile. 'Yes, the very same group that was brutally disbanded during the thirteenth century.'

Harker shook his head in disbelief. He'd managed to keep quiet throughout Brulet's monologue, but this was getting too much. 'Mr Brulet, I'm aware of the stories—or should I say legends—but you don't honestly expect me to believe you are the head of an organisation of almost mystical status that's had more books written about it than the Queen of England.'

Brulet held out his arms in a welcoming gesture. 'At your service.'

Harker stood up from his chair and rubbed at the lines of frustration developing across his forehead. 'I'll admit this collection of books and texts is extraordinary.' He gazed around at the wealth of historical knowledge that sat neatly ordered on the shelves. 'And truth is they would compete with any museum in the world,' Harker slid back into his seat, 'but you'd better have something more than this to convince me that you're the head of an organisation that the history books declare hasn't existed for over seven hundred years.'

Brulet's glistening malformed pupils stared deeply into Harker's eyes with all the intensity of a predator eyeing its prey.

'I certainly do, my friend, and by the time I'm finished here, I'll be accepting your apology.'

Chapter 18

Prince Genges twisted his fingers in quick succession, each one releasing a loud and satisfying crack. He wasn't a natural knuckle-cracker, but it was a habit he had acquired during the past few months whilst being holed up here in the basement of the Monte Mario observatory. It may have been Rome's primary astrological telescope steeped in history, but for the Magi Prince, it was turning into a jail cell, and he was going stir-crazy.

The Monte Mario observatory sat atop the city's highest hill and was only two miles north of Vatican City. It made up one unit in a trio of telescopes located around the province, known simply as the Rome observatory and had enabled the Magi high command to track a streaking comet that had been illuminating the night sky for the past seven weeks.

The comet had originally been discovered by a Swiss scientist some years earlier, but before he could announce the discovery, he had been killed in an unfortunate car crash. Of course, in the world of the Magi, there were no such things as accidents.

The secret organisation had been searching for a galactic phenomenon such as this comet for many years, and, on being made aware of the Swiss scientist's discovery through their network of informants, the high command had leapt upon it immediately. The occurrence of the comet would tie in with their plans nicely, and all written evidence of the Swiss astronomer's work to date had immediately been transferred to their associates at the Rome observatory, who subsequently took full credit for the exciting find.

When it came time to setting things in motion, the powers that be had arranged for refurbishment of a large disused basement underneath the main complex, creating an HQ for the coming months. This base of operations was complete with all the facilities a five-man team—which included both Genges and his brother—would need to remain self-sufficient for the duration. From this operation's centre, the last elements of the grand plan had been carefully choreographed, and all had been running smoothly until that idiot Dwyer had screwed everything up. The priest's intervention had provoked so many unnecessary killings, and, now this Harker person had turned up, things were becoming intolerable. It was for this reason that Genges now found himself involved in a heated discussion.

'I'm only saying', he was insisting, 'that we should be ready for a full assault, should the need arise. At the very least, allow me to put a unit on standby. I could gather them together in ten minutes, and then they'd be ready to go at a moment's notice.'

'No.' Lord Balthasar slowly shook his head. 'We can ill afford the kind of attention such an action would bring. You know this, Brother.'

Genges slammed his fist down hard on the brightly illuminated map table, not in anger but in frustration. 'And what if this Harker character is already in British custody or, even worse, holed up in the British embassy? What then?'

Balthasar got up from his red leather armchair and strode over to the heated aquarium, where two satisfied-looking red-bellied piranhas were contently gnawing on a thick chunk of beef. 'There's no reason to presume the UK authorities are involved, and, more importantly, we've heard nothing from our British contacts. No, the good professor is in the hands of someone else—someone we've not considered.'

'And what if these "someones" are measured in large numbers? What then?'

The Magi leader stared into the aquarium and then gently tapped his forehead against the glass, causing the two fishes to pause momentarily before continuing with their bloody meal.

'Then, Brother, we will deal with it silently and subtly. But until we hear back from Lupis, we wait.'

Genges grunted in annoyance as an uneasy silence descended upon the room like a thick fog. He had always been labelled as the less patient, less level-headed of the two brothers, and, though he tried not to show it, deep down, resentment clawed at his innards like an ulcer. If it were up to him, he would have grabbed Harker much earlier, taken him somewhere private, and squeezed the information from him by force. By now, both relics would have been safely in their possession, allowing them simply to count down the clock till crisis hour. *As for that idiot Heldon . . .* well, Genges continued to be appalled at how much faith his sibling had in the lumbering fool, regardless of whatever history the two of them shared. That alone was not reason enough to assign the hulking assassin with such a delicate and crucial assignment. Heldon was Magi, sure, but he was a broadsword, not a scalpel, and the events of the past few weeks had proved that fact time and time again.

Genges watched his older brother sink heavily back into his chair with a wince, and he wondered if their father had made the right decision in choosing his successor. Had Balthasar been chosen to lead the Magi because of his patience and cunning, as his father proclaimed, or because there were few other areas of clan activity he would have been any good at? After all, a boss could not be allowed to get his hands dirty, which, in his mind, may have been a saving grace for his brother.

Genges banished the thought. No, his brother was a great leader, and his position was deserved, but if his father had known of the illness that now hung around Balthasar's neck like a heavy weight, he might have chosen differently. Balthasar's blood disorder had continued to ravage his body during the three years since being originally diagnosed, but it wasn't until the last few months that his physical symptoms had truly begun to show. The sores and welts that now covered his body must be painful but relatively easy to conceal. Other symptoms, however, were more difficult to keep secret such as nosebleeds, stiffening of the joints, and extreme fatigue. But the most difficult to conceal were the droplets of blood that formed in his tear ducts as small capillaries in his eyelids ruptured. Most of the men knew that their master had medical issues, but it was not something to be openly discussed *ever*.

Genges glanced down at the fish-shaped silver brooch fastened to his lapel and smiled. In recent years, it had been hijacked by funky new-age Christians, but for the previous two millennia, it had, and still was, the symbol of the Magi. *Damn hippies with their sacrilegious pretensions to Catholicism, what a joke!* He thumbed at the badge with the small emblem of a sword underneath it, which signified his position in the hierarchy.

As head of the Magi's diplomatic division, he was directly responsible for the enforcement of its will, whether it require a peaceful resolution or a violent one. The role gave him certain freedoms within the administration, which, in turn, provided him the sense of power he so craved. Genges bit his lip at the thought: he had been telling himself exactly that since Balthasar had been chosen to lead the clan five years ago as a result of father's dying wish. It was a tradition which passed from father to eldest son, thus ensuring that the family line survived. In truth, to himself anyway, he still attempted to justify his contentment with his own role and that he felt satisfied about the real power being passed to his elder sibling. Anyway, in just a few more hours, the goal which had steered the Magi over the past forty years would finally come to fruition, and with it, would result a new world and—just as importantly—more power.

The heavy thud at the door broke the silence, much to Genges's relief.

'Enter,' called out Balthasar, throwing his younger brother an inquisitive look. 'Some good news maybe?'

Marko Lupis burst into the room, the eighteen-year-old Magi associate's face flushed with excitement. 'My Lord, we've received word from one of our contacts. The professor was taken to an estate just outside Rome. It seems the British consulate wasn't involved, after all.'

The long pause that followed only served to increase the exhilaration emanating from the messenger, who was clearly thrilled by the news he brought.

'C'mon, Lupis, spit it out,' Genges snapped, becoming impatient.

The young associate immediately composed himself, the flush in his cheeks draining away, and he snapped to attention as a soldier does. 'Yes, sir, but it's just you're not going to believe who has him now.'

It was Balthasar's turn to air his annoyance. 'Are you asking me or telling me, boy?'

Lupis shook his head forcefully, his long black hair lashing against his cheek. 'It's the Templars, sir. The professor, as of this moment, is in the company of Sebastian Brulet.'

The name shattered the expectant atmosphere like a blow from a sledgehammer. The Magi lord's mouth dropped open, his eyes widening like those of a maniac. 'Genges, assemble your team immediately, and get them geared up for a full-frontal assault on Brulet's hideaway. I want a total breach. Recover Harker and the item and then bring them straight here to me.'

Genges was already out of his seat and heading towards the door, iPhone in hand, when Balthasar's voice stopped him dead in his tracks.

'And Genges . . .'

He turned around to face the piercing gaze of his brother.

'Leave no Templar alive.'

Genges put the mobile phone to his ear, waiting for the call to connect. 'And what about Brulet?'

Lord Balthasar clenched both fists, the tensing of his muscles making both arms quiver. 'Before you kill him, make him suffer.'

Chapter 19

'So you're saying the Templars and the Magi aren't that dissimilar then, in that they both serve Christ?' Harker suggested as he dabbed a fresh napkin against his still damp thigh, where Lusic had clumsily spilt coffee on him moments earlier.

'Yes, in a way. They are the yin to our yang, opposite sides of the same coin, but that is where the similarities end.'

Harker was riveted, if not a little confused, by the point being made, and Brulet sensed this immediately.

'To truly understand the relationship between the Templars and the Magi, you must look back to the very beginnings of the Catholic Church and the last wish of the emperor who instigated it all.'

'Constantine?' Harker said, knowing full well the story because there wasn't a priest in the world that didn't.

'Yes, exactly, the last true ruler of the united Roman Empire who from his deathbed made one final order, demanding the conversion of every citizen in the realm to Catholicism. From that moment onwards, it was the bishops and the burgeoning clergy that ruled all aspects of a citizen's life from cradle to grave. They acquired control of everything through the persecution of any dissenting Christians.'

'But surely the establishment of the Catholic Church put a stop to such persecution?' It sounded as if Harker was taking Brulet's comment a little too personally.

'No, that's exactly what people have been taught to believe. In fact, up until this time, the early Christians were not persecuted with any more zeal than were other smaller religions. Those stories of Christians en masse being fed to the lions in Nero's circuses are purely fictional.' Before Harker could protest, Brulet was already signalling him to be quiet with a wag of his finger. 'Yes, yes, of course, some prisoners were fed to wild animals as part of the general Roman practice *Ad Bestias* or condemnation to beasts, but it was fairly rare and certainly not just because they were Christians.'

Content that Harker was mollified by this answer, he continued after a grunt.

'No, no, the Romans treated all minor dissenting religions with the same contempt.'

Brulet deliberately took a slow, long sip from his cup as if testing Harker's ability to remain quiet and just listen. Satisfied that no more interruptions would occur, he carried on with a gracious nod. 'When Constantine established the Catholic Church, it meant that the bishops now joined the bureaucrats in composing a new governing class of the empire. The bishops of Italy became the heirs of the Roman senate, and the bishop of Rome became the emperor's successors. But once this official version of Christianity was established, it meant that all others, even older branches of Christianity, were now seen as a threat—alongside the pagans, druids, and anyone else that commanded spiritual power over the population. And so began a prelude to the dark ages, a period when the old ideologies of the western world were destroyed and replaced with the new.'

The Templar Grand Master finally relinquished control of the conversation by relaxing into his armchair, a glint in his eye encouraging debate.

Harker had heard similar ideas expounded by a lecturer at King's College, London, but he had never taken them seriously. 'I've heard that theory before, but it seemed pretty far-fetched.'

Sebastian Brulet wagged a finger dismissively. 'It's no theory, Professor, I assure you. It actually happened, and both my forebears and the Magi were there to witness it.'

Harker once again relapsed into silence, willing to hear Brulet's case further.

'The descendants of the early Magi had followed Christianity devoutly from one generation to the next and thus became involved in the newly growing religion, but it did not last. During the beginnings of this new religious shift the Church leaders called a great assembly to best decide how this new religion would be constituted.'

'The first Council of Nicaea,' Harker murmured.

'Yes, it was determined how Catholicism would function and by following what system of beliefs. The very mechanics of the Church were decided upon, and every aspect of the new faith was scrutinised and voted upon, including its most important doctrine: that Jesus Christ was truly the son of God, rather than human, and made flesh by his Father. The descendants of a certain group were supposedly present amongst the adjudicators, already casting themselves in the role of rightful enforcers of the faith.'

Harker had already figured it out before the sentence was finished. 'The Magi?'

Brulet gave a gentle nod. 'Yes, the same secret faction that is now responsible for holding your friend Claire Dwyer captive.'

The very mention of her name sent a rush of apprehension through Harker's stomach, and he immediately pushed the painful thought to the back of his mind as he allowed Brulet to continue.

'Several self-appointed groups grew in strength alongside the Church itself. Then in AD 1118, a new order was created by a Frenchman Hugh de Payens ostensibly to protect pilgrims travelling to Jerusalem. That order was called the Knights Templars, and Hugh de Payens is one of my ancestors.' Brulet let out a sigh of dismay. 'The Magi, on the other hand, assumed the role of financial administrators, which, as they knew all too well, was where the real power of the Church lay. And that is how things stayed until a single event changed everything.' Brulet rubbed his hand together awkwardly as if trying to rid himself of some unseen stain. 'Even though my ancestors were amongst the first to embrace the church of St Peter, many of the ancient truths passed them by because it was not until the crusades that such truths were finally unearthed.'

Brulet stole another sip from his coffee cup, the ensuing silence only enhancing Harker's curiosity. 'Towards the end of the second crusade, in the aftermath of the battle for Jerusalem in AD 1123, the surviving Templars began to excavate the area of ground where King Solomon's Temple had once stood. It was long believed that buried in the ruins of that building lay evidence revealing Christian truths of such importance that they could weaken the Catholic Church, possibly irreversibly, at a time when other major religions were fighting for global dominance and for the hearts of mankind. As righteous defenders of the faith, the Templars believed these truths must be protected at all cost, lest they fall into the wrong hands. After almost two years of excavation, the foundations of King Solomon's Temple were finally discovered, and with it, a wealth of Christian relics.'

Sebastian Brulet drained his cup with a wince of disgust. 'You know, that man couldn't make a good cup of coffee to save his life!' He shook his head in disgust, pushing the china cup to the other side of the table as if distancing it would somehow rid him of the aftertaste. 'As I was saying, they recovered a wealth of Christian relics—ones whose importance shook their beliefs to the core, thus bringing about the beginning of the Templar reformation that transformed it into the secret organisation of today.'

Brulet rose to his feet up and made his way over to the nearest bookshelf. He tenderly extracted a leather-bound volume and returned to his seat, all the time tapping at the book's binder with one long slim finger. 'This is only one of many relics that were discovered, but it is the one that changed my family's relationship with the Church forever.' Brulet laid the book on to the table and carefully nudged it in Harker's direction. 'This is only a copy, Professor, since the genuine article is far too valuable to leave lying about on a library shelf.'

Harker excitedly pulled the book towards him and cradled it in both hands. The dark brown, cracked leather cover bore no title, and, judging by the wear and tear, it had been perused many times before. Cautiously Harker opened it up to find the pages inside were a high-resolution colour photocopy of such clarity that he could make out the minute scratches covering what must have been the original papyrus. The words had been written in a dark-red ink, the brush strokes consistent with the very basic type of pen generally used prior to the Middle Ages. The ink had hardened over time, causing cracks in the lettering, but the language was instantly recognisable to Harker as Aramaic—the same language a number of the Dead Sea Scrolls had been written in. It had originally been adopted by the Persians as the unifying language of their empire but was discarded after Alexander the Great had conquered the superpower, which was then carved up into smaller territories after his death. These nations adopted their new conqueror's home language of Greek, with the exception of just one, for the Kingdom of Judah was the only nation to retain Aramaic as its official language.

Brulet watched silently, a hidden satisfaction lying deep in those mysterious star-shaped black pupils, as Harker thumbed his way across the first page, muttering quietly to himself. It took him just a few seconds to decipher the title, and with it, he experienced the most overpowering surge of excitement yet. He glanced across the table at Brulet, whose thin knowing smile said it all, and then shook his head in complete disbelief. He turned back to the text and deciphered it just to confirm the incredible reality of what he was reading.

'This is . . .' Harker broke off mid-sentence, and he swallowed hard, struggling to control his emotions.

Opposite him, Brulet's smile widened. 'Yes, Professor, you hold in your very hands a copy of the "Word of God"—and the very reason our order still exists to this day.'

Harker tried to steady his shaking fingers as he read the title line out loud: 'The Gospel According to Jesus of Nazareth!' He continued to scan the lines of text, his mind still overwhelmed. He had spent so much time excavating sites over the past seven years—the digging and scraping of earth, the supervision of workers, the death of friends, as well as the political problems like arranging permits—and yet, here in the comfortable surroundings of this library, rested in his hands an item of more archaeological worth than anything he had ever dared hope to find. It gave him a momentary sense of sadness to consider how he, along with rest of the archaeological world, continually scoured the bowels of the earth for clues to the origins of human culture, religion, and everything in between, and all the while here, in a library on the outskirts of Rome lay one of the greatest historical discoveries never to have been made. He pondered that thought, for how many other crucial links to our past sat collecting dust in a private collection somewhere, never to see the light of day.

'You seem sad, Professor.'

He looked up to catch Brulet looking genuinely concerned, his silver-tinted eyebrows raised demurely. Harker shook his head and offered him a smile. 'No, just somewhat overwhelmed.'

Brulet resumed his smile. 'Difficult not to be, isn't it? Now, before you read on, allow me to enlighten you further to the events you currently find yourself embroiled in.' He reached over and gently scooped the book out of Harker's hands. Settling back in to his seat, he opened it to a special page with a flick of his tongue much as a schoolteacher would. 'Our lord Jesus Christ wrote this account during the last two years of his life, and, of course, the title was added later. Some pages were missing when it was unearthed, and, much to your relief, no doubt, much of it verifies what appears in the King James Bible with one notable exception.'

Harker found himself leaning forward, like an enthralled pupil, as the surrogate teacher ran his finger across one particular passage in the book.

'And so I say to all God's children who wish to follow my teachings, do not do so in a place of worship set apart from where it truly matters. If you wish to honour me, observe my teachings in your daily life and in full view of the world around you. For my message is not something to be regulated, like in a Roman court, but must roam free in the hearts and minds of those who wish to see the Lord's kingdom beyond, and in doing so will change the face of man and earth forever.' Brulet let the words hang for a moment in silence before closing the book and placing it back on the table. 'So you see, Professor, Jesus Christ—the son of God—had no wish for his fellow man to be entrapped in psychological bondage. The Church we know—the hierarchy that has lasted over one-and-a-half thousand years—brought about by the Romans, the very people who crucified him, should not have been. But nothing so important changes overnight. The Templars still largely believed it was their duty to protect the Church from these subversive truths. So the relics were hidden away for safekeeping, and the Order continued in its duty of protecting the status quo. It carried on in this way for almost two hundred years until, finally, it took the betrayal of a pope to convince the Knights that they had made a mistake in suppressing these facts. Tell me, Professor, have you ever heard of the Templars' treasure?'

Harker knew the legends well but wanted to hear it from Brulet's own mouth. 'I know bits but not much.'

Brulet looked disappointed at this response. 'Then I shall give you a history lesson. During their years of service, the Templars saw their coffers swell. They even introduced the first banking system by allowing pilgrims to deposit money in their home country and pick up the same amount on reaching Jerusalem. Robbery was common in those days, and the road of pilgrimage was a long one when you're dependent on riding a horse or, even worse, walking. These types of transactions and papal donations enabled the Order to amass a fortune—worth billions, even trillions, in today's money. During this time, the head of the Catholic Church, Pope Clement V, wanted to merge the newly formed Knights Hospitaller with the Templars in an effort to diffuse the Order's power. Clement brought to light accusations from an ousted Templar that the Order was in fact anti-Catholic and involved in the most sordid activities. The pope even went as far as approaching King Philip IV of France, who was by chance an old childhood friend, for assistance in mounting an investigation. Now Philip was already heavily in debt to the Templars, following years of wars with the English, and he seized upon this chance to resolve his finances by getting his hands on their fortune. So, with the help of Clement, he had the Templars disbanded and arrested, including Jacques de Molay, their last Grand Master, on Friday the thirteenth, which is one of the reasons the date still holds such a bad reputation almost seven hundred years later. Most of the Templars were executed, but some, including my ancestors, evaded capture, and when King Philip raided the Templars' treasure vaults, he found them empty. All the Templar riches had disappeared. Of course, that is where their official history ends, but, in fact, it was only the beginning for the Templars. The few who remained gathered all the wealth and a fleet of ships and headed to Scotland, which had been excommunicated and was thus out of papal reach. These survivors placed my family line in charge of the Order and simultaneously pledged a new oath to undo everything the Catholic Church had done and to restore the Christian religion to the ideals that Jesus Christ had originally intended. And, from one generation to the next, we've been honouring that oath ever since, working to ensure observation of the true word of God and the true teachings of Christianity.'

Everything Harker had ever been told or taught urged him to dismiss the story instantly as a childish fantasy, yet his gut instinct was pushing him in a different direction altogether. There was a dark truth in what he was hearing, and the deeper Brulet drew him into this rewriting of history, the more intense that feeling became.

'It is to these ends that the Templars have striven to pursue for almost a millennium, namely trying to drag the Church back on to its original course.' Brulet settled into his seat, a look of triumph lighting up his features. 'And we have succeeded in doing just that.'

'But the Catholic Church still exists, and it doesn't seem to have changed that much.'

The Templar steepled his fingers. 'Hasn't it? It was Templar influence that encouraged Protestantism, fostering a departure from the strict tenets of Catholicism to a new and more liberal branch of Christianity that has now spread around the world. In fact, the Catholic Church seems only able to make headway today in those Third World countries where people are at their most desperate. This Protestant branch of Christianity is much closer to Jesus's ideology than any other before. In fact, it is so engrained in western life that people no longer see it as a religious belief but rather simply as their way of life, one's own cultural identity, encompassing almost all the same morals and principles, but . . .' Brulet leant forward aggressively. '. . . the Magi have always believed in the Catholic Church as it was and that they must use it to control mankind. And that is the ground on which our secret war is fought, each generation attempting to turn the tide.' He pointed to Harker's suit pocket. 'And, with that relic and others, they think they can do just that, although how is not yet clear to us. But one thing is certain—they believe it, and they will stop at nothing to get their hands on what you have there.'

The tingling in Harker's stomach was quickly turning to a sickly feeling of apprehension. 'I need a drink,' he croaked.

Brulet nodded sternly and pushed the now familiar plain brass button on the wall next to him. 'Lusic, two vodkas and Red Bull, hold the ice. Quick as you can, please, as I'm not sure how long our guest can wait.'

So many questions were running through Harker's mind that he was finding it hard to concentrate on any single one. He picked up the leather-backed gospel and began to translate the first page again to himself as Brulet sat quietly and watched his new associate fully absorb what he'd just been told. Harker had barely made it to the end of the fourth sentence when the silence was shattered as Lusic briskly entered with their two drinks in half-pint slim jims. The large German rolled his eyes as Harker deliberately covered his lap with both hands as the tray was placed on the table. He then nodded silently and left as quickly as he had come. Harker took a deep swig of his vodka, allowing the fiery liquid to slowly trickle down his throat, leaving a comforting warmth in its wake. He then slowly inhaled a deep breath and let the soothing effect of the alcohol vapour settle in his lungs as he attempted once more to gather his thoughts.

'OK, for argument's sake, let's say I believe everything you're telling me—about the Templars, the Magi, this Gospel of Jesus, all of it. What the hell has any of that got to do with the suicide of Archie Dwyer?'

A serious frown appeared on Sebastian Brulet's forehead, and he clasped both hands together, vicar-style.

'When we two met back in Britain, I told you that vast sums of money had been siphoned off from Vatican funds for some unknown project?'

Harker nodded and took another slug of his drink.

'Well, this project is and has been run by the Magi since the 1970s but, despite many tries, we have never been able to penetrate the high level of security around it. What we have known since the '80s is that Christian relics are somehow involved. We know this because one of our underground security vaults was broken into by a known Magi associate, and the thorn crown was stolen from us. It was an item that had been in the hands of my forbears since Jesus's death and was then passed on to the Templars. We were able to trace the thief, but by the time we got to him, he was already dead—his reward for helping the Magi. In our world, Alex, secrecy is everything, but when it comes to protecting that secrecy . . .' Brulet shaped his hand into the form of a gun and pointed it directly at Harker's chest. '. . . The Magi use murder as their first line of defence.' He dropped his hand to the table. 'For the Knights Templars, it is the last.'

Most of the uneasiness Harker had felt was beginning to subside, although that may have had something to do with vodka he was still gulping and with every passing moment he began to eye his new acquaintance with less scepticism.

'About six months ago, one of our contacts intercepted a transmission from the Magi hierarchy. It revealed that the entire project had been moved to the Vatican, more accurately to the Academy of Sciences. And that's where Father Dwyer enters the picture, since he was asked by a Cardinal called Rocca to work as part of a small team on a project charged with finding solutions in the fight against world hunger.'

'World hunger?'

'Yes. From what Father Dwyer told us, it was aimed specifically at increasing the natural size of fruit, vegetables, and even animals that could then be farmed in poorer countries.'

'You mean like the Frankenfish?'

For the first time during the conversation, it was Brulet who looked confused. 'I'm not sure I know what a Frankenfish is.'

Harker himself had read about the Frankenfish in a news week article only a few months earlier. 'It's a type of Atlantic trout that an American company has genetically modified to grow faster and bigger than the natural variety. Twice as big in half the time. The papers have been calling it the Frankenfish. It's not been approved by the FDA, yet, but, if it is, they hope it will provide a step towards solving world hunger.' Harker suppressed the excitement building on top of his words. 'And, like battery chickens, it will also line their pockets through the domestic sales.'

Brulet gave a nod of interest. 'I'd not heard that, but, yes, that's exactly the kind of project Father Dwyer ended up working on—or so he thought. But it turned out that world hunger research was just a cover for a secretive restoration project involving ancient relics, including the crown of thorns. However, I'm afraid that's all we know about it.'

'So why did Archie end up getting into contact with you?'

Sebastian Brulet pinched his lips thoughtfully. 'Well, I don't suppose it matters now, but one of our associates, a cardinal priest called Vito Malpuso, made contact and told us all about Archie Dwyer and the thorn crown—the same item which eventually ended up in the possession of someone you met today. I refer to Father Maddocks.'

Harker felt himself cringe as a fresh image of John Maddocks's limp body dangling from a sword flashed through his mind. 'Rings a bell, yeah,' he replied noncommittally.

Seeing the painful memory in Harkler's eyes, Brulet gave a respectful nod before continuing. 'Vito spoke to Archie Dwyer privately and explained his connection to us, and, much to my surprise, he promptly got in touch and agreed to pass over the artefacts. He seemed most desperate to rid himself of the objects. Why, I'm honestly not sure, but, before he could, he disappeared, and that's when Maddocks went into hiding with the thorn crown. Vito refused to come to us for protection, choosing instead to wait for Maddocks to contact him so he could then take possession of the crown and place it safely back in our hands. But someone got to him first.'

Only one person surfaced in Harker's mind. 'Heldon, the Magi's assassin?'

Brulet tapped the top of the table with a finger, his frustration and anger obvious. 'Yes, we believe so. They call him the butcher of Račak, a nickname he picked up whilst participating in the ethnic cleansing of Yugoslavia during the late '90s before being recruited into the Magi. A Serbian national born in Croatia, Heldon was responsible for the murder of hundreds of civilians, and his weapon of choice during this period was a large wooden sledgehammer—need I say more? He's powerful, merciless, and completely void of conscience.' The Grand Master wore a look of disgust. 'The majority of associates within the Magi ranks are most often morally corrupt. Their only true allegiance is to one thing and one thing only—power and those that wield it.' He swigged down the last mouthful of his drink. 'Luckily for us, Father Dwyer mentioned your name, and we contacted you first via our associate Mr Caster. And here we are.'

As Brulet wrapped up his account of events, Harker found himself not just being convinced but also, weirdly enough, he wanted to believe it. The story itself, the relics, it was all becoming intoxicating. 'So why go to all this trouble just to get hold of the crown? I mean, its value as a religious artefact is priceless, but what more is there to it than that?'

Brulet shook his head. 'As I've said, what they intend using the relics for is unclear, but we have intercepted phone calls between Magi members, talking about a pivotal event in human history—an event that will occur when these items are brought together.'

Harker polished off the last sip of his own drink, the vodka having provided him with a newly restored focus. 'You said relics in the plural? That's what Father Maddocks said too.'

Brulet gave a nod, some of his white hair slipping over his shoulder. 'Yes, Professor, you see Father Dwyer took more than just the thorn crown. He also made off with a second object—another unidentified relic.'

The Templar brushed the lock of hair away from his cheek and curled it up neatly behind his ear. 'And once you've returned the crown to me, and the note that came with it, I will send an escort of our Knights to pick the second item up and then secure them both so that the Magi can no longer pursue whatever wickedness they have planned.'

He reached out an open palm. 'So, if I may have it now, I will then get in touch with our contacts within the echelons of power and have the murder charges dropped against you. With your reputation restored, we will find Ms Dwyer and if need be barter for her life. We already have a solid lead on her whereabouts. Is that plan OK with you?'

Harker relinquished himself to a soothing sense of relief at the thought, though things were by no means guaranteed. Throughout this brief history lesson, he'd felt worry and guilt over Claire's absence hanging over him like an invisible weight. 'Mr Brulet, you know these people, the

Magi, and you know what they're capable of. If they don't get what they want, she's dead.'

Brulet snapped his fingers to summon Lusic, who came in holding a wooden case identical to the one that had contained the crown. Even the engraved symbol of Caesar looked as genuinely ancient as the original. The German carefully lifted the lid to reveal two separate strips of intertwined thorns identical to the ones in Harker's pocket, even down to the transparent hermetically airtight case that housed them.

'We will barter for Claire Dwyer's life with this, and by the time they manage an analysis, she . . . We, will be long gone.' His confident smile was back. 'You see, we have everything under control.'

Harker dug deep into his pocket and retrieved the sealed plastic case containing the crown and gently placed it into Brulet's waiting palm. 'Really? Try telling that to Father Maddocks and Father Valente to name a few!'

Brulet gave a sad but understanding nod before pocketing the relic inside his silk-lined jacket. 'I'm very sorry to say there is little I can do now for those unfortunate people.' He stood up, gesturing for Harker to do the same. 'But believe me when I tell you that Claire Dwyer will survive her ordeal. On that you have my solemn word as Grand Master.'

As Harker got to his feet, Brulet courteously took his hand and shook it firmly.

'Professor, you are clearly a good man with an untainted soul. From this moment on, you have trusted friends amongst the Knights Templars.'

Harker had just begun to squeeze his new friend's hand in return when David Grant and two other men abruptly burst in through a side door.

'Sebastian, the house is being breached. We must leave here immediately.'

Brulet's white hair flicked to one side as he swung around to face Grant's alarmed expression. 'Breached by whom?'

It was now the turn of one of the other soldiers to respond, 'They're dressed in traditional combat garb, My Lord. I think it's a Magi death squad.'

A venomous scowl spread over Brulet's face. 'How the hell did they track us here?'

'I don't know, but there's about ten of them—and only four of us, or five if you count the professor.' Grant gave a brief nod in Harker's direction.

'Sir, we are heavily outnumbered, and clearly we've been set up. Caster and Lusic are already making their way out to the jet. We need you both to join them immediately.'

In an instant, Brulet's hand wrapped itself around Harker's arm like a vice, the firmness of its grip surprising for such a spindly limbed man. He immediately began marching Harker towards the rear door as the three remaining Templars stood guard, scanning the dimly lit library for any movement. They were only a few steps from the doorway when a Magi henchman clothed in a black Kevlar combat uniform smashed through the main window, landing only a few feet from them both with an MP5 sub-machine gun gripped firmly in his gloved hands.

Before Harker could react, Brulet had shoved him towards the rear door, and, in one swift movement, he slapped the barrel of the MP5, spinning it 180 degrees, out of the intruder's hand and into his own. He then pulled the trigger, and, amid a short series of flashes, the Kevlar-dressed assassin fell back on to broken glass with a crunch, his black leather boots flicking violently in to the air as his muscles went into spasm.

'Sir, we have to go now,' Grant shouted as he kicked open the door with his boot and pushed Harker through it, followed by Brulet. More gunfire blasted behind them, and Harker turned in time to see the youngest Knight being flipped backwards against the wall under the force of a dozen bullets hitting his chest.

There followed a few more seconds of frantic running down a long dark corridor before a rough shove in the back pushed Harker through an open doorway into a pantry and on to a hard, terracotta-tiled floor. He was followed closely into the room by Brulet and then Grant, who slammed the metal door shut and slid a hefty bolt into place.

Harker scanned the large, chilly meat pantry for an exit but saw none—they were trapped. Behind him, bullets rattled against the closed door, compelling him to hurl himself to the floor, until the cold tiles were pressing against his face.

'I can't see a way out, any ideas?' Harker shouted in an effort to be heard above the now continuous thudding of bullets against metal. Bulbous indentations began appearing in the door as each successive bullet struck with such force that the whole thing jerked back and forth on its hinges. Panic began building in Harker's chest; and then it suddenly evaporated as he felt a wave of calm surge through him. But this wasn't due to his own self-control but rather the confidence and strength emanating from the star-shaped pupils of Sebastian Brulet, who was staring at him directly as Grant manhandled a large freezer across the doorway.

The Grand Master's yellow-tinged eyes widened as he surveyed the walls around them, his attention finally settling on the end wall, whereupon Brulet gave Grant a sharp tap on the shoulder and pointed towards it. Without another word, the younger Templar pulled a small narrow disk from a Velcro-fastened pocket on his shoulder pad and passed it to Brulet, who leant over to the same wall and stuck it against one of the bricks. He secured it in with a click and returned to join Harker, lowering his head in both hands.

'I'd keep your head down if I were you.' The advice was offered loudly yet calmly, and it took Harker only a moment to comply.

As the small explosive ripped through the masonry, the pantry was consumed in a shower of dust. Outside the room, the gunfire ceased, and the guttural voice of Genges could be heard from behind the bullet-ridden door. 'Brulet, have you no honour? Come out and face me like a man, you murdering albino freak. It's time to pay for the murder of my father.'

'Not exactly my number-one fan,' Brulet murmured with a dry smile. 'It's time we split up because, as you can see, I have unfinished business.' He motioned to the gaping hole in the wall and to the cold night air beyond. 'Now get yourself to the airstrip where Lusic and Caster should be waiting for you.'

Brulet reached into his pocket and passed back the thin plastic case carrying the crown of thorns. 'It seems we will be needing your services a little longer, Professor Harker. Go and find Dwyer's other hiding place and secure the second relic. But, whatever happens, don't allow them to fall into the hands of the Magi even if it means destroying both artefacts.'

The very thought of such a sacrilege caused Harker to gulp, but he managed to ask, 'How about you?'

Brulet gave another smile. 'Don't worry about me. I'm not down by a long shot, trust me. Now go.'

Harker felt a quick sharp shove to his chest, and then he was falling backwards through the hole and tumbling on to soft grass.

The high-pitched whine of a jet roared nearby, and he looked up at the craft to see Lusic crouching in the open hatch, beckoning him over. The *Cessnar Citation's* twin turbines sent shockwaves rippling through the earth underfoot as it throttled its engines, readying to take off from the private tarmac runway. Harker picked himself up and began heading towards the jet, just as gunfire started up again from the gap in the wall behind him, encouraging him to run flat out.

The jet aircraft was already moving as he reached the hatch, where Lusic hauled him up into the cabin with a firm grip before slamming the pressurised door shut behind him. Suddenly, everything was quiet except for the muted howl of the engine. A face intruded into Harker's vision, and he looked up to see a worried-looking John Caster. 'What the hell's going on, Professor?'

He grabbed the lawyer's clammy hand, pulled himself up on to one of the seats, and looked out of the window as the engine throttled up further, the g-force pressing against him. It was hard to see anything happening inside the villa as all the lights were now out, but, as the jet rumbled along the airstrip and lifted itself into the darkening sky, he could make out sporadic flashes of gunfire as the building began to fade into the distance.

'Well? What the hell's going on?' Caster repeated, his eyes bulging in alarm. Lusic nudged the older man back into his seat before he himself sat down opposite.

'It was an ambush by the Magi,' Harker spluttered in explanation.

'The Magi!' Caster looked horrified. 'How the hell did they find us?'

Lusic shot Harker an accusing look before turning back to the lawyer. 'Don't you get it? We were set up.'

The lawyer rubbed his balding crown vigorously. 'And how about the chief?'

Lusic smiled confidently. 'I don't know, but Sebastian's got more lives than a cat. If there's a way, he'll make it.'

Caster cleared his throat with a grunt and wiped away the bead of sweat that had broken out on his forehead with a white handkerchief. 'The real question is where do we go now?'

Both men turned to face Harker, who was still trying to gather his thoughts. He recalled how Maddocks had mentioned London as one of Archie's destinations but nothing more. At least, it was a start. 'London,' he said firmly. 'Tell the pilot to plan a course to London Heathrow.' He turned his attention to the window and stared at the scattering of house lights a few thousand feet below whilst he attempted to figure out their next move.

Damn it, Archie, what the hell did you get yourself involved in?

Chapter 20

Drazia Heldon slammed his massive fist down on to the kitchen counter, causing the entire surface to shudder before pulling his hand away and peering at the black smudge that had been a bluebottle fly only moments earlier. 'At least you won't be annoying me any more,' he muttered, wiping his hand on a grubby dishcloth before heading back to the lounge with his steaming cup of Capo Colombo. The seven-foot tall, three-hundred-pound assassin set his coffee on a cheap metal table and stared out through the grit-stained window and across the small floodlight airfield spread out below.

He had always felt at peace in this flat despite its filthy conditions. To anyone else, this place looked and smelt like a crack den, somewhere to be avoided at all costs, but to him, it was a sanctuary. He had used the airfield safe house many times over the past couple of decades, and practically nothing had changed in that time period, which, for some reason, he found extremely comforting. Outside, a small single engine *Piper Lance* awkwardly lowered itself on to the overgrown grass runway. This jerky landing brought a smile to the giant's lips.

'That's a newcomer to night-time landings, if ever there was one.'

The small private airfield was snugly located between the foothills of the Monti Tiburtini and was used mainly as a pilot school. Situated just twenty miles outside Rome, it was a perfect place for beginners and was far enough from any main roads to not draw any undue attention. The old airstrip had been purchased by the Magi seventy years previously, and the small pilot-training school had been set up there in order to hide its true operational purpose. It was one of many such landing strips composing a flight network that allowed agents of the Magi to travel around the globe without attracting the watchful eyes of border controls. Couple this advantage with the scores of customs and excise agents on the organisation's payroll, and it ensured that flying from country to country was a very private affair.

The apartments bordering the northern edge of the airfield had once been furnished to the highest standards, but, as the years had progressed and the interiors faded, they now looked almost ready to be condemned. At a glance, even the exteriors would now convince most people to stay away for fear of getting mugged or raped. This provided a perfect location for a safe house.

At the northern apex, a rusting, though well secured, hanger concealed a fleet of five Lear jets, allowing quick access to anywhere throughout the world. There was even a rota of eight pilots undertaking specific shifts so that there would always be one on call, twenty-four seven. It was a sharp set-up that ensured Magi operatives could reach their destination within hours of receiving their orders.

Outside, on the rain-sodden grass runway below, the trainee pilot of the small single-prop *Piper* peered triumphantly out of the cockpit window as he pulled into a floodlit, demarcated parking space. Heldon pulled himself away from the window, not wanting to be spotted, and slumped on the dirty brown sofa with a gasp of discomfort. He cursed both his lungs and the cigarette that was jammed between his lips. He really had to give up this filthy habit; it was so dirty, so unhealthy but, unfortunately, *so fucking necessary*. The thought of not being able to light up a cigarette first thing in the morning made him even more anxious than the prospect of contracting lung cancer.

Heldon pulled out a silver Zippo and, with one oversized thumb, flicked open the lid with a metallic click. He then lit his cigarette before closing the lighter with a flick of his wrist. He took a long, deep drag and settled into the sofa as an episode of *Star Trek* began showing on the small TV balanced precariously on a rickety wicker chair in front of him.

He wasn't a natural fan of the show, but this old colour television set could only receive two channels, and because *Momma's Family*, which he hated, was on the alternative, *Star Trek* had won his vote outright. Heldon had never understood why his superiors spent so much money on these secret hangars but were far too cheap to buy him a decent TV. *And if they thought he was going to waste his own money on acquiring one, then they could forget it. What did they take him for, a total mug?*

Outside, another light aircraft began flaring its engines as the pilot attempted a textbook landing, its wheels touching down with a few brief thuds that sent a light tremor through the apartment building and the TV.

As the show's credits began to roll, the assassin's stomach clenched once again, his anger suddenly spiking as it had done at the monastery earlier that same day. *What a mess,* he reflected, *to have been so close to ending the game that had begun with Archie Dwyer stealing what did not belong to him and should have finished with the death of that prick Harker.* How could he have fallen for such an obvious trick—allowing the professor to slip away right between his legs? It was almost unforgivably stupid. He punched his own cheek with such force that he felt his teeth rattle.

'Idiot.'

Balthasar had taken it relatively easy on him, but he could tell his mentor was furious, and he had promised himself no more slip-ups. Heldon thought back to a meeting a few weeks earlier with Lord Balthasar and Cardinal Rocca: how Rocca had held no faith in his ability to track down and acquire the relics, and how his master had defended him.

Cardinal Rocca had even declared to his face that, whether Drazia was a member of the Magi or not, he wasn't smart enough to do this job quietly and such an important task shouldn't be left to a simpleton.

Simpleton!

Heldon had needed all the restraint he could muster just to stop himself from grabbing Rocca by the neck and snapping it in half like a breadstick. Luckily, Balthasar had rallied to Heldon's defence by taking the decision out of the cardinal's hands.

The giant let out an uncomfortable sigh. And now here he was fucking everything up. Thank God, he had at least captured the Dwyer woman and managed to smuggle her into the Vatican without anyone seeing. Otherwise, they might have turned their backs on him completely.

Heldon stubbed out his cigarette and clasped his thick skull with both hands. Throughout his life, he had never before failed his master, but to do so now during such an important mission was . . . well, it was really fucking bad. When Lord Balthasar had inducted him into the Magi, almost two decades ago, it had been merely a blessing, but now it had become the only family he had and he would do anything to protect it.

After the war in Yugoslavia during the '90s, he had spent a whole year evading those wretched war crime tribunals, who insisted in sticking their noses into affairs that did not concern them. With time running out until they finally caught up with him, the hulking giant had seen it as a godsend when someone approached him with an invitation to meet the master. Heldon had never even heard of the Magi, but, they, nonetheless, sought him out because he had, as it was explained, the right aptitudes and character to serve their organisation, and he formally entered their ranks that very same day. On further training as an assassin, the younger Heldon discovered he had a special talent for it, even if things often ended up getting a little messy. Brute force, he had already discovered during the war, was his major strength, and he now put it to good use. If the powers that be wanted a quieter, more subtle message to be delivered, then someone else was sent to do so, but if they wanted to cause fear and destruction, then he was the one they called on. In hindsight, therefore, he may not have been the right candidate for this job, but once Cardinal Rocca had referred to him as a simpleton, he was forced to protect his reputation and had begged Lord Balthasar to give him the task. Heldon gave an annoyed shake of his head. No, he didn't want to think about that now, and next time, he would not fail.

He slid another cigarette from the pack and once again flicked open his Zippo, ready to spark it up, when suddenly the phone in his trouser pocket began to vibrate. He put down the cigarette and flipped open his mobile.

'We have a location on the second item. Our contact is currently with the professor on a jet heading there right now, so time is of the essence.' Balthasar's voice sounded rasping and shrill, obviously excited by this new information.

'Yes, My Lord. I will prep the plane immediately. Where to?'

'London. Get going, and I'll call you with more instructions.'

Heldon unconsciously nodded in agreement at the mobile. 'Yes, sir, I'm on my way.' There was a brief awkward silence before the line crackled back to life.

'And Drazia . . . My friend, there is no more room for any mistakes. Do you understand what I'm saying? You know what happens to those who don't fulfil their tasks, don't you?'

'Yes, sir, I do.'

'Good. Then do not fail me again.'

'Thank you, my . . .' He had not even finished before the line cut out, and within seconds, he was heading for the door, already scrolling through his address list for the pilots' contact number. Heldon gulped nervously as there would be no second chances this time around; if he screwed up again, he would end up dead just like that professor was soon to be.

Chapter 21

Superintendent Perone lit one end of his tightly rolled Villager cigar and sucked on it until the tip glowed bright red before blowing out the match and dropping its smoking corpse over the edge of the police station roof, down on to the pavement thirty feet below. He took another deep refreshing drag and let the thick smoke seep slowly from his mouth into the night air, enjoying the bitter aftertaste on his tongue.

At the end of a working day, he enjoyed coming up to the roof for a well-earned smoke and the chance to gaze out across the city he protected. The police station was one of the older buildings in the area, and many newer structures had grown up around it. The top storeys of them now hid most of the natural skyline, giving the view a closed and slightly claustrophobic feel, but, to Perone, it nevertheless felt cosy.

In the sky above, a full moon was just beginning to rise, bathing the crowds of hurrying people below in a white-yellow hue as its clear light blended with the street lamps. The bustling activity of people coming and going brought comfort to the greying superintendent, and after such a shitty day, he deserved a little uplifting. He leant over the handrail to get a better view of an attractive blonde mother with two young children in tow, and the feel of the leather wallet containing his police badge jutting into his ribs made him smile.

'Yes, sir, even cops need a little moment of comfort from time to time,' he murmured to himself.

He took another drag on his cigar and flicked some ash over the roof edge before spitting out a small piece of tobacco that had got stuck to his lips into the dried-up potted rose bush to his left. He gave a sigh of deep frustration at the day's events involving the Cambridge professor, his chief suspect in at least five murders, who had been politically wrestled from his grasp. The muscles in his cheeks bulged as he cursed his superior's decision to let them haul the professor away like that, right in front of his team. *Christ, what a morale killer!* He had contacted the chief of police immediately and argued furiously with the man, even making this call in front of the entire station team so everyone would know that he had done everything possible. But that hadn't made a blind bit of difference, and Chief Diego had refused even to discuss it, making it clear that the decision had been made by someone well above his pay grade, in the government itself, and if he wanted to complain, he should start there. Apparently the chief had been assured by the minister of the interior himself that Professor Alex Harker was not guilty of the charges and that instead the real suspect should be found and arrested without delay. It was at this point that Perone had laughed out loud; after all, there wasn't another suspect except for this Dwyer woman Harker had kept squawking about—of whom, by the way, there was absolutely no trace whatsoever.

Within minutes of arresting that British bastard, his team had searched the monastery from top to bottom, and the only thing they had discovered were the mutilated bodies of two monks. As for the seven-foot assassin with a sword for an arm and the body of a professional wrestler, there was no evidence of him. And although the murder weapon had not been found, it would probably turn up somewhere in the monastery grounds, wherever the professor had dropped it.

Perone shuddered at the memory of Father Valente's head roasting amongst the smouldering embers of the open hearth. He was not much of a religious man, but to have a priest's death go unsolved—let alone two—was not something he wanted resting on his conscience. He puffed away on his cigar, once more allowing that feeling of contentment to fill his mouth. No, sir, he didn't need that kind of shit weighing on his shoulders.

Behind him, the fire door creaked open, and a young officer in plain clothes poked his head through the gap. 'Sir, I'm sorry to disturb you but . . .'

Perone cut him off straight away. 'It's pretty clear you're not sorry, or you wouldn't have disturbed me in the first place. I only asked for five minutes, a crappy five-minute break, that's all.' He sighed deeply and took another puff of his cigar.

'Understood, sir, I'll come back in a few minutes.'

The older man growled loudly, 'Kid, you've already ruined the moment. Don't you fucking dare now disappear without telling me what you want.'

The junior officer cleared his throat with a cough. 'You asked Benito and Gaetano to follow the consulate car carrying the professor. Well, you were right. They didn't go anywhere near the British embassy. They followed them to a large villa on the edge of town, and now they're reporting gunfire. I've told them to hold off until a back-up team arrives.'

A satisfied grin spread across Perone's lips. 'I fucking knew it. Is the team tooled up?'

'Yes, sir, awaiting your orders.'

The superintendent nodded approvingly. 'Then get them in the vans and over to that villa, now.'

The subordinate gave a jerk of his head and was already disappearing down the fire steps when his superior called out after him.

'And, Detective, no one goes in there until I'm on site, understand? I don't care how bad it is.'

'Yes, sir.' And with that, the officer was gone, leaving Perone free to take one last drag of his cigar before lobbing it over the roof edge and heading downstairs. The feeling in his gut told him this was going to be a long night—just the kind he loved.

On the street below, an old man with a wicker shopping basket and a light but sturdy wooden cane hobbled home after an hour's shopping. It wouldn't be until he arrived there and unpacked that he'd notice the large hole burnt into his basket and the half-smoked cigar that had caused it.

Chapter 22

A loud rattling sound assaulted Father Reed's eardrums.

'Wake up, you treacherous wretch.'

Reed clasped his ears with both hands and glanced towards the source of the din, his vision blurry and eyelids heavy.

'That's it, Father. Over here.' Again, Cardinal Rocca swiped a metal drinking cup back and forth across the prison cell bars, each clink mercilessly increasing Reed's already throbbing headache.

'Enough, I'm awake!' he protested, massaging his aching skull as a flickering light bulb overhead added to the violation of his senses.

Rocca threw the cup to the floor and grasped the bars of the cell door with both hands. 'I want you to clear your head and take a good look at your surroundings, Father Reed, because if you don't answer my questions truthfully, then I swear by Christ you'll spend the rest of your life in this dark, dank shithole. Do you understand me?'

Reed scanned his dimly lit surroundings: a cell about six feet by eight feet, furnished only with an iron bed and a somewhat grubby mattress. The walls glistened with condensation, and the stone floor was . . . well, stone cold. Shithole was about right. He would have laughed at the thought, but Rocca's menacing stare demanded an answer. 'I understand, Cardinal. So perhaps you can tell me why I'm here, wherever here is.'

Rocca eyed him scornfully. 'That's a question you should be asking yourself since, after all, you were following me. Who sent you?'

'No one sent me. I'm new to the Vatican, and I just wanted to see the academy for myself, simple as that.'

Rocca nodded sarcastically. 'Right, simple as that.' He reached inside his robe and pulled out a doubled-up sheet of A4 paper which he gracefully unfolded. 'Whilst you were taking a nap, I did a little research into your background.' He ran his finger across the words typed on the page. 'It seems you led a somewhat exotic, if not questionable, lifestyle before entering the Church, Father.'

Reed said nothing. He had made ample amends for his 'questionable lifestyle' many years ago.

'It says here that a great part of your early youth was spent in and out of juvenile detention. You were quite the little hellraiser. But what really caught my attention was your enlistment in the marines at age eighteen and a year later in to the special forces.' He raised his eyebrows sarcastically. '*Semper Fi,* indeed!'

Reed ignored the dig at his past. He wasn't about to take personally a taunt from the man who had just kidnapped him.

'Almost two decades of secretive black ops, then—quite extraordinary—you gave it all up to join the priesthood. I wonder why.'

Reed remained silent and continued to rub his aching head.

'Well, that's OK,' the cardinal continued. 'I'm not interested in the whys and whats of your chequered past, but I am going to insist that you tell me why a man of your background is spying on me and for whom.'

Father Reed gave one final rub of his temple before answering. 'That's one heck of an intelligence dossier you have on me—pretty accurate, too. The truth is there are a lot of people in the Vatican who've been troubled recently by your running of the academy and administrating finances. So I was asked to look into it on behalf of the Church. And, since waking up in this place, I'd say their reasons for concern were spot on.'

Cardinal Rocca stood po-faced and silent, allowing his captive to continue.

'But here's the real question. Why would a cardinal of the Vatican, head of the Academy of Sciences, abduct a fellow member of the clergy and imprison him in a cell? I'd say, therefore, you've more to hide than just a few black holes in your finances.'

Rocca shook his finger dismissively. 'Well, you don't have to be Sherlock Holmes to figure that out. No, the reason you're here is because of your unwelcome curiosity—or the curiosity of Cardinal Vincenzo, should I say?'

'I'm not at liberty to reveal, but even if I were . . . I'd tell you to go screw yourself, my son.'

'I'll take that as a yes then. Good, good.' Rocca clasped his hands together. 'So all I need to do now is take care of good old frail Vincenzo, and no one's the wiser.' He sounded almost joyful at the prospect. The manic glint in his eye was back. 'Well, I've enjoyed our chat, Father, and I must say you have been extremely helpful, but I'm afraid I must leave you and go and attend to some important matters of the Church.'

He had taken only a step when Reed called out after him. 'Damn it, Rocca, you're a cardinal at the heart of the Vatican, an institution representing a billion Catholics. What the hell are you doing?'

Rocca's smile disappeared and was replaced with an unnervingly, prophetic stare. 'The reason you have been detained, my Christian brother, is an unfortunate but necessary evil, I'm afraid. It's rather difficult to explain.'

'Then please, Cardinal, try to enlighten me.'

Rocca crossed his arms and pursed his lips as he assumed a deep frown. 'In just under twelve hour's time, something special is going to happen—something wonderful, something world-changing.' He paced slowly back and forth in front of the cell door. 'It will change the entire face of Catholicism and usher the Christian world into a new golden era we could not have even dared dream of. And with it will come a new order: light will finally once and for all triumph over darkness, good will dominate evil, and the earth will become a utopia, second only to the kingdom of heaven.' Rocca pulled open the outer exit door, pausing as Reed called after him yet again.

'Cardinal Rocca, you've left your slimly trail everywhere. Vincenzo already suspects you, and, with me missing, he'll have you in his grasp within hours.' It was a lie, of course, but Reed hoped it might just discourage this madman from going after the head of the Governorate.

'Slimy trail? Why, Father Reed, are you likening me in some way to a slug?'

Reed shook his head gravely. 'Not at all, Cardinal Rocca. I'm likening you to a skid mark and a nasty one at that.'

Chapter 23

The Cessnar's twin engines sent a steady ripple of tremors through the cabin, causing Harker to experience a fleeting sense of panic. He had flown many times in this kind of weather, but when that was coupled with the day's events, he was feeling altogether sick to his stomach.

'It's only turbulence, my boy.' John Caster was sitting in the seat opposite, his eyes now brimming with concern. 'You were trained as a pilot. Surely you must have experienced this before.'

The lawyer's comment drew a sheepish smile from Harker; indeed, he had flown in much worse weather than this as a pilot but not so often as a passenger. The truth was that he had only ever started taking lessons in an attempt to conquer his fear of flying. The real problem had emerged in his late twenties after a particularly stormy flight from Rome to Belfast, when he had experienced what the stewardesses had referred to as a total freak out. A combination of turbulence and sporadic bolts of lightning had resulted in a minor electrical problem causing the cabin lighting to flicker on and off. This in itself had rattled Harker's nerves, but when a yellow oxygen mask dropped down in front of him, courtesy of the same electrical fault, he'd snapped. Two minutes of shameful panic later, followed by three minutes of pacification by two burly stewards, he had managed to regain his composure much to the relief of everyone else on board. The embarrassment of facing all those accusing eyes for the rest of the flight had convinced him it was time to sort out his fear once and for all.

Six months later, he had acquired his private pilot's licence and, soon after that, his instrument rating, enabling him to fly at night and in bad weather. Harker had taken to flying like a duck to water, so his instructors told him, and he was even convinced to attempt his jet licence. Unfortunately, the lessons had only just begun when the opportunity to dig in Jerusalem dropped into his lap, and his spare time had fallen to zero. Becoming a pilot had certainly cured him of his phobia, but when not at the helm, it still brought out a nervousness in him that courted odd stares from surrounding passengers, similar to the one he was getting now. 'I'm more of a pilot than a passenger.' Harker said in a strained voice, attempting to sound confident.

'Ah, control freak,' the lawyer said, patting Harker's forearm. 'A man after my own heart. I'm a terrible passenger myself.' He sported a sly grin. 'I even fake car sickness so I always get to drive.'

Though Harker managed a reassuring smile for Caster, he was finding it difficult to think of anything but the close shave they had just experienced at the hands of the Magi hit squad. The whizz of bullets zipping past him had been truly terrifying, and Harker's muscles were still going into occasional spasm as if an unconscious instinct was still prompting him to dodge them.

'Here, drink this.' Lusic pushed an opened can of Coke into his hand. 'Sugar and caffeine are a good antidote for shock.'

Harker gulped down a few mouthfuls. 'Is it that obvious?'

The German answered with a smirk. 'People are so used to seeing murder on TV that they think they know it all. But seeing it in the flesh has much more of an impact than most would like to admit.'

Caster nodded agreeably. 'The first few times are the worst, but I'm rather sad to say you do get used to it.'

Harker found his brave smile failing him. 'I don't know if I could ever get used to seeing people get killed in front of me.'

'I served two tours of military duty in Korea and three in Northern Ireland,' the lawyer remarked with a grimace. 'Trust me, a person can get used to pretty much anything, given time.'

Lusic nodded in agreement. 'You see enough blood, and, yes, over time, the colour does fade, if you know what I mean.'

The German's remark was chilling, leaving Harker feeling completely out of his depth.

'Well, that's the third murder I've witnessed today, and it's not getting any easier.'

Caster offered a sympathetic nod before leaning in and whispering quietly. 'Now, perhaps you could show us this item that's causing everyone so much trouble. After all, we've heard about it, but we're more than a little excited about seeing it with our own eyes.'

The comment surprised Harker, since he had assumed all the Templars would be well familiar with the relic. 'You mean you've never seen it?'

Both men shook their heads in unison. 'When a Templar comes of age, he is inducted into the Order via a ritual involving many of the sacred items originally discovered at the Temple of Solomon, but the crown of thorns is not one of them,' Lusic replied with an unyielding stare. 'Only a very select few have ever had access to the crown. So it's somewhat irritating to the rest of us that you, an outsider, have it in your possession.'

He extended an open palm in Harker's direction. 'If you'd be so kind?'

Harker reached into his jacket pocket and pulled out the slim plastic case, gently laying it down on to the table in front of them. 'This is it,' he declared.

The Templar was the first to examine it, followed closely by the lawyer, who peered at it over the top of his spectacles as if appraising an antique, which wasn't so far from the truth. 'It's much smaller than I'd imagined.'

Lusic shot Caster a dirty look as if he was actually insulting the relic.

'Lawyers are so materialistic.' He clicked his tongue. 'It's not just about size.'

Caster ignored his associate's angry stare and returned his attention back to Harker. 'Well, Professor, it seems we are now in your hands. Where to next?'

Harker felt a knot tighten in the pit of his stomach, as all eyes focused on him. 'I'm honestly not sure.'

This reply drew blank expressions from his crew mates till it was Lusic who finally broke the silence.

'What do you mean, you don't know?'

'I mean I don't know. There was nothing else with the crown, no note, no directions . . . Nothing.'

John Caster gave a disbelieving shake of his head. 'There must have been something. Maybe somewhere in the packaging.'

'No, nothing.' Harker pointed down at the plastic case. 'There was only this container and a wooden box.' His words trailed off as a disheartening thought crossed his mind. How could he have been so stupid not to think of it? A strong sense of guilt began to take hold of him. 'There was the box it came in, and it's possible a note was hidden inside it. But . . .'

'But what?' The tone of Lusic's voice indicated curiosity, but the Templar's dulling gaze confirmed that he already knew the answer.

'I had to leave it at the monastery as part of creating a diversion. The Magi giant, the one you call the Butcher of Račak, he's got it.'

The German slammed a clenched fist down on to the table tray, sending Harker's can of Coke flying. 'What possessed you to leave anything so precious in the hands of that murderer?'

'It was the only way to distract him and get away. If I hadn't done so, I'd be dead, and the crown would be in the hands of your enemies. Would that have made you happier?'

The Templar's muscles were tensing furiously. 'Well, getting rid of you might have been a bonus.'

It was Caster who jumped in to act as referee, raising both hands in the air. 'Shut up, both of you. This won't solve the problem. If something vital is in the hands of the Magi, then there's nothing we can do except regroup with the Templar Council and formulate a new plan.'

Lusic tightened both hands into fists and nodded stiffly. 'OK, I'll give the pilots new heading instructions.' He stood up and disappeared into the cockpit, leaving Harker and Caster alone.

'Ignore him, he's . . . Well, he's an idiot who's unable to control his emotions. Not something the Templars encourage. Anyway don't blame yourself, Professor. What occurred could not have happened any other way.'

The statement was a nice gesture, but Harker was still struggling not to feel responsible.

'Thank you, that's very philosophical of you. Not sure it's true though.'

Caster took off his glasses and cleaned the lenses with his silk tie, which, to Harker's mind, was an odd thing to do, given the lawyer's immaculate appearance. 'We've been dealt a blow, but we're not out of the game just yet.'

He slid the spectacles back on to his nose and brushed off his tie. 'Anyway, how could you have known that the box was important as well?'

This last question caught Harker's attention, and his mind latched on to the connection it created.

'I wouldn't, but Archie would have.'

'Sorry, old boy, but I can't see where you're going with this.'

Harker reached down and picked up the plastic case containing the crown of thorns. 'It's something that Archie used to say to his parishioners when they brought gifts for the poor at Christmas or during a harvest festival. Some would wrap them up in fancy paper and bows, whilst others just used plastic bags.'

Caster was now looking totally confused.

'So Archie would always tell them that it didn't matter what wrapping the presents came in, only what was inside. He also joked that man could not live on bread alone, but he most definitely couldn't live on the pretty packaging it came in.'

'Very funny, I'm sure.'

Harker shook his head. 'I know, Archie was a lightweight when it came to humour, but . . .' He ran his fingers around the edge of the transparent case, searching for anything unusual—there was nothing. He was almost giving up when something else caught his eye. The case had been heat-sealed on all four sides, leaving dark lines where the plastic had been melted and so keeping the container airtight, but this was not what caught his attention. On each of the corners was a marking—a very small marking too small to make out. 'Can I borrow your glasses?' He reached over and swiftly pulled off the lawyer's spectacles.

'Easy on, I'm as blind as a bat without those things,' Caster complained, his beady eyes struggling to focus.

Harker positioned one of the lenses over a corner of the case and moved it back and forth until the marking became readable. 'It's the letter D.' He moved to the next corner. 'And a B.'

Harker followed the corners left to right and then flipped the case over to find a further two letters. 'It reads: DBBMNH.' He passed the spectacles back to Caster, who couldn't get them back on his nose quick enough.

'What the hell does that mean?'

Harker shook his head. 'Not sure yet.'

The lawyer picked up the plastic case and also examined its corners, his squinting causing his forehead to crease upwards like a Shar Pei dog. 'Ah, yes, I see the letters. But I don't recognise them. Maybe it's an anagram.'

His pondering was interrupted by Lusic, who appeared from the cockpit and stumbled over to his seat just as the jet hit a small pocket of turbulence.

'I've contacted the council, and the pilots are adjusting our flight plan even as we speak.'

'We may not need them to. The professor's found something else.' Caster pointed to the tiny black letters on each corner of the case. 'Apparently, we're not out of the running just yet.'

'What does it say?'

Caster shrugged his shoulders. 'That's what we're now trying to work out.'

Harker read them out loud once again. 'They go DBBMNH, and I don't think it's an anagram.'

The lawyer tapped the case mindfully. 'Are you sure you've read them in the right order?'

Harker nodded confidently. 'There are four corners, of course, on each side of the case. On one side, all four corners carry a marking.' He pointed to them in turn. 'But on the other side, only two corners have markings, so it stands to reason that this is the last side to be read. Like an unfinished sentence. And anyone brought up in the West reads from left to right, from top to bottom. So . . .' He moved his forefinger from the top left to the top right and then bottom left to bottom right. 'We then flip the thing over and do the same thing, and you get DBBMNH.'

Caster and Lusic sat still, both of them looking stumped, whilst a shiver of excitement ran through Harker's body as he made the connection. 'I think I've got it.'

He sat in silence for a few moments, enjoying this feeling, much to the irritation of the others.

'Well, are you going to let us in on your discovery or not?' Caster finally enquired as calmly as he could.

'OK. Let's consider BMNH. It's a common abbreviation for one of the oldest and most renowned scientific establishments in the world. I refer to the British Museum of Natural History.'

Lusic still looked confused. 'And the DB?'

Harker gave him a wide grin. That refers to one of the curators, a certain Mr David Blix.' He laughed out loud. 'He's an old work colleague of mine through the Macmillan Archaeology Department at Cambridge, and so Archie knew I'd recognise it—and I alone. Even if someone else cottoned on to the Natural History part, few people would be familiar with the name David Blix. That's because he freelances and doesn't even appear on the museum's list of staff. Archie, you're a bloody star!'

Both Templars stared at him blankly. 'Well, I'd have never got that,' Caster admitted.

'That's the whole point: no one would have got it except me and a couple of other people. I've known David for years ever since the university put on a biotech exhibition in 2006, and we borrowed some exhibits from the museum. I organised that directly with him, and we've kept in touch ever since. The world of archaeology is no different to any other. It pays to have as many contacts as possible.'

'So he must have the second relic, then, but how did he get it?' Lusic sounded just as excited as Harker felt.

'It was Archie Dwyer who introduced him to the university. Archie knew David better than I did, so he must have left the relic with him for me to collect.' Harker placed the crown of thorns back in his pocket, much to the displeasure of Lusic, who began aggressively tugging at his chin.

'Well done, Professor. But, seeing as you've now figured out the clue, I can't see any reason why you should keep hold of the crown.'

'Why?' Harker suddenly felt revitalised, and his confidence returned with a vengeance. 'I'm keeping it because your boss entrusted it in to my care, and he also made me swear to find the second relic and ensure that neither would fall into the hands of the Magi.' Harker pulled out his iPhone and tapped the recall button. 'And I'm going to make sure that's exactly what happens.'

Caster gestured to the mobile, now pressed against Harker's ear. 'And who exactly are you calling?'

'A friend, his name's Thomas Lercher. He's a dean at Cambridge University. The Natural History museum will be closed, but he can arrange special passes for us with security.'

'Won't this David Blix be off site once the museum's shut?' the lawyer asked.

Harker answered the question with a shake of his head. 'We'll have to chance that, but, so far, Archie's hasn't left any part of his paper trail to chance, and I've no reason to think this occasion will be any different.'

His mobile suddenly crackled into life with a voice echoing from the earpiece.

'Hello, Dean Lercher speaking.' The reception was terrible, and the faulty feedback caused Harker to instinctively pull away.

'Doggie, it's Alex.'

'Attics? Attics who?'

'No, Doggie, it's Alex.'

'Alex! Where the hell are you? I've been worried sick. The Italian authorities told me you'd been taken to the British Consulate, but when I phoned them, they knew nothing about you. Frankly, they were as helpful as a kick in the teeth, so I . . .'

'Harker cut him off, knowing how Doggie could rattle on whenever he was anxious.'

'Tom, listen. I need a favour, and I need it now.'

Chapter 29

The cold evening air stung in Genges's lungs as he ushered the remaining members of his hit squad into the dank, dripping drainage outlet that acted as a back entrance to the Rome observatory's basement. 'Get yourselves cleaned up,' he barked, 'and remain on standby in case you're needed later.'

Genges slammed shut the side door of the black transit van and followed his masked hit squad through the murky fifteen-metre-long entrance tunnel. This old drainage pipe hadn't been used in years, and deep cracks in the cement were a testament to that fact. Up ahead, a door swung open, flooding the entire passage in a bright yellow fluorescent light. A seven-foot-high steel cage surrounded the inner doorway, and two Magi guards, wearing black Kevlar combat suits, each equipped with an MP5 machine gun, stood guard at either side. Once the crew had been identified, one guard swiped his key card across the lock, and, with a green flash from an LED light, the cage door popped open.

Genges pushed past without a word and headed along a series of narrow cedarwood-panelled corridors towards the war room. There his elder brother would be waiting, eager for an update. Their assault had gone as planned, catching Brulet and his followers off guard, but to allow Harker and the precious item to slip through their fingers was inexcusable.

He stopped outside the office itself and rubbed the back of his neck nervously. His brother would be livid, but, so long as they had someone on the inside, this Professor Harker wouldn't be hard to track. He glanced down at his wristwatch and noted the hands at 23.00. Good, they still had time, and his brother would surely be mollified by the news of Brulet's death.

Genges thumped his fist heavily against the door before heading inside without waiting for an answer. He found Balthasar sitting at his brass-trimmed oval desk, sporting a deeply unhappy grimace and, with his complexion, an unhealthy shade of grey.

'What happened, Genges? Things did not go as they should have. Explain.' He pointed to the frayed leather-covered armchair in front of the desk, and Genges dutifully slid on to the seat, its wooden legs creaking in dismay under the weight of his body armour.

'Brother, the assault went well with three Templars being dispatched.'

The Magi chief relaxed his thick shoulders and settled back deeply into his armchair, one eyebrow raised knowingly. 'But it wasn't without loss, Genges. Four valuable warriors have been lost to us.'

The prince swallowed hard under the piercing stare of his older brother.

'And Harker and the item got away from you, didn't they?'

The remark caused Genges to swallow nervously. 'Unfortunately, yes. I see you've been in contact with our man on the inside then.'

Lord Balthasar nodded, emitting a weak gasp. He pulled a white handkerchief from his pocket, pressed it to his mouth, and let out a cough, which spattered dark red specks of blood on to its white cotton fabric.

Genges was already making his way solicitously around the table when he saw a rigid finger directing him back to his seat.

'I'm fine,' Balthasar croaked as he grabbed for the glass tumbler of iced water standing next to him and took a deep sip, his lips leaving red wisps of blood fusing with the contents like dancing ribbons. He retrieved a silver pillbox from his pocket, shook out two pink-coloured tablets, and wolfed them down.

'Yes, I received a call from our man. It appears the second relic is in London, and they're on their way to retrieve it as we speak.'

Genges was already on his feet, tapping at his iPhone before his brother again motioned him back to his seat.

'No, Brother, I've already sent the giant to intercept them. He's already in the air.'

By his expression, the Magi prince made no effort to hide his displeasure at this news, but he kept quiet. His brother already knew of the misgivings he had about using that brash oaf, but, seeing as he'd just lost the opportunity to bag the crown himself, he was in no position to complain. 'Very well. I suppose, as long as you trust the giant.'

Balthasar scoffed at the comment. 'You know I do. You must be mindful of your prejudices, Genges, and not forget your place in all this.'

The younger brother nodded dutifully and pulled an imaginary zipper across his lips.

'Good. Now tell me of Brulet and his men.'

Genges relished getting the chance to elaborate on the good news. 'We ambushed the building as planned, and before they knew what was happening, we had ended two of them before driving Brulet into a corner.'

Balthasar was already losing himself in the joy of hearing about his arch-nemesis's suffering, and the stabbing pain in his lungs momentarily eased.

'And what then?'

'We threw in a few frag grenades and collapsed the roof, squashing him like a grapefruit. There wasn't much left.'

The Magi lord clapped his hands, basking in the warm glow of such a victory. It had been almost five years since Brulet had murdered their father in such a cowardly way that even now recalling the event stirred up a powerful hatred within him. The Templar had received exactly what he had deserved, and to have accomplished his demise on tonight, of all nights, was surely a good omen.

'And you left nothing at the scene?'

Genges shook his head. 'We torched their library and gathered the bodies of ours and theirs with the exception of Brulet. I doubt that even his dental records would help identify him after a sandwiching like that. We then had the dead incinerated, once the blessing was performed as the code requires. The trail is clean.'

Balthasar dipped his head approvingly. Since the Templars and Magi were intertwined by history, and the discovery of one could lead a trail to the other, bodies from either side were always destroyed to guarantee that either organisation remained a secret from the outside world. It was a code that both sides had vigorously adhered to for hundreds of years.

'I'm glad to hear it, my brother, because the cardinal was most displeased with our brazenly open attack on the Templars. It is of critical importance that the coming hours are handled with the same shrewdness our organisation so normally observes.'

Genges nodded. 'Yes, My Lord. So what now?'

His sickly older brother coughed another bloody offering into his handkerchief. 'Because of the unforeseen attack on Brulet, we must vacate the observatory as soon as possible. The Templars' hideout is not far from here, and we cannot allow ourselves to become embroiled in any judicial entanglements. I want you to leave for the Vatican immediately and link up with the cardinal. Make sure that preparations are running smoothly for tonight's summit, and I will meet you there in a few hours.'

'You're not coming with me?'

'Not yet, Brother.' Balthasar shook his head. 'I want to oversee the clear-out of this observatory and make sure no trace of its use as a safe house is left behind. I fear some of our men have been getting a little sloppy of late.' He shook his head in disappointment. 'And now we wait for the giant to succeed where we have failed and, with it, the rebirth of the world.' He let out another painful grunt. 'As well as my own body.'

Chapter 25

'No bodies? What the hell do you mean no bodies?' Superintendent Perone shouted in disbelief. 'Angelo, there's blood everywhere, for Christ's sake.'

His young subordinate could only shrug his shoulders. 'We've searched the whole villa, sir. It's huge, covered in bullet holes, and totally empty.'

Perone moved aside from the library doorway and allowed a couple of firemen to bustle past, each with his own personal fire extinguisher. 'And what the hell are they doing here? This is a fucking murder enquiry, not arson.'

Detective Angelo Barbosa allowed himself a satisfying smirk as he watched the two fire fighters disappear into the depths of the building. The old man had been furious ever since those two embassy men had turned up and seized his prime suspect, so everyone was now giving the boss a wide birth. Of course, it was particularly difficult to keep out of the way when you were second in command.

At only twenty-six, Angelo Barbosa was one of the youngest officers in the Rome jurisdiction to make it to detective. On graduating from the academy, he'd immediately enlisted into the Guardia di Finanza, where he had spent the previous six years as part of a team dedicated to taking down the three major families of the Sicilian mafia. During a time of great upheaval within the ranks of organised crime, violence had spilt out on to the streets with a string of high-profile murders, which had outraged the entire country. After that, the police had redoubled their efforts, and a crew of young fresh-faced cops, untainted by corruption, had been recruited to pursue the Sicilians with everything in their arsenal.

Angelo had chased the assignment with all his energy and was eventually chosen because the rival candidate had recently got married, and, it had been decided that all crew members should be single. It was considered far better to have a single man who only had to watch his own back and didn't have the additional worry of a young wife that could easily be threatened.

Six long years of investigation had led to over one hundred arrests and a crippling of the main Mafia clans. Afterwards, Angelo had been given the option to pretty much choose where he was to be assigned next, and the Polizia di Stato division, based at the Questura in Rome, was rated as one of the most respected and incorruptible jurisdictions in the country. It also had a lot to do with the station's most famous incumbent officer, Superintendent Rino Perone, one of the toughest cops on the force and renowned for being morally untouchable. Just the way Angelo liked it, even if his new boss was also a tremendous pain in the arse.

Perone's husky voice snatched him from his thoughts. 'Angelo, you fucking deaf? Why the firemen?'

'Sorry, sir, but someone set fire to one of the rooms and there's a lot of smouldering plasterwork out the back, near the pantry. Looks like an explosive device went off—we'll know more about that soon. As for bodies, the boys have done a thorough sweep of the property, and there are no stiffs, despite the blood.'

The superintendent let out one of his typical growls as he pulled a Villager cigar from the top pocket of his Armani blazer and jammed it between his teeth. He then lit it with a match and tossed the smoking splinter to the floor, attracting a glare from a passing fireman.

'Fuck! OK, what else have we got?'

'There are surveillance cameras mounted all over the property. We checked the DVD storage disks, and they're all empty so that's a dead end. But . . .'

Perone's frown turned to look of impatience. 'But what? Tell me you got something for Christ's sake.'

The young officer shot him a knowing glance. 'Well, the internal surveillance is a washout but I checked the footage of a CCTV camera on the main road outside the front gates and found this.' He thrust a black-and-white photograph into the superintendent's hand and tapped the image of two black transit vans travelling in convoy. 'The time's about right, and there was no activity on the road until we got here, so I'd say those are our suspects.'

Perone brought the photo closer to his eyes and peered at the fuzzy licence plate of the lead vehicle. He really needed glasses, as his eyesight was getting worse year on year, but the idea of showing any physical weakness in front of his men was galling. He had considered contact lenses, but the prospect of inserting them in and taking them out every day convinced him otherwise. Anyway, surely, he still had a few years left in him before that would become necessary.

'Can you blow up a copy of that licence plate?' Perone grunted.

'We've tried, but it's too grainy, sir. I've got the tech guys checking all the cameras on their departure route, going from road to road, and if the van appears on them, we may be able to track them to their next location.'

Perone passed the surveillance photo back to his lieutenant and gave him a firm slap on the back. 'Well, what the fuck are you waiting for? Get on to it right away.'

As the young detective headed for the main doorway, clutching the photograph in his hand, Perone took another puff of his cigar, mulling over dozens of unanswered questions—but two were at the top of his list. Who exactly was this Professor Alex Harker? And, more importantly, where the fuck was the officer who was fetching his cappuccino?

Chapter 26

Balthasar tapped the large glass aquarium with his fingertips and admired the two well-fed piranhas that were scouting the outer limits of their tank. The Magi leader loathed, having to dispose of these pets that had brought him so much pleasure during his past few months of being locked away inside the observatory, but sneaking two flesh-eating piranhas into the Vatican was not an option. It was a shame to have to destroy them, but he could purchase a new pair. Balthasar smiled to himself, reflecting that there was no better way of instilling fear into one's subordinates than the threat of losing a finger or two to these ravenous little eating machines. It was a lesson one of his associates had learnt first-hand, as it were, when he was disciplined for failing to track down the priest Vito Malpuso just a few days earlier. The task had then been assigned to Drazia Heldon but not before the red bellies had munched their fill on the unfortunate man's index finger.

The recollection was interrupted by a knock at the war-room door. 'Enter.'

Marko Lupis came in and stood to attention. 'Sir, the safe house is almost clean. Another hour, and no one will know we were ever here.'

'Good.' Balthasar gave an approving nod. 'Once we're finished, you and Toledo head off to Munich and wait for further instructions. Oh, and make sure these fish are burnt to a crisp.' He signalled towards the aquarium. 'Their bellies could still contain traces of DNA—not something I wish for anyone to find.'

Lupis instinctively rubbed his fingers together and winced. 'Yes, My Lord, I will have them properly disposed of.'

The young Magi officer was already making his way out of the room when the piercing, high-pitched shrill of an electric buzzer reverberated from a grey unit linked directly to the observatory entrance. Both men locked eyes, each thinking the same thought, which preceded a single word: 'Who?'

Lupis didn't need his master to bark an order and was already heading through the grey concrete bunker and into the main observatory by the time a second buzz had sounded. On reaching the entrance, he took a moment to compose himself before unlocking it and then pulling open the heavy wooden door to find a rain-soaked man holding a newspaper over his head.

'Open up, my friend,' Detective Angelo Barbosa ordered, pushing his way into the observatory's reception area and wiping the rain from his thick black hair. 'There's a bloody downpour out there. I should have brought a mac.'

The young officer had barely taken a step inside before Lupis began waving his hands in protest.

'I'm afraid we're closed for the evening.'

Barbosa stopped brushing himself off and glared at the blonde-haired man making the objection.

'You'll have to come back tomorrow when we're open.'

The detective pulled out his Polizia di Stato ID card and brandished it in front of him. 'For me, you'll make an exception.'

Lupis examined the card thoroughly. 'Detective Barbosa. Yes, of course. I'm the manager here. What can we do for you at this late hour?'

Angelo slipped the ID back into his pocket, never taking his gaze off the now fawning custodian. 'There was an incident about ten miles from here earlier this evening, and I'm checking it out.'

Lupis eyed him innocently. 'And what, may I ask, has that got to do with us?'

The question sounded reasonable, and Angelo thought nothing of it, apart from that the manager was a bit of a wise ass, but, in his experience, most wannabe scholars were. 'CCTV cameras caught the suspects leaving and heading in this direction, so we're checking all the nearby locations.' He passed over the same grainy picture of the black transit van he had shown Perone earlier that evening.

'No, sorry, Detective, can't say I've seen it. Or anything else out of the ordinary tonight, for that matter. It's been pretty quiet here.'

Angelo flicked the photograph between his fingers, obviously frustrated. 'OK. Mind if I have a look around?'

'Of course not, Detective.' Lupis smiled agreeably, 'If those people you're looking for are dangerous, then we're certainly safer with you around. Please, feel free to have a proper look.'

Detective Barbosa nodded graciously and began inspecting the main room, which, to him, looked more like a library than a base for the province's primary observation telescope. The large, round chamber was lined with rows of shelves filled with astrological charts and books, allowing a circular space at the centre of the room, laid out with eight workstations. Angelo scowled at the heaps of printed works, which were beginning to produce a strong sensation of claustrophobia in him. As a child, some fellow pupils had locked him into the school library one night for a joke. His parents, thank God, had the whole village out, looking for him within hours of his missing supper. When a search party finally located the young Angelo, he was curled up under one of the reading desks, crying like a baby—not his fondest memory and the reason he still detested libraries to this very day.

As the detective continued his tour of the room, Lupis could not help but marvel at how a person could become so focused on the objects immediately surrounding him that they missed spotting the most obvious things. Namely the black transit van parked out at the back and just visible from one of the side windows, not to mention the semi-automatic black Glock handgun lying on a leather seat next to one of the bookshelves. More importantly, the Magi warrior lurking in the shadows behind it, dressed head to toe in bulletproof armour with an automatic MP5 aimed directly at the police officer's head through a gap in the bookcase.

'What's in there?' Angelo pointed at a metal door over to one side of the room.

'It's where we keep our stock for the gift shop: postcards, pens ... All the usual stuff.'

The detective gently rapped his knuckle against the door inquisitively. 'Can I have a look?'

Lupis shook his head. 'I'm afraid I don't have a key myself, but if you'd like to come back tomorrow, I could ...'

Angelo cut him off mid-sentence. 'You don't have a key? So what happens if you suddenly need more stock!'

For the first time since the detective's arrival at the observatory, Lupis looked rattled.

'Um, well, we'd have to wait until the manager arrives in the morning.'

'But I thought *you* were the manager?'

From the corner of his eye, Angelo caught a glint of something metallic, and he spun around to find himself facing the hollow-chambered barrel of an MP5 machine gun.

'Thank you, Detective, but I don't think we'll be needing your services any more.'

The assault rifle came crashing down on Angelo's temple, knocking him to the ground. As he slipped into unconsciousness, he felt someone tug his magnum revolver from its holster.

A voice continued above him. 'Tie him up and bring him with us. We'll dispose of his body on the way. Now get everything packed up. We need to be gone within the hour.'

Chapter 27

'Gonna see the T. rex, are ya, guv'nor? Hell of a sight. Almost filled me kecks when I saw that creature.'

The black hackney cab bounced its way over another sleeping policeman, lifting Harker a couple of inches into the air, then setting him back down on the plastic-covered seat with a bump. He'd asked for a quick ride, and that's exactly what he was getting.

The flight to Heathrow had taken a little over an hour, and fortunately, they'd been met by an extremely accommodating customs officer, who had recognised the archaeologist immediately. A few handshakes later, and he was in a taxi on his way to the Museum of Natural History. Unfortunately, both Caster and Lusic had realised mid-flight that neither of them had passports with them. It seemed that being a Knights Templar carried a number of perks, including a sort of diplomatic immunity due to the organisation's many well-placed associates within every level of government. At every level, that is, except Heathrow Airport customs and excise, so both men had been forced to wait behind in the jet.

The taxi bounced alarmingly once more as the cabbie continued setting the world to rights.

'Shame, though, that most of the stuffed animals 'ave been replaced with pictures—something to do with political correctness or some such rubbish.' The middle-aged Londoner scratched his shiny bald head as he guided his taxi between two narrowly separated road bollards, causing Harker's heart to skip a beat. 'I mean, I'm all for equality, but political correctness is just a load of old bollocks, aint it? I mean, take a gander at me.' He glanced back towards his passenger before giving his shiny scalp a good slap. 'I aint folically challenged. I'm bloody bald, son. I call's a spade a spade, and that way you always know where's you stand, eh?'

Harker nodded enthusiastically in the hope his new friend would give up delivering his take on the world at large and concentrate on the road instead. Not a chance, he realised, because after all there are three things a London cabbie does better than anyone else: drive expertly, give top directions, and, most of all, talk for Britain.

'Gotta say, it's been a while since I picked up anyone off a private jet. Is it yours?'

Harker shook his head. 'I wish. It's a friend's.'

'Nice bit of kit that, the kinda one the Arabs use, I reckon.'

The black Hackney cab did a final lurch forward before coming to an abrupt halt.

'Here we go. Quick as I promised.'

Harker jumped out on to the pavement adjoining Cromwell Road and slung on his overcoat.

'That'll be spot on thirty pounds, sir.'

Harker passed over two twenty-pound notes and gave him a thumbs up. 'Keep the change.'

The burly cabbie grinned wildly and pointed a pudgy finger in Harker's direction. 'Good man, much appreciated and happy holidays.'

At this time of night, the streets were empty with the exception of a few midnight wanderers, and, within minutes, Harker had made his way through the still open gates and was heading for the imposing entrance of the museum. As he drew nearer, the unusual sight of two policemen in yellow reflective jackets guarding it suggested that something wasn't right, but before he could get close enough to enquire, he felt a tap on his shoulder, and he spun round to see the brilliant white teeth of Tom Lercher smiling at him.

'Well, fancy meeting you.' The dean let go of Harker's shoulder and motioned him to one side.

'Doggie, what are you doing here?'

Wearing a tweed jacket and light corduroy suit trousers, his old friend looked as if he had walked straight out of a lesson.

'Are you joking?'

It was hard for Harker to tell whether his friend's question was merely rhetorical. 'What do you mean?'

'You disappear off to Rome at a moment's notice only to call me from a private jet, shortly after being charged with murder and asking for my help. So how could I not be curious about what's not going on?'

Dragging Doggie into this whole affair could result in the Cambridge dean getting hurt. All the same, Harker was glad to see him. 'Well, I'm really pleased you're here.' He gestured back towards the two policemen. 'But what's going on?'

'There's just been a bomb threat. That's what they told me anyway.'

'Bomb threat from whom?'

'Not sure.' Doggie shrugged his shoulders. 'This is London, so maybe its terrorists. You know, the usual stuff. But they're not letting anybody in.'

'Did you manage to speak with David Blix yet?' Harker asked impatiently.

'No, when I arrived, the police were already on the door.' He gently took Harker by the arm and pulled him further away from the two policemen, who were now beginning to take an interest. 'Alex, what the bloody hell's going on and why were you in the custody of the Italian police? More importantly, what are you doing here? Shouldn't you be awaiting trial or something?' Dean Lercher's face sagged as a worrying thought came to mind. 'Oh, bloody hell, tell me you're not a fugitive, will you? Because Interpol will track you down. They're like bloodhounds!'

Harker didn't feel he had time to give him the whole rundown and, more importantly, telling the dean everything could make him a target also. But the look on his friend's face persuaded him otherwise. When Doggie's curiosity was piqued and he got his teeth into something, he rarely let go. Harker would have to tell him something eventually, but for now, attempting a fob off was worth a shot.

'No, I'm not a fugitive.'

The dean released a deep sigh. 'Thank God, because I could be charged with aiding a criminal, and I wouldn't last long in jail. I'm not the type.'

Harker grasped Doggie's shoulder and gave it a gentle shake. 'Look, I'll tell you everything, but right now I need to get inside the museum, and I'm short on time. Really short.'

Dean Lercher's curious smile was back with a vengeance as he eyed his associate. 'How big is this, Alex? I mean are we talking BIG?'

Harker placed both hands on his friend's shoulders and went eyeball to eyeball, his expression as serious as he could muster. 'Tom, they don't get much bigger than this. What I'm on to makes the Dead Sea Scrolls seem like an old *beano* annual.'

The dean's eyes widened, and he instinctively licked his lips in anticipation.

'And I'll let you in on *everything* eventually, but time is of the essence now, and I need to see David Blix right away.'

Doggie was already nodding in agreement before the words came out of his mouth. 'OK, OK. But I'm coming with you.'

It was pretty obvious the dean wasn't going to miss out on whatever was going on, and Harker knew it.

'Deal.'

'And once we've found him, you'll tell me *everything*?'

'Yes, everything. But whatever I tell you could get you hurt—maybe even killed.'

The mention of death really lit a fire in Doggie's eyes.

'My God, you're serious, aren't you?'

Harker's grave nod in response wiped none of the intrigue and excitement from his friend's eyes.

'OK, then, follow me. There's an old service chute near the west side, and we should be able to sneak in through there. Dr Blix and a few others use it to pop out for a cigarette, so it's always left unlocked in the evening.' The university dean let out a knowing laugh. 'And they say smoking is a *bad* thing!'

Chapter 28

'Who on earth would want to blow up the Natural History Museum? It's not exactly what I'd call a high-priority target. Not unless you're one of those madcap creationists!'

Dean Lercher had been waffling on in such a fashion ever since getting inside the building, and Harker was doing his level best to remain pleasant. His old friend could be a talkative handful at the best of times, but, after the day's events and with his head still aching, it was starting to sound like verbal diarrhoea.

Doggie had been right about the fire exit, and, after easily gaining access to the main halls, they had navigated their way down to the lower levels within a few minutes. Harker had visited the museum on numerous occasions for exhibits and galas, amongst other events, but he had never seen it looking so empty, and, in truth, it was a little creepy. The dean, on the other hand, was understandably far more concerned about the terrorist threat and had been talking non-stop in an effort to quell his nerves, an endeavour that seemed to be working successfully even if he wasn't making a lot of sense.

'It's much more likely to be fundamentalists hell-bent on destroying one of our great institutions. My God, think of the exhibits that would be lost, the specimens destroyed. Now, I know that many at Cambridge see me more as a fund-raiser than an academic, and a few still question my appointment as head of archaeology, but I ask you this. Without funding, there can be no digs, and no digs mean no finds, and no finds mean no archaeological evidence, so you tell me, who's the real professional in all this? I'll tell you who.' Doggie raised his finger rigidly and confidently towards the ceiling. 'Dean Thomas Lercher, that's who. And you can bet your sweet arse I will be successful in that mission.'

In the past, Harker had never minded his friend's periodic nervous rants; in fact, on most occasions, he found them highly amusing. But this was not most occasions. 'Take it easy, Chancellor. You are indeed a consummate professional, but no one's going to blow this building up, as I'm sure the terrorists have much better things to do. Now let's keep our thoughts to ourselves and go find David.'

Harker's stern tone of voice caused his old friend to realise how foolish he must be sounding, and he immediately calmed his outburst.

'Yes, of course, you're right, I'm sure. Oh and Alex, don't be sarcastic. You know I don't like it.'

'Well, stop acting like a tool then! Now, do you want to know what this is all about or not?'

Any shred of indignation on the dean's face vanished. 'OK, tell me what you've done?'

'It's not what I've done, but what I found.'

Harker reached into his inside jacket pocket and carefully pulled out the slim plastic case containing the crown of thorns. 'Allow me to present to you possibly the most significant Christian relic of all time. It's the crown of thorns that Jesus himself wore on the day of his execution.'

Doggie's jaw slumped, and his eyes widened like camera lenses as he moved closer to examine the encased object. 'Oh, my God, is it genuine?'

'Apparently so.' Harker slipped the item back into his pocket after allowing his friend just a quick glance. 'And there's a second relic here at the museum, and, before you ask, no, I don't know what it is, but I'm not exaggerating when I tell you that finding it could literally mean the difference between life and death.'

Doggie was now chewing at the bit, his mouth already open and ready to jump in the moment Harker finished his last syllable.

'And before you bombard me with questions, Tom, be aware that I'm not telling you anything else until we've seen David and recovered the second item. After that, I promise I'll give you the whole story, chapter and verse. So the sooner we find Dr Blix, the sooner that unbearable feeling of curiosity gnawing in the pit of your stomach will be satisfied, OK?'

At first, he thought the dean's head was about to explode, the way his whole neck was trembling, but, instead, Doggie leant closer and whispered, 'Then what the hell are we doing standing around here? Let's move it.'

It took them another few minutes of silently navigating the subterranean corridors before they reached the research department's electrically operated glass doors. The lights were on, but the place looked empty, and Doggie was already rapping forcefully on the glass before Harker even had time to raise his fist. Seconds later, a familiar face appeared, rising from behind the computer sitting on one of the large desks.

David Blix was a man in his mid-forties, but with a boyishly round face, curly red hair, and a youthful complexion, that made him look like he had barely reached his thirties. The image was accentuated by his red bow tie and brown jumper with a black zigzag pattern running around the edges, making him look like a youngster trying to appear older than he was. After a moment of squinting, a glimmer of recognition flashed across the academic's face, and, with a wave, he pressed a red button on the wall next to him, so the glass doors slid apart.

'Alex Harker, but . . . Tom Lercher? Well, how about that?' David Blix shook both their hands. 'I expected you Alex but Archie never mentioned Tom as well!'

The remark lifted Harker's spirits immediately. 'Good to see you, David, and glad to hear you say that. So you know what's going on then?'

Blix shook his head. 'Absolutely no idea, but Archie asked me for a favour, and here I am. I still can't believe he died just a few days after I last saw him. All feels like a bit of a dream, really.'

Harker managed a nod. 'Yes, for you and everyone else that knew him, but it seems he's left me a path to follow from beyond the grave. David, why did he visit you?'

'And why are you still here during a terrorist alert?' Doggie almost shouted the question, his outburst catching the naturalist by surprise.

'Easy, Tom, I have my reasons. When Archie turned up a couple of weeks ago, he seemed fine. He was a bit more enigmatic than usual, but you know how eccentric he could be, and it wasn't until he got ready to leave that things got serious.' Blix pointed to a couple of metal stools, and he waited for both Harker and Doggie to settle on them before continuing. 'We spoke for about half an hour, talking about Janice and generally catching up on things.'

When David Blix's wife had passed away from lung cancer a few years back, he had come close to committing suicide. In fact, he was so overwhelmed with the feelings of loss and guilt that he had locked himself away, refusing to speak with anyone except eventually Archie. Archie had managed to reach him, and not a moment too soon for it later turned out that, just a week earlier, Blix had renewed his shooting licence and even bought himself a twelve-bore shotgun with cartridges. Archie's timing, as always, had been impeccable, and he had managed to pluck his former parishioner from the clutches of suicidal depression and place him on the road to a new life. Blix had never forgotten this, and whenever Archie was in the country, he would make sure they met up for a coffee or a meal, and their last meeting had proved no exception.

'We had several cups of coffee, and I was about to walk him to the door when he said he needed my help. He made me swear I'd stay on site, at the museum, and just wait for you to contact me. He was also just as adamant that I must not contact you first. If it had been anyone else but him, I'd have told them to get knotted, but I could never have refused Archie. So I stopped off at home, grabbed what I needed, and came back here to the museum. Had I known I was going to be stuck here for over two weeks, I would have brought some more clothes. All I can say is thank God, there's a shower in the utility area, or I wouldn't have made it. Unfortunately, that packed up three days ago and still hasn't been fixed.' Blix lifted his jumper upwards in disgust. 'It gets very hot down here next to the boiler room, and besides, I'm not sure I can take another night of Domino's pizza!' He motioned briefly to the stack of empty delivery boxes piled neatly in the corner. 'Anyway, Archie made me swear to stay here, and when I found out he had died, well, I had to keep my promise to him.'

Harker was just about to comment when Doggie beat him to it.

'Did he leave anything with you for safekeeping?'

Dr Blix gave a nod and a sigh. 'Yes, he did, a small package. He made me swear to keep it safe and tell no one about it except for you. Real cloak-and-dagger stuff—very unlike Archie.'

'And do you have the package here?' Harker enquired with such urgency that Blix was prompted to stand up.

'Sure. I can fetch it right now.'

Both Harker and Doggie were already out of their seats and heading for the glass doors with such enthusiasm that Blix had to hop a few steps just to keep up with them.

'Wow, you two gentlemen are really in a rush, aren't you?'

Harker moved aside, allowing the academic to precede them. 'Bad luck has been shadowing me all day, David, and I don't want it rubbing off on you. The sooner I take that package off your hands, the better. So where is it?'

Blix smiled shrewdly. 'I put it in the safest place I could think of. It's in a whale.'

'A whale?'

'Yes, some of the security guards used to sneak drinks in so they could enjoy a tipple and make their nightshift that bit more enjoyable. Very cheeky of them. The museum's director was furious when he heard the rumours, but, despite his best efforts, he never caught them with any alcohol.'

Blix paused as they reached a small glass-enclosed service elevator just off the main corridor and he pressed the call button before progressing with his story. 'So he repositioned all the CCTV cameras one night without telling anyone and managed to catch them in the act. It turned out they were hiding their bottles in the mouth of the blue whale exhibit, which you can now only reach by ladder since they suspended it from the ceiling last year. Great idea, but it means none of the staff goes near it now, which made it a perfect hiding place for Archie's package—even if I do say so myself.'

He was obviously proud of his hide-and-seek abilities, but Harker said nothing. He would only be happy once back on the plane with the item secure and the sooner, the better.

The elevator doors slid open, and Blix was already inside it when a thunderous stomping sound echoed along the corridor towards them, grabbing everyone's attention. The passageway turned a corner fifty metres ahead, so they couldn't see what was causing the commotion. But one thing was for sure: it was getting closer and coming fast.

A sickly feeling of dread churned in Harker's stomach as the sound became clearer, and he recognised they were the sound of footsteps. Big, heavy, footsteps.

'No, it couldn't be . . . could it?'

His worst fears were immediately realised as the hulking mass of Drazia Heldon came hurtling around the corner, his arm-sword raised in the attack position, and a look of absolute bloody murder etched across his face. Harker instinctively pushed Doggie into the elevator before diving in after him. Blix was already frantically tapping the door button. Seconds later, the elevator sprung into life, and its doors slid shut just as the dark, forbidding shadow of Drazia Heldon fell across them.

'What the hell was that thing?' Blix hissed croakily, his whole body frozen.

'That was the bad luck I was telling you about.'

No sooner had Harker spoken than the slender blade of Heldon's arm-sword sliced through the elevator door with such force that it buckled the metal before imbedding itself into Blix's shoulder. The museum curator yelped in pain as the sword was summarily retracted, leaving a slit in the door. Beyond it, the Magi assassin stood silently watching them through the puncture as the elevator rose upwards and out of sight.

'David!' Harker moved to his friend's side as Blix clutched at the stab wound and sank to the floor.

'How deep did it go?'

The academic gave a shake of his head. 'Deep enough to bloody hurt, but I think I'm all right.'

Harker pulled his hand away and examined the wound. Luckily, the blade had only penetrated a fraction into his shoulder, and, satisfied there was no need for a tourniquet, he pulled Blix to his feet.

'I'm sorry to heap all this on you, David, but it's essential I get hold of that package before he does.'

'Who the hell was that?' Blix huffed, his face still marble-white with shock.

'It's better you don't know, but he's not someone you ever want to meet again.'

'No shit, Alex, you think?'

The quip made Harker expel a sigh of relief. The professor was going to be fine, and, as he turned round, he realised that Blix was not the one he should be worrying about. In one corner, Doggie was still standing in a pose of sheer terror, his mouth wide open in horror, his eyes wide, and his hands outstretched as if clasping something invisible in front of him.

'Doggie, are you OK?' Harker asked, tapping the dean on his shoulder only to feel the resistance of tensed muscles.

'Alex,' Doggie managed. 'I, I think I've wet myself!'

Harker glanced down at the man's trousers but saw there was no telltale dark stain. 'You're just imagining that. Now get it together, Doggie. I need you.'

The elevator jolted to an abrupt halt, its doors sliding back to reveal the massive exhibit room known as the blue zone, and above them hung the plastic hundred-foot-long blue whale replica, suspended from the ceiling by two thick cables bolted in to its back. The bones of a further two leviathans were on display below, along with a host of other exhibits. The museum's blue zone housed a variety of dinosaur, reptile, and mammal exhibits amongst others, but the whale exhibit was possibly the most famous.

'Did you see the size of that man? He was the biggest I've ever seen,' mumbled Doggie, still rooted to the spot.

'And he's on his way up to get us right now, so move your bloody arse, Thomas,' Harker yelled at him uncharitably.

The dean finally snapped out of it and made his way shakily out of the elevator, followed closely by Harker and Blix.

'OK, where's the ladder?'

Blix pointed over towards an African savannah exhibit, where a folding stepladder was resting against a grouchy-looking rhino. Within seconds, Harker had positioned it directly below the whale's gaping mouth.

'David, is there somewhere safe you can call the police from?'

Blix gave a nod. 'There's a staff lounge with a phone just down the corridor.'

'OK, make the call and then wait for the cavalry to arrive. Don't worry about the sword-wielding psychopath because it's me he's after. Doggie, I need you to stay and hold the base of the ladder whilst I climb up and get the package.'

'Maybe I should go with David?' Doggie suggested nervously, but Harker silently shook his head and pointed to the ladder, clicking his fingers, before returning his attention back to Blix.

'David, I know this is going to seem strange, but you can't mention either me or Doggie to the police. I know it sounds dodgy, but I promise you . . .'

Blix waved a hand, signalling for Harker to not say another word, and gave him the biggest smile possible considering the degree of pain he was in. 'I already promised Archie I wouldn't tell a soul, and that's a promise I intend to keep. Besides, the day I start believing that you two are embroiled in a life of crime is the day I lose all faith in humanity. Now, you'll have to climb all the way inside because it's tightly wedged at the back of the throat, about twenty foot along. You'll need to use this because it's pretty dark in there.' He pulled a small metal pen torch from his pocket and handed it to Harker. 'Once you have it, you should make your way out by the same exit you came in through to avoid those policemen out the front. Good luck to both of you, and, the next time you're setting up another treasure hunt, do me a favour . . .' He smiled bravely. 'Leave me out of it!'

With a final wave, Blix was gone, which left a still shaking Doggie struggling with the ladder. 'Come on, hurry up, my boy,' he pleaded. 'Let's get that package and skedaddle. I have no wish to come face-to-face with that giant again anytime soon.'

Within seconds, Harker was steadily making his way up the steps until he reached the whale's mouth, all the while keeping an eye on the exits for any sign of the Magi assassin.

The opening was easily large enough to squeeze through, and Harker hastily pulled himself inside, letting out a grunt of pain as he caught his kneecap on the whale's lower lip. The cavity he now found himself in was so large that he could almost stand upright. He flicked on the torch and ran a beam of light slowly around the hollow space. The mouth itself was empty except for some leftover tools and a small pile of plastic shavings directly underneath a hole that had been drilled to admit the thick cable and bolt used to suspend the exhibit from the ceiling. There was also an empty vodka bottle, no doubt left by the night guards as a tribute to better days.

Harker made his way to the back of the mouth, which was sectioned off by a plywood partition that stopped him from going any further into the belly of the beast, and he began to make a search with his torch. It didn't take him long to find the eighteen-inch long rectangular package comfortably jammed between two of the struts holding the wooden framework in place. He reached over and gently pulled it from its perch before placing the torch between his lips and loosening the thick string that secured a large brown-paper bag around the box.

A loud thud behind him caused Harker to bite down on the metal torch, and he cursed at the sharp pain shooting through his teeth as he spun around to find the source of the noise, the beam of light zigzagging back and forth.

There, in the mouth opening, stood Dean Lercher, and, as the torch beam settled, Harker could see the sheer look of panic on his face.

'Doggie, what are you doing? I told you to stay where you were,' Harker complained, walking over to him. But, before the dean could reply, a deep voice booming out from somewhere down below answered the question for him.

'Meeting twice in one day—that's extremely rare in my line of work. Usually one encounter is enough, but you're proving to be a real challenge, Professor.'

Harker peered out over the edge to see the intimidating amber eyes of Drazia Heldon glaring straight up at him. The lumbering Magi enforcer tapped the tip of his arm-sword, the blade still stained with David Blix's blood.

'I don't know who your friend is,' the killer gestured towards Doggie, 'but for his sake, I hope he stays out of the way. Meanwhile, Professor, you and I have unfinished business, and if you're prepared to hand me down the two items I seek, then you may both keep your lives. I'm short on time because soon those guards will realise the bomb threat I phoned in was a fake, and we don't want any more unnecessary bloodshed. This is a one-time offer, and I will allow you thirty seconds to decide. Consider this a goodwill gesture, but if you decline, then rest assured, I will dice you both into mincemeat.'

The assassin gave an unsettlingly playful wave of his arm-sword and then pointed to his watch, making Harker instinctively pull his head back from the edge.

'Alex, I vote we give him what he wants,' Doggie yelped, but Harker shook his head. He knew they were trapped, but even if he did hand both packages over, there was no way that psychopath would let them go. That was a lesson he had learnt at the monastery.

'Whether we give it to him or not, trust me, Doggie, he won't let either of us walk out of here alive.'

Harker's blunt response drew a high-pitched protest from the dean. 'So what the hell do we do? We can't bloody fly out of here, can we? Good God, think of something, man.'

Doggie's shrill reply gave Harker an idea—it was a crazy idea, but they were running out of options. He knelt down amid the mishmash of abandoned tools on the floor and began to scrabble through them, stopping at a weighty-looking torque wrench.

'You're right, we can't fly, but we can fall.' He lifted the wrench up to the thick metal screw nut, securing the suspension cable in the roof of the mouth, and adjusted the tool's aperture accordingly. 'How much do you reckon this whale weighs?'

Doggie firmly shrugged his shoulders and tried to hazard a guess. 'I don't know, ten, twenty tons, why?'

'Because once I unloosen this bolt, the weight of it is going to snap the other suspension cable and then, my friend, we're going for a ride.' Harker's idea elicited little positive response from Dean Lercher who was already looking totally mortified.

'A ride! To where, for Christ's sake? We're in a plastic whale!'

Harker finished the wrench's size adjustment, so it was now firmly positioned around the large screw nut, and gave it a hard shove that turned the bolt slightly, with a screech of metal.

'Look, we need a distraction, and this is the best I can come up with. And, who knows, this thing might even land on top of that psychopath down below. Either way, this is happening. Now grab on to something tight.'

Doggie was now looking horrified. 'Grab on to what?'

Harker loosened the nut further, pushing on the wrench with all his strength. 'I don't know, but you better find something now. I can already feel it going.'

He gave one last muscle-aching tug on the wrench's handle as Doggie pressed his back to the wall and grabbed one of the thin overhead struts with both hands.

With an ear-splitting crack, the screw nut spun off, sending the thick cable zipping upwards through the hole in the roof. And then they were falling, the front end of the whale crashing down on to the complete skeleton of a genuine blue whale, causing the bones to splinter in all directions and sending Harker and Doggie violently tumbling out of the exhibit's mouth and skidding across the floor only to end up in a heap at the base of a chubby-looking hippopotamus.

The following moments became much of a blur to Harker as he struggled to focus on anything at all. He had felt something smack against the side of his head as they hit the floor, possibly the wrench, but he couldn't be sure. Next to him, Thomas Lercher was groaning something unintelligible, which Harker took as a good sign because it meant at least the dean was alive.

As his vision became clearer, he could see plumes of white dust from the splintered whalebones gently sinking to the floor. He grabbed hold of the hippo's thick plastic whiskers and pulled himself to his feet. Harker steadied himself before bending down to offer his spare hand. It was grabbed immediately by the Dean, who stood up with another loud groan.

'Did we get him?' Doggie asked as he rubbed at the scarlet bruise forming on his cheek.

'Not sure. Hold on.'

Harker looked back to the crash-landed whale, which was still intact even if the skeleton beneath it had been smashed into two. He scanned the wreckage thoroughly until he saw a sight that brought him close to vomiting. Drazia Heldon was pinned underneath the whale's huge bulk, with a thick white shard of fractured bone jutting from his thigh. The Magi enforcer was conscious, however, and already trying to pull a silencer fitted pistol from his pocket, its sights getting snagged in the fabric of his coat jacket.

Harker instinctively made for the exit, with Doggie staggering behind him, still dazed by the knock he had received. They were only metres from the main corridor, which would get them to the fire exit, when a bullet zipped past them and embedded itself with a ping into the brickwork to their right. The second shot was closer still, and then they were out of the exhibit room and heading towards the way out.

Harker's head began to cloud, and he stumbled to his knees, his vision becoming more blurry. He was close to passing out when he felt Doggie's arm slip under his shoulder and haul him forward. Neither man spoke a word, instead using all their energy and determination on one objective—getting out of there. As they finally reached the elevator, which would take them to their escape route, a deep voice resonated along the corridor behind them.

'Harker, there's nowhere you can hide that I won't find you. You're a fucking dead, man!'

Doggie bundled Harker inside the lift and pushed the button for the first floor. At the very last moment, he stuck his head out of the lift door to yell one final comment to the still trapped assassin.

'Maybe so you gigantic oaf, but not today, not today.'

Chapter 29

The balding, road-weary tires of Superintendent Rino Perone's sliver Alfa Romeo crackled over the gravel as it entered the Rome observatory driveway and pulled into an empty handicap zone. Inside the superintendent lit up his cigar with an A. C Milan lighter, wound down the window, and took a deep puff before picking up the mobile phone from the seat next to him. He tapped in a number and placed the cheap twenty-euro mobile next to his ear. The familiar engaged tone reverberated from the earpiece, and he slammed the phone down in frustration, cursing under his breath.

Where the hell was Angelo? He'd been trying to get hold of the detective for the past half hour with no joy, and it was unlike the young policeman to remain out of contact for long, especially considering the night's events.

Perone had sent his young subordinate to check out the observatory whilst he himself searched an old farmhouse further down the road. The building turned out to be empty except for a rather rambunctious family of porcupines that hadn't appreciated him poking around and had forced him into making a hasty retreat to the safety of his car. Satisfied there were no humans about, he'd then called Angelo for an update. But, after getting the engaged tone for over ten minutes, he'd called the office and arranged for his team to meet him at the observatory itself.

It wasn't regular procedure to send out an armed response unit just because he couldn't establish contact with one of his boys, but every member of his team knew to keep their lines open and always be ready to receive his calls. Furthermore, he had developed a gut feeling about this one.

The tech team had traced the van to this particular area through a network of roadside CCTV cameras, and all the likely buildings had been empty, with the exception of those ill-tempered mammals. The observatory was the last place on their list, so if they weren't there, then it was likely they had switched vehicles somewhere and were long gone by now. He made sure the Romeo's inside light was turned off before he opened the door and stealthily made his way towards the building's main window.

Somewhere in the field beyond, an animal howled suddenly, catching him off guard and causing him to drop to his knees. 'Shit,' he whispered, annoyed at this overreaction because now was not the time to develop a case of the willies. Perone raised himself up quietly and cautiously made his way over to the window and peered inside.

The main reception lobby was empty, and the inner doors beyond were closed. He'd been here a few years before with his wife—or ex-wife as she was now—but he couldn't remember the basic layout. Ducking down again, he slunk his way around to the rear pathway, keeping low and hugging the stonewall, deliberately avoiding the low-set windows.

A narrow path followed the circular contour of the observatory building, gently descending downwards to a small car park at the back, surrounded by clumps of heavy-set pine trees, creating a private courtyard free from prying eyes. At first glance, it looked empty, but, as the superintendent moved in for a closer look, a glint of metal caught his eye. There in the corner of the yard, hidden in the shadow of an overhanging pine tree, was a black transit van similar to the one they had been looking for. Perone drew his revolver from its holster and moved over to the side of the vehicle so as to peer in through the passenger window.

The van was empty except for a PC and monitor snugly secured by an elastic tether and, much more interestingly, two pairs of black Kevlar combat jackets of the kind usually worn by security forces.

'Bingo.'

The superintendent turned his attention to the wide-access drain, which tunnelled into the building's lower level, but the grating that covered it was firmly locked from the inside. Frustrated, he made his way back to the observatory's front door, re-holstered his gun, and gently turned the door handle. It too was locked, so Perone pulled out a small zipped leather case from his inside jacket pocket and quietly slid it open to reveal a set of thin metal picks. He took out two of them and began working the lock ever so carefully until, within seconds, the bolt clicked open. If Angelo was in trouble, then the next few minutes could make all the difference between life and death; therefore, Perone couldn't risk waiting for his team to arrive. Gun drawn, the lawman headed inside.

The lobby seemed empty, but, not one to take a chance, the veteran officer steadily made his way around the corners of all the bookcases. Satisfied he was alone, Perone proceeded past the reception desk towards a metal door behind it. He paused and quietly pressed his ear to the door, holding his breath and listening out for any sign of movement inside.

There was nothing to be heard except for the constant ticking of the wall clock above him. He slowly opened the door, checked the coast was clear, and headed inside.

Perone found himself in a large circular main room with shiny cedarwood panels covering the walls, all beneath an exquisite gold-coloured tray ceiling from which hung four green-shaded lights that gave the place the feeling of a war bunker.

The room was totally empty, but on the thick blue carpet, he could make out deep indentations in the fibres where desks and chairs had stood, suggesting that place had until recently been a hive of activity.

There were no windows in the room, just six beautifully crafted Royal Cuesta doors, each with a thick strip of mahogany running down the centre. The doors were set into the curvature of the wall and spaced evenly from left to right, not unlike the hours on a clock face. They were all closed except one, which was ajar just a few inches.

Perone warily made his way across the carpet towards it, pulling out his black revolver. He raised it up to his chest as he peeked through the crack.

The room beyond looked empty except for a stout oval table at one end, a couple of leather armchairs, and an aquarium containing two rather chubby-looking fish. Piranhas? This on its own wasn't cause for concern, but what sent a shiver through him was the gold pinkie ring lying at the bottom of the tank, nestling amongst the multicoloured gravel.

The sight made him gag as a feeling of revulsion spread from the pit of his stomach. 'Gun battles, flesh-eating piranhas . . . who the hell were these people?'

Such thoughts evaporated instantly at the sight of Detective Barbosa lying face down on the floor, gagged and hog-tied directly in front of the aquarium. Perone cautiously gave the door a nudge with the muzzle of his gun, and it swung open with a creak, bringing Angelo's head whipping around, his eyes sagging in relief at the sight of his boss.

The superintendent made one last visual scan of the room and had only taken a few steps inside when he caught a flicker of movement to his right. He spun round just in time to see Marko Lupis swinging a combat knife towards him, but instead of burying itself in his back, it ended up impaling his biceps. Perone let out a deep growl as the pain shot up his arm. The knife quivered wildly as Lupis began pulling at the six-inch blade, but, before he could retrieve it and have another go, Perone swiped the barrel of his revolver across the Magi's temple with a sharp thud, sending him to the floor like a lead weight. Perone toppled back against the wall and sank on to his haunches, lowering his revolver to one side as he inspected the serrated metal blade now protruding from the thick dense muscle of his biceps. Bile gathered in his throat as shock began to take hold, but Angelo's muffled yells pulled him out of it, and, squinting through watery eyes, he grabbed hold of the handle and, in one brisk movement, slid the knife out.

The wound spat out a stream of blood as the blade exited but, despite a quivering lip, not a sound left his throat. He dropped the slim blade to the floor with a clunk, the sound encouraging the semi-conscious Magi guard to lurch upwards on all fours in a wobbly attempt to stand up. But another swift swipe of Perone's revolver sent the attacker crashing back to the floor, this time knocking him out cold.

'Bastardo,' the superintendent hissed at the unconscious man, spittle dribbling down his chin. 'The only person allowed to treat one of my boys like shit is me.'

He drew a white cotton handkerchief from his top pocket, slipped it under his armpit, and wrapped it around the haemorrhaging cut using his teeth to tighten the knot. Satisfied it was pulled as tight as the pain would allow, he turned his attention to the young detective and used the jagged blade to cut off the ropes with a few swipes.

Angelo staggered to his feet, rubbing at the deep red marks left on his wrists by the tight nylon rope. 'What took you so long, boss?'

The cheeky smile on his subordinate's face was the only thing that stopped him getting smacked around the head with Perone's revolver too. The superintendent ignored the comment and nodded towards the unconscious man sprawled on the floor. 'Use those ropes to tie him up.'

Angelo bound Lupis's hands and feet together roughly and then slapped his erstwhile captor hard across the head, producing a semi-conscious groan. 'We should call for back-up, sir. Can I use your radio?'

'They're already on their way,' Perone snarled. 'How many others are there?'

'I'm not sure. I only saw two.'

The superintendent managed a smile. 'Only two of them? You're getting sloppy, Angelo. Is that how you broke the Mafia?' He wearily patted his young subordinate on the shoulder. 'Don't worry, kid. We can't all be superheroes.'

Angelo said nothing and simply shrugged his shoulders in defeat. What could he say that would make any difference?

'Now you get sleeping beauty there, and let's go outside and secure this guy properly. We'll check the rest of this little den once the back-up team arrives.'

Without warning, the door behind them flung wide open with such a force that the metal knob hit the inner wall, snapped off, and was sent hurtling through the air just missing Angelo's head. Lord Balthasar thundered towards them, seemingly punching the air, and, instantaneously, a foot-long sword zipped out from underneath his sleeve and clicked into place like a giant switchblade. With a bloodthirsty glare, he raised both arms upwards as if ready to strike, his teeth gritted so firmly that both jaw muscles looked close to popping.

Two shots rang out, the first slicing through Balthasar's right cheek in a puff of red mist, which the man simply ignored as he continued lunging forward, his eyes glazed over in a ferocious rage. The second shot penetrated squarely through his Adam's apple, leaving a gaping, bloody star-shaped hole just above the neckline of his body armour.

Balthasar dropped to his knees with a deep thick gurgling sound, a spurt of dark crimson blood oozing from his mouth, before falling face first on to the floor, his arm-sword still extended towards the two police officers.

Angelo turned around to see Perone holding the smoking revolver still aimed at the motionless body of Lord Balthasar.

'To get caught off guard once is unfortunate,' Perone growled. 'Twice would be un-fucking-forgivable. Now grab that bastard, and let's go.'

Angelo gave a nod and hoisted the still unconscious Lupis over his shoulder. He followed the still shaky superintendent who stayed a few feet ahead of him, gun drawn all the way, back to the front lobby.

On entering the room, he came face-to-face with four policemen wearing navy-blue balaclavas and heavily armed with semi-automatics and M4 machine guns.

'It's about fucking time, boys. Have to wait for the bus, did you?'

The armed-response team began lowering their weapons as the shortest member of the unit offered a response. 'We brought the weapons van, boss.'

Perone snorted with laughter through gritted teeth, the wound in his arm throbbing mercilessly, 'You fucking slow coaches, all the actions over. Now how about giving us a hand?'

Angelo swiftly deposited his unconscious prisoner on to the waiting shoulder of the nearest team member, in exchange for an M4 machine gun, whilst Perone holstered his weapon and tenderly massaged his wound. He had only taken one step further towards his team, when Angelo raised the M4 directly towards him and pulled the trigger, the weapon spewing out a series of shots that whizzed past Perone's ear by mere inches. The stunned superintendent dropped to his knees and let out a yelp of pain as his pierced biceps instinctively attempted to support his weight as he keeled over to one side. He hugged his arm protectively and glanced behind him, grimacing at the sharp pain that burst through the ruptured tissue.

There, motionless in the doorway to the corridor, lay the twisted body of the Magi henchman Toledo, his eyes staring blankly at the ceiling and a double bullet wound to the forehead. On the floor next to him lay an MP5 machine gun, cocked and loaded. Angelo lowered the smoking barrel of his M4 and threw Perone a cocky grin.

'Superheroes, aren't we all?'

Chapter 30

'Professor, can you hear me?'

Harker awoke with a searing pain in his head and, through bleary eyes, gazed upwards at Lusic hovering over him with an uncharacteristic look of concern in those big blues of his.

'You're safe, Professor—as is also your assistant. We're on-board the jet heading to Vatican City.'

Opposite him sat a pale-faced Doggie, struggling to gulp down some pills with the aid of a can of Tango. Lusic picked up a silver pack of Solpadeine Plus from the side table and tapped a couple of them into Harker's palm. 'Take these. They should help with your headache.'

He happily obliged, washing them down with a can of diet Coke. Damn, his head hurt.

'I'm sorry, but there's no water left on-board. It's either soft drinks or champagne.'

Harker nodded thankfully, trying to ignore the sharp pain in his right shoulder where it had collided with either one of the whale's rib bones or the steel wrench. 'Where's the relic?'

The German reached down and pulled out the brown-paper package from under a seat. 'Your assistant took good care of it until you woke up.'

Harker let out a hefty sigh of relief at the sight of it, allowing himself to take another sip of his drink as Lusic continued, 'When you arrived, I had to spend five minutes searching the taxicab for any sign of this package, since your assistant took it upon himself to keep it from me.'

Doggie glared up from his can of Tango. 'I keep telling you, whoever you are, I'm not his assistant.'

Lusic gave a courteous nod in the dean's direction. 'I apologise, Mr Lercher.'

The comment once again stirred Doggie's anger by omitting his academic rank.

'Alex is the only one here I trust, and once we got airborne . . .' The dean let the sentence trail off as his friend shot him a sympathetic look. 'Well, it's not like anyone's going anywhere, is it?'

Harker might have laughed had his head not hurt so much. It had taken one hell of a wallop back at the museum, but still that was far more preferable than a bullet to the brain. He now noticed the big bruise that had fully developed on Doggie's cheek. 'Are you OK?'

The dean offered a wry smile. 'Oh, fine considering we've just been chased by the mother of all psychopaths and taken a ride inside a whale, Jonah-style.'

Lusic nodded gravely. 'I've since heard on the radio that your giant psychopath was arrested coming out of the museum. You're obviously lucky to be alive. The report said it took a whole troop of officers to take him into custody.'

Harker took another swig of Coke, the sugar providing him with a much-needed boost of energy.

'Where are we right now?'

'Somewhere over the English Channel. We've been airborne for about fifteen minutes. Professor, I . . .' The change of tone in Lusic's voice sent an unpleasant tingle down Harker's spine, and he readied himself for some bad news. 'I have some unsettling news regarding Mr Caster.'

'Caster?' For the first time, it dawned on Harker that the other man was missing. 'Where is he?'

The German rubbed the back of his own neck gingerly. 'A few minutes after you left us for the museum, Caster came up behind and knocked me out. When I woke, he was gone. Apparently, he did have a passport, after all.'

Harker slumped back in his seat, his mind rushing to connect the dots as Lusic continued furiously. 'That bald-headed little shit must have contacted this ogre of yours and advised him of your destination.'

'So Caster is the Magi infiltrator Brulet spoke of? It's hard to believe, though. He seemed OK.'

'I know.' The Templar nodded sombrely. 'I was pretty shocked myself, because I've been working with John Caster for years. But by keeping hold of this item, his betrayal will have all been for nothing.' He gestured to the brown-paper package sitting in Harker's lap. 'So shall we see what all this effort has been for?'

Harker placed the packet on the table in front of him, pulled loose the coarse string securing it, and slipped off the paper bag to reveal an old and scratched wooden box identical to the one that had contained the crown of thorns. The same image of Emperor Tiberius Augustus Caesar was etched on the lid, and Harker instantly found himself experiencing the same tense anticipation he had felt back at the monastery.

Next to him, Doggie was already kneeling to examine the metal engraving more closely, rubbing the grime of ages from the symbol with his thumb. 'It's Roman. I know that much.'

Harker nodded. 'It's the seal of Emperor Tiberius, exactly the same as on the other box.'

The dean shot his friend a confused look. 'You've already shown me the thorn crown, so isn't it about time you told me everything?'

Under the increasingly unhappy glare of Lusic, Harker proceeded to give the Cambridge dean a rundown of the last few days' events but omitting any reference to Brulet, the Templars, or the Magi. Instead, he blamed the murderous actions of Drazia Heldon on a consortium of thieves hell-bent on stealing the relic from its lawful private owner. Harker wasn't sure if the dean would actually buy that, but, as he described the dark affair, Doggie merely sat silently, listening attentively like an obedient schoolboy.

Harker told him about the secret room found in Archie Dwyer's house, the fire at the orphanage, the monastery, his first encounter with Heldon, and, finally, the shootout at the villa. By the end of it all, the dean was close to salivating.

'Christ alive, Alex, are you telling me that right there in that box there might be another relic associated with Jesus of Nazareth?'

Harker couldn't suppress a wide grin. 'I told you this was big.'

Doggie reached over again and lovingly stroked the top of the wooden casket. 'So you're saying this is part of a secret history lost in the sands of time for over two thousand years? A part of history the entire Western world was founded on? And now it's right here in front of us, ready to be brought in to the daylight once more.'

The dramatic turn of phrase was typical of the dean, who, it seemed, was already coming up with a press release, much to Lusic's displeasure.

'Gentlemen, might I remind you this item does not belong to us but to the private collector you spoke of?'

Doggie almost fell off his seat at the remark. 'If this turns out to be whatever Alex thinks it is, then it belongs to no one and to everyone, which means it belongs to us just as much as to your collector friend.' He turned his attention towards Harker, his eyes beaming with possibilities, and ran a trembling hand through his greying hair. 'Well, Alex, I think you should open it up. Let's see what we've got here.'

The excitement was infectious, and once more Harker's stomach was buzzing. He delicately grasped the container's small metal key and, with a creak, carefully opened the lid till it was upright.

The interior of the case was lined with fresh velvet that must have been part of a recent restoration, and a strong smell of foam rubber began spreading throughout the aircraft cabin. In the very middle, sealed inside a now familiar vacuum-packed transparent plastic case, lay a single rectangular piece of wood no more than six inches long and about eight inches wide.

Doggie tugged at one corner of the container, trying to get a better look, and was immediately dealt a sharp slap across the wrist by Lusic.

'Easy, Dean.'

The swipe restrained him, and, instead, he craned his head sideways for a better view.

Harker meanwhile picked up the plastic case and ran his fingers across the length of the object inside it. The piece of wood had blackened around the edges—no doubt as a result of age—and one end of it had been cut off with a saw.

Scanning the uneven surface, he began to make out a series of markings or symbols carved across it. In many places, the engravings had worn away completely leaving only abrasive scuff marks, but some of the characters were still legible, and Harker soon began to recognise them.

'They're words,' he stated confidently, 'or at least they were.' Harker pointed to the visible text. 'They're a mixture of Hebrew, Latin, and Greek, I think.'

As he traced the lettering with his fingertips, Doggie and Lusic remained silent, their breathing becoming shallower, neither man wanting to disturb Harker's train of thought as he attempted to visualise the original texts.

'OK, there are three lines of writing,' he summarised. 'The top is in Hebrew, although in this condition, it's difficult to make out complete words, the same for the last line in Greek but', he tapped a finger against the middle sentence thoughtfully, 'the one in Latin I can just about make out.'

Harker ran a finger across each faint letter in turn. 'There's a capital *I* followed by a lowercase *S*, then a capital *N* and a capital *R* followed by a lowercase *E* and an *X* . . . IsNRex?'

As the other two men crowded over Harker, each jostling one another for a better look, it suddenly dawned on him exactly what he was looking at. The strip of wood had been severed just after the *X*, and had it not been for the discovery of the thorn crown earlier, Harker wouldn't have twigged so quickly. 'I think I know what this is.'

Both men fixed their attention on Harker as he considered the possibility. Could this really be what he thought it was? After all, the crown of thorns had already blown a hole in his sense of rational, so should this be anything less?

'Well, Alex, you bastard, don't leave us in suspense,' Doggie blurted out, rubbing his hands together impatiently.

Harker swivelled the object around so it was facing them and pointed out the three letters in turn. 'Only focus on the capitals, OK. That's an *I*, an *N*, then an *R*. Now, look closely, after the *X*, the wood has been cut away, so we're missing the last piece of the sentence.'

Lusic remained silent, not wanting to reveal his ignorance in front of the dean, who, was looking just as clueless as he felt. 'Are they initials?' Doggie ventured.

'No, they're the first letters of words, on a rectangular piece of pine wood, dating back to the era of Tiberius.' Harker said, trying to coax the answer.

A blank and frustrated look continued to hang about Tom Lercher's face.

'God, Doggie, you should know this! Especially considering the Rex part.'

Lusic raised his eyebrows sarcastically, at the dean's lack of knowledge, whilst surreptitiously trying not to get the question directed his way.

'Add on an *I* where the wood's been cut off, and you get INRI!' Harker eyed him encouragingly, but he could tell that his old friend still had no idea what he was talking about. Still, it did not stop the dean from appearing shocked and even mouthing the word *INRI* dramatically through his tight quivering lips as Harker explained further.

'When Jesus Christ was crucified on the hill of Golgotha, two items made him stand out from the other crucifixion victims that day. The first was the crown of thorns that a Roman soldier placed on his head and the other was a sign nailed to the foot of the cross which read,—Iesvs Nazarenvs Rex Ivdaeorvm—INRI—which in Latin translates as "Jesus of Nazareth the King of the Jews".' He looked down at the fragment of wood lying in his hands. 'The sign has been chopped in half at some point, but, two thousand years later, here it is.'

Lusic reached over and carefully took the relic into his own hands, bowing his head respectfully as he did so. 'Yes, I know of it, and keeping it out of the wrong hands now is all I'm concerned about.' The bulky German was beaming with pride. 'We'll be eternally honoured for this.'

He then passed the relic to Doggie, who took it in his arms and gently pressed it to his chest. As he lovingly gazed down at the engraved words, tears began to form in the corners of his eyes.

'Yes, we will, my German friend, but more importantly, we're going to make a bloody fortune!'

Chapter 31

Cardinal Rocca burst into his office at the Academy of Sciences with such force that the door handle struck the wall behind with a loud bang, making his waiting visitor jerk upright in his seat.

He glared over at Genges with a judgmental scowl before more calmly closing the door behind him and making his way over to the cherry-wood desk, ready to confront his younger brother. 'You already know that this day has been so very long in the making. Perhaps forty or fifty years,' Rocca began, settling into the leather-padded armchair and resting his hands on the wooden arms like a troubled monarch. 'Reflect on the time, the effort, the patience, not to forget the hundreds of millions of dollars we've invested in anticipation of this moment.'

Genges said nothing, fully aware of where this conversation was heading, as the cardinal rubbed his brow and let out a deep sigh of frustration.

'When that imbecile Archibald Dwyer stole those items rightfully belonging to the Magi, it almost ruined our plans, jeopardising the most significant event to occur in over two thousand years. So when I entrusted my own brothers with the crucial task of retrieving our property, I felt confident.' He stroked his chin bitterly. 'No, I felt certain that you would get things back on track. And now two weeks on, you are sitting here in front of me, and only one thought keeps running through my mind.' Rocca's nostrils flared, his whole body twitching. 'How did you two *idiots* manage to fuck everything up?'

Spittle flew from the cardinal's mouth as he actually shouted the words. 'I'm actually totally surprised you even dared to enter my office. And where the hell is Balthasar anyway?'

'He'll be joining us shortly,' Genges replied, not wanting to bring up the men's carelessness that Balthasar had mentioned earlier; his brother was furious enough. 'There have been many complications that could not have been anticipated.'

Rocca cut him off, 'Oh, yes, the ex-priest. A professor no less—quite the action hero that one.'

The sarcasm in Rocca's voice stirred a frisson of rage in Genges, and he struggled to maintain his temper, his jaw clenching ever tighter. 'He had help from Brulet whom—as I might I remind you, Cardinal—we disposed of earlier this evening.'

Rocca's face immediately calmed at this mention of the Grand Master of the Templars. 'And that's been your saving grace, Genges: the death of our enemy and the payment of a blood debt. It has undoubtedly landed a damaging blow on them. Well done! But I'm sure you can see that it does not help with our predicament, and I'm also sure you understand why I am so angry.'

The tension in Genges's face subsided, and he nodded shamefully. 'I know, and for that I'm truly sorry, but Balthasar should not have put so much faith in that idiot Heldon.'

Rocca settled back into his seat, somewhat chastened by his brother's comment.

'Yes, that was a definite mistake. Drazia is only truly useful when butchery or macabre violence is needed—scare tactics, but that's all. He should never have been entrusted with such an important task, and allowing himself to be caught by the British authorities is inexcusable. To use him at all was a bad call.'

'He would not have been my choice, that's for sure.'

Rocca greeted the statement with a dismissive flick of his hand. 'However, luckily for you, I have everything in hand, and our inside man is proving himself a most useful tool. As we speak, a plan has been set in motion to bring both relics back to us within the next few hours. So you need no longer feel quite so concerned.'

The cardinal sat back in his chair. 'Therefore, feel ashamed of your own failure, but take consolation in the thought that your brother is taking care of everything you yourself were unable to achieve.'

Genges forced a grudging smile. Apart from enduring the stream of criticism that Cardinal Rocca was dishing out, he was furious at having to change his own strategy at the last minute because of Heldon's failure. It meant his team going dark until after the main event, and he didn't like that one bit. To be out of contact for so long was dangerous, especially after the assault on Brulet's hideout following which every policeman in the area would be out searching for them. 'Then, if you have everything in hand, as you say, why did you request the presence of both myself and Balthasar here at the Vatican?'

A thin smile crossed Rocca's face as he let the question hang in the air, his expression challenging Genges to hazard a guess. When none was forthcoming, he shrugged his shoulders. 'My dear Brother, the reason is simple. I don't want either of you screwing things up any more than you already have.'

This response set Genges's jaw muscles tensing again, but he kept silent, his eyes never breaking contact as the cardinal stood up before making his way to the door.

'Now, Brother, follow me. For our destiny awaits us—and the birth of a new world order.'

Chapter 32

'This is not about personal glory, you garlic-stinking, Bavarian sausage-gobbling weirdo! This is about protecting two of the Christian faith's greatest relics.'

Tom Lercher sat back regally in his seat and watched the German digest this insult through taut lips. 'A find of this magnitude belongs in an institution worthy of it, and Cambridge University is one of the oldest and finest in the world.'

Lusic looked on with contempt as Doggie raised a forefinger towards the cabin ceiling and proclaimed, 'Good God, man, Cambridge produced Sir Isaac Newton, not to mention the very foundations of science itself!'

The Templar's lips puckered condescendingly. 'Oh, yes? And what has it done for the world lately?'

Doggie's reddening cheeks quivered, and his fingers whitened as he gripped the seat's leather armrest. 'My young German friend, if we're going to trade insults, then allow me to delve into my Nazi repertoire. I can assure you it won't disappoint.'

'I just don't get it!' Harker's unexpected remark brought their bickering to a sudden halt.

'What do you mean you don't get it? The man's a bloody Kraut!'

Harker ignored the dean's jibe and gently placed the vacuum-sealed bag containing the wooden artefact on to the table, patting it broodingly with his fingers. 'I mean why this relic? Look at the crown of thorns. It's a universally known treasure, cause for celebration, but this fragment . . .' His words trailed off, his gaze still fixed on the piece of wood. 'It just seems a bit, well . . .' He shrugged his shoulders. '. . . unworthy, don't you think?'

Doggie looked aghast. 'I'd hardly call it unworthy, Alex!'

Harker shook his head. 'The crown of thorns is a central feature in the account of Christ's demise. The Bible makes significant reference to it, but the sign INRI is barely mentioned. It's not integral to the story, just a footnote really.'

'It's still an important piece of history worth protecting,' Doggie insisted, as Lusic gave a nod of agreement. 'You see, even Lusic gets that!'

The Templar shrugged off this latest slight with a roll of his eyes, clearly not wishing to continue with the pointless bickering he had allowed himself to be drawn into earlier. Harker meanwhile picked up both relics and placed them on to the table side by side.

'Archie's message said that the Vatican had other items relating to Christ's life hidden away. In fact, he said there were so many that an entire team was set up to preserve and care for them. But he also said that these two relics were the most prized of all, and it seems to have been that way for decades.'

Doggie leant forward, a deep frown developing across his forehead. 'Sorry, old boy, but I'm not exactly sure I know where you're going with this?'

'Think about it, Tom.' Harker placed one hand on the sign and the other on the crown. 'If you had so many items pertaining to Jesus, which ones would you prize amongst all others?' He tapped both items questioningly. 'The crown of thorns? Without a doubt.' Harker now turned the focus of his attention to the dark fragment of two-thousand-year-old pinewood. 'But a sign put up by a Roman soldier with little mention in the story of Jesus related afterwards. It's just strange. If Archie was correct, then they must have possessed far more precious relics than this one, yet these *two* are the ones our opponents want most of all. Why?'

The other men's eyebrows rose simultaneously as this oddity finally became apparent to them.

Harker held the tight-fitting plastic container in his hands and carefully traced the lettering inside as if merely touching the relic would provide him with an answer. 'Lusic, you must know more about what's going on here than I could ever hope to. Feel like sharing?'

The bulky German sucked in a deep breath and sighed heavily. 'I'm sorry, Professor, but I was never made privy to the ultimate motives of the man I work for. Neither do I have any knowledge that would help provide an answer to your question.'

Harker stared deeply into the German's eyes, searching them for any hint of a lie. After ten years in the priesthood, he had grown rather good at spotting an untruth in a member of his congregation—a flicker of the eye, a dilation of the pupils, maybe a split-second loss of direct eye contact. They were all signs that a person was lying—not definitive proof, of course, but a good starting point. As he stared into the Templar's near black pupils, he saw nothing to suggest the man was any less confused than he was. 'No, I don't suppose you do.'

Lusic gave an unhappy grunt, glanced at his watch, and stood up. 'Well, if that's all you want to ask me, I'm going to check with the pilot to find out when we're due to arrive in Rome.' He disappeared into the cockpit, closing the door behind him with a distinctive slam.

'He's a bit of a baby really, isn't he, Alex?'

Harker gave his old friend a firm punch on the arm. 'Nazis! Honestly, Doggie, what a stupid thing for you to say.'

'My dear boy, if someone attacks me verbally—or physically—then I strike back.' He adopted a Churchillian pose and pointed a finger up to the ceiling. 'And I make no apology for striking back with vigour.' He held the pose for a moment before settling back into his seat with a smug grin.

'Yes, Doggie, you're quite the little soldier.'

The dean let out a grunt and sipped at his mini-can of slimline tonic water before delicately placing it down on the table with all the finesse and poise he could muster. 'I know you're being sarcastic, Alex, but you're right nonetheless. I'm a natural fighter, and I wish you'd stop calling me Doggie. Now I need to spend a penny, where's the loo?'

Harker pointed to a sealed-off section towards the back of the plane.

'Right, I'll be back in a moment.' Lercher rubbed his midriff uncomfortably and made his way towards the toilet door. 'In case I forget to tell you later, this is all terribly exciting. Thank you for involving me, Alex. It means a great deal to me, it really does.'

The comment brought a smile to Harker's face as he watched his old friend struggle with the toilet's safety lock. After all, it had never been his decision, for as usual, Doggie had involved himself.

Dean Lercher gave one last hard tug on the steel-panelled grey door, and, without warning, it flew open, throwing him back against the cabin wall. As he repositioned his glasses, the sight that appeared in front of him made him jump back quickly, smacking his head once more against the cabins interior. 'Oh, my God!'

Perched like a stuffed animal on top of the plastic toilet seat was the blood-soaked body of John Caster. His lifeless eyes were wide open and his hands tied with a cord to the disabled users' bar directly above, causing his head to loll grotesquely to one side. Underneath his chin, a deep knife wound ran from ear to ear, revealing the glistening white cartilage within. His tweed waistcoat was spattered red with drops of clotted blood originating from the thick gash in his throat, and it had also left trickles running down his neck which looked like roots burrowing themselves into the depths of his chest. Harker had to clamp his hand over his mouth to stop himself from gagging.

'Holy shit,' Doggie gasped, pulling out a white handkerchief from his top pocket and pressing it to his mouth as the nauseating, coppery smell of John Caster's blood assaulted the back of his throat. 'Lusic, you sick bastard.'

Harker reached over to the lawyer's limp body, and gently closed each of his eyes with one stroke of his palm. 'Rest in peace, John.' It wasn't much to offer, but it was the best Caster was going to get, given the circumstances.

'What are we going to do?'

The dean's voice was shrill, and Harker could tell Doggie was a few moments away from total panic. After all, the sight of blood was one of his friend's phobias.

A chill ran through Harker's body, knowing the murderous German was stronger than both of them put together, and, within the jet's compact interior, their options seemed limited. He tried to steady himself, as he attempted to determine the best course of action. 'OK, we're both going to play dumb,' he decided. Harker closed the toilet door and grasped his friend firmly by the shoulders. 'As long as we play along, Lusic's got no reason to do anything crazy. So we're going to sit back down and pretend everything's normal. Then, once we've landed, we'll alert the police, understood?'

Doggie stared back at him blankly, his left cheek twitching wildly.

'That's going to be a difficult one to pull off,' a voice intruded.

Harker felt the solid tip of a gun barrel jab into his upper back, and he turned his head to see the stern and unyielding face of the murderous Templar directly behind him.

'No games now, Professor.' Lusic gestured with the gun towards the front of the cabin. 'Take a seat, both of you.' He then reached over and retrieved both relics from the table, placing them one by one into a dark brown leather satchel. 'I must thank you both.' He patted the bag. 'You've made my job exceedingly easy.' The German tipped an imaginary hat politely and smiled. 'But don't beat yourself up. Considering tonight's events, there was no way you could have known who to trust.'

'What did it take for you to sell out your own brotherhood to the Magi?' Snarled Harker, his voice shaking with anger.

Lusic scowled at the remark. 'Brotherhood! The Templars aren't a brotherhood, they're nothing more than a self-serving organisation that's had its day. And with these two relics, I'm helping to land the fatal blow.'

Behind him, Doggie mumbled in surprise on hearing mention of the word *Templar*.

'So you sold out your own people to a bunch of zealot murderers and assassins?' Harker continued, barely managing to contain the fury he was feeling.

'You speak like a man of conviction, Professor Harker, but you're nothing more than a failed priest who stumbled into today's events by chance, simply because you were a friend of Archie Dwyer. You don't even have the faintest idea what these relics are intended for, do you?'

'So why don't you illuminate me?'

Lusic let out a sarcastic laugh. 'I don't think so, but, I will tell you this much: these relics will provide the stepping stone for the rebirth of the Catholic Church.' His eyes widened into an ecstatic gaze as only a true believer can achieve. 'And then a new religious order will emerge with the Magi positioned at its side.' A broad grin spread across the German's features. 'And our first order of business will be to put the Knights Templars out of their misery once and for all.'

To Harker, the look consuming the disloyal Templar's face could easily be mistaken for one of insanity, but he had seen that expression many times before. It was the look of a fanatic, which meant that trying reason or logic would prove a total waste of time. 'So what now? You shoot us here and risk depressurising the cabin. That way, you'll kill us all.'

Lusic shook his head. 'No, nothing quite like that.' He unzipped his thick leather jacket to reveal a parachute harness underneath and then, with one hand, stuffed the handgun into his trouser pocket before grabbing the emergency-exit handle with his other.

'Thank you for the help, gentlemen, but your journey ends here.' He shot a wink in Dean Lercher's direction. 'Next time I'm in Cambridge, I'll stop by and send them your regards, you arrogant prick.' With that, he twisted the handle around ninety degrees, and, with a deafening bang, it disappeared off into the cold, black night air, along with Lusic still attached to it. In an instant, the entire cabin became a freezing whirlwind of chaos, and both Harker and Doggie found themselves clinging to their seats as the cabin pressure was mercilessly sucked outside with a high-pitched whine.

As the aisle lights flickered and debris swirled around the jet's interior, only one thought popped into Harker's mind, and it wasn't for himself or Doggie or even the fear of death itself. It was just a single reflection that squeezed out any other thoughts from his mind.

'I'm sorry, Claire. I'm so sorry.'

Chapter 33

A burning ice-cold wind seared Harker's face as the air continued to escape from the jet's cabin, and his tear-filled eyes struggled to make out his surroundings. Just to his left, he caught snapshot images of Doggie also clinging to his seat for dear life, his tweed jacket flapping uncontrollably as the cabin floor lights continued to flicker erratically.

Within seconds, the roaring of the wind subsided as the cabin air pressure equalised, and it was replaced with a high-pitched whine from the aircraft's engines, struggling to counterbalance the drag from the open exit hatch.

Harker's heart beat heavily in his ears as he mustered all his strength to overcome the sheer dread he was now feeling, attempting to focus on his next move. Overhead, the oxygen masks, with their telltale yellow plastic mouth pieces, were whipping back and forth, slapping painfully against his head and then the cabin ceiling. The good news was that he hadn't passed out yet due to lack of oxygen, which meant the plane must be at a low altitude, but it also meant they were closer to hitting the ground. He had to reach the cockpit.

Harker grabbed the safety belt and began to drag himself from one seat to the next, each passing second seeming like a lifetime as a suffocating sense of urgency tugged at his lungs. He heaved himself forward until he was opposite the cabin exit, which looked like some swirling black vortex mercilessly consuming anything not bolted down, out into the night air. The terror Harker was feeling came close to paralysing his muscles as he imagined the horrendous sensation of disappearing through it and falling thousands of feet through the pitch-darkness to his death.

Ignore it, Harker. Just focus. You must focus.

He finally forced his arm towards the next seat belt and continued to pull himself forward, each step painfully testing his ever-stiffing muscles as he fought the fear vying for control of his body.

After a few more such efforts, he reached the cockpit door and searched for the handle, his eyes aching from the wind. Seconds later, he had a hand clasped around it and, with one forceful twist, pushed it open. A pocket of turbulence caused the jet to drop suddenly, the force almost knocking him backwards towards the open exit, but he clung on to the handle, pulling himself inside and up to one of the pilot's seats only to find himself staring into the dead lifeless eyes of the aircraft's captain. The flashing green lights of the dashboard grotesquely illuminated the deep dark knife wound that ran from ear to ear, and Harker imagined Lusic catching the young pilot unaware with the same brutality he had shown to John Caster.

He was still flinching from the gruesome sight when the plane hit another pocket of turbulence, which, this time, threw him sideways into the adjoining seat. He instinctively grabbed the yoke with both hands before trying to level the plane out. The resistance he felt in the wings confirmed what he already knew. The jet was struggling to stay aloft, and the open exit was pulling them into a stall.

Harker scanned the glowing instruments in front of him in search of the altimeter, finally finding it just beneath the artificial horizon. It read: *Four thousand feet.*

Below it, the automatic pilot glowed brightly. The treacherous Templar had wisely not been prepared to take a chance on the aircraft, making a sudden dive before he could parachute himself to safety. Harker gritted his teeth in anger at the thought of the back-stabbing bastard, swearing silently that, if he survived this, he'd be paying the German a visit.

From behind, a hand firmly clamped down on to his shoulder, and he spun around to see the deathly white face of Tom Lercher staring at him through squinting eyes.

'Jesus fucking Christ.' The dean's voice was barely audible over the whirring of the jet engines.

'Close it, Doggie,' he yelled, gesturing to the flapping grey cockpit door, but his old friend now seemed frozen to the spot. After a few more seconds of pointing and swearing, Doggie finally let go of Harker's shoulder and slammed the door shut with his foot. Both men felt their ears pop as the closing of the door produced some stability in pressure. All around them sheets of paperwork torn from the captain's flight bag began floating down to the floor, and once again, the drone of the jets became bearable.

Harker reached over to the seat next to him, undid the safety belt, and pulled the dead captain to the cockpits' walkway with a thud. 'Doggie, sit down and get yourself strapped in,' he instructed, surprised at how controlled his voice was sounding. As the dean fastened his belt, Harker felt a renewed sense of confidence flow through his body. He reached down to his side and pulled a map off the captain's thigh pad, and then passed it to Doggie who merely nodded in a daze whilst clutching it to his chest.

'We need to find a suitable place to touch down!'

Doggie's head bobbed back and forth, his face getting ever paler. 'Can you do that?' he croaked.

Harker nodded back at him without hesitation. 'Yes I can, we just need to find a place to land.' He wasn't even sure it was possible, but what other choice did they have?

'Keep an eye on this.' He pressed his finger to the altimeter. 'This indicates our altitude in feet. As we get lower, I want you to shout out our height.' Harker raised three fingers and counted down, 'Three thousand, two thousand, one thousand—and then every two hundred feet. Got it?'

Doggie nodded as a solitary teardrop trickled from the corner of his eye. 'I don't want to die, Alex.'

The remark provoked a powerful surge of anger deep down in Harker's chest, fuelling his determination further. 'Neither do I.' He snarled and gripped his friend's arm firmly. 'We're not going to fucking die, Doggie. Do you understand? Now concentrate on our height.'

With a shaky nod, Doggie returned his attention to the white dial which continued to fall rapidly. It was something that Harker was all too aware of, even though they seemed to be flying straight and level.

The drag created by the blown emergency hatch was slowing their air speed. The plane itself was slowing down, and if they stayed at this angle of flight any longer, they would eventually stall and drop like a stone, and there was nothing he could do to prevent that. They were only going to get one chance at landing, so every move had to flow perfectly.

Harker glanced over at the large, well-lit GPS display and noted their current position. He then pulled the map from the dean's hands and laid it across his lap before tracing these two coordinates to their exact location.

'Three thousand feet,' Doggie hollered, the fear in his voice barely contained.

Harker didn't reply, keeping his attention fixed solely on the flight map. Rome Airport was only eighteen miles away, but, at their current trajectory, they would hit the ground within five. Lusic had timed his departure well, that was for sure, because down below them was nothing but dense forest in all directions. Harker scrutinized the map but he couldn't locate anywhere that would suffice as a landing strip. It was then that he noticed a large blue circular area labelled with the name Bracciano, just four miles from their present position. The sight of it inspired an unnerving mixture of fear and relief in Harker's chest as he recalled the name. Bracciano was a vast lake occupying the crater of a volcano that had ceased erupting over forty thousand years ago. Situated in the province of Lazio, it had become a major tourist attraction in recent years. The massive crater had long since filled with rain water, creating the second largest lake in the country with a surface area of about fifty miles and a maximum depth of well over a hundred metres. It now provided most of Rome's drinking water ever since a filtration plant had been constructed during the early '70s to counteract the use of it by people as a dumping zone for their raw sewage. The only reason Harker knew so much about this lake was because he had once taken a tour here whilst still studying at the Vatican years earlier.

A warm glow began to spread inside his stomach. It was still a long shot, but at least now they had an option. Landing on water had maybe a 30 per cent chance of success, but, compared to a forest which was certain death, those odds suddenly looked pretty damn attractive.

'Two thousand feet.' Doggie's voice was getting even jumpier, and he was visibly shaking. 'Alex, what are we doing?'

'There's a lake down below. It's our best chance. We're going to slow down close to stalling speed, keep our landing gear up, and skip across the surface like a seaplane.' This idea didn't get the response he had hoped for as the dean's face turned an even paler shade of white.

'Oh shit, is that even possible?'

'Not only is it possible, Doggie, it's doable, but there's just one problem.'

The Cambridge dean raised both eyebrows in surprise. 'Just one?'

Harker mustered the best smile he could. 'It means we're going to have to take a swim, and I know how much you hate swimming.'

The beginnings of a grin began to emerge from his old friend, replacing some of the panic.

'Actually, swimming doesn't seem so bad, Alex. Just get us down safe, OK?'

'OK, let's take a dip.'

Down below, lights were becoming visible as the jet broke through the cloud layer, and Harker almost yelled out in joy as the dark foreboding outline of Lake Bracciano came into view. They had passed below the clouds at just the right moment and were now squarely lined up with the two-mile stretch of water.

'One thousand feet.'

Harker initiated the first stage of the aircraft's flaps, causing the entire cabin frame to judder wildly as it continued to lose speed.

'Eight hundred feet.'

'Make sure you're strapped in securely, Doggie.'

The dean gave a hard tug on his belt, his eyes locked on the altimeter. 'Six hundred feet.'

Harker pulled back on his second stage of flaps, the whole aircraft now shaking more violently still as their air speed dropped further.

'Four hundred feet.'

The jet hurtled past half a dozen well-lit tourist boats lining the shoreline with such ferocity that he could have sworn he saw someone fall overboard in shock.

'Two hundred feet.'

Harker remained silent, continuing to wrestle with the yoke, attempting to keep the wings parallel with the water-line. It seemed a battle he was winning when Doggie called out: 'One hundred feet. Good luck!'

Suddenly everything went into slow motion as Harker's thought processes disengaged, and his core instincts took over. When landing a plane, such instinct is everything. It involves a feel for the controls, a feel for the speed and the external forces. But, most importantly, a feel for the resistance of air pushing up against the wing, giving the aircraft sufficient lift and allowing the controls to ride that same resistance, allowing you to glide safely to the surface below.

The only problem being that it was near impossible to glide a jet comfortably in to land. They were just too heavy, so you had to keep up the speed, but that meant hitting the water harder. It was a balancing act like walking a tightrope but blindfolded and with only one's senses to guide you. Couple this with the fact that when an object impacts with water at more than 60 mph, it's like hitting concrete and makes for one hell of a rough touchdown.

Harker smiled as he remembered his flight instructor's parting words of wisdom just before he had attempted his first solo flight at Biggin Hill. 'And as for luck, Alex, there's no such thing. In this world, it's up to us to make our own luck.'

An intensely violent jolt rippled through the entire craft as the jets underbelly connected with the lake's surface, sending deafening sounds of scraping and twisting metal reverberating throughout the cockpit. For a moment, the g-force was almost unbearable, both men feeling their eyes coming close to literally popping from the sockets. The entire plane rose up on its back, virtually flipping over, before finally crashing downwards on to its underbelly with a backbreaking wallop. The seat harness tightened itself around Harker's chest to the point of crushing him, and then everything went black.

Chapter 34

'Damn it!' Father Reed murmured as the lock clicked back into place with a now all-too-familiar clink. Since his talk three hours earlier with Cardinal Rocca, he had been attempting to pick the lock on his cell door, and he was still getting no closer.

'Damn, he was rusty!'

Reed glanced instinctively down at his wrist, only to find a white band of untanned skin where his watch strap used to be. Apparently, Cardinal Rocca had added petty theft to his ever-increasing list of criminal activities. Reed was finding it hard to accept just how crooked the senior cleric had evidently become. He had never known a man of the cloth go rogue, and the thought made him laugh. He had heard of rogue marines, rogue cops, even rogue politicians, but a rogue priest! The image of a muscle-laden Rambo-type with a lopsided dog collar elicited a deep chuckle. It was totally inappropriate, given the circumstances, but humour was the only thing keeping him going at this point.

Reed inserted the strip of metal back into the lock and began manoeuvring it again. It had taken him about forty-five minutes to shape the lock pick, fashioned from one of the bed springs, and, so far, that had been the easy part. When it came to picking locks, the older varieties were easy, but these newer, more resilient, devices were tough.

The cell lock clicked back into place yet again, whilst his home-made key slipped from his hand and fell to the floor. 'Shit!' If he ever managed to get out of this place, he'd resolved himself to spend the next couple of weeks saying Hail Marys.

He picked up the fragment of metal and started over again. If anyone had ever told him that his early lessons in lock picking would serve him well as a man of God, he'd have thought them crazy, but then again, he had never envisaged becoming a priest.

Reed wasn't sure where he was born exactly, but it was in a Texas orphanage outside Dallas that he'd been brought up. All he knew was that his birth mother had become pregnant with him as a teenager and had placed him in care, unable to cope with the responsibility.

Responsibility? The word made him ponder. In the past, he'd always imagined himself an inconvenient burden to her lifestyle, and that had been the reason she'd discarded him. But the simple truth, on reflection, was that a young girl with no family and no experience of life and fearful of the future had faced limited options in the 1950s. As time passed, he was able to forgive her for what had seemed like an extremely personal rejection, like taking offence at his very existence. As a result of his neglected childhood, the young Father Reed had turned into a considerable hellraiser, and, by the age of eighteen, the judicial system was beginning to take notice. At fifteen, he was boosting cars and selling them to chop shops. By seventeen, he was an enforcer for a local gang, ensuring that all the neighbourhood businesses paid their weekly insurance. That is if they didn't want their shops burnt down. By eighteen, he was into everything from running numbers to loan sharking. And that's when his crooked little empire came tumbling down.

A rival from another gang had ties within the local police department and, on seeing how well the eighteen-year-old was doing, had decided to take it all for himself. Reed had wound up with a ten-year sentence for racketeering, though it turned out to be the best thing that could have happened to him. The judge presiding over the case had recognised something in the young man standing in the dock, 'a glimmer of hope' as he had put it, and Reed was offered an alternative to jail—the United States Marines.

The idea had seemed crazy at first, but then, after a month behind bars, Reed had a change of heart. Jail was not a place he would ever get used to, and one week later, he found himself in sunny Wyoming, decked out in army fatigues whilst being verbally abused by a hard-nosed drill instructor. It was a move that had changed his life.

In the Marines, he'd found a family and the sense of belonging he had always craved. After eight weeks of basic training, he was fighting communists in Vietnam and, within months of that, was offered a position in the Special Forces, sniper division. The next seventeen years saw him deployed all over the world, from Cambodia to Somalia, and Reed had relished every moment.

His comrades in arms were a mixed bunch: some loved the action, others simply loved to kill, but most were just proud to serve their country. Not him, though. For Reed, it was about doing the right thing, the good had to be safeguarded from the bad, and, to those that deserved it, he offered what his mother had never given him—*protection.*

These were the principles that had guided him through the years, and they served him well until his deployment to Bosnia in '93. The Serbian government under Slobodan Milosevic had set about systematically murdering every Muslim in the country in an operation ominously labelled as ethnic cleansing. It was Reed's first posting to the country, and, even though the war was coming to a close, there were still numerous pockets of militant Serbs furious at the West's intervention. His unit had been tasked with pacifying a company of twenty Serbian soldiers that had gone AWOL. The group had been terrorising villages in north Bosnia for months, raping or murdering every Muslim they found—and all in the name of Christian purity. In one case, they'd even cut off some kid's balls and then forced him to perform fellatio on the pet dog—really sick stuff.

The troop was led by a malevolent one-eyed ex-special force's captain named Vladimir Ivenco, or, as the locals had named him, the Cyclops of Death. The only thing that seemed special about this guy was that he had his genitals blown off during a skirmish with British forces years earlier. Unable to enjoy the finer things in life, Ivenco had taken to debasement and torture as a way of satisfying his urges and feelings of resentment—a true sadist in every sense of the word.

Two United Nation units had already been sent to bring him in, but he and his vile gang were always one step ahead. There was talk amongst Reed's unit that someone inside the UN was tipping the group off, but it was never proved, and, after three months of failed ambushes by the UN peacekeepers, many were starting to believe they would never get rid of him. As one UN commander had so elegantly put it, 'With the tracking equipment we have, this bastard should be easier to nail than a Bangkok hooker. So what the fuck is going on?'

Two days later, Reed and his team had been assigned and were already deep inside Bosnian territory. It took just under two weeks to catch up with the group of renegades, simply following the carnage from one village to the next. They had massacred hundreds of villagers in ways that, even to this day, he still found hard to accept. Reed's unit eventually caught up with them in a small village, near the town of Travnik, where the murderous soldiers had been camped outside its church all morning. About forty residents were holed up inside, and its priest, Father Zivota, had been trying to negotiate with the Serbian leader for a peaceful solution. The village was 90 per cent Muslim, but the priest had made no distinction when it came to saving human lives, and this was the first time the Serbs had attacked a Catholic church for by now most of the soldiers were becoming indifferent to the idea of killing Muslims and Christians alike.

Zivota had kept these animals at bay for over six hours with nothing but his dog collar and words to combat twenty armed men with assault rifles, grenades, and the experience to use them, yet he had held the attackers off. When Reed's unit arrived, it wasn't a moment too soon because the Cyclops of Death had reached the end of his patience, and it was just a matter of minutes before the situation turned into a bloodbath. What had impressed Reed most was how this little man, no more than five feet tall, had held the brutes off for so long, even slapping the Serbian captain across his face and berating him for such treatment of his fellow man. Honestly, it was the bravest thing Reed had ever witnessed, this ability to hold off total carnage by just the power of belief and conviction. For the first time in his life, he had realised that you didn't have to carry a gun in order to prevail and that anything was possible with God by your side.

He and his unit had taken down every one of the Serbians in under fifteen seconds, and all the villagers had survived. That single event had changed Reed's thinking for good, and once back on US soil, he had resigned his commission in order to join the clergy. That was twenty years ago, and he'd never regretted his decision even once, saving more lives with faith and words than he had ever succeeded in doing so at the end of a gun barrel.

With one last flick of his wrist, the cell door made a metallic click and gently swung open. 'Thank the Lord for unsavoury skills,' he whispered, gratified by his achievement. Another couple of tries, and he would have given up for sure. Reed made for the exit door further along the corridor, and finding, to his relief, that there was no lock, he pressed his ear up against its cold, steel surface and listened. After a few seconds of silence, and satisfied there wasn't an ambush waiting for him on the other side, he quietly opened the door and headed on into the gloom. The room he now found himself in was almost pitch-dark except for a solitary light suspended from the ceiling, illuminating everything within its reach with an eerie orange glow. Reed's gaze travelled around the room, finally settling on the silhouette of a side lamp perched on top of a table just a few feet away. He made his way over and, after some fumbling, located the switch. The intense brightness from the small halogen bulb made him recoil for a moment, his vision suffused with red spots.

Despite the bare stonewalls, the room was furnished rather cosily with thick, navy-blue Saxony carpets throughout, and a handsome oval conference table about eighteen feet long surrounded by costly-looking wooden chairs with white satin coverings. At the head of the table, a red leather Victorian spoon-back chair stood imposingly, and behind it, two steel doors had been set into the stonework. To his right, a massive wooden noticeboard covered the entire upper half of the wall, giving the room a classroom feel, and although it was now void of any notices, he could see signs of it having been in use.

'What are you up to, Rocca?' Reed muttered as he made his way over to the nearest bookshelf and thumbed through the wide array of titles. The books on this shelf ranged from atlases to hotel guides, all except one. It was a thick, leather-backed personal notepad with the name Dr M. Sephris, DDS, gilded on to the cover in silver lettering. Reed flicked through the pages only to find them empty, and although the name meant nothing, he recognised the initials. He'd seen them often when visiting the Vatican's dentist.

DDS stood for doctor of dental surgery.

Why would Cardinal Rocca have need of a dentist down here?

An unsettling thought entered his mind as he recalled the Dustin Hoffman film *Marathon Man*, one of whose characters was an ex-Nazi dentist played with terrifying realism by the late, great Laurence Olivier. His character had worked in the concentration camps during the World War II and many years later had begun to ply his trade of oral torture once more whilst involved in a quest for stolen diamonds smuggled out of Germany. The film had given him nightmares as a kid, and the thought of a sociopathic dentist operating down here in this sinister place made him uneasy, to say the least.

Reed took a deep breath to calm his nerves and told himself how ridiculous he was being. Whatever was going on here, it had nothing to do with a crazed oral-hygiene specialist brandishing a dental syringe and mouth mirror. No, this was something else altogether. Something worse.

Along the sides of the room, every metre or so, were glass-fronted refrigerators containing a variety of food and drinks. Reed swung open the door of the nearest one and selected a small carton of orange juice. He'd had nothing drink since just before meeting Cardinal Vincenzo and was now severely parched. Tearing open the top, he downed the contents in one go and then placed the empty carton back in the fridge. The sugar rush gave him a new clarity of thought, and his curiosity was replaced with an immediate sense of urgency.

I need to get out of here now.

As Reed began making his way towards the nearest exit, the four strip lights above him suddenly flickered into life and footsteps could be heard on the other side of the door. Without hesitation, he dived under the stout conference table, dragging his robe with him and out of sight. Seconds later, the door opened, and two men entered, immersed in conversation. Although Reed could only see them from the waist down, he recognised one of the voices immediately. It was Cardinal Rocca.

'We are ready to move at a moment's notice, and once we have the relics, there's no obstacles left in our way. It will be time to give back to the world what has been denied it for so long. Now watch this.'

The sound of grinding gears resonated through the room, making the floor vibrate heavily, and Reed peered up to see the noticeboard covering the wall opposite slowly rising into a slot in the ceiling above. The screen disappeared entirely, revealing a plate-glass window of equal dimensions.

'Well, Genges, what do you think?'

The Magi prince offered a satisfied grunt. 'My men did a fine job here, eh? It's good to finally see the results of two months' secret construction.'

Cardinal Rocca raised a thin slender finger. '*Our* men, dear Brother.'

The younger sibling gave a submissive nod. 'Yes, of course. Now, please allow me to inspect the fruits of our toil.'

Rocca gave a brief nod and disappeared into the room beyond, followed closely by Genges. Reed pulled himself out from under the table and peaked through the glass observation window. The room beyond was similar to a private hospital suite, with grey carpets, magnolia walls, and a host of flashing monitors he wasn't familiar with. Over to one side, a waist-high wall jutted out, concealing something. Whatever it was, both men were now staring down at it intently.

Reed quietly made his way to the far end of the window, eager to see the object of the men's intense scrutiny, but it was impossible without getting too close for comfort. Regardless, Reed had seen enough. He slid back under the conference table and was slowly beginning to make his way over towards the other door, when a voice called out from behind him.

'So you must be the ex-Marine my brother told me about. You're not very stealthy, are you?'

Reed looked up to find the barrel of a 16 mm Beretta aimed directly at his forehead.

'You're a bad lad, breaking out of your cell, tsk, tsk,' Genges mocked sarcastically, cocking the gun with his thumb. 'What are we going to do with you, I wonder?'

Reed crawled out from under the table and stood up, holding his arms high, before noticing on the younger brother's face the same manic look that he had already seen on Cardinal Rocca's earlier. *Damn*, he thought, *how many of these crazies are there?*

Genges nodded towards the door leading back to the empty cell. 'C'mon, there's a good boy.'

Reed did all he could to quell the sense of despair overwhelming him, but only one positive thought came to mind: *At least there's no sign of a dentist!*

Chapter 35

'Alex, can you hear me?'

Harker jerked his head fiercely upwards, but the pain in his chest immediately forced him back down again.

'Take it easy, my boy. You're safe and sound.'

He rubbed at the swelling on his temple and winced. Everything was still a bit hazy, and he couldn't quite remember where he was or, for that matter, why his clothes were drenched. But he did recognise the face hovering above him. 'Doggie?'

Dean Lercher knelt beside him, also dripping wet from head to toe but with a wide smile on his lips. He let out a deep sigh of relief, loosening the soggy red tie around his neck. 'Thank God! For a moment there, I didn't think you were ever going to wake up.'

Harker raised his head, more gently this time, and glanced down at his chest, which was aching more with every passing moment. His white Oxford shirt had been ripped open, and, across his torso, a thick black bruise was developing nicely in the shape of a seat belt. 'Damn, what a mess!' He tried grasping Doggie by the arm, but his hand remained floppy and unresponsive, slipping instead back down to his side. 'What happened?'

247

'You saved both of us. Hellish close thing, my friend, but we made it.' He gestured to a group of motor boats that were frantically circling the still sinking tail section of the Templar's jet. 'Although the plane is a definite write-off.'

Suddenly, everything came flooding back to Harker in one painful flash: the plane journey, Lusic, the crash landing, and, with it, an enormous sense of relief. 'I crash an aircraft better than anyone I know.'

The dean let out a deep bellow of laughter. 'That you do, my friend. That you do.'

For the first time since coming round, Harker suddenly became aware of the shocked-looking group of people, all dressed in expensive designer clothing, who were jostling to get a better view of the spectacle unfolding. 'Where exactly are we?'

'You were knocked unconscious during the crash,' Doggie explained, briefly glancing over his shoulder at an inquisitive group of onlookers and offering them a courteous wave, 'but I managed to drag you out before the jet sank, and then I paddled water until this tourist boat showed up. By the time I'd got us clear of the sinking fuselage, the boat was already waiting to haul us on-board. We were only in the water for a matter of minutes.'

'It sounds like I should be thanking you,' Harker offered as the dean donned the proud expression of a yeoman.

'Well, yes, you could say I played my part in this rather incredible adventure.' He paused and leant in closer, looking slightly embarrassed. 'But when we regale people with our heroic story, let's miss out the part where I cry like a baby.'

Harker shot him a wink. 'It's funny, but I don't remember that bit. Now help me up, will you?'

Doggie nodded appreciatively and gently pulled Harker to his feet, not letting go until his woozy friend had steadied himself against the side rail.

'Take it easy, Alex. You took one heck of a bump to the head—and that's the second time in the space of a few hours. You're lucky to be standing upright at all.'

Harker patted his friend's shoulder reassuringly and turned to gaze out across the calm, black waters of Lake Bracciano. The lights of the various villages surrounding the massive inactive volcano were brighter than any of the many thousands of stars hanging in the night's sky overhead, and he found himself gasping at such simplistic beauty. *Thank God for those*, he thought, *for no villages meant no boats*, and without a rescue, they could have easily drowned. Doggie was a terrible swimmer at the best of times, and frankly he was amazed that his old friend had managed to get out of the sinking plane by himself, let alone with Harker in tow.

Harker remained at the side rail, taking another moment to appreciate still being alive before surveying the vessel that had helped make it so. The boat they stood on was actually more of a ship: over one hundred feet long, with two huge internal engines spewing out thick jets of water that were now propelling them speedily towards the shore. The chipped paintwork and yellowing perspex betrayed the vessel's age, but to Harker, she was the most beautiful thing he had ever seen.

As he watched its thick foamy wake ripple out across the glistening waters of Lake Bracciano, apart from the pain in his head, there was only one thought on his mind, and it weighed heavily. *Where were the relics?* The Magi now had them both, the only bargaining chips he had for Claire's life, and without them, well, the thought was too troubling to contemplate, and he tried to push it from his mind. 'I'm sorry, Claire, but I've failed both you and Archie,' he whispered to himself, the pain of his failure far worse than anything his battered body was serving up.

'Mr Harker, you're awake and standing! Excellent.'

The voice behind him bellowed with such ferocity that Harker almost tumbled over the side rail in surprise. He swivelled around to see a swarthy olive-skinned man wearing a well-worn, white naval jacket with a gold-crested hat perched coolly upon a nest of dazzling white hair.

'The gods are smiling down on you today, eh?' The captain's husky voice was, no doubt, a result of smoking too many cigars similar to the one currently dangling between his forefingers.

Harker nodded graciously. 'Anything for a good story.'

The quip brought a smile to the Italian's lips. 'And you still have your sense of humour. Very admirable, very British. Allow me to introduce myself. My name is Sergio Anatoly.'

Harker shook the captain's hand with a wince, his muscles beginning to ache. 'It's a pleasure, Captain, and thank you for picking us up.'

'Not at all. As I was telling your friend, Mr Lercher, I'm just glad to have been a part of this.' Anatoly licked his lips, searching for the right words. 'This death-defying miracle.'

Harker noticed Doggie raise his eyebrows comically. Captain Anatoly indeed seemed excited by this evening's events—perhaps a little too much excited.

'Here, we must keep you warm, eh. We don't want you dying of pneumonia so soon after you've cheated death.' He leant over and draped a bright yellow beach towel around Harker's shoulders, which had the words ANATOLY'S PARTY CRUISE. BOP TILL YOU DROP tailored across it. 'And you too, Mr Lercher.' The enthusiastic captain said, passing an equally colourful one to the dean. 'Now, both of you, please come sit down and relax.'

He ushered them both to a wooden bench situated in the middle of the deck, firmly pushing away some of the gawking passengers who were continuing to hover. Anatoly took a quick glance round at his paying customers, and then with a roll of his eyes, he leant forwards so only his two new best friends could hear.

'You're lucky you arrived when you did, otherwise in a few more hours, my clientele would have all been pissed out of their minds. Booze hounds the lot of them,' he shrugged his shoulders acceptingly 'but they're my bread and butter, so maybe I shouldn't complain.'

As Harker and Doggie settled themselves on the bench, Captain Anatoly's demeanour became more serious.

'As I was telling, Mr Lercher, I've contacted the police and they should be here shortly, so you'll be in good hands.' He straightened his cap importantly. 'Also I believe the press have been alerted to this evening's events. They may want to talk with the two survivors, but I'd gladly offer to speak on your behalf if you're not feeling up to it?'

Harker threw Doggie a knowing glance. Clearly, the party-boat captain wasn't one to miss an opportunity for self-promotion. 'That would be *so* helpful, Captain, thank you.' He hadn't meant to sound sarcastic, but it just came out that way. Luckily, the Captain was far too absorbed in thoughts of his upcoming interview that he completely missed it.

'So then . . .' Anatoly pulled a small pad and pencil from his top pocket and surveyed them both with all the poise of a journalist. 'What were the series of incredible events that drew you to the safety of Anatoly's party boat then?'

Chapter 36

The worn floorboards of interrogation room 1A squeaked loudly under Superintendent Rino Perone's weight as he sat down opposite the young man he had arrested earlier at the Monte Mario observatory. Next to him, Detective Angelo Barbosa shifted in his seat, the cheap plastic chair proving less comfortable than it looked.

'OK . . .' The superintendent took another long drag on his cigar and blew it across the interview table towards his suspect, who was securely cuffed to a pair of steel ringlets on either side of his chair. 'Let's try this again.'

The interrogation had been rattling on for over two hours by now, almost three if you included the time it took for Perone to get back from hospital where the on-call doctor had attempted to keep him in overnight. The policeman had laughed right in the young medical practitioner's face. Like that was going to happen when bodies were turning up faster in one night than was usual for an entire month. He had needed sixteen stitches for the wound in his biceps—a personal record—before heading back to join the interrogation where Angelo had been having about as much luck as he himself was having now. In all those hours, the suspect hadn't said a word, hell he had hardly moved an inch, his stare unflinching and constantly fixed on the table throughout. This kid was either very tough or totally fucking retarded. Whichever the case, he wasn't talking.

'You're due to be charged with the kidnapping and attempted murder of a police officer. You're also a suspect in the homicide of six people and a string of other offences including resisting arrest. My young friend, you're racking up years in prison as if they were loyalty-card points.' He took another drag on his cigar but, this time, blew it courteously towards the air-vent above. 'You're set to end up doing the hardest time there is and, seeing as you look too young to have ever spent much time in a correctional facility, allow me to enlighten you to the predicament you'll find yourself in.'

Perone stubbed out his cigar in the makeshift ashtray, much to the relief of Angelo who had been throwing irritated glances his way ever since he'd first lit up in the strictly non-smoking interrogation suite.

'For the first few days, you'll be getting used to spending the rest of your life in an eight-by-nine cell. Then, just when you beginning to get settled in, the wolves will come a knocking because all animals need companionship, and, in prison, the inmates get lonely, real lonely. Some of them know they'll probably never even see a woman again, let alone be with one. And that's where you come in: young, supple-skinned, and looking all fresh.' Perone rubbed his chin and winced painfully. 'Usually, the first time round, a bunch of muscle heads will run a *train* on you. They'll just line up outside your cell, all wanting to welcome you to the neighbourhood. Afterwards, your poor little sphincter's gonna feel like someone's pried it open with a fucking crowbar. A few more years of the good life, and you'll be able to crack off the biggest fart you can, and kiddo, no one will hear a goddamn thing. It'll just sound like you're letting out a deep sigh.'

The superintendent placed his elbows firmly on the table and cradled his head in both hands, offering a genuine look of sympathy. 'I'm not trying to scare you. I mean, no one likes the thought of having their arsehole ripped to the size of an exhaust pipe. I'm simply trying to let you know what to expect, for if you don't start playing ball "what will be, will be", and I'd rather not see a young lad like you go down that road. *Capisce?*'

Perone's robust description even had Angelo clenching his bum cheeks, but the young Magi associate said nothing. No words, no movement, no eye contact . . . nothing. He just continued to stare downwards as he had been trained to do.

This was one tough kid!

The interrogation room was getting pretty rank with the potent stink of sweat and body odour, so Perone got up and opened the interview room's door, swinging it back and forth a few times to circulate the air before slamming it shut again.

'Well, kid, get used to that sweet aroma of sweaty men because that's what you're in for.' He reached into his pocket, pulled out a couple of painkillers, and gulped them down. The doctor had prescribed them for the ache in his arm where the stitches were getting uncomfortably tighter as the skin began its healing process. He took another sip from the white Styrofoam cup resting on the table, the coffee inside it cold and unpleasant. Perone wasn't sure what was proving more painful—the wound in his arm or the lack of any response from this Lupis character. Back at the observatory, Angelo had overheard one of his kidnappers refer to him as Associate Lupis, whatever the hell that meant? At first, he had assumed they were part of some weird cult, but, after three hours of hard but useless interrogation, he was starting to think differently.

'Was this youngster ex-military?' It was hard to believe so since he looked no older than seventeen, just a boy. But the way he carried himself suggested otherwise.

'You ever served in the forces, Lupis?' Perone said, finally sitting back down at the table. 'I find it pretty hard to believe that because you barely look old enough to have fluff on your balls, let alone military training.' He sighed at the suspect's vacant stare and began thumbing through a pile of colour photographs in a box file on the chair next to him. 'But look at all these weapons we found at your little hideout, all in such good shape and properly taken care of.'

Perone dropped the images on to the table, one by one. 'AK-47s, MP5s, silenced berretta. Shit, you've even got a military Barrett M107 sniper rifle. And . . . oops!'

The last picture to hit the table was of the dead Magi associate Toledo, whom Angelo had gunned down in the observatory's lobby. The man's jaw hung open loosely with two dribbles of blood running down from the blackened bullet holes in his forehead.

'Your friend here, the one we had to put down, dumb bastard . . . he had the tools but not the talent, eh?'

Lupis didn't show a shred of emotion.

Christ, Perone thought. *It would have been easier to antagonise a Telly Tubby!* In any other circumstances, he would have happily let this crook stew in the cells for three or four days and nights with his officers waking him up every time he looked to be getting comfortable, but the situation here was more urgent.

Since the brutal murder of the Vatican's chief science advisor, Vito Malpuso, a few days earlier, coupled with the shoot-out at the villa, the top brass had been all over him. High command were worried it was the beginning of a new mafia turf war and were demanding prompt answers that they could feed to the press without creating a panic. After decades of effort, mafia violence had finally been contained, and no one wanted a return to the old days.

Perone massaged the back of his neck irritably. And how about the professor from Cambridge? His gut told him that man was somehow at the heart of this whole mess, yet he didn't even know his current location. The Brit had simply disappeared. Yes, they needed answers—and they needed them right now.

As he stared across the desk at Lupis's unresponsive gaze, he finally began accepting the inevitable: there was no way this kid was going to talk. Whether it was through brainwashing or a misguided sense of ideology, the boy intended going down in flames without saying a word. In Perone's mind, there was only a single option left open to him if he was going to get the answers he needed. He didn't like resorting to it and rarely did, but needs must as the devil drives, and tonight the devil's upstairs were driving him hard.

'Detective, why don't you go and get a sandwich or something? I'll continue this interrogation for the next hour or so.' The instant the words left his mouth, he knew his second-in-command wasn't going to swallow any of it. The glare Angelo sent his way was a firm mixture of unease and a wholehearted 'Fuck you, boss' as the younger officer guessed what would come next.

'Not really hungry, sir. I'll stay here if it's all the same.'

Perone let out an unhappy grunt. Angelo was a good cop; no, he was one hell of a cop, but his generation was becoming altogether too honest. Most officers like Detective Angelo Barbosa had been taught to behave whiter than white if they were to succeed in dismantling organised crime. It was a way of thinking that Perone's own generation had not been educated in. Still, he couldn't help but admire the officer's resolve, just a little.

He was still mulling over whether to approach this difference of opinions through force or diplomacy when there was a knock at the door to interrupt the uneasy stare passing back and forth between the two policemen. 'Come.'

The door swung open, and one of Perone's team strode briskly over and whispered into the boss's ear. 'The tech guys have managed to access the SIM card we found in the suspect's mobile phone.'

When they had searched the prisoner earlier, only two items were found on his person apart from the weapons. They were a small metal crucifix and a BlackBerry, which the techies had gone to work on immediately.

'They've been able to pull a contact number from it.' The officer paused apprehensively, much to Perone's annoyance.

'Well, for Christ's sake, cough it up,' Perone barked before glancing over at Lupis, who, for the first time, was starting to look nervous.

'The number was traced, and, because it's not been turned off, the techs were able to triangulate its location. The recipient's mobile signals are coming from somewhere inside the Vatican.'

The answer was gobsmacking to both interrogators, and they turned in unison to face their increasingly twitchy-looking suspect. A few beads of sweat were even forming across the Magi youth's brow, although his gaze was still glued to the table top. Half a dozen murders, military hardware, and now the Vatican! Perone felt an uncomfortable knot tightening deep in the pit of his stomach.

This was turning into one long fucking night.

Chapter 37

The entire shoreline of Lake Bracciano was now alive with a mixture of concerned locals and inquisitive camera-toting tourists, all jostling to get a prime view of the feverish activity on its dark waters. The plane had come to rest on a rocky plateau one hundred metres offshore, and a group of boats were eagerly circling the white tip of the *Lear Jet*'s tail still jutting above the waterline. On the shore, local television crews had spotlights shining towards the wreck, illuminating the fuselage's reflective white paint and giving it the chilling appearance of some ghostly leviathan lurking just below the water's surface.

From the porch of a beach house just off the sands, Harker watched as the organised chaos unfolded. He wondered if this was what Brulet had in mind when he told him to keep everything low-key.

Harker gulped down the last dregs of the effervescent painkillers that had been supplied to him by the owner of the beachside property he was now sitting outside. The pills were supposed to help with the pain, but instead, they were making him feel sick, and he was struggling to keep them down. The police had not arrived yet, even though representatives of local news stations had appeared within minutes of them reaching dry land and had been hustling to interview the survivors ever since. He couldn't believe how well Doggie was coping with the incident, for not only had his friend managed to escape without injury of any kind but was also brilliantly holding at arm's length the same journalists and cameras that Captain Anatoly had been courting so passionately.

The savvy captain had made them both comfortable before setting off on a promotional campaign which included handing out free *Anatoly's party cruise ship* towels to all the assembled newsmen. The skipper's talent for PR was definitely being wasted out here in the midst of the Italian countryside.

On his return, Doggie left Anatoly in charge and headed back to join Harker inside the waist-height wooden fence that was keeping the excited crowd at bay.

'What a commotion!' Doggie exclaimed. 'Honestly, you'd think they'd never seen two men fall out of the sky before.' He glanced over his shoulder to make sure there was no one within hearing distance. 'Alex, all those things Lusic mentioned about. The relics . . . the Templars. Isn't it about time you came clean, again?'

Harker had been waiting for the question to arise ever since regaining consciousness and dreading it too, but if he ever wanted to rescue Claire, he was going to need every ounce of help he could get. The importance of keeping things secrets suddenly seemed immaterial and pointless. 'OK, but, before I begin, I need you to swear on your life that you won't utter a word of what I'm about to tell you unless I say you can.'

The Cambridge academic immediately nodded without hesitation.

'No, Doggie, I need you to think seriously about this. You can't tell a soul on pain of death. Do you hear me? No exceptions. Now say it. Swear on your life.'

His friend considered it for a moment, and then, with one eyebrow raised and in the most sober manner possible, he nodded slowly. 'Fine, you have my word. I swear on my life I will not tell a soul.' He paused, chewing his bottom lip pensively. 'Unless you say I can.'

A profound feeling of angst now swept through Harker's stomach. He wasn't sure that Doggie would believe him, after all, it was a tale even he was struggling to accept—and he was living it!

Over the next few minutes, Harker ran through the events of the past twenty-four hours, from the meeting with Brulet at Bletchley Park, the children known as the Angels, the attack at the monastery . . . This time, he told him everything, including the Templars, the—two-thousand-year-old quest of the Magi to dominate the Church and the role he himself was being forced to play in bartering for Clarie's life. As Harker gave up more of his story, Doggie's breathing became noticeably heavier, each new revelation drawing louder gasps as the dean looked increasingly flabbergasted.

'Jesus Christ! I mean, I knew you were embroiled in something serious but this . . . It's hard to believe, Alex, but, damn it, Templars? Magi?'

Harker actually felt an invisible but, nonetheless, heavy weight lift off his chest as if the very act of saying it all out loud had removed a massive burden from his soul. 'I know it's all incredible, unbelievable.' He struggled, and failed, to find a word that was suitably worthy for the story he was telling. 'But my only concern now is Claire Dwyer. I have to find her immediately because if Brulet is telling the truth, then come nine o'clock this morning, she's likely to disappear for good. Doggie, those relics were my only leverage, but, with that bastard Lusic pulling his skydiving stunt, I've only got one choice left now, and it's a long shot at best.'

Their discussion was interrupted by a lone reporter attempting to jump over the fence and falling face first on to the concrete paving stones with an awful thump. The red-faced intruder was immediately dragged to his feet by a furious-looking Captain Anatoly, who heaved him head first back over the fence and into the crowd beyond. 'That's it, no interview for you, idiot,' the seaman yelled, pausing to pose amid the flood of camera flashes that concentrated on him for one brilliantly lit moment before resuming his role as security guard, surveying the onlookers with an even more steely resolve.

Satisfied they could not be heard, the two men resumed their conversation. 'So all the events involved in this whole conspiracy seem to revolve around one place: the Vatican's Academy of Sciences—specifically its northern corridor. I need to get myself inside if we're to have any hope of getting her back.'

This idea clearly didn't appeal to Doggie, who was woefully shaking his head. 'If you're right about the Magi and other powerful elements of the Church being involved, then how the hell do you expect to gain entry? You'd be arrested on the spot, and I don't have to remind you, Alex, that the Vatican City is considered to be a sovereign country under international law.' He threw his hands up into the air passionately. 'Not to mention the fact that they're hosting a summit of world leaders there tonight.'

It was the first time Harker had heard of this event, but, having been so busy with the Dead Sea Scrolls exhibition, he'd totally lost track of general news over recent weeks. 'Summit? What summit?'

'A summit of world leaders will take place in St Peter's Basilica later that morning, hosted by the new Pope himself. Even the American President is due to be there. Not sure what it's about, though. The news reports have been pretty sketchy about it. It's been labelled as some kind of official meet-and-greet for the new pontiff. Whatever the purpose, you'd never get past security in the first place.' He paused anxiously. 'You don't think this has anything to do with that, like a bomb or something?'

Harker shook his head. 'No, I can't believe they would blow up St Peter's. The Magi want to control the church, not destroy it.' But Doggie was right about one thing: with world leaders now congregating at St Peter's Basilica, security would be higher than anywhere else on earth. Still, there was one important thing his friend knew nothing about—one thing that might just enable Harker to gain admission. *Time to play my last card,* he thought.

'What if I could get an audience with Pope Adrian?'

A disbelieving smile fell across Dean Lercher's face. 'You'd never get to see him. Not tonight. Not with this summit going on.'

Harker persisted. 'Yes, I know, but what if I could? If the Pope knew elements in the Vatican were involved in kidnapping and murder, he'd have to take me seriously, wouldn't he?' He could see a glint in Doggie's eyes as his old friend began to weigh up the possibilities.

'OK. That could work if, indeed, Claire is actually being held in Vatican City. But we're still stuck with the same problem: how do you get an audience with the Pope?'

Harker leant in closer to the dean, preparing to speak of a secret he had sworn never to reveal to another living soul. 'I never told you why I left the church, did I, Doggie? I've never told anyone, not even Archie Dwyer, and he never forgave me for it.'

The noise of the chattering crowd on the other side of the fence seemed to suddenly fade away.

'My last clerical posting was just outside Norwich.'

'East Harling, wasn't it?'

'Yes, but what you don't know is that, a few months after taking over the parish, it came to my attention that one of the young altar boys had been sexually abused by the former priest. I was horrified, disgusted, and immediately contacted the Vatican, who, in turn, sent someone to investigate the allegations I had made.' Harker sucked in a deep breath, rubbing at his chest, as if the words themselves were painful to expel. 'After two months of investigation, it was agreed that the matter be laid to rest without any publicity and the priest be quietly moved to another parish under the watchful eyes of the Church.'

Doggie's jaw almost hit the floor at the news. 'What did the boy's parents say?'

Harker gritted his teeth as these painful memories he had forcibly buried were allowed to surface. 'The boy only had a mother, and she, being a devout Catholic, agreed it would be best for all concerned to forget that it ever happened.'

'And the poor boy?' Doggie said looking outraged, his cheeks flushing slightly.

'The boy and mother were given a financial settlement by the Church, which they accepted, so I found myself fighting a battle that quiet literally no one wanted to fight. I was so disgusted and incensed that I saw no other option but to resign, which is exactly what I did. I couldn't continue serving a church that would seek to bury such a hideous crime for no other reason than PR.'

'My God, Alex, is that why you never told Archie?'

Harker nodded solemnly. 'I knew it would shake his entire faith, and I couldn't do that to him. So I didn't tell him.'

Doggie moved back a step, his eyes wide open. 'So what has this got to do with the current Pope?'

Harker cleared his throat as if subconsciously a part of him was trying to restrain himself from saying anything further. 'The man selected to investigate the affair was none other than Archbishop John Wilcox, who only two weeks ago was inaugurated as the new bishop of Rome and head of the Catholic Church. Pope Adrian VII himself.'

This latest revelation sent Doggie reeling back even further, and Harker had to grab his friend's arm to steady him.

'And that's not all. You've often asked me how I managed to acquire the Dead Sea Scrolls from the shrine of the hand in Jerusalem.'

Judging by the vein now bulging in his forehead, Doggie already had an idea of where this conversation was heading.

'Well, Wilcox happened to have a huge amount of sway amongst certain officials in the Israel Antiquities Authority, and he helped me secure a loan of the collection and bring it to Cambridge for the exhibition.'

Dark shadows were now appearing underneath Doggie's eyes as his brain processed the inescapable conclusion. 'Fuck me, you blackmailed the Pope?'

Harker shook his head fervently. 'No, he wasn't Pope then, and it wasn't like that at all.'

The dean rolled his eyes in shock. 'Holy fucking shit, you blackmailed the Pope, didn't you?'

'No, I didn't. I had already spent three months negotiating the deal with the Israeli government when one of their officials, for no reason, rescinded his vote. I was completely at a loss and didn't know what to do. That's when I got a call from Wilcox, who offered me help in securing the deal if I promised never to mention his involvement in that molestation case.' Harker rubbed at the wrinkles now appearing on his forehead, blood rushing to his cheeks in shame. 'After a lot of thought, I decided to take him up on his offer. I'd already quit the Church by then with a clear conscience, and I never intended to mention it anyway, so I finally thought why not. The problem is that now I really do need to blackmail him into doing the right thing and allowing a thorough search of Vatican City for Claire.' He could tell by the despondent look in Tom Lercher's eyes that these revelations were tearing at his friend's ethical compass.

The dean had never been a particularly religious man, but, even so, he had always taken pride in his high moral standards and, on the surface, Harker was now coming off looking pretty bad.

'Look, Doggie, you've known me for what . . . over ten years. In all that time, have you ever known me to be deceitful or sly in any way?'

Doggie shook his head without any hesitation.

'Then I need you to trust me now when I say it was never blackmail.'

The lack of direct eye contact told Harker he was losing the argument, and he reached over and firmly grasped his old friend's forearm, more determined than ever to make him see the truth. 'Look, you may believe me right now or you may not, but if we don't find Claire Dwyer in a little under three hours' time, then she's dead. Can you really have that on your conscience for the rest of your life, knowing that you could have done something but failed to act?'

Dean Learcher rubbed his palms together and clicked his teeth nervously as he deliberated the question. 'Honestly, Alex, do you really think these people—these Magi or whatever—would kill her?'

Harker stared out beyond the crowd of bustling people still gathered nearby and towards the ring of boats circling the downed aircraft. 'Doggie, they crashed a plane and murdered the pilot, John Caster, and nearly us as well simply to tie up loose ends. So do you really think they'll even give a second thought about doing away with a woman who no one, except ourselves, even knows is missing?'

This last point hit its mark, for the dean immediately sucked in a lungful of air, and, with it, the confidence and determination he had shown earlier returned to him. 'As usual, you're absolutely bloody right.' He slapped his hand on Harker's shoulder with a wet squelch. 'OK, I believe you. And if that's what you say happened, then that's what happened. OK, fuck it! Let's go and blackmail the Pope!'

Harker pulled open his blanket and peered down at his soaking-wet shirt and trousers. 'First, I need some dry clothes and then a way out of here and to the Vatican before the police arrive.'

Doggie nervously scanned the surrounding area for any law officials but found none. 'OK, what do you need from me?'

'I need you to stay here, Doggie. If we both leave simultaneously, those reporters won't take long to realise we've made a break for it.'

'Right, I stay here and work the crowd, giving you as much time to get away as possible. I can do that whilst . . .' He struggled to articulate the words. 'Whilst you go and blackmail the Pope.'

Harker almost laughed out loud but, instead, exhaled a deep sigh, simply relieved that his friend was up to the task. 'Ok, by road, we're only about forty minutes from the Vatican. All I need now is a ride.' Harker eyed the road running parallel to the shoreline. All the vehicles he could see were parked alongside the beach—except for one. It was a rusty grey minivan with the faded black logo NANDOS TAXIS stencilled across the passenger door. Inside it sat a man wearing a tasty Hawaiian-style red shirt with short sleeves, and protruding from his mouth was a smouldering cigar nestled comfortably under a bushy grey moustache. The driver was touting a man and woman for business, but for the time being, they seemed far more interested in getting on to the beach rather than heading away from it.

His perusal of the van caught Doggie's attention, and the dean nodded understandingly. 'Right, my boy, now all you need is a fresh change of clothes.'

Chapter 38

The high-pitched screech of an amplifier echoed through the immense domed interior of St Peter's Basilica as a young priest fretfully tapped at the pulpit microphone. Standing below, Cardinal Vincenzo clasped both hands around his ears and was mouthing urgently, 'Turn it down!'

The young priest peered down at him and shrugged, unable to hear anything over the speaker's reverberation.

'I said turn the volume . . .' Vincenzo was halfway through his sentence when the deafening noise suddenly cut out, and the cathedral was once again filled with the clatter of workmen rearranging chairs for the world summit taking place that morning. 'Down!' The cardinal cleared his throat sheepishly. 'Well done, Alberto. Now adjust the pitch and that should do it.'

The priest made his way down the pulpit's solid stone steps and, offering a pleasant smile, headed towards the main PA system, eager to rectify the problem.

Vincenzo glanced down at his watch: 6.20 a.m. already. This was going to be tight.

Arrangements for the event had been completed days earlier, and everything had seemed ready to go until, twenty minutes ago, when his Holiness had decided to modify the seating arrangements.

Not very helpful, thought the cardinal. He took a moment to survey the majestic interior of the cathedral. Even after all these years, he still struggled with the emotions that surfaced when he was in the presence of such overwhelming beauty. It was the first time since the World War II that a Pope had invited so many world leaders to the Vatican at one time, and it signalled a change in the way the Church would operate in the future.

This event had originally been conceived as a way for the new Pope to meet with world leaders but had evolved into representing a new era in relations between the Catholic Church and every other culture and religion in the world. With the number of church-goers dwindling across the globe, the new pontiff believed that a fundamental change was essential within the Church's way of thinking if it were to continue as a progressive force for good in people's lives. Vincenzo agreed with this viewpoint wholeheartedly, for, Pope Adrian VII himself had proclaimed, 'How can we spread the word of *god* if no one is listening?'

Though Vincenzo had never thought of himself as a liberal, there was no doubt in his mind that the Church needed a degree of change in its dialogue with the people, and this summit would provide a good start. Unfortunately, much of the media had portrayed the forthcoming event in a rather negative light with ill-thought-out headlines such as: 'Adrian's twenty-first century crusade', and harping on about his wish to 'create a new empire amongst Christian nations'.

Vincenzo shuddered at the thought, for Christianity was a force for good throughout the world and not just for Catholics, and tonight's summit would begin to endorse that fact. After his inauguration, the Pope had immediately invited the leaders of the Muslim, Jewish Orthodox, Protestant religions, and all in between. It was a show of faith to everyone that in a modern world, the Catholic Church was more concerned with humanity's progress as a whole rather than just on its own patch. The message was of right over wrong, good overcoming evil, and decency triumphing over the debasement common to all cultures, regardless of their beliefs. The ideology that the new Pope was preaching was, in Vincenzo's mind, estimable, but he still felt a pang of doubt because the road to change was always painful, regardless of the final outcome.

It was the young priest Alberto who disturbed him from such thoughts. 'Sorry about that, Cardinal, but I think it's now set at the right pitch.'

Currently a student at one of the local churches in the Rieti district of Lazio, a mainly farming community, Alberto was a good-hearted young man, though occasionally a bit slow.

'Which is it, Alberto? Do you think so, or are you sure?'

The priest glanced at him thoughtfully before replying with a swift nod of his head. 'I'm sure, Cardinal.'

Vincenzo shot him a confident glance. 'Good, then so am I. Now find out what that man is doing, and why?' He pointed to a greasy, leathery-skinned builder who was about to drill a hole in one of the glossy marble pillars soaring up to the ceiling. 'And hurry, please, before he does any damage.'

Alberto set off towards the workman, waving his hands in protest, leaving Vincenzo to survey the hive of activity around him. It was bad enough that the PA system should break down just hours before the summit was due to begin, but even worse that he himself had been tasked with rescuing the situation. Most of the evening's VIPs were already meeting with Pope Adrian at his private quarters, another informal touch that the new pontiff had prearranged for his guests, so time was now of the essence.

As Vincenzo attempted to foresee any more problems likely to raise their heads, he found himself consumed with only two concerns. Firstly, what was Cardinal Rocca up to? At least he would have a chance to catch up with the man later, as they were both selected to attend the summit. But, secondly, where was Father Reed—and what had he learnt at the academy? Vincenzo had not spoken to him since yesterday's discussion at the Governorate, and he was eager to get, as one of his young priests had put it, 'the low-down'.

Chapter 39

Officer Rico Lombardi slapped his report on to Superintendent Perone's desk with a thud and headed back to the police station's reception desk. He was still furious at having been charged with processing the day's paperwork whilst the rest of the team tracked down the mobile signal they had got from Lupis's SIM card. He let out an irritated sigh. 'Fuck!'

His frustration caught the attention of a passing lieutenant, who raised his eyebrows disdainfully before heading off to wherever he was going.

'What a shit end to a great day!'

Lombardi had never seen so much action since finishing his training over a year ago, and not being allowed to see it through to the end was truly painful.

He arrived in the main lobby to find the duty manager, Sergeant Anonzo, contently filling in forms.

'How you feeling, kid?'

'How would you feel getting left out at the last minute?'

The response drew a smile from the veteran officer, who replaced his pen in its holder and adjusted his thick, black-rimmed bifocal glasses. 'Don't let it get you down. You've done a good job today.'

'Yeah, then why leave me behind here? To fill out the reports?'

Anonzo gave him a friendly slap on the back. 'Because the superintendent trusts you to get the job done.' He made a clicking sound from one corner of his mouth. 'Plus you're the youngest on the team, and they always get the shit jobs.'

Lombardi nodded unhappily because that was the truth right there. If he had been a year or so older, then you could bet he would be heading towards the Vatican right now, and some other shrub would be filling out that bullshit report. He took in a deep breath and expelled it through his nose, trying to release his frustration.

'Hey, Perone put that suspect of yours on high alert, and I'm supposed to check him every fifteen minutes.' The sergeant glanced at his watch. 'Only a few minutes till his next check, so why don't you do it for me? Who knows, maybe he's ready to talk.'

Lombardi knew the older man was just trying to cheer him up because he had seen the look in Lupis's eyes and that boy wasn't going to be talking to anyone. But what the hell! It would at least give him something else to do until the others got back. 'Sure, I'll check for you, but don't hold your breath. I doubt he'll say a word.' He lifted the master key from a brass hook behind the desk and headed towards the cells.

Sergeant Anonzo wagged a warning finger after him. 'Hey, just talk. No funny business.'

'You know me better than that, Sarge!' Lombardi bellowed over his shoulder as he unlocked the thick, grey metal security door and headed on downstairs, all the while shaking his head in disbelief at the sergeant's comment. In the old days, violence and intimidation in order to get a confession had been as prevalent inside police stations as it was out on the street, but the younger generation—his generation—had been brought up to believe that the only way to change things was to be cleaner in behaviour than the crooks. For young officers like Detective Angelo Barbosa and his contemporaries, this new ideology had evolved out of a hundred years of organised crime and corruption at every level. Acting like a crook made an officer of the law vulnerable and also open to blackmail. That was a cycle that, once started, never ended. No, the only way to ensure and maintain proper law and justice was to practise what you preach—something the older sergeant, although basically a straight shooter, had little appreciation of.

Italy had seen big changes over the past thirty years, but, to Lombardi's mind, it all began with the murder of an anti-mafia judge by the name of Giovanni Falcone in '92. The fifty-three-year-old lawyer had relentlessly chased after the mafia and exposed their activities with all the tenacity of a pit bull terrier at a time when his colleagues were too scared of the reprisals such activity would bring. Falcone's distinguished career climaxed in '87 when the well-publicised Maxi-Trial convicted 360 Sicilian mafia. The judge then continued to drive organised crime out of Sicily until he and his family paid the ultimate price by being assassinated in a road bomb.

In an interview given shortly after a previous attempt on his life, involving an abandoned sports bag and fifty-eight sticks of plastic explosive, Falcone had said, 'My life is mapped out. It is my destiny to take a bullet by the Mafia some day. The thing is I don't know when.'

Falcone was proved absolutely right just a year later at the hands of the Sicilian mafia led by boss, Salvatore 'The Beast' Rina, who had wanted to make a point regarding picking a fight with the mob: you could start it, but they would inevitably finish it.

His murder was tasked to an up-and-coming mafioso named Giovanni Brusca. Brusca was a vicious enforcer who had infamously tortured the eleven-year-old son of a mafia turncoat and had even sent pictures of the boy being beaten and abused in an effort to ensure the father's silence. It hadn't worked, however, and Brusca had finally strangled the youngster to death after eighteen months of enslavement before dissolving the body in a vat of acid. Endowed with such credentials, Falcone's appointed killer and his gang had spent a week tunnelling under the road they knew the judge's police escort would be taking and filled it with metal drums containing half a ton of explosives. The detonating button was said to have been pushed by Brusca himself as he and his lackeys watched from a nearby building. The explosion had ripped through the motorway with such force that it left a forty-metre-wide crater in its wake.

Giovanni Falcone and his wife had died instantly, along with three bodyguards, but the atrocity produced an opposite effect to the one the mafia had hoped for. Within days, the Italian people, tired of almost a century of mafia violence, had rallied in outrage and pushed the country's politicians into doing something drastic. The event had even inspired youngsters like Lombardi to join the police and reclaim their country's honour from the hands of organised crooks.

It was to this exact police station, and within these very cells he was now passing, that the scruffy, unkempt Brusca was initially brought to after being tracked down and arrested by elite members of the State Police's special service in '96. Indeed, Detective Barbosa had been one of the arresting officers, and Brusca had ended up in prison for life.

As Lombardi approached the barred door of the suspect's cell, he wondered about these Magi Angelo had overheard reference to whilst he'd been tied up at the observatory. Could it be a new mafia family branching out? The young officer gave a deep confident grunt since, if that was the case, then the law would take them down just like they had done before. Because there was one thing that ran true with most gangsters these days: given the choice between long sentences or selling out their friends, 99 per cent sang like birds to cut a deal, and the other 1 per cent never again saw the light of day.

He stopped at cell ten and peered into the well-lit interior to find Lupis perched at the foot of his steel-framed bed, with his back turned towards the door, resting against the bars. Lombardi was almost tempted to reach in and give him a little nudge with his fist but thought better of it. If he hoped to get a word out of this suspect, it might pay to be nice.

'Hey, Lupis, how you doing? You need anything—food, a drink?'

The young Magi henchman didn't move an inch.

'You know you're going to be here a long time, so you might as well accept some hospitality.' Lombardi's offer was met with further silence. 'OK, but remember I'm only trying to . . .' His sentence trailed off as he noticed the suspect's right hand hanging limply over the edge of his bed at an odd angle. But that wasn't what caught his attention; the really strange thing was the suspect's fingers. They were a light shade of blue.

'Hey, Lupis!' the young police officer called out before reaching through the bars and tugging on the boy's shoulder.

In one swift movement, Lupis lurched towards him and then collapsed in a heap, his head cracking loudly against the white-painted concrete floor. The prisoner's face was a deep shade of bluish-purple, thick veins bulging from his temple, and both eyes had rolled upwards in to their sockets, displaying numerous ruptured capillaries throughout the whites of his eyes. Lombardi fumbled frantically with the cell door key, but he already knew the boy was dead.

An autopsy would later reveal that the boy had managed to swallow his own tongue, choking himself to death and, in turn, forcing Lombardi to reconsider his theory that Lupis was a mafioso because a crook's first instinct was to protect themselves at any cost—a concept this boy had shown little, if any, understanding of.

Chapter 40

Harker's temple once again jolted against the metal roof of the yellow minicab, maybe for the tenth time since their journey to the Vatican had begun. Nando, the elderly yet surprisingly muscular driver, had initially apologised, blaming the suspension, but after the forth bump, he'd simply resorted to a sympathetic grunt.

'There you go, sir. How's about that for a view?'

Harker tilted his head to peer along the wide expanse of Via della Conciliazione towards the wonderfully lit dome of St Peter's Basilica in the distance. Even though he had seen this view many times before, it still gave him goosebumps.

The largest church in Christendom, St Peter's, was built originally in the fourth century by the Roman emperor Constantine and, today, could hold around sixty thousand people. Situated on the west bank of the Tiber, St Peter's had dominated Rome's city skyline for the past one and a half thousand years, and the very sight of it filled Harker with a sense of awe. Strangely, a part of him felt as if he was arriving home after a long trip abroad, and he resisted the comfortable feelings that began spreading throughout his body. This was not his home any more, and many residents of the Vatican would have him banished if they knew why he was here except one, Cardinal Vincenzo, who was perhaps the most descent man Harker had ever known.

On his first day here, Vincenzo himself had shown Harker, and the other new arrivals, around Vatican City, and the two men had immediately struck up a rapport. At the time, Vincenzo was in charge of overseeing the scriptural department, which maintained and stored the huge volumes of religious writings contained within the Vatican's archive. Few people realised how many of these religious works had never even been examined, let alone been properly maintained, and that was a job that had gained importance only in recent years. The younger Harker had been fascinated by how much history was locked away within the library's walls, and his keen interest had immediately been picked up by the cardinal. Vincenzo had soon taken Harker under his wing, and a close relationship developed between them. Even when Harker quit the priesthood, Vincenzo stuck by his side, and, although truly disappointed by his friend's action, he had never berated him for it. But, just as Harker had kept his secret from Archie Dwyer, the same was true of Cardinal Vincenzo. Harker had never wanted to create a difficulty between his mentor and the Church, besides, what good would it have done in telling him, since certain elements within the Church would never have changed their policy of closing ranks on a subject such as child abuse. Vincenzo would have been shocked, of course, because he possessed an extremely simplistic view of right and wrong, of good and evil—which was why, at this moment in time, he was the only person Harker felt he could trust.

The taxi arrived in front of the red-striped barrier of Vatican City's Petriano entrance on the edge of St Peter's square. As a security guard waved them to a halt, Harker wound down the passenger window and poked his head out.

'My name is Alex Harker, and I've an urgent appointment with Cardinal Vincenzo.'

Thankfully Harker's iPhone had survived the cold waters of Lake Bracciano, and he had managed to make a few calls from the taxi, in between suffering concussions. He had first left a rather frantic message for Pope Adrian himself at the Vatican's main switchboard, but, realising it would never be passed on, he had followed that up with a call to Cardinal Vincenzo who, although a little agitated, had agreed to meet him.

The security guard eyed him disconcertingly before referring to the metal clipboard in his left hand.

'Professor A. Harker?'

'Yes, to see Cardinal Vincenzo. I spoke with him earlier.'

On the other side of the taxi, another guard ran a mirror attached to a metal rod underneath the length of the vehicle. Then, satisfied the car was bomb-free, he gave a signal to his colleague who lifted the barrier and waved them through. 'You're expected, Professor. Follow this road all the way to Governorate building.'

'Thank you, I know the way.'

The guard gave him an appraising glance and continued to urge them through. Though being part of the Vatican police force, the border cops were not required to wear the traditional multicoloured uniform of the Swiss guards. In the old days, they had become an object of such interest to tourists wanting to take photographs that a change of policy on clothing had been necessary. The thought made Harker smile. *The old days!* He had finally reached an age when the expression became relevant. Getting older wasn't much fun until you learnt to accept it.

The taxi headed on through the Piazza del Santano Uffizio and past the impressive walls of the archpriest's residence. Everything in Vatican City was magnificent, as it perhaps should be, because it had been constantly rebuilt over the centuries to impress Catholics with its importance as the closest point on earth to the Almighty Himself, and it didn't disappoint.

The taxi came to a gentle halt outside the grand fortress-like Palace of the Governorate, which was the centre of executive power in the Vatican State. Situated directly behind St Peter's and surrounded by stunning gardens, the Governorate was comprised of many departments, all working in tandem to run the state's day-to-day affairs, and its president wielded influence second only to the Pope himself. Not a bad contact to have in one's arsenal. The palace itself had the feel of a parliamentary building, composed of three huge interlocking rectangular buildings looming over one hundred feet in height and casting a somewhat foreboding shadow across the white marble steps leading up to the main entrance.

'Here we are, and no more than the ninety euros I said it would be.' The husky-voiced taxi driver offered him a proud smile and tapped a wrinkled finger to his forehead. 'I'm never wrong, you see, so that's got to be worth another ten.'

Too preoccupied to care, Harker slapped one hundred euros into the driver's palm and stepped out of the cab. He had been getting ripped off by cab drivers all day, so what difference was once more going to make? 'You've got a talent, my friend, no doubt about it.'

The comment delighted Nando, who slipped the two 50 euro notes into his top pocket and, with a friendly salute, headed for the exit, the taxi's frame wobbling from side to side on the geriatric suspension that had made the journey feel more like a sea voyage than a road trip.

Harker waited for the taxi to disappear before making his way up the steps and through the thick bulletproof doors, heading into a wood-panelled reception area and then towards the priest who manned it.

Harker always had a soft spot for the department of the Governorate, and not just because his old friend Vincenzo was now its president. To him, it was like the home office, foreign office, the chancellery, and MI6, all rolled into one. Certainly, it was not as dark and mysterious as its British counterparts, but, nonetheless, just being there sent a frisson of butterflies rippling through his stomach.

'May I help you?' the priest's unimpressed glance of appraisal said it all, and, in that moment, Harker would have sold his own mother for a clean white shirt and tie.

'My name is Professor Alex Harker, and I'm here to see his eminence Cardinal Vincenzo.'

The young priest was just picking up one of the grey digital phones from the front desk when a deep voice boomed out from behind him, a voice Harker knew all too well.

'Alex Harker!' Cardinal Salvatore Vincenzo strode down the marble staircase with his hands outstretched. 'My old friend.'

The two men embraced tightly. Harker had forgotten what a vice-like grip Vincenzo possessed, and the years had not diminished any of its strength. 'Salvatore, thank you for seeing me at such short notice. It's great to see you.'

Vincenzo took a step back, his arms still firmly gripping Harker's shoulders. 'Let me take a look at you. You're looking well.' He stared him up and down. 'Except for your taste in clothes. "Bop Till You Drop" The cardinal chuckled as he read the words on Harker's T-shirt. 'You're quite the fashion victim these days, Alex?'

Harker laughed out loud. He had missed the cardinal's honest dry wit, which seemed exceptionally British for an Italian. 'What can I say? I'm a trendsetter.'

'Still as cocky as ever.' Vincenzo wrapped a fatherly arm around Harker's shoulder and pulled him up the steps, his expression suddenly sagging. 'Your timing is awful, Alex. You know we've got an important gathering here tonight with leaders from all around the world?'

'It's one of the reasons I needed to see you.'

Vincenzo raised his chin inquisitively. 'And what are the other reasons?'

'Why, to see you, of course, old friend.'

The cardinal gave him a gentle nudge on the back of the head. 'Don't lie, Professor, it doesn't suit you.'

Harker let out a grunt. 'OK, maybe that wasn't the main reason, but it's still good to see you.'

Vincenzo hesitated for a second before assuming a broad smile, his nostrils wrinkling. 'The feeling is mutual. Now come to my office, and tell me all about it. It's not like I have anything else to do right now.'

Harker relished the irony in Vincenzo's voice. The cardinal had a wonderful way of mixing sarcasm with genuine affection or *sugar-coated insults* as he liked to call them.

Thirty seconds later, and they were in the president's office, Vincenzo pouring two glasses of orange juice from an antique glass decanter. 'You know I don't drink alcohol, so this is about as hard as it gets around here.'

Harker accepted the crystal tumbler and took a sip. 'It's good enough for me.' The sugar gave him a fresh boost of energy, loosening the stiffness in his shoulders that had been getting tighter since taking a dip in Lake Bracciano.

Vincenzo clinked his glass against Harker's and raised it to wish his guest good health before taking a generous sip himself. 'So, Alex, what brings you to Vatican City?'

Harker found himself grasping his glass firmly, surprised at how nervous he suddenly felt. 'It's about Archie Dwyer,' he began. No sooner had he mentioned the name than Vincenzo's eyes began to dull over, and his shoulders slumped. The relationship between those two men had been difficult, to say the least. Archie had been a little wild in some of his beliefs, and the Irish in him had inspired a lot of backchat. Vincenzo had even felt Father Dwyer might be a bad influence on the young Harker and had been as glad to see Archie leave the Vatican as he was sad to see Harker go.

The president of the Governorate let out a deep uncomfortable sigh. 'Ah, yes, Father Dwyer.' He emptied his glass and began refilling it. 'I know you two were close friends.' He placed the stopper back in the juice decanter and turned towards Harker with genuine sorrow in his eyes. 'But, Alex, his suicide and the manner in which he committed it . . .' He shook his head woefully. 'It is a difficult sin to forgive in someone of seemingly sound mind. The truth is that I'm not sure I would have attended his funeral even if I had been allowed.'

Harker was confused by the remark. 'What do you mean *allowed?*'

'Well, His Holiness the Pope decreed that no one from the Vatican should attend, owing to the nature of his death. He was quite adamant about that. Shame, because Archie still had friends here.'

Suicide was considered as an automatic gate pass to hell by the Catholic Church, even if in recent years, people with psychological problems had been deemed absolved of the sin. But Archie, although deemed eccentric, was far from mentally ill, and it hadn't helped that he'd chosen to hang himself from St Peter's.

'Salvatore, at his funeral yesterday, there was a cardinal present. Cardinal Rocca, I think.'

Mention of the name drew a wide-eyed disbelieving look from his friend. 'Rocca?'

Vincenzo slammed his replenished drink down on to the lacquered wood cabinet beside him. 'Rocca, Rocca, Rocca . . . that man seems to be breaking all the rules left right and centre. Are you sure of the name?'

Harker nodded. 'About six foot, mid-forties, black hair, glasses, sallow complexion.'

'That sounds like him all right. He's head of the Academy of Sciences and causing me untold grief at the moment.'

'The Academy of Sciences?'

'Yes, the good cardinal seems to be responsible for a rather large hole in the academy's budget, and he has been dodging me for weeks.'

And just like that, a huge piece of the puzzle fell straight into his Harker's lap. Cardinal Rocca was clearly the Magi's contact within the Church. It was too much of a coincidence and also the connection to the academy. He couldn't involve Vincenzo in the events of the last twenty-four hours, but he had to find a way inside.

'Salvatore, you've known me for a long time, and I've always been honest with you, haven't I?'

The old cardinal seemed somewhat insulted by the remark. 'What on earth are you talking about?'

'If I were to tell you something about why I'm here, but without giving you the whole picture, would you believe me?'

Squinting over his glasses, Vincenzo was looking confused. 'I'm not sure what you're talking about, but, yes, I trust you.'

Harker swallowed hard. He would have to be liberal with the truth, and it made him uncomfortable having to be less than honest with his friend and mentor. Harker swallowed hard. 'I believe that something terrible is going to happen this morning—possibly aimed against Pope and the world leaders gathered here for the summit. I think there's going to be an assassination and an attempted takeover of the Church itself.'

'An assassination?' Vincenzo's arm dropped to his side in disbelief. 'Alex, a large number of the world's secret services are here in force. Believe me when I tell you this is probably the most secure place on the globe at this moment in time.'

Harker opened his mouth but was cut off before he could get another word out.

'And as for taking over the church . . .' he laughed incredulously. 'No one person or group can just take over the Church. We're not a company with shareholders!'

Harker couldn't blame the older man's disbelief. If their roles were reversed, would he take it seriously either? He moved closer. 'Salvatore, I can't tell you how I know, but if you ever had any faith in me, then I beg you to draw upon it now. Something terrible is going to happen here today, and I believe the academy and Cardinal Rocca may be involved. I need you to arrange for me an audience with the Pope, today, before the summit takes place.'

By the look on the Cardinal's face, you would have thought Harker had asked him to murder someone.

'An audience with His Holiness! The summit begins in under two hours, and he's entertaining world leaders even as we speak.' Vincenzo sucked in a sharp, frustrated breath. 'And you don't even know for sure why you need to speak to him. Alex, you're like a son to me, but you ask too much—and without even so much as a reason. The Vatican has rules and procedures as you well know.'

Harker allowed a few seconds of silence before continuing, hoping to disperse some of the tension. 'Salvatore, I would never ever ask this of you if I didn't have a good reason. But I need to see the Pope.'

Cardinal Vincenzo folded his arms and eyed Harker contemplatively for a few moments before giving his answer. 'I'm sorry, Alex, but there's only one man who can grant you an audience with the Pope at such short notice, and that's the Pope himself, but, seeing how he is currently entertaining leaders from all around the world, well, it's not going to happen. I'm sorry.'

Before a knot of despair had even begun to fully form in Harker's gut, a light yet gruff voice sounded behind them.

'Then it's lucky I'm here, is it not, my sons?'

Both men turned to see Pope Adrian VII standing at the open doorway of Vincenzo's office, in full ceremonial garb. Behind him stood four members of the Swiss Guards, each wearing the famous multicoloured uniform with pride.

'So would someone like to tell me what's going on, or did I just abandon the company of the most powerful political leaders in the world simply to catch up with you, Professor Harker?'

Chapter 41

'Your Holiness, I wasn't expecting you,' Cardinal Vincenzo swiftly made his way over to Pope Adrian VII and respectfully kissed the papal ring adorning the pontiff's finger.

'Neither was I expecting to visit you, Cardinal, but the professor here left an urgent message for me, so I asked the pontifical guard to inform me of his arrival. And here I am.'

Harker deliberately maintained a look of surprise longer than he felt it necessary for Vincenzo's sake, since the cardinal was doubtlessly curious as to why the Pope himself would take time out from such an important gathering merely to meet with an old acquaintance.

'Cardinal, would you be so good as to allow us a moment alone?'

'Yes, of course, Your Eminence.'

Vincenzo threw Harker a smile totally void of animosity before leaving the two men alone and going to join the colourful security team in the hallway outside. Pope Adrian remained silent until the doors had been firmly shut behind him.

'Professor Alex Harker . . .' He strode over with his hand outstretched. 'Welcome back to the Vatican. It's been a while since you were last here.'

Harker shook the pontiff's hand, surprised by the strength in it. 'Thank you for sparing time to speak with me, especially at such short notice.'

Pope Adrian raised a hand to silence him. 'Alex, before we speak any further, there is something important I need to say.' He cleared his throat. 'I know we have had some disturbing issues to contend with in the past, which have proved difficult for us both, but you need to know from the outset that my reason for granting you a meeting this evening is nothing to do with trying to prevent those issues seeing the light of day. I came here to meet with you simply because, despite our differences, I know you to be an honest man, and if you say, it could be a matter of life and death, then put simply, I believe you.'

The sincerity in his words caught Harker off guard, and he tried to hide his surprise. Could John Wilcox's progression to the papacy have changed his character? He wasn't sure, but the man standing in front of him seemed far less like the Cardinal Wilcox he had once known.

'I appreciate that, Your Holiness, as I do also your willingness to hear me out. And I know that you have an international summit to prepare for.'

Pope Adrian smiled graciously. 'When someone I trust warns me that we are all in imminent danger, I listen. Now, if you please, what is going on that warrants such an urgent message?'

Judging from how Vincenzo had responded to his desperate pleas for understanding, Harker decided to approach the subject with a bit more finesse this time around. 'Some information has recently come to my attention suggesting there's a plot to seriously harm the Church—and possibly you, here this morning.'

His gaze holding firm, the Pope said nothing, as Harker continued.

'It seems there is a group either active within the Church or closely connected to it that is seeking to remove and replace you in a coup of sorts.'

The pontiff remained silent, but a single raised eyebrow betrayed his growing curiosity.

'I am sad to say that during the last twenty-four hours, I've witnessed several deaths perpetrated by this group in their efforts to keep this coup secret, including an attempt on my own life and the kidnapping of a friend.'

A growing frown of concern now appeared on the Pope's face. 'Who is this group?'

Harker knew he couldn't say much without making himself sound like a conspiracy theorist. 'I don't know their name, only that they exist and are in some way connected with the Academy of Sciences and . . .' He paused, unsure whether to take a gamble on suggesting Cardinal Rocca was involved. What the hell! If he was wrong, what difference would it make now? 'With Cardinal Rocca.'

Pope Adrian's mouth fell open, his eyes widening in disbelief. It was an expression similar to the one Vincenzo had worn earlier. 'Rocca?'

'Yes, I believe so. I also believe whatever they're planning is due to take place very shortly.

The Pope went pale as if in shock, and he began to rub his forehead furiously. As Harker watched the head of the Catholic Church reel from what he was being told, it began to dawn on him that the man's reaction was more of a sudden realisation than complete shock. He had known something was going on.

'Your Holiness, is there something you suspect already?'

The cleric said nothing, but he just stood silently gazing at the floor.

Ten seconds went by, then twenty . . . a whole painful minute passed by with neither man saying a word. Until, finally, Wilcox gave a slow, solemn nod of his head. 'There has indeed been some gossip, over the years, concerning Cardinal Rocca's character and of behaviour unbefitting a man of the Church. Mainly . . .' he gave an uncomfortable gasp as if embarrassed or ashamed. 'To do with a preoccupation with ambition and power. But whenever I heard such stories, I always dismissed them as misinterpretations. Cardinal Rocca has a determined will and a strong clarity of focus, which is one of the reasons I appointed him to oversee the Academy of Sciences. But to even presume there is anything more is . . . well, shocking.'

Harker watched in silence as the pontiff digested the possibilities, his look of dismay rapidly being replaced with resolve. 'Do you have any proof of what you're telling me?'

A cold spike of uneasiness jolted through Harker's body. He didn't have anything except . . . 'Your Holiness, I do know that the Vatican has been restoring certain sacred relics in secret.'

'Go on.'

'Before Archie Dwyer died, he sent me a note pertaining to certain relics that he had taken illicitly from the Vatican. He hid these same relics for me to find, and I did.'

Harker let the dust settle around this bombshell as the supreme pontiff's eyebrows rose a little higher.

'Do you still have these relics, Professor?'

Harker shook his head. 'No, not any more. The same group I mentioned earlier snatched them from me as I was returning them to the Vatican.'

If Pope Adrian had looked in any way surprised before, he now looked completely dumbfounded. 'You were bringing them back to the Vatican?'

'Of course.' Harker nodded. 'Relics such as those should be in the safe hands of the Church. I'm guessing that Archie's decision to hide them was because he believed this rogue group was planning to steal them. For what purpose, I have no idea, but the man who took them from me boasted that they would usher in the end of the Catholic Church as we know it.'

Pope Adrian's expression began to darken, and his eyes seemed to sink further into his skull. 'You appear to know a great deal, and, yes, it's true, the Church is in possession of many relics unknown to the rest of the world. Such items have been carefully guarded for years, and they were never meant to pass beyond the Vatican's walls until Father Dwyer saw fit to steal them. I wasn't even aware of their existence until my coronation a few weeks ago. For it is only the Pope and a handful of cardinals who, at any one time, know where these items are kept. It is a responsibility that is passed on from one appointed principal to the next.'

Little of this information offered anything new to Harker, who had already experienced the initial excitement of this knowledge earlier in the day. But, above all else, there was one question still niggling at him. 'Why has it been necessary to keep these relics a secret?'

Pope Adrian let out a cough as if he had just been punched in the stomach. 'I'm sorry to disappoint you, but the answer is very simple, if not long-winded.'

He made his way over to the window and gazed out towards St Peter's Basilica, where a huge number of TV crews and onlookers were congregating in the sunlit square below.

'As children we believe, and are taught, that the world and all its rules are set in stone, we believe that nothing will ever change—and that includes us. It is a reasoning that we never completely lose, albeit in a lesser form, and so when culture or social change occurs around us, we rarely notice it because we change alongside it. In fact, it's not usually until we reminisce about it in later years that we come to realise the huge changes that have taken place. It has been that way since mankind first existed, as part of the human condition, and has evolved to provide us with comfort and to help our minds deal with the truth—the truth that everything is in a continual state of change. So here we are, in the dawn of the twenty-first century with modern communication, new technologies, and knowledge that have begun to awaken people to this reality more than at any other time in human history. People these days actually want change more than ever before, and they want it now.'

Pope Adrian turned to face Harker, with an expression full of absolute conviction. 'I, therefore, believe it is time that the Catholic Church give its flock the change they so keenly desire. I'm not speaking of a total reshuffling of ideology all at once but simply the beginnings of a change to make the Church more relevant in the modern world. And the worshipping of these relics has no place in that.'

The pontiff moved closer, his hands pressed together respectfully. 'When you yourself saw these relics, how did you feel?'

Harker thought back to the moment when Father Maddocks had shown him the crown of thorns. 'I don't think I've ever felt so exhilarated in my life. It was a feeling of total euphoria.'

'Exactly,' Pope Adrian declared assuredly. 'But you felt such a strong connection over nothing more than an inanimate object, and there was no truth to those underlying feelings. Relics have been used unscrupulously like this in the past to control the faith of many, but that is a way of thinking that will soon come to an end. The Church has long taken such faith for granted. People are expected to follow the Church and its spiritual path blindly because that is the way of things, end of story. But I believe the opposite. I believe that we, its servants, should begin earning that faith. We should be showing, explaining, and convincing people of why it is the right path for them to follow, and for that to happen, the Church must begin to modernise. The ideology, the message, must never change, for that is God's will, but the way the Church is administered . . . that is down to us, his servants. I will not fail the Christian faithful of the world in my responsibility, and that is why I want those relics to stay hidden as have so many popes before me.'

By the end of this speech, Harker was feeling altogether giddy. To hear a man of God, let alone the bishop of Rome, speak so liberally about the role of the Church was as refreshing as it was worrying—refreshing because, deep down, he believed everything the Pope had just said, but worrying because it went against everything that he had been led to expect since childhood.

'I understand, Your Holiness, and agree, it is the right time for change, but the group now in possession of these relics will, I fear, do anything to stop you. And everything they've planned seems to converge on the Academy of Sciences. I know you have a lot to consider, but I must find my friend, and I'm almost out of time.'

Pope Adrian barely hesitated in his response. 'Then we must find this friend of yours at once, and we can be at the academy within five minutes. I will not wittingly allow anyone to defile Vatican soil with a crime.'

'And your guests?'

'They will survive. And we must make sure your friend does likewise.'

Chapter 42

'I've already told you, Superintendent Perone, that's just not possible.'

Lorenzo Rossi, head of the Vatican's pontifical police, stared at the Italian lawman and his detective scornfully. 'You might have noticed that we've got most of the world's leaders here tonight, and what seems to be the entire global media camped outside my door, every one of whom is looking for a story. So if you honestly think I'm about to authorise a manhunt on Vatican soil, then you're nuttier than the men you're chasing!' He rested both hands on his hips and glared at his visitors uncompromisingly. 'My decision on this matter should be as clear as a child's conscience, understand?'

It was an odd analogy but the sarcastic tone of it made Perone's face begin to turn a dark shade of red. He stroked back his silver hair with a quivering hand, concluding that this bunch of wannabe cops were more frustrating than his own in-laws.

The grey-painted interior of the Vatican's pontifical police headquarters was as musty as it was drab, and, after almost twenty minutes of heated discussion, Perone was no closer to gaining access. Standing next to him, the much calmer Detective Barbosa now took over the conversation. 'Captain Rossi, we understand your predicament, but the criminals we're seeking are responsible for a kidnap and the murder of at least five people, namely two priests and three church workers. If you don't allow us in now, we're likely to lose for good the signal we've been tracking.'

The finality of Angelo's statement created a sense of dread in Perone's stomach, and Rossi's stern, swift shake of the head compiled it. This wasn't going to work, and Perone knew it, leaving him only one option. He gave Angelo a gentle prod backwards and stepped closer to the Vatican policeman.

'If you don't let us in to do our job, then we're likely to lose any chance at all of capturing this murderer and child rapist.' He could feel his younger colleague's stare burning into his back at the lie, but the mere suggestion of a paedophile always brought out the best in people's willingness to help. 'Now there's no way I'm letting this sick bastard escape, so you either allow us to find him discreetly or I head right over to that crowd of paparazzi camped on your doorstep, and I tell them how the Vatican is harbouring a vicious child molester and how their chief of police is helping cover it up. And before you make a decision, just remind yourself how potent the power of the media now is because these days, Captain Rossi, it's almost as powerful as the Church itself.'

The lack of reaction on the Vatican official's face spurred Perone on yet further. 'Just think, Captain, how you alone will be held responsible for a worldwide news story accusing the Catholic Church of harbouring murderers and rapists simply for the sake of PR. Imagine the scandal that will result in—and all down to you.' He returned to Barbosa's side, allowing the captain to regain his personal space once more. 'Now, Captain Rossi, I'm asking you again. On behalf of the Italian judicial system, will you allow us to do our job?'

Almost twenty seconds of uncomfortable silence passed before the muscles in Rossi's jaw began to twitch, and Perone knew they were getting in.

'Very well, Superintendent, you can conduct your search. But a member of the Pontifical Guard will be with you at all times, and you'll have to leave your weapons here at the guardhouse.'

The two policemen immediately passed over their handguns. That was no surprise because the only professionals allowed to carry guns inside the Vatican walls were secret-service agents, and even they needed to seek permission months in advance.

Captain Rossi opened the secure metal door to one side of the reception counter and ushered them inside, his face now seething with fury. 'Now it's my turn to make the threats, Detective Perone, and I know of your reputation, so I'll get straight to the point. If you disturb tonight's important events in any way or handle yourself in a disrespectful manner, then I will do everything in my quite considerable power to destroy your career. The Vatican Police may be small in numbers, but what we lack in size, we more than make up for in dogged determination. We make honourable friends but a powerful enemy. Are we clear on that, Detective?'

A mischievous smile crept across Perone's face as he and Angelo followed one of the guards towards the exit. 'As a child conscience, Captain Rossi. Clear as a child's conscience.'

Chapter 43

'It seems you've been grossly misinformed, Professor. Whoever this group are that you are referring to, they are clearly not here.'

There was a note of frustration in Pope Adrian's voice, and, after forty-five minutes of searching the north corridor of the Academy of Sciences, Harker couldn't blame him. Even he himself was beginning to have doubts.

Where was the secret entrance to this room of whose existence Father Maddocks had been so convinced existed? The thought conjured up images of Valente's decapitated head roasting amongst the red embers of the open fire back at the monastery, but Harker immediately pushed this grisly image from his mind. Too many people had died in getting him to this point, and he was not about to give up after only forty-five minutes of investigation. 'Bear with me, Your Holiness.'

The pontiff tut-tted loudly and then sat down on a black granite bench beneath a sixteenth-century oil painting of St Francis of Assisi, his impatience becoming obvious. 'Very well, Alex, but we don't have much time left. The summit begins in under an hour.'

Harker surveyed the long extent of the north corridor. He had visited the academy occasionally when studying at the Vatican, but its refurbishment had left the decor very different from what he remembered.

'What happened to all the other paintings and statues?'

'Most of the paintings were destroyed in the fire, and the statues are still being restored. It was a bad fire, and it's only by the grace of God no one was killed.'

Harker nodded agreeably as an idea came to him. 'Or maybe it was planned that way?' His remark drew a confused look from the pontiff.

'Planned? Why would anyone plan such an act of destruction?'

'Well, for one thing, it would create an opportunity for building a secret entrance, without anyone's knowledge, whilst the refurbishment took place.'

Pope Adrian scoffed at the notion. 'That seems fairly improbable, and, besides, there doesn't seem to be any secret entrance, regardless of what you have been told.'

'OK, maybe the fire was an accident, but it could still have provided an excuse to install a . . .'

As Harker's eyes darted up and down the corridor, desperately searching for a clue; he noticed something odd. The walls were adorned with paintings from different time periods replacing those consumed by the fire, but more importantly, they were focused on a single theme—each image, unsurprisingly, related to Christianity or the Church in one form or another. A view of St Peter's Basilica hung next to an image of St John the Baptist. Next to that was a pastel landscape of Vatican City, and beyond that, hung a Botticelli depicting the crucifixion, and so on. They were all, therefore, devoted to religious or Catholic themes except one.

Harker hurried down the corridor towards the penultimate painting on the left-hand side. In between, a depiction of the crucifixion and an oil painting of the apostle Saint Peter was a contemporary portrait of Sir Isaac Newton dressed in his finest attire. Harker gazed at the painting in front of him as a twinge of excitement rose in his chest, and he found himself thinking again about the last words of Archie Dwyer's message: 'Trust your logic, not your faith.'

Initially, he had thought it was just the password for the monastery coupled with Archie's way of telling him to view everything he encountered logically and not get caught up in any religious symbolism, but as he studied the picture in front of him, he realised he had misunderstood. Archie had meant those words literally, for Newton had been a man totally consumed by the *logic* of science.

Harker slid his fingers down each side of the frame as far as the lower corners and then along the bottom edge till his fingers met in the middle, directly underneath a gilded cartouche bearing the words: 'Isaac Newton 1642-1727. Artist unknown.'

He gently prodded it with his forefinger, and, from underneath, there was a click followed by a low rumble. The entire painting then retreated into the wall by three inches and gently slid downwards to reveal a gap about a metre high allowing the admittance of an average-sized man. No sooner had the panel receded out of sight than a strip light flickered into life, revealing a brick-lined passageway. Another light came on a few metres beyond the first, followed by another and then another, creating a succession of lights that illuminated the gloomy passage running for many metres ahead.

Pope Adrian was already at Harker's side by the time the last light came on in the distance.

'I don't believe it. You were right, Professor.'

Harker rubbed a finger across the corridor ceiling, causing fresh dust to float down. 'And recently built too. This might be a good time to call the gendarmes, Your Holiness.'

The pontiff's face filled with concern. 'No, I think we should find out exactly what this is before we get others involved.'

This response confused Harker. 'Why not?'

'Because if this does involve any of the criminal elements you described, then I want to keep it between as few people as possible. Consider it damage control . . . No, we first take a look, and, if there is anything serious, I will call upon officers of the pontifical police who can be counted on to be discreet.'

Harker felt his heart sink. He had been starting to believe that the ex-cardinal's transition to Pope had marked a change in his character, but this was pure Wilcox to cover anything up at the expense of truth and bury the very morals that should be guiding the Church.

The pontiff caught the disappointed look on Harker's face. 'You're so naive, Alex. Everything I have ever done is to protect the Church and, in doing so, protect the faith.' The Pope genuinely looked saddened. 'Why do you think I'm appearing so lax about the protocols of being Pope? Why I'm changing how the Catholic Church works? It's to make it more relevant in people's lives. But that won't happen overnight.' He stared deeply into Harker's eyes, his own full of sincerity. 'The Church cannot survive another crisis of faith, not now. I need time to bring Catholicism into the twenty-first century, just as our saviour Jesus Christ would have done if he were alive today.'

That remark struck a chord with Harker for Jesus had been a visionary but also a revolutionary, a man with a message of change that eventually reshaped the world. He hated himself, for what he was about to say next. 'For the time being, OK. But if anything happens to Claire Dwyer don't expect me to keep quiet.'

The Pope nodded in agreement. 'Thank you for your discretion. Now let us see where this passage leads, shall we?'

Harker pulled himself over the brick ledge and into the cold, dank passage beyond. There he waited as Pope Adrian speedily removed his robe to reveal the customary black and red cardinal's costume underneath before placing them in a neat pile and following closely. They had made it only a few metres along when the entrance behind them slid shut, causing both men to instinctively race backwards, only to have the door slide open again.

'It must be activated by a pressure switch,' Harker surmised. 'Clever construction.'

He turned around and began venturing further into the tunnel with the pontiff in tow. Behind them, the stone panel slid back into place once again with a loud grinding noise.

'That entrance may be new, but the further in we get, the older it looks.' Harker rubbed at one of the walls, which crumbled away under his hand. 'This corridor must be over fifty years old at least.'

The Pope gave him a nod. 'There are scores of tunnels underneath Vatican City, mostly unexplored.'

It was something Harker knew all too well, and he had always been fascinated by the reports of excavations under the Vatican. 'I'll bet it dates back to the war.'

Judging by the silence, he figured the new Pope was unaware of the city's underground history. 'During World War II, there were genuine concerns that the Nazis would enter the Vatican and attempt to kidnap the Pope himself. Hitler decreed that the Vatican would remain exempt from occupation, but, with a track record like his, the promise fell upon deaf ears, and Vatican officials dug escape routes from many of its major buildings. This could be one of them. There was even a route leading from the Pope's inner chamber, but if my memory serves me correctly, it was filled in during the 1950s for security reasons.' The vague look in the pontiff's eyes convinced him to cut short his papal history lesson, and not wanting to embarrass the man any further with his ignorance, Harker swiftly moved onwards through the dank musty tunnel.

Another fifty metres brought them to a sturdy-looking black metal door, and Harker pressed his ear against it, listening for any sounds. There were none. 'Right, let's take this slowly. If we do find Claire Dwyer in here, I must insist that you go back immediately and get reinforcements whilst I stay. Is that acceptable?'

The pontiff shot him a firm look 'Yes, it is. I only hope the room behind this door is empty.'

It was a strange thing to say, considering a woman's life was at stake, but Harker shrugged it off. 'And I hope you're dead wrong. Otherwise, I'm out of leads, and out of time.'

Chapter 44

Cardinal Vincenzo pushed his way past the sprawl of secret service agents littering the steps of St Peter's Basilica with all the grace of a water buffalo. The last few hours had been testing enough without the Pope taking a midnight stroll with less than an hour to go before he was due to address this summit of world leaders.

When Alex Harker had turned up, it had been an unexpected, if not pleasant surprise, but, with all his talk of conspiracies and bomb threats, the cardinal's nerves were beginning to fray, and an uncomfortable feeling had been building in his stomach ever since. This was not what he had envisaged when the Pope originally outlined tonight's event, describing it as 'a chance to remake the Church in the world's image'. Had Vicenzo known it would reflect the more troubling aspects of the globe, he would have argued strongly against it.

He halted in front of the enormous doors of the basilica overlooking St Peter's Square and thumped his fist against them. *What a day!*

The eyes of numerous secret service men watched him doggedly as he waited for the doors to open. Most had been there since the early morning, completing every safety check imaginable, from manhole covers to cloakrooms. Even the pontifical guard, the Vatican's own police service, had been required to undergo a complete security check, encompassing every single member of its staff. That was no real surprise since, where there was a congregation of world leaders such as tonight, safety and security had to be of the upmost importance. Vincenzo once again rapped on the massive doors. With so many eyes fixed upon him, it was hard not to feel guilty about anything.

Finally, the double doors swung open, and the cramp in Vincenzo's stomach got even tighter at the sight confronting him. The young priest acting as a doorman offered the president of the Governorate a nervous look as he glanced back at the fervour of activity behind him. 'It's a little busy in here, Cardinal.'

The hall was brimming over with prime ministers and presidents taking their seats, already discussing politics and swapping pleasantries. For a brief moment, the entire crowd went silent as they turned to the entrance, expecting to see the Pope. But finding only the startled-looking cardinal, they turned their attention back to one another, and the low-level rumble of chatter continued once more.

Vincenzo forced a smile and battled his way to the rear of the Cathedral and through a plain wooden doorway just behind the pulpit where Pope Adrian would soon be making his speech. The room beyond was not empty as Vincenzo had suspected, and he found Cardinal Rocca sitting coolly on one of the stonewall benches covered with red and gold Camomilla cushions. In one hand, he held a sheet of paper which he was carefully scrutinising and with the other was running a finger across the page line by line, his lips murmuring the words he traced.

Vincenzo gently swung the door shut, allowing the room to quieten from the chatter in the main hall. He then turned to face the younger cleric, who had still not looked up from the document he was reading, completely engrossed in the text. 'Cardinal Rocca . . .'

Rocca glanced up towards the Governorate president with wide eyes, the focus of his thoughts elsewhere.

'You've been extremely difficult to get hold of.'

A thin grin spread across the younger man's lips, and he placed the sheet of paper face down on the bench beside him. 'Salvatore, I'm glad you're here. I was just about to send for you.'

Vincenzo ignored the irony. 'Well, I'm glad about that, too, because I've been trying to get hold of you since this morning.'

He sat himself down on the bench opposite, noting the sarcastic glance on Rocca's face, and he realised there was no point in tiptoeing around the situation further. Whatever the younger man was up to, he seemed hell-bent on continuing with it.

'I sent Father Reed to check up on you today at your office. Did you meet with him?'

Rocca's expression morphed into a curious smile, and he shook his head. 'No, can't say I've had the pleasure, but it's interesting to know you've been checking up on me. For what purpose?'

Rocca's conceited response stirred a deep anger in Vincenzo, but he immediately quashed it, not wanting this conversation to dissolve into a shouting match. 'You know why, Cardinal. It concerns the black hole in the academy's budget and the secretive way you've been handling yourself over the past few weeks.'

'Hmm, as much as I would love to sit here and talk to you, I'm afraid my workload just won't allow it,' Rocca replied drily, gesturing to the piece of paper lying on the bench next to him. 'Can we reschedule?'

Vincenzo eyed him with contempt before resting back against the white-painted wall of the waiting room. 'Very well, Cardinal Rocca, if that's going to be your attitude, then all you need do is listen. After our meeting yesterday, I asked a member of the Governorate, Father Reed, to take a closer look into your dealings at the academy, of which I am still awaiting his findings. But that wasn't all. I also tasked members of the pontifical guard to place you under a watchful eye, which they've been doing ever since you left my office. Apparently, Father Reed entered the academy yesterday afternoon, followed shortly by yourself, but later, only you were seen coming out, and Father Reed, it seems, has now vanished.'

Vincenzo finally saw a chink in Rocca's confidence begin to open up, and the younger Cardinal's thin smile started to evaporate. 'Then, in the early hours this morning, you were seen allowing an unknown man access to Vatican City, whereupon you took him into, where else, but the Academy of Sciences.' He let out an ironic laugh. 'And again, would you believe, after an hour or so, only you emerged. Another mysterious disappearance. You're somewhat of a magician.'

Rocca's jaw muscle twitched irritably as Vincenzo continued.

'Still there's more. The gendarmerie took some photos of your friend and had them checked through the appropriate channels, and this is the truly worrying thing—no one knows who he is! For all intents and purposes, that man doesn't exist. I'm still waiting to hear back from Interpol, but I've got a feeling they won't be able to identify him either. So the real question I put to you, my Catholic brother, is who is he and what business does he have in Vatican City?' Vincenzo sat absolutely motionless as he waited for a response.

Cardinal Rocca's jaw muscle suddenly relaxed, and all concern disappeared from his face as he tapped the sheets of paper next to him. 'You're absolutely correct, Salvatore, there are things going on here that you have been left out of. Plans that are going to reshape the Catholic Church as we know it. Plans I wish you to be a part of.'

'Plans *you* wish me to be a part of?' The older man was fuming now. 'Whatever plans you may have, *you* are not head of the Catholic Church and *you* have no right to attempt at any reorganising . . .'

Rocca cut him off mid-sentence. 'No, you're right, I cannot, but our highest authority can and will.' He picked up the typed sheets from the stone bench and handed them to Vincenzo, who pulled out a pair of bifocal reading glasses from inside his robe and placed them on the bridge of his nose. 'This is the speech Pope Adrian will deliver to world leaders shortly, and it will mark an end to the old Church and the dawn of a new one.'

As Cardinal Vincenzo scanned the two printed pages, his chest grew tighter and tighter with every sentence he read. 'I don't believe it. This is pure fantasy.' He glanced up to find Cardinal Rocca eyeing him coldly, his pupils alight with the forbidding glint of a man unsure of his next move.

'Not fantasy, Salvatore, but reality.'

Vincenzo struggled to comprehend what he had just read, the implications churning his stomach and pushing a single thought to the forefront of his mind, above all others. 'You're insane, Rocca.' He shook the piece of paper in front of him. 'This is blasphemy of the highest order. You'll not see it happen as long as I live and breathe.'

In an instant, Rocca was swiftly upon him, clamping a palm across Vincenzos' mouth before he could sound off a cry for help.

'Well, then, we'll have to remedy that fact, won't we, old man?'

Chapter 45

It only took a few moments for Harker's eyes to adjust to the darkness and until then, he clung to the door handle, half expecting to topple into some deep pit. Luckily, such fears were unjustified.

The room was large and bathed in a dim orange glow from a lamp hanging over a conference table surrounded by chairs, which stretched the entire length of the room. He stepped over to one of the bookcases lining the walls and attempted to scan the contents through scrunched-up eyes, but nothing in particular stood out.

'Anything interesting?' Pope Adrian whispered as he bumped into one of the shelves, making Harker jerk backwards in alarm. 'Sorry, it's very dark.'

'I'll see if I can find a light,' Harker decided. He ran his hand across the wall until his fingertips found a switch protruding from underneath one of the shelves. 'Here we go.'

All around the room up-lighters flared into life, illuminating not only a table, chairs, and bookcases but also numerous items of what looked like scientific equipment, neatly piled up in the far corner.

'What on earth is that?' The Pope frowned as he tried to make sense of the scene in front of him, understandably rattled by the existence of this mysterious subterranean chamber they now found themselves in.

Harker, on the other hand, immediately recognised most of the assembled equipment. On the left stood a dialysis machine as used for patients suffering from kidney failures. Next to it was a material splicer used for taking cross section cuttings of flesh and bone. He'd seen both in operation whilst attending a charity event at St Olmand's children's hospital. Cambridge University had generously provided the neonatal intensive care unit with new incubators, and a group of alumni, including himself, had been given a grand tour of the research department which contained similar apparatus. Whatever was going on down here it certainly had nothing to do with religion.

'It's medical equipment at least, I think it is.' Harker turned to the increasingly pale-faced pontiff. 'I believe now would be a good time for you to contact the pontifical guard.' He gently nudged the Pope, who was looking increasingly glassy-eyed with each passing second. 'Your Eminence, I think it's safe to say the Magi are up to something rather ...' The moment the word left his mouth, he cursed himself for the slip.

'The Magi! That's who this is about!' The pontiff recoiled in disbelief. 'But the Magi aren't real. They're just made-up stories ... false legends. Those old tales have been around since I first entered the Church.'

Harker firmly grasped the Pope's arm and gestured with his other hand to the equipment arranged against the wall. 'Does this look like some old tale?'

The pontiff didn't say a thing, his eyes now darting wildly over the room's contents as he tried to formulate a more rational explanation. 'The Magi are not real, Professor, and even if they were, what would bring them down here with all this equipment?'

'The Magi are real. I know this for a fact, your Holiness, and this is their doing. I don't know what they're up to, but I intend to find out. Now, please, alert the pontifical guard.' Harker managed to guide Pope Adrian to the passageway, without any resistance, unlocking the metal door and gently pushing him through it. 'Now please send guards. I'm going to look for Claire Dwyer.'

The pontiff offered a reluctant nod, his eyes filled with disbelief and confusion. 'I'll send security immediately as there is obviously something very wrong going on here. But believe me when I tell you the Magi are nothing more than a myth created to keep the pious alert at all times.'

Harker almost choked at the Pope's analysis, his conviction wanting to set him straight but instead settling for a conciliatory nod. What was the point? 'You may be right, but the sooner you get help, the sooner we'll know for sure.'

With that, Pope Adrian disappeared back the way they had come, carefully closing the door behind him.

Finally, Harker was alone, and with that came an enormous sense of relief. He had no idea who was down here, but his recent experiences with the Magi told him he had every right to worry. He was in enough trouble as it was without adding endangerment of the spiritual leader of over one billion Catholics to his ever-growing list of charges. There wasn't a chance he was going to take on that responsibility as well.

He made his way past the medical equipment, heading alongside the unusually large, yet empty, drawing board that spanned the entire length of the wall until he reached a grey door on the far side of the room. Cautiously, he grasped the cold brass handle and turned it slowly until the door began to open. As he poked his head into the dimly lit room, only one thought preoccupied his mind. *Claire Dwyer, are you in here?* His heart sank when instead he came face-to-face with a tall man dressed in a cardinal's robe, standing behind the bars of a prison cell.

'So you're another of Rocca's lackeys,' the prisoner growled before staring down at Harker's tracksuit bottoms and then up at his red Anatoly's T-shirt. 'Nice threads. I see you're going for the hobo look. Either that or Rocca's not paying you enough.'

The man stood well over six feet with broad shoulders, and Harker was momentarily thankful there was a cell door standing between them. 'I don't work for Cardinal Rocca, and I'm now guessing you don't either. Who are you?'

The man instantly looked relieved, and he placed his face closer to the bars. 'Cardinal Priest John Reed. And I'm very glad to meet you.' He extended a hand, and Harker shook it warily. Had the Cardinal not been wearing his official robes, he might have thought twice about it. He had always found it odd that human beings could be so easily reassured by a uniform. 'Professor Alex Harker.'

Reed retrieved his hand and once more grasped the bar till his knuckles whitened. 'I'm a consulate working for the Vatican Governorate. I was asked to look into Cardinal Rocca's irregular dealings, and, as you can see, I found something.' From the exhausted look in Reed's eyes, he had obviously been stuck here sometime, and it was obvious he didn't want to stay a second longer.

'I'm looking for a woman called Claire Dwyer,' he explained. 'Have you seen any sign of her?'

'No, but there was something going on in the other room. I don't know if that's connected with the person you're looking for.'

Harker felt his heart begin to sink. 'There's no one next door—only some conference room full of equipment.'

A smile crossed Father Reed's face. 'No, there's a secret room, too. I've seen it. Just get me out of here, and I'll show you.'

The fact that Father Reed had been locked up by Cardinal Rocca seemed reason enough to set the man free. And he was a priest, after all, but there was something else. Harker had always prided himself on his ability to assess a person's character just by looking at them—the way they held themselves and the way they talked. His father had once claimed, 'The eyes never lie.' As he stared hard into Father Reed's, he couldn't detect any malice whatsoever.

'OK, Father. Let me see what I can do.'

He headed back into the main room and searched for something that might help. After just a few minutes, he had found a thick metal rod discarded behind the dialysis machine. He couldn't tell what its proper use was, but it would serve as a perfect makeshift crowbar. Harker headed back into the cell and jammed the rod in between the lock and the door, slowly edging it in deeper until it could go no further.

'Stand back.' Harker pulled on the crowbar, shifting his weight more and more until, finally, his whole body was pulling against it with every ounce of his strength until, without warning, the door sprang open, sending him hurtling to the floor with a thump, the iron bar slamming against the bruise on his chest where the Cessenair's safety belt had dug in during the crash landing. 'Damn, that hurts!' He rubbed at the painful swelling on his chest as Father Reed reached down to pull him to his feet.

'You OK?'

Harker nodded uncertainly: if he got hit in that same place once more, he was likely going to pass out. 'If we can just find Claire and get out of here, I'll be fine.'

'Good. Then follow me.'

Harker followed his new ally back into the adjoining room and observed as Reed pulled aside a fuse box located next to a heavy bookcase and pushed the button behind. Overhead, the grinding of rotating gears could be heard from somewhere above, and Harker watched in astonishment as the wall-length drawing board rose into the ceiling, revealing an impressive glass observation deck behind it. His skin was now prickling with anticipation, and he fought to steady his breathing as he surveyed the interior. Inside, it looked like a regular hospital room equipped with everything you would expect, from the oxygen mask linked directly to the wall to the magnolia-painted walls and a vase full of fresh lilies.

'What the hell is this place?'

It was like looking on to a movie set where everything appeared normal, but you knew it was an illusion—like being in a waking dream.

'I don't know what all this stuff is for,' Reed said, aware of the questioning look that was now developing on Harker's face. 'But there's definitely something not right over there.' He pointed over to the bed in the corner of the room which was now visible.

It took a few seconds of squinting past the heart monitor and a web of tubes and wires for Harker to see a hand jutting out from beneath the bed covers. *Claire?*

'How do we get in?' he demanded, surprised at how erratic his voice sounded.

'Through here.' Reed pushed a small red button on the adjacent wall and a single glass panel about a metre wide swung open to allow them access.

The air inside the room was fresh, not stuffy like in the observation area, and it smelt just like any hospital: that curious mixture of chemical concoctions and cleaning products ensuring the required cleanliness.

Harker rushed over to the bed and gazed down at the occupant. It was undoubtedly a woman, but a large breathing mask covered her entire face, like a diving mask, and he could not see more because the inside of it was steamed up with her breath, so he gently slipped it off, and what he saw made him shudder.

It was a girl who could not have been more than eighteen years old with thick black curly hair and soft olive-coloured skin. Beads of condensation peppered her silky cheeks, and both eyes flicked back and forth under closed lids. She was beautiful, but she wasn't Claire Dwyer.

'Is this the woman you're looking for?' Reed asked hopefully.

Harker shook his head despondently. 'No, it's not. I've never seen her before, but she sure as hell doesn't belong down here.'

Harker pulled back the sheets and began to gather the girl into his arms when he noticed something that stopped him dead in his tracks. He felt his legs crumple under him, and he slumped against the wall as Father Reed leant over the women to see what had caused such a reaction. The girl looked normal, healthy even, but one thing did stand out, though he couldn't see what was so disturbing about it.

'She's pregnant. What does that mean?'

Harker managed a deep breath and rubbed his temple intensely. 'Oh my God, what have they done?'

'Not God, Alex,' a sudden voice declared behind them.

Harker and Reed recoiled in shock, and they both turned towards the glass doorway to find Pope Adrian VII grandly flanked by Lusic Bekhit and another man dressed in black holding a silenced berretta, unwaveringly trained upon them.

'But his son.'

Chapter 46

Perone took another drag of his stogy and exhaled a wisp of blue smoke above the crowd waiting in front of him. 'Take a good look, Angelo.' The veteran officer pointed down towards the twenty or so news vans lining the edge of St Peter's Square. 'That's what rules the world these days, not the Church. For better or worse.'

The two officers were standing halfway up the white steps leading into the basilica, from where they could see clearly across the massive tiled expanse of St Peter's Square.

'It's the way of the world, boss, and maybe not a bad thing either,' Angelo declared firmly.

The superintendent gave his second-in-command a grimace, shaking his head doubtfully. 'It used to be personal morality and religious beliefs that guided people to their own conclusions, but now we're all being told by the press what to think and how to act.'

'Sounds just like the Church then,' Angelo replied sarcastically as he eyed the slim figure of a female CNN reporter rehearsing her lines in front of a cameraman. 'And it looks better, too.'

Perone let out an unimpressed sigh and turned his attention back up towards the cathedral entrance, looking out for their guide. He wasn't about to get involved in a philosophical debate with someone whose hobbies, amongst other things, included collecting porn films with titles such as *Butt Buster* and that hardcore Roman epic *I came, I saw . . . I came again.*

Back at the station, Perone's tech team had managed to trace the mobile phone signal to somewhere inside the basilica itself, but their appointed gendarme chaperone, Officer Greco, had refused to let them go inside. Perone had then caused such a scene that some nearby news reporters had begun taking an interest in the sudden disturbance. Faced with half a dozen camera lenses aimed in his direction, the flushed-faced Vatican cop had retreated into the building to seek permission for access, and the two officers had been waiting outside ever since.

Down below them, scores of well-wishing Catholics mingled with the tourists, all wanting to witness the morning's events. The summit had generated far more public interest than Perone had imagined it would. He'd read about it in one of the papers but hadn't paid much attention; he wasn't particularly interested in the everyday news, most of which was as depressing as anything he regularly encountered at work.

Up ahead, the huge doors of St Peter's swung open, flooding the steps outside with bright light. Seconds later, a still flushed-looking Officer Greco reappeared and briskly made his way down towards them.

'Good news, you have been granted temporary access to the cathedral, but we must be gone before the Pope begins his speech. Until then you're free to carry out your inspection.' The gendarme leant towards Perone, not wanting his words to be overheard. 'If the man you're looking for is inside, then his apprehension must be handled discreetly. Is that clear, Superintendent Perone? There are secret service agents from all over the world inside, and to create a disturbance would undoubtedly cause a reaction. And the last thing we want is the attention of over a hundred armed agents, so low-key diplomacy is essential.'

The superintendent gave him a courteous nod. 'We've no wish to draw any undue attention, but we will remain inside as long as is needed, Officer Greco.'

The gendarme frowned unhappily. 'Very well, gentlemen, but may I remind you there are many world-famous faces inside, so please, no ogling.'

Perone nudged Angelo in front of him as all three men began to climb the steps. 'They're politicians, not school kids, so I'm sure they'll survive a few stares.'

Greco ignored this last remark and began to make his way through the crowd. He did not want these scruffy beat cops creating any undue problems over imaginary conspiracies. The last thing security needed tonight was an unseemly ruckus of any kind.

The young officer courteously pushed his way deeper into the massive interior of St Peter's, creating a path for his two guests, but had he known what chaos was about to erupt around the two policemen, he would never have let them on to Vatican soil, let alone inside the basilica.

Chapter 47

'Well, what a relentless pain in the arse you've turned out to be, for a man who gave up his faith so easily!'

Pope Adrian snorted in contempt and strode furiously into the room, stopping just a few metres short of the hospital bed. His anger was directed solely at Harker. 'If you had shown this much determination back when you were a priest, then maybe you would be Pope now instead of me.'

He glanced back at the man still standing in the doorway, glaring angrily at the two intruders. 'What did you liken the Professor to, Genges?'

'Like a turd that just won't flush, Your Holiness.'

The pontiff gave a momentary smirk, tickled by the remark. 'Like a turd that just won't flush? Never has an analogy been more apt as I'm sure Lusic here can attest to.'

The traitorous Templar merely emitted a deep grunt as Pope Adrian continued, 'And so here you are. I can't tell you how surprised I was to get your message, followed by your unexpected arrival this evening.' He let out a deep dramatic sigh. 'Finally, we can do away with the charade because I can't tell you how much I detest having to lie.'

Harker steadied himself against the hospital gurney positioned next to him as he struggled to take in what he was witnessing. Behind him, Reed stood motionless in silent astonishment.

'So you're the fourth Magi brother, then, Wilcox?'

John Wilcox gave a gracious bow. 'In the flesh, Professor. But John Wilcox is no more, only Pope Adrian VII remains. I have been reborn, and with it comes the total absolution of all my sins. I am truly a man renewed.'

Harker glanced down at the young girl lying on the bed, with a look of revulsion. 'And it hasn't taken you long to commit all new sins. My God, Wilcox, what are you doing?'

The mention of Popes Adrian's former identity once more caused the man's smile to disappear, and he frowned in displeasure. 'I said do not call me by my former name, Alex. Wilcox is no more. You will address me now', he smiled slyly 'as your Holiness.'

'Holy Father, what are you doing?' Reed interrupted as he struggled to understand what he was hearing. 'This doesn't make any sense.'

Wilcox placed both hands behind his back in a statesmanlike manner and eyed the cardinal priest unflinchingly. 'I'm sorry it had to be like this, Father, and that you have become embroiled in something that was not yours to know, but, once explained, I hope you will understand the truth in it and join us.' He glanced up at the grey wall clock hanging above the young girl's hospital bed. 'In just under twenty minute's time, I will give a speech to world leaders revealing to them what I'm about to tell you. Of course, I'll be obliged to omit some unpalatable truths, though ones I'm happy to enlighten you on right now.'

The door behind Harker swung open, making everyone jump—even Wilcox himself—as a scruffy-looking man in thick glasses with greying hair and a thick moustache, poked his head into the room, appearing even more startled than anyone else.

'What's going on in here?' The accent sounded German, and Harker instantly recognised it as from Berlin.

'Do not be concerned, Dr Sephris.' John Wilcox waved a dismissive hand in the air. 'Everything is under control, so please return to your work.'

Dr Spheris's thick-lensed spectacles made his eyes look bulbous, thus exaggerating his appearance of dismay as his stare darted back and forth between Harker and Reed. 'Yes, sir, but we must begin the procedure as soon as possible. I've already administered the drugs necessary to reverse the anaesthetic, but she will still need another shot to fully regain consciousness. The schedule must be rigidly observed and adhered to, so I must ask everyone to leave immediately. Of course, with the exception of Your Holiness.'

'I understand, perfectly, Doctor, I only need a few minutes, and then you may begin.'

The white-coated doctor assessed Harker and Reed once more, his eyes full of contempt, before slipping back through the door and closing it gently behind him.

'How big is this place anyway?' Harker asked, having glimpsed the corridors beyond over the doctor's shoulder.

'Bigger than you would think, but we'll get to that later.' Wilcox resumed his lecturing pose with his hands linked behind his back. 'Allow me to start at the beginning and allow me to introduce ourselves. We',—he indicated to both himself and Genges—'are Magi. Who have existed alongside the Christian Church since its inception by Emperor Constantine during the fourth century.'

'Christianity goes back further than that,' Reed interrupted defiantly.

'That's true, Father, but it had not yet evolved into the universal church we know today. It was still being defined simply by its followers until Constantine established it as the official creed of his entire empire. Once he had given his blessing, religious leaders set about deciding how this new church would be governed.'

'You're talking about the first Council of Nicaea?'

'That's correct, Professor. It was then decided by what system of beliefs it would be guided and the very methods by which Christianity would operate were resolved. Every aspect of faith scrutinised and voted upon, including the most important—the insistence that Jesus Christ was the son of God made flesh by the Father and not just a simple human being. This religion was to provide the unifying ingredient in a mighty empire that had begun tearing itself apart.'

John Wilcox smiled proudly as he continued to pace the black lino-covered floor. 'My forbearers . . .' He stopped and glanced in Genges's direction. 'Our forbearers were present at the first council but also present was a dissenting family, one of whose current spawn I believe you have already met?'

'Brulet.' Harker surmised.

'Yes, that freakish bastard who murdered our father.' A large grin spread across his face. 'A murder that was avenged earlier tonight, but I digress. My Magi ancestors believed that the new Church should have the prime authority to create and control the culture of the world and to shepherd its people like a flock. Brulet's predecessors, on the other hand, believed that the Church should observe more closely the path which they claimed Jesus Christ envisaged, where people were not a flock to be guided but merely individual followers of the new religion—followers that practised the tenets of the Church as they interpreted them and did not rely on guidance from the necessary higher authorities to steer them through their daily lives. That might sound great in theory, but it meant there was no control. And, my friends, human beings need to be controlled, for that is part of their genetic make-up. In the modern age, there are many who argue differently, but I can assure you they are wrong. After the instinct for survival, the need to belong, to follow a leader, is without question the strongest of all human characteristics. Indeed, it is built into the core of every living person on this planet, whether in terms of fashion, social customs, or religion. We all need to belong to *something* and freedom of thought', Wilcox shook his head knowingly, 'is just a myth.'

Genges and Lusic nodded in agreement, their eyes never leaving Harker's as if their stares alone had the power to convince him.

'After much debate during the Nicaean Council, it was thankfully the Magi's sense of logic that prevailed, and so the Catholic Church as we know it was born. Brulet's ancestors, on the other hand, continued to disagree, and, worried through concern that they could do real damage to the fragile structure of the new Church, that motley crew of beggars were stripped of all positions and authority before rightly being banished from the Catholic world. But, as with all vermin, they did not disappear entirely, and as the Church grew in strength, bringing enlightenment to the peoples of the Roman Empire and beyond, so did Brulet's predecessors lurk nearby in the shadows, always a step behind yet gaining strength, wealth, and followers. Their only aim, thereafter, was to sway the path of the Catholic Church towards their own misguided set of beliefs. The clan spent hundreds of years on the periphery of Christendom, building up this political power and wealth until the formation of the Templars gave them an opportunity to infiltrate the Church once again. In that guise, for almost two centuries, they concentrated on amassing a fortune in treasure and land, mainly donated by the gullible, and, only after years of operation, were they finally discovered for the dogs they were. It was then that the Templars were formally disbanded by Pope Clement V but not before they had arranged to have him murdered under the facade of natural causes.'

'That's not the way they tell it,' remarked Harker sarcastically.

'I'm sure they don't, Professor. Still, if you knew them as well as I do, then you'd know never to trust a Templar. Anyway, the remaining few fled to Europe with a vast fortune capable of buying nations, and they did just that. It was they, in the guise of advisors, who were responsible for convincing the British king Henry VIII to divorce his first wife and thus break with the Church. In doing so, he unwittingly laid the foundations of protestant heresy throughout England. And as England grew in power, so did the Protestant faith which eventually spread around the globe, taking authority away from the true church and placing it squarely in the hands of secular interests.'

Wilcox rubbed his fists as if preparing for a fight. 'And where has that got us? We now live in a world where most people are solely out for themselves, caring little for anyone else. They still like to think of themselves as good Christians, but that's all a facade. You only have to witness how such people ignore the plight of the homeless and less fortunate members of society to understand that. They are perfectly happy to complain about how unfair and difficult life is for such unfortunates so long as they don't have to be in the same room with them. Hypocrisy has become the standard in our daily lives and the norm is something people rarely question.'

Harker glanced towards Father Reed who stood motionless and silent, simply gaping in disbelief. As for himself, he felt more disturbed than shocked, since the real bolt from the blue regarding this situation had hit him earlier during his session with Brulet. But what really concerned him was that some of what Wilcox was preaching did resonate with him—not a lot but some of it.

'That's a pretty bleak outlook you have there, Wilcox. And besides, how do the Magi fit into all this? They are sure as hell not an accepted part of the Catholic Church.'

Wilcox eyes glinted with an unsettling anger. 'As I mentioned, the Magi were formed by my ancestors shortly after the first council of Nicaea. Many others deemed our beliefs too radical, and, even though they accepted our ideas on the nature of the Church, we were also seen as having become too powerful. The truth is that we were seen as a potential threat to the new Church's leadership and so were relegated to the fringes. But we survived, building up wealth and guiding Catholicism's path when we could—but more importantly, we kept the Templar threat at bay. Over the centuries, we have protected the Catholic Church from liberals hell-bent on idiotic changes and have even managed to install our own people into the upper echelons of Catholic hierarchy. But I am the first of the Magi ever to be ordained as Pope, and I intend to make it count. Do you know why, my good Professor?'

'I think I might have an idea,' Harker replied.

Wilcox laughed sarcastically. 'Of course you do, you know everything, don't you?'

Before Harker could say more, the Magi leader stepped forward and leant calmly over the hospital bed. 'But you're my guest here, so allow me. You know what changed during the nineteenth and twentieth centuries more than in any other? Religion, and more importantly Protestantism. This new diluted form of Christianity has emboldened people to speak their own minds and forget God's very laws that generations before them have adhered to. Eventually, television took over and, with it, a new form of social commentary. Suddenly, our culture and morals were decided upon by newspapers and popular entertainers, regarding what's acceptable and what is not. And with that came the collapse of traditional Catholic values. Community spirit and clear morality have been replaced by hard liquor, hard drugs, and even harder pornography. Some now speak of a broken society and broken homes, but the truth is that it is people's minds that have been broken. And that's when the Magi decided to save the world from itself and to restore spiritual order from the ashes of psychological chaos. Throughout the sixties, the standards in Catholic morals began to lower and with it church attendance, a trend that has steadily worsened with every passing decade. So a plan was formulated that would bring people back into the fold. It has taken over forty years to prepare for this, a plan to resurrect the only entity that could stem the tide of evil that has plagued human consciousness for too long. The entity of Jesus Christ himself. So the Magi set about collecting those very relics you had in your possession earlier tonight until they were returned to us by our newest associate and ex-Templar . . .'

Lusic offered a quick bow as Wilcox continued, taking great delight in the revelations.

'And once these items had been discovered in the depths of the Vatican archives, two programmes were initiated. One was to place as many Magi into the Vatican hierarchy as possible, which as you can see has been a stunning success. The other was to begin the process of bringing Jesus Christ himself back to life.'

Wilcox then gently placed his hand on the side bar of the metal bed in which the young pregnant woman lay sleeping. 'And this too has been a success.'

Harker's mind began to soar as he digested this latest disclosure. 'You're telling me that this girl is pregnant with Jesus Christ?'

Wilcox interrupted, his excitement barely contained. 'Well, a clone of Christ. The DNA was extracted from the relics and worked upon with huge sums of funding from both Magi coffers and siphoned off by our operatives placed within the Vatican. It is only in the past ten years that science finally caught up with our aspirations, and even then, there was a degree of trial and error and a few casualties along the way in order to get the process absolutely right. We then had to wait until a Magi Pope could be elected before the final stage might be undertaken.'

Those images of the contorted faces of the Angels in the orphanage flashed through Harker's mind. 'Casualties? You're saying that those poor children were . . .' He could barely voice the words. 'The result of your failed attempts at the cloning process . . . Christ's clones gone wrong?'

Wilcox nodded sadly. 'Yes, I'm afraid so, and, unfortunately, it could not be helped. Like I said, trial and error, but once born, they were cared for in that orphanage you yourself visited.'

'Cared for!' Harker yelled, struggling to contain the sheer revulsion he was feeling. 'Those poor children were burnt alive. *Deliberately.*'

Again Wilcox nodded. 'Yes, a sad but unavoidable occurrence—one that was brought about by your friend Archie Dwyer. When requested to safeguard the relics, it seems he nosed around far more than he should have. He uncovered Magi documents pertaining to the cloning process and the Angels, as he later called them. When I found out that he continued to visit them, I realised it was just a matter of time before he dragged everything out into the open, and so the evidence had to be destroyed.'

'You mean you burnt those kids alive just to keep your twisted plans a secret?' Harker shouted.

Wilcox smiled wistfully. 'Yes, I gave them life and then took it away again. As I said, unfortunate but necessary.'

From behind Harker, Father Reed suddenly sprang forward, his arms outstretched, clearly outraged at what he was being told, but he made it only a few steps before Genges was upon him with lightening speed and precision, his arm-sword halting the larger man, the blade nuzzling into the crook of his neck.

Wilcox hardly moved an inch, the confidence in his younger brother's abilities absolute. 'I will put that down to natural reaction, Father Reed. I, too, was appalled when I realised the corner Archie Dwyer's actions had backed us into.'

Reed struggled uselessly in Genges's steel grip. 'You're a monster,' he gasped.

'I know,' Wilcox agreed 'But I have become a monster only so all Christians can regain what they have so sadly lost over the past hundred years—belief and confidence in their faith. This is a burden I must bear like Jesus, who never wanted to give himself up to the Romans but did so in order to save the souls of all people.'

'Don't even dare compare yourself to the son of God, you sick bastard.'

'So how did you get Archie to kill himself?' Harker cut the ex-marine off mid-sentence. He could see this was about to turn into a slagging match and that wouldn't get him any closer to finding Claire. 'Did you have to use blackmail?'

'No, nothing like that.' Wilcox looked genuinely insulted. 'Father Dwyer took the whole tragedy on to his own shoulders. He felt personally responsible for the deaths, and, in a way, he was right. If he had not got involved, those children would still be alive today. And with the realisation that he was the instigator of Christ's death four times over . . . Well, his suicide then becomes understandable but not before he stole our relics and sent the letter which dragged you into all this.'

Harker rubbed the back of his neck as he tried to assimilate the fantastic yet horrifying final few pieces of the puzzle. 'But why did you need those relics? You already had your clone.'

Wilcox's face began to pale, and a grim smile appeared. 'Why? Because shortly I will reveal to world leaders a story destined to become the new gospel—a story calculated to affect every Christian mind on the face of the planet. It tells how a virgin peasant girl came to the Church miraculously with child and how we came to realise this was Jesus Christ himself and the beginning of the second coming. I will explain how we tested the newborn baby's blood with that found on sacred relics held in the Church's possession for over two thousand years and how the DNA matched perfectly. Then independent scientists from every nation on our planet will be given access to these relics, whose carbon dating will corroborate our claim. Millions of people, Christian and otherwise will realise they are witnessing the second coming of Christ and will flock to the Catholic Church with a renewed fervour, revitalising the faith and imbuing it with a power that has been draining away for too long. The returned messiah is to be brought up by the Magi, who will supervise the young Christ child until he is old enough to become the Church's voice. This glorious event will herald a new golden age for the Catholic Church, but this time its hegemony will last not just for two thousand years but for two hundred thousand. It is this renewed faith that human colonies will eventually transport to the stars.'

Wilcox seemed to lose himself in wonder at the very idea, gazing up towards the ceiling as he imagined the possibilities. 'And it is on the teachings of Catholicism and the events that transpire here today that their faith will be based upon. No longer will the biblical stories be passed merely by book from one generation to the next, but there will be visually documented evidence for believers to see with their own eyes for millennia to come. For if the Catholic Church lasted two thousand years on just the existence of a book, then imagine how long it will last with undeniable proof of Jesus Christ himself.'

The new Pope gazed down at the young woman lying on the bed in front of him and lovingly stroked her head. 'But without those relics, this would be just another boy. The question of this child being Jesus Christ himself must be undeniable, and the more relics, the more evidence because after tonight, the whole world will be scrutinising our future actions, and so everything must be in place.'

Harker glanced down at the sleeping beauty. 'And how about her? She must suspect something.'

Wilcox shook his head. 'Dr Sephris, who you just met, is a trusted Magi associate, and he runs a dental clinic here in Rome. Once a suitable female candidate had been chosen by us, she was offered a free check-up. The woman is Ms Maria Genova, chosen for both her religious beliefs and her strong constitution, was then booked in and given an anaesthetic in the guise of deep root-canal work. The good doctor inserted the cloned foetus into her without penetrating her hymen, with techniques developed by the Magi for just this purpose, and thus maintained the physical semblance of her virginity. When she discovered her pregnancy some months later, I was on hand to lend my advice and support. She was brought here to the Vatican in secret and watched over dutifully by my brother Cardinal Rocca and, of course, by Dr Sephris. Some hours ago, the girl was given a strong sedative, and she will be woken up once we have left and the birth induced.'

'And what then? Surely, she'll want a hand in how her own son is brought up,' Harker protested.

'I'm afraid this girl won't be around long enough to see the young boy's first birthday. She will be assassinated in a few months' time by a Muslim extremist—an act that will enrage and incite Christians to embark on a modern crusade.' John Wilcox pressed a palm lightly against his chest. 'But not before she has signed a will naming me her most trusted priest, as the child's guardian—the guardian of Jesus Christ, the son of God, returned to mankind in the twenty-first century.'

Harker was suddenly overcome with a deep feeling of dread. In truth, Wilcox's plan was just crazy enough to work and, if brought to fruition, could initiate the greatest deception of all time—or second greatest at any rate.

The fact of having just revealed his entire plan for world domination was either a testament to Wilcox's supreme arrogance or his confidence that neither Harker nor Reed would survive to divulge it. Either way, he had managed to omit the one piece of information that had originally drawn Harker to Vatican City.

'Where's Claire Dwyer?' he demanded.

Mention of her name drew an excited grin from the Magi operative. 'I've been waiting for you to get around to her.'

The sarcasm was completely lost on Harker. 'Enough with the talk, Wilcox. I want to see her now.'

Wilcox shook his head unconcernedly. 'Does the life of that woman mean so much to you, considering the world-changing events that will transpire here today?'

Unbelieveble, Harker thought. This man wasn't fit to wear a dog collar, let alone be Pope. 'One step at a time, Wilcox. One step at a time.'

'Cocky? I like that. You really believe you can influence tonight's proceedings, don't you? Very well, Alex, if she means that much to you. You know, it's funny, but I was convinced you'd be far more concerned about the implications of today's events than the location of Ms Dwyer.'

'Then you really don't know me at all, John.'

Wilcox sucked in a deep breath and then let out a bellowing laugh. 'Well, then, with that in mind, this will be all the sweeter.' He clicked his fingers in the direction of Lusic, who disappeared for a few moments before reappearing with a ruffled-looking Claire Dwyer. She appeared OK apart for a few scuff marks on her forehead. 'Alex' She leapt towards him and wrapped her arms around his neck.

'I never thought I'd see you again.'

'Did they hurt you?'

'No. They were a bit rough but no.' She pulled away and eyed him closely. 'What the hell is going on?'

The relief Harker felt was palpable, and he gazed at her. *Damn she looked like Archie.* 'Apparently, Pope Adrian here is behind everything, including Archie's death.'

Wilcox tut-tted impatiently as Harker continued. 'All the murders, the assassinations, everything that's happened was organised by him in an attempt to gain absolute control of the Catholic Church.'

Claire Dwyer pulled back further, her face full of confusion. 'No, that's not what I meant. Why did *you* come here tonight?'

'What?'

'You weren't meant to come chasing after me because your job was already done. Oh, Alex.'

A surge of nausea rose in Harker's stomach as he watched her walk calmly over to Wilcox's side, who was now grinning like a madman.

'Oh, you should see the look on your face—it's a picture. Almost worth all the trouble you've caused us. Almost. How do you think the Magi were able to track you down so effectively? We're not psychics.'

Harker could barely believe what he was hearing. *Claire Dwyer a Magi associate!* 'What the fuck is going on, Claire? Archie was your brother! How could you work for these people? When did it start?'

She looked genuinely sad, but her words painted an altogether different picture. 'When Archie stumbled across the Magi's plans, he called and told me everything. About Cardinal Rocca, the relics, the angels, the Magi cloning process . . . everything. But where he was horrified by it all, I saw the benefits it could bring to the Christian faith. So I contacted Cardinal Rocca and agreed to find out the whereabouts of the relics' location from Archie, and, in return, the Magi would leave him alone. But before I could do that, he committed suicide. He had mentioned your name in our last conversation, so when you turned up unexpectedly at his funeral, it set everything into motion. All I had to do before calling a taxi was to alert the Magi to our location, but then, that idiot Drazia turned up and almost ruined everything.'

'Yes, that damn ogre really threw a spanner in the works.' Wilcox shook his head disappointingly at the thought. 'Thank goodness Brulet had you picked up from the police station, which brought Lusic into play—or we would have struggled to keep tabs on you.' Wilcox offered a grateful nod to the ex-Templar before continuing his devious omission. 'My oversight was in keeping Claire's true allegiance from my brothers, but until you arrived at Archie's funeral yesterday, we didn't need her to be involved. And now that bloody fool Drazia has managed to get himself arrested by the UK police. Still, at least he'll keep his mouth shut. That's about the only positive side to the oaf's personality. But I assure you, it's the last time I will entrust my brother Balthasar with any such important task.'

Harker felt totally stunned. Claire Dwyer had always seemed the most loyal sister a brother could have. From the first time he met her, she had protected Archie like a watchdog, castigating anyone who dared bad-mouth her brother and even throwing punches when the insult offered was harsh enough. What had changed?

'Don't look at me like that, Alex. I'm not evil. I'm a realist and a Catholic, and I believe in what's being done here. The Church has been hit hard in recent years. Remember how you struggled to retain the numbers of your congregation? Well, that's being repeated all throughout the Western world, and something drastic needs to be done.' It was now Claire who was struggling to hold back her anger. 'That erosion of the Catholic faith over the past fifty years was causing my brother more pain than anything else, and he wanted above all to see Catholicism recover its rightful role as a force for good in this world, and you know that, Alex.'

Harker could tell by the look in her eyes that she believed what she was saying emphatically. Whatever her reason for assisting the Magi, it was still rooted in a warped belief that she was helping her brother. 'Maybe so, Claire, but at what cost? There's one thing I know in my heart, and it's that Archie would never have wanted you involved with people who consider the murder of children as justified collateral, regardless of the reason. And I think *you* know that!'

Claire Dwyer shook her head solemnly and eyed Harker with the same unflinching expression that had adorned John Wilcox's face minutes earlier. 'What *I know*, Alex, is that sometimes the end does justify the means. And with the faith of over one billion people at stake, I'd say without question this is one of those times.'

Wilcox reached over and gently pulled Claire towards him. 'Well said, my dear, but you've no need to explain your actions to a man with no faith. Now we must be going. I've got a speech to deliver, and we need to find a safe place for you to hole up in until we've dealt with any police concerns. Remember, you're still listed as a kidnap victim.' He smiled deviously in Harker's direction. 'If the authorities actually believed anything the good professor told them in the first place, which is unlikely. Well, I've said all there is to say, and so I shall say goodbye for the last time.' He turned and faced Harker in a formal manner. 'Goodbye, Professor Alex Harker, you will not be missed.' He then offered a limp wave of his hand and headed towards the door, stopping only momentarily. 'Oh and Father Reed, I will grant you a few more days to make your decision, and then, well, I'm afraid you can either join the new world order or follow in the footsteps of your new-found friend.'

Reed once more strained against the razor-sharp sword that Genges was still holding to his neck. 'You can have my decision now. Go screw yourself!'

Wilcox shrugged his shoulders uncaringly. 'Very well then, you'll die with your best buddy here. Goodbye.' He then briskly stepped through the door, followed by Claire who shot Harker a final disappointed look.

'It didn't have to be like this, Alex.'

Harker responded with a nod, barely able to look her directly in the eyes. 'Yes, it did.'

With that, she was gone, the door slamming behind her with a jolt.

'Well, boys,' Genges rasped, releasing his grip on Father Reed, who stumbled back against Harker as the Magi retracted his arm-sword with a click. 'Let's get this party under way. Lusic, take this automatic and keep them covered.' He thrust a stubby Glock handgun with a silencer attached into the hands of his German counterpart. 'We'll do it in the corridor outside and use the academy entrance to get the bodies removed. I'll check the coast is clear and organise a car to take us from there.' He leant in closer, out of earshot for both Harker and Reed. 'We'll tie them up first and strangle them as we don't want any bloodstains down here. This place is destined to become a shrine after todays events.'

Genges slunk off through the door in his usual fluid, catlike motion, leaving the three men alone.

'Well then,' Lusic's contempt was obvious, 'looks like you chose the wrong team, Professor. Strange for you to think that this girl in front of you will be the key to the beginning of a new world, just as your own life is coming to an end.'

As Lusic wallowed in self-satisfaction, a movement caught Harker's attention, and he glanced down at the young girl. She still seemed fast asleep, and he was about to turn his attention back to the still gloating German when he noticed it once more. The girl's eye flickered once and then again. Next, her mouth began to prise itself open, her dry lips sticking to each other. She was waking up, the drug administered by Dr Sephris was taking effect.

Harker glanced furtively at Reed, who had noticed too, and, as both men locked eyes, a plan was hatched.

It had been well documented that over 80 per cent of human communication is non-verbal, a fact not lost on either of them. Neither man was quite sure what their plan was, but the girl's awakening represented an opportunity—one that would be lost the moment the other henchman reappeared.

'You know what, Lusic, you're a complete tool.' Harker's insult brought the ex-Templar's joviality to a standstill. 'And if you weren't so busy congratulating yourself, you would have noticed that the girl's waking up. And if she sees you waving a gun at us, well, she's going to realise things aren't exactly kosher. What do you think?'

Lusic gestured both men away from the bed and moved in for a closer inspection, his eyes focused on the girl's head, now lolling from side to side as she struggled to regain consciousness.

He leant over the bed, lowering the silenced Glock to his side, and, in that moment, both men seized their chance.

Harker was immediately wrestling the pistol away as Reed locked both his arms around the traitor's thick neck, applying pressure to the windpipe just like his military training had taught him. Lusic's muscular frame swung them both around like rag dolls, smashing Harker into the wall with such ferocity that the impact came close to knocking him out. But he still clung to gun and to the forearm wielding it, holding on for dear life.

After twenty seconds or so, the German's strength began to ebb as Reed's grip on his throat became tighter and tighter, cutting off the supply of blood and oxygen to his head. After a further twenty seconds, all three men collapsed to the floor in a wheezing pile.

'Is he dead?' Harker gasped, struggling to recover his breath.

Reed shook his head, staggering to his feet. 'No, unconscious. But he'll wake up with a banging headache.'

Harker rubbed at his forehead. 'He's not the only one.'

A high-pitched squeak sounded off behind them, and both men turned around sharply to see the young girl staring at them through bleary eyes. '*Che passa?*' She only managed these two words before her eyes rolled upwards, and she slumped back on to the bed, the anaesthetic not yet entirely flushed from her system.

'We need to get her out of here—and now,' Reed said firmly as he sucked in a few more restoring breaths. 'But we can't get her out through the academy itself without running into Genges and his Magi friends. There must be some other way out.'

For the first time in years, Harker felt the urge to do something he rarely did any more, but he suddenly felt compelled to do it. He clasped his hands together briefly and stared up towards the ceiling. 'We could use a little help here, if you're free.'

Ahead of them, the room door was flung open, and an irate-looking Dr Sephris hobbled into the room with all the grace of a man with severe piles. 'What's going on here?'

Harker raised Lusic's pistol to aim at the doctor's groin, and the medic instantly flung his arms in the air and froze. *Some Magi warrior he was.*

'Tell us how to get out of here, Doctor, without having to go through the Academy of Sciences. Otherwise, I pull this trigger right now. No games: you answer me or you die.' It was a bluff, of course, since Harker wasn't the type to kill someone in cold blood, but he was definitely considering a leg shot.

Without hesitation, Dr Sephris pointed towards the door they had entered by. 'Through the door, go right, and you'll end up in the academy. But left takes you into an unexcavated part of the necropolis. Follow the path, and you'll come to a secret doorway leading into one of the grotto's chapels.'

The last part of the Sephri's directions brought a thin smile to Harker's lips. 'A secret entrance underneath the basilica! Are you serious?'

The nervous man gave a nervous, shaky nod. 'It was specially constructed as an escape route during the World War II. We discovered it whilst building this facility—that's what I was told anyway. Now please go, but leave the girl.'

'I'm afraid not, Doctor. She comes with us.'

Before Sephris could protest, Harker slammed the butt of the pistol across the man's face, dropping him to the floor in an unconscious heap.

'OK, Father, would you please get her to her feet.'

In a matter of seconds, Reed had hauled the unsteady young woman upright. Still groggy, she struggled to remain conscious, her eyelids flickering and her lips mouthing soundless words. Reed gently slipped his arm around her waist and moved towards the door, where Harker was already making sure the coast was clear.

'You know, Alex, for a man who's lost his faith, you don't seem to be entirely convinced of that decision.'

Harker said nothing; this wasn't the time for a spiritual debate, and he simply beckoned Reed into the empty passage outside, taking a left towards the underground necropolis. The city of the dead, as it had become known, was a vast underground burial chamber that housed the bones of some of the earliest Christians but more importantly offered their way out of this place.

He glanced back into the observation room and checked the unconscious body of Dr Sephris sprawled out on the floor before, once again, raising his eyes to the ceiling. 'Thanks for the help, but we need some more if you can spare it.'

Chapter 48

The cold, decay-filled air of the necropolis was nauseating, and Harker had begun breathing through his nose in an effort to keep the bitter taste from his mouth. In front of him, the Cardinal had taken the lead and was slowly navigating the dusty path running the length of the ruins with the flickering yellow flame of Harker's Zippo offering fleeting images of crumbling tombstones spread across the massive open space.

Harker never visited this part of the ancient burial site but knew one thing for certain: this wasn't on the tourist itinerary. Pressed against his side, the pregnant girl was using him as a crutch as she continued her struggle to regain full consciousness.

'It's only a few minutes' walk from here, past the main layout of crypts and then upwards,' Reed announced as Harker strove to keep up with the remarkably fit cardinal. He was surprised at how agile the fifty-seven-year-old was, but what really preoccupied his thoughts was why this good man of the cloth did not volunteer a hand with the semi-conscious pregnant woman he was struggling with.

'How do you know this place so well?' Harker finally puffed.

'During my first week here, Cardinal Vincenzo gave me a quick tour. And thank the Lord he did, because it's a total maze down here.'

The metal door Dr Sephris had directed them to led straight into this dark untended section of the necropolis. On the other side, the door was hidden from view by an unkempt mass of ivy serving as a curtain to hide the secret opening to the Magi's underground lair.

'It's a shame I didn't discover that entrance earlier,' Reed declared. 'It could have saved both of us a lot of trouble.'

Harker managed only a groan.

'I gotta be honest, Alex. I'm still struggling to get my head around the Pope, and these Magi crazies, and then there's this cloning project. It seems as fantastical as it is despicable, and I can't decide whether their infiltration of the Vatican is a testament to their abilities or shameful proof of our ineffectiveness.'

'Don't take it personally,' Harker advised. 'These people have been pulling strings from the shadows for hundreds of years, and it's near impossible to stop something you've no idea exists in the first place. Just look at the American Mafia. Now, how about you lend me a hand?'

Reed looked a little embarrassed. 'Of course. Sorry.'

Before he had even taken a step, there was a high-pitched ping as a bullet whizzed past their heads and embedded itself in the crumbling stonework of the wall in front of them.

Reed ducked to the floor as Harker lowered himself more slowly for fear of hurting the girl. He gently laid her against the side of a grey stone mausoleum as another bullet tore over their heads. Further along the necropolis, they could hear the scuffling of leather-soled shoes on the dusty flagstones as they slowly approached. The cardinal priest snapped the Zippo shut with a click, plunging them into the darkness. There were a few seconds of silence as the footsteps paused, and then a familiar voice echoed through the vast underground chamber.

'Professor Harker, there is no need for all this melodrama. I'd rather not harm you. We merely want the woman and her child. Please don't prolong this ridiculous game of cat and mouse any further.' The Magi's voice sounded sincere, but, in the gloom, Harker could hear Reed quietly mumbling in disbelief, echoing his own sentiments as Genges continued with his plea.

'Gentlemen, I've no wish to harm either of you,' the voice continued civilly. 'I only want what is ours.'

Reed prodded Harker to move forward, but the scraping of his shoes attracted their pursuer even closer, now perhaps only fifteen metres away.

'I will not beg you, Professor, or you either, Father Reed, but the decision you now make will either ensure your life or terminate it. The girl with you knows not a word of English, so we can clear this up and she'll be none the wiser.' All the while the Magi killer continued to draw closer to them both. 'Please, gentlemen, I am armed and you are not, so there's not a chance of you escaping.'

Ten metres behind them, a thin beam of torchlight now flickered into life and began slowly shifting from one headstone to the next, searching for the slightest sign of movement.

Reed leant over towards Harker and whispered in his ear, 'He's right. There's nothing else we can do.'

Harker winced at the thought and tightened his grip on the young girl. 'Not a fucking chance,' he hissed.

Reed's face screwed up tightly in the dim torchlight, and then he shook his head. 'Not what I meant, I'll make a play of surrendering to him, and, meanwhile, you get her out of here.' He pointed towards a dim glow of light visible some twenty-five metres up ahead. 'If Dr Sephris told us the truth, the exit should be right about there.'

Reed carefully slipped off his red-and-black outer robe and gently laid it over the still barely conscious body of Maria Genova. He then lovingly stroked the young girl's cheek and, with sadness in his voice, urged Harker, 'With that world summit going on, she'll stick out like a sore thumb. So put that robe around her and move as discreetly as possible. Then you get her straight to a hospital or somewhere safe. You must defend her with your life, and above all else, don't let these Magi devils get their hands on her. Do you understand me, my brother?'

The cardinal's emotional plea stirred a renewed strength in Harker's muscles. He remembered this as the way men of the cloth spoke to each other—as friends, as equals, as family. Harker nodded silently and placed his hand on top of the cardinal's before squeezing it as one would do to a sibling.

Reed's smile was barely visible. 'You're still a man of God, Alex Harker, whether you accept it or not. You may have turned your back on *him*, but *he* will never turn his back on you.'

This simple comment almost caused Harker to shed a tear, and he fought back his embarrassment as Reed gestured him away. 'When I stand up and head towards him, I'll cause as much distraction as I can to cover your escape. Now get her out of here. And good luck.'

Before Harker could say anything, Father Reed was already standing up and swaying about wildly, giving the impression that he was trying to find his footing whilst preparing to cover the sound of Harker's movements with his own. 'All right, you win, the girl's yours. I'll come to you.'

In the same moment, Harker dragged the girl to her feet and, ducking as low as he could, took off towards the dim outline of a doorway ahead, turning briefly to see the torchlight pick out Father Reed, its dazzle making him squint and raise a hand to his eyes.

'Where is she, Father?' Genges snarled.

'She's lying here, unconscious.' The cardinal priest continued to shuffle around before pointing towards a wall of crumbling masonry just a few metres away. 'She's OK, but she'll need a blanket. It's freezing down here.'

Genges cautiously edged towards him, the torch now shining directly into Reed's face. 'Where's the Professor?' he demanded.

Father Reed took a step back as the blinding light drew nearer. 'That coward made a run for it. He said he'd had enough of people trying to kill him over something that wasn't his fight.'

By the time he had finished speaking, the Magi prince was no more than a few feet away and, shifting his torch, revealed the grimace of anger that was spreading across his face. 'Now now, Father, you don't expect me to believe that for a second, do you?'

The cardinal shook his head woefully. 'No, but it did bring you closer.'

In an instant, Reed lunged towards the other man, his hands reaching for the gun, but, still blinded by the light, he missed, instead managing only to clasp both hands around the torch instead. Instantly, he felt the hard muzzle of a gun dig into his ribcage, followed by a blinding flash. The explosion in his chest caused his legs to buckle and sent him to his knees. With a struggle, he raised his head to see the flashing white teeth of his attacker, his grip now tightening on the killer's jacket.

'You lose, Magi. All your years of work have been for nothing. All your hopes and dreams are over.'

Genges smiled mockingly. 'As is your life, Priest.' He cocked the pistol, staring down at Father Reed who was drawing upon his last pockets of energy to pull his head up as close to the killer's face as possible. The cardinal could only manage a whisper, but his words sent a shiver down Genges's spine. 'My soul is prepared for the afterlife.' He coughed, bloody spittle running from his lips. 'But is yours?'

Up ahead, Harker was only a few metres from the dim outline of the secret doorway when he turned and glanced back fleetingly into the gloom of the necropolis. In that moment, a second shot rang out, and the flash of the gun provided a glimpse of the two men together like a photographic negative. Genges was towering over Reed, the gun pressed against the man's chest as the cardinal clung to his attacker, before they were both enveloped in darkness once more. Ignoring the fear the image had conjured up in him, Harker turned and pressed against the door in front of him.

Despite its bulk, the door swung open easily with nothing more than a scratchy grinding sound, and he was instantly bathed in yellow brightness from a light above his head. He swiftly lifted and carried Maria Genova through it and then pushed the door shut behind him. There was no lock or handle, for the exterior did not even resemble a door, but a beautifully sculpted white marble wall slab depicting the Virgin Mary in prayer.

The vaulted room he entered was decorated with gold and red tiles of magnificent craftsmanship, and Harker recognised it immediately. Directly above the modest stone altar behind him was *The Madonna della Bocciata,* a fresco as famous as any found in Vatican City and, in English, was better known as the bruised Madonna. The legend dating back to the fifteenth century told of a soldier who, angry at losing his florins in a game of chance, hurled a stone at the virgin's face. The impact left a lesion on her cheek, and soon afterwards, drops of blood oozed from the cut before dripping to the stone paving below. Harker had viewed the scene of this miracle for himself on numerous occasions and knew that the chapel of the Madonna della Bocciata was located directly beneath St Peter's Basilica and not more than twenty feet from the Tomb of St Peter itself. The recognition gave him a sliver of comfort as he realised they were only seconds away from two potential exits. One led up to the necropolis or Scavi tourist office, which would get them outside, but there was a problem. The gates would normally be open at this time of day, but, seeing as the world's entire political elite were here for the summit, they would no doubt be locked for issues of security. And with Genges less than a minute behind them, he could not chance running into a dead end. That meant there was only one other way.

Harker tugged at the girl, who had finally found the strength to stand on her own, though barely able to keep her eyes open, and began heading away from the small underground chapel. Once reached, he continued onwards past the impressive grey marble slabs that led to the tomb of St Peter and then further still until he reached a spiral staircase next to the small chapel of St Andrew. The steps led directly up on to the main floor of St Peter's, emerging only a few metres away from the main altar where Pope Adrian VII would be delivering his speech to the world at large.

Harker wrapped the clerical robe Father Reed had given him around Maria Genova's shoulders, fastening it in place with its scarlet sash and quickly brushed her hair back from her face as best he could.

'OK, here we go.'

Chapter 99

'Honoured friends and guests, I give you His Holiness Pope Adrian VII.'

Superintendent Rino Perone watched Cardinal Rocca with accusing eyes as the clergyman raised his hand in the direction of John Wilcox, who was slowly progressing down the long aisle of St Peter's Basilica towards the great altar and the majestic baldacchino directly above it. Bernini's masterpiece towered thirty metres above the altar itself, supported on four massive legs of bronze, and, at the corners of the canopy, gold angels sat studiously, watching over the expanse of the cathedral floor below.

The pontiff was flanked by five high-ranking cardinals who continually nodded greetings to the hundred or so world leaders that had assembled for the summit that morning. Every pair of eyes was fixed on the papal procession, except for two. Both Perone and Barbosa instead focused on the pulpit in front of them. To be more accurate, both men were concentrating on one man, Cardinal Rocca, who was making a final adjustment to the height of the microphone. Once that was done, the cardinal stepped to one side where he stood waiting calmly.

Angelo discreetly nudged his boss's arm with the LCD-display tracker unit nestling in his palm. 'The signal's definitely coming from him, sir. There's no doubt. He must have the phone on him.'

Perone gave a small nod. 'Once the speech is over, we'll introduce ourselves.' He glanced back at their personal security guard, Officer Greco, and smiled pleasantly before returning his gaze towards Cardinal Rocca, who was now joining in with the rapturous applause for the new Pope. 'We'll wait until afterwards, when all the political types are outside, and then we'll have a chat.'

Angelo sighed slightly. 'You know I'm with you, boss, but I have to be honest. Questioning a cardinal about murder on his own turf is, well . . .'

Perone raised an eyebrow questioningly as he listened to the young detective's concerns.

'Well, it's a bit above my station, if you know what I mean.' Angelo nodded towards an elegantly dressed man in the front row who was now kissing the Pope's ring on bended knee. 'And I'm not sure if you're aware of it, but that's our prime minister and the minister of the interior—our boss.'

If Perone had noticed the Italian prime minister, he didn't show it, his face remaining the picture of a man at ease. 'I don't care if Jesus himself walks in and pulls up a seat. If this so-called cardinal has anything to do with our murderer, then we're taking him in, even if that means dragging him across the Vatican border by the scruff of his robe.' The apprehensive look in Angelo's eyes was clear, and he understood his subordinate's reservations. If this all went wrong, it could constitute an international incident, and there was a shit load of ways it could go tits-up. 'Don't worry, Angelo, I'm the commanding officer here, so it's my responsibility.' He leant in nearer as officer Greco closed in behind them, straining to get a better view of Pope Adrian VII making his way leisurely up the altar steps towards the waiting microphone. 'And if it's God you're worried about, believe me, boy, if this guy's crooked, then the old man upstairs will be cheering us on.'

This last remark coaxed out the smile Perone had been looking for, and he returned his gaze to Rocca who was now taking his seat, along with all the other guests, as Pope Adrian tapped at the mike and waited calmly for the sound of shuffling feet and creaking chairs to die down.

'Ladies, gentlemen, leaders of the world, I myself, the Vatican and the entire Catholic Church welcomes you here on this special day.' John Wilcox surveyed the hundred or so delegates seated in front of him, each eager to know why the head of the Catholic Church had called on them to attend.

'When I first made the invitation to all the heads of state to attend here this morning, without offering a good reason, I wasn't sure how many of you would actually turn up. But seeing so many of you present, from so many different countries and belonging to so many different faiths, representing six-and-a-half billion people around the globe, it imbues me with a renewed sense of faith. Not religious or ideological faith, but a faith in humankind and its ability to come together regardless of our differences.' Wilcox smiled proudly, and his audience smiled back. 'On the day of my inauguration as head of the catholic church, a tragic event occurred. For, as you will know, one of our cardinals committed the awful sin of taking his own life in a very public way. It was an incident that has left many of us with a great sense of sadness and shame.'

Wilcox shook his head woefully from side to side. 'Yes, I say shame because those of us who knew Father Archibald Dwyer did not see the tragedy coming. That oversight in itself will haunt many of us for years to come'—he gave a deep sigh—'but there is another reason that our shame is so great, and it is why I have invited you here this evening. It is also the reason I have insisted there be no direct broadcast or reporting of what I am now saying, so please allow me to explain. Eight months ago, a young woman arrived at the doors of the Vatican with a story so unbelievable that there were those of us who found it impossible to accept and It is for this disbelief that we are also shamed. Aged in her early twenties, she was born in the village of Monte Massaruccio just outside Rome, no more than thirty kilometres from where we now sit. For the time being, I will refer to her simply as Maria and tell you only that she is a good Catholic and a child of Jesus Christ. She is an extremely special young woman, not just because of her religious faith but because of her caring, loving, and honest nature. It is for these same reasons that I now believe she was chosen.'

A confused murmuring began to fill the cathedral as the audience struggled to understand where this announcement was leading.

'Please allow me to explain. For what you don't know is that Maria was with child, and she was utterly convinced that the child, still only one month in her womb, had no father. She insisted she had never had carnal knowledge of a man and had simply woken one day to a bout of morning sickness. Now as you can all imagine, most of us here at the Vatican believed her to be mistaken or simply making up the story to gain attention. But . . .' Wilcox let the words hang for a few seconds as the majority of his congregation's eyes began to widen like saucers. 'We organised a doctor to investigate further, and a medical examination confirmed what Maria had been insisting upon all along. She was indeed pregnant but had never been with a man.'

As Wilcox paused for breath, whispers of disbelief began to circulate amongst the crowd.

'After this revelation, we called upon the best medical advice we could find, and a sample of the child's blood was taken through the most non-invasive way possible to provide us with the child's DNA. That on its own does not convey anything, simply indicating the blood type of the unborn child, even if its conception was unconventional. The story might well have ended there if it had not been for comparison with certain items that have been in the Church's possession for over two thousand years. I refer to sacred relics that have been protected and kept secret from the outside world until now.'

Emerging from a side door to the left of the pulpit, six cardinal priests in full ceremonial robes made their way towards the altar. Three carried caskets, each wrapped in a purple velvet cloth, whilst the others carried wooden stands which they positioned side by side on the flat marble surface of the altar. Once that was done, the first group of priests each placed a box on its stand and then simultaneously pulled away the cloths to reveal the three ancient reliquaries of Emperor Constantine, each now contained in their own transparent Perspex box.

Wilcox stretched out his hand towards these showpieces, his eyes never leaving the increasingly puzzled-looking faces of his audience. 'These caskets contain three items pertaining to our lord which were thought to be lost two millennia ago. One is the wooden sign fixed to the cross that Jesus Christ was crucified on. The second is the loincloth our saviour wore on the day of his execution.'

The sounds of shock and intrigue from those assembled now turned into a low rumble as many of them leant forward in their seats, attempting to get a better glimpse of the display contents as the Pope continued with his astonishing story.

'And the third is perhaps the most coveted relic of all: the crown of thorns Christ was forced to wear on that same terrible day.'

As the murmurs from the crowd began to rise to a crescendo, the pontiff raised both his arms in an effort to calm them. 'Please, ladies and gentlemen, allow me to finish.'

As the ripple of excitement abated, he went on, 'On each of these holy relics were found bloodstains, and under analysis, although degraded, we were able to extract a complete strand of DNA from all three. I can reveal to you now that they are an exact . . .'

Wilcox's voice tailed off as he caught sight of a familiar-looking figure making his way down the Cathedral nave towards the main doors. Clutching his shoulder for support was a young woman enveloped in the familiar red-and-black robe of a cardinal. The man glanced back for a split second, and, in that moment, John Wilcox locked eyes with Alex Harker who, with a wink, continued towards the main entrance.

A nervous unsettling sensation ran through John Wilcox's body, and he spun around to see an equally concerned-looking Cardinal Rocca already making his way towards one of the side doors at the rear of the basilica.

Standing in the nave, Detective Barbosa nudged Perone in the ribs as the superintendent stared disbelievingly at the Pope, straining to take in what this announcement actually meant.

'Boss, Rocca's on the move.'

It took another moment for the superintendent to snap out of it and a few more to wonder why his second in command was not as shocked as he was by the Pope's revelation until he recalled that the young officer didn't speak a word of English. 'OK, you stay here whilst I go and check on what Rocca is up to.'

Perone made his way quietly past the seated rows of politicians and interpreters and over to the door Cardinal Rocca had just disappeared through. His mind was buzzing with what he had just heard, and he felt light-headed, almost euphoric. Could it be true? The second coming?

Reaching the door, he made his way inside only to come face-to-face with Cardinal Vincenzo, hog-tied and laid out on one of the stone benches. Beyond him, Rocca was busily tapping at the numbers on his mobile phone, and Perone instinctively reached for his holster before remembering that it was empty. Even before he could withdraw his hand from underneath his jacket, Rocca was hurling himself forward with fists outstretched, sending both men to the ornately tiled floor with a thud.

The heels of Perone's leather brogue skidded vainly, attempting to maintain a grip on the polished surface as the cardinal clasped both hands firmly around the detective's throat and began squeezing with all his strength. If he intended to subdue the superintendent quickly, he failed totally, for Perone immediately thrust his knee violently into the cardinal's groin. Rocca released his grip and, with a yelp, retreated towards the opposite wall, cupping his crotch, but Perone was not about to allow him an inch. Still panting for breath, he was immediately on his feet and pressing his advantage. With both hands planted firmly around the clergyman's collar, he lifted him up and slammed him up against the door, which crashed open, sending the two men sprawling across the Cathedral floor before the eyes of the entire assembly. The two men stood up quickly and faced each other, but only Perone seemed aware of their shocked audience. A furious glare transformed Cardinal Rocca's face as he confronted the superintendent, seemingly oblivious to whatever else was going on around them. In this moment of utter insanity, he pulled a silver dagger from beneath his robe and lunged at Perone with a blood curdling cry. So lost was he in this moment of pure psychosis that he never even noticed that the two secret service agents protecting the French president were raising their 9 mm Glocks towards him. Cardinal Rocca made it only a few feet before he was struck by a fusillade of bullets, all in the chest and well grouped. The impact sent him flying backwards on to the floor with a crack to his skull, the glinting blade dropping from his hand and sliding into the office he had just hurtled out of.

No sooner had his body come to rest than chaos erupted, and dignitaries were being jostled out of their seats by suited agents and hustled efficiently down the long nave of the basilica towards the main entrance. Back at the altar, Perone was still frozen, his hands raised upwards in surrender as they had been since the first gun had been fired, but a high-pitched scream from behind made him spin around to see Pope Adrian VII raising his hands to his face, his mouth agast with an excruciating look of despair.

The Pope sank to his knees, his gaze fixed on the motionless body of his brother. There were many things that could have been running through John Wilcox's mind during such a moment—damage control or the whereabouts of the young mother pregnant with the Christ child—but as he stared into those dull eyes of the lifeless corpse no more than a few metres away, only two thoughts occupied his tormented mind.

How much he would miss his younger brother, and how the Templars and their lap dog, Alex Harker, would pay.

Chapter 50

Harker heard the muffled sound of two gunshots ring out from somewhere inside the cathedral within seconds of exiting its towering doors, but he was not about to go back and investigate. He had to keep moving, and, thankfully, the priest on watch at the basilica's entrance had hardly batted an eyelid at the odd couple. He was no doubt far too preoccupied with the Pope's earth-shattering disclosure to notice the man wearing a red party shirt and the young woman next to him swaddled in a cardinal's robe.

Up ahead, the majestic circular piazza was buzzing with activity because of tonight's event the area had been cordoned off, allowing access to media crews only. Scores of reporters, trailed by cameramen, were hovering only fifty metres away whilst further out were gathered crowds of ordinary well-wishers eager to witness the event first-hand. Apparently, no one had heard the two gunshots coming from inside the cathedral, to which Harker counted his blessings because the last thing he needed was a media frenzy. That would no doubt come later. His first instinct was to head for the journalists since there was no way even Genges would try to kill him on international television, but Harker's sense of logic now kicked in. Appearing in front of the world's press with a semi-conscious, half-naked pregnant woman would not look good, and, considering he had been wanted in connection with five murders earlier that day, he would undoubtedly be taken into police custody immediately. With him out of the way, it would only be a matter of time before the Magi had Ms Genova picked up, and that was not an option. No, he had to find a hospital and get her into the care of a doctor. From there, he could make some calls and figure out what to do next, but, first, it was all about the girl and the unborn child inside her.

The Italian girl was at least standing upright, but, without a reducer drug to reverse the effects of her anaesthetic, there was no telling how long it would take until she snapped out of it completely. He kept his arm firmly wrapped around her waist and began making his way down the open-air corridor towards the Arco delle Campane, keeping hidden from public gaze as best he could. In decades gone by, the arch had housed two large bells used to announce mass, but they had been taken down years earlier, and the entrance was now used by the cardinals and priests as an easy access to the basilica without having to plough through the general crowds before and after prayers. On the other side of the wall, there was a car park and public payphone he could use to call a taxi—or at least there used to be.

It was a chance he would have to take. They were already through the arch, down the stairs, and heading towards the car park when he heard the clang of the basilica's heavy doors being flung wide open and the chaotic sound of security people running around the open space behind him. In the car park, he could hear several vehicles revving into action when he finally caught sight of the payphone up ahead. On reaching it, Harker started furiously rummaging around in his pocket for some change, propping Maria Genova on his knee, her head bobbing up and down as if she was a life-size ventriloquist's dummy. He finally located the one coin he had been looking for, trapped in the lining of his trouser pocket, and was just about to insert it when he felt something hard poke into the base of his spine.

'I don't think so, Professor.'

Genges stood directly behind him, tight-lipped and looking severely pissed off. 'You've caused us more than your fair share of trouble tonight, and that ends now.'

Nearby, more politicians were hurriedly being bundled into their respective limousines, completely oblivious to Harker's predicament.

'Now, let's move slowly and calmly, or I shoot you right where you stand.' The Magi prince dug the gun barrel in deeper.

'Over there,' he ordered, gesturing them towards an open gateway, and suddenly, they were in the serene surroundings of what looked like a mini-forest, a perfectly maintained courtyard filled with an assortment of trees, flowers, and tombstones. The smell of damp earth was strong as was the sap from the palm trees towering above them. They were greeted by two marble statues: a cardinal complete with a shepherd's crook on one side and the Emperor Charlemagne on the other. A sign over the gateway announced what Harker already knew—THE TEUTONIC CEMETERY.

It was on this very site that the Emperor Nero's circus had been built to give the people of Rome the excitement of fights to the death for their entertainment, and more famously where St Peter had been crucified upside down—as was his last wish so as not to emulate his mentor Jesus Christ. Millennia later, the site had been turned into a cemetery here in the centre of the Vatican, honouring the many Christians that had died there.

'An appropriate place for you to meet your end,' Genges spat, still trying to control his rage, 'and fully deserved considering the amount of trouble you've caused us.'

Maria Genova clung to his arm as Harker turned to face the Magi assassin. 'You're nothing but a cheap hood, a career criminal Genges. You and your brothers deserve everything you get.'

The man's expression of anger was gradually replaced with an expression of confidence. 'What we are doing is for the benefit of over one billion people through the restoration of their faith. There are times, as your girlfriend, Claire Dwyer, already stated Professor Harker, when the ends *do* justify the means.'

Harker recoiled instinctively. 'And that includes killing Father Reed in cold blood does it? He was a good man, a true man of God, and yet you seemed to enjoy it.'

Genges shook his head slowly. 'Your precious Father Reed belongs to the old world and would have as much relevance in the new Church as you yourself do.' The same psychopathic grin Genges had displayed down in the necropolis was now back with a vengeance. 'It's not my fault if I enjoy my work, and, with that in mind, it's time to say adieu, Professor Harker.'

In one swift motion, he unsheathed his arm-sword and swept the steel blade across Harker's chest, cutting deep into the sinew of his ribs and sending him back on to the grass verge. At the same, and with no one to support her, Maria Genova dropped on to the hard gravel path like a rock. Tears began to well in her eyes as she instinctively rolled on to her back, clutching at her stomach, the pain finally dispelling the last vestiges of anaesthetic in her system. Harker tried to call out to her, but the shock of seeing a diagonal red line oozing across his chest made him choke.

'You see, Professor, all your meddling will not have changed anything,' Genges snarled as he stood over the fragile Italian woman and gestured with his sword at the red bloodstain pooling between her legs. 'Except for the timing. We Magi have waited over a thousand years for an opportunity like this. We can wait a little longer.'

He pressed the tip of the blade against the girl's face who immediately pushed it away. Her eyes were now fully open, but she let out a whimper as if not sure whether she was awake or asleep. 'As for this creature, she is no longer of any use to us, though she could have been the next holy mother.' He let out a deep sigh. 'Now the honour will have to go to another. Goodbye, my lady.'

Genges had raised his arm-sword above his head, ready to plunge it into the girl in front of him, when a familiar husky voice called out from behind.

'Just like the Magi to cut down a helpless woman.'

Harker turned his head towards the dark silhouette standing in the cemetery entrance, trying to catch a glimpse of the man's face. But he already knew who it was because the voice was unmistakable.

Sebastian Brulet strode out of the shadows to face his sworn enemy. He was dressed in a long black overcoat with the now familiar black Kevlar combat armour underneath. A thin brimmed trilby covered his silver hair, and his steely gaze was fixed on the quivering sword still raised above Genges's head.

'When will you people learn that murder is not the only solution?'

Struggling to accept the person standing in front of him, it took a few seconds for Genges to respond, 'Brulet? No, that's impossible! I saw you die.'

The Grand Master of the Templars shook his head gracefully. 'No, Genges, you saw the room you believed me to be in blown-up, and there's a difference. Luckily, I have had escape routes built into every room of every Templar safe house for just such an occasion.'

The Magi captain's jaw muscles tightened as he realised the novice's mistake he himself had made.

'Always check your kill and always dispose of it,' Brulet added. 'Without your help, however, I wouldn't be standing here. If you had just slung in that grenade before mouthing off a lot of useless rhetoric, the blast probably would have caught me.' The Master Templar gave a snort. 'Thank the Lord, your mouth is bigger than your brain.'

Genges lowered the sword and took a step forward. 'Maybe it's just as well you aren't dead. It means I get to dispatch my father's murderer in the ways of the old code.' He raised the blade upwards as Brulet now released his own arm-sword into place with a sharp click. 'And I'm going to enjoy it too.'

Both men stood facing the other with no more than a few metres between them and each displaying a mutual scowl of contempt.

'Be warned, Brulet, there is no better swordsman than me. In the art of steel, I have no equal,' Genges boasted confidently. 'We both live by the sword, Templar filth, but today, only you will die by it.'

A thin smile crossed Brulet's lips, and suddenly his sword retracted upwards into his sleeve. Then, in the blink of an eye, he reached into his pocket, pulled out a black silenced pistol, and aimed it directly at the dark prince's forehead. 'You're absolutely right.'

A single shot from its barrel splattered the back of his skull against the trunk of a palm tree directly behind him, and the Magi's body went limp before dropping to the ground with a heavy thud, dark blood seeping out on to the grass underneath.

Within seconds, two other men appeared at the entrance and carefully lifted up Maria Genova, wrapping a warm blanket around her as Brulet made his way swiftly to Harker's side. Without a word, he ripped open the Party Cruise T-shirt, now saturated with blood, and began to examine the deep cut.

'Don't worry, Professor, it's just a flesh wound,' Brulet announced assuredly.

'It doesn't feel like it,' grumbled Harker, exhaling frothy bubbles that dribbled down his chest. In fact, the sword had punctured his lung, and a severe pain descended on his abdomen as it tried to re-inflate with every breath he attempted. *Oh God, is this it?* he wondered, instantly trying to dismiss the odious thought. No, surely it couldn't be. He wasn't ready to go yet, and there was so much still to see in the world.

Harker clutched at his wounded chest as the pain continued to intensify. By now, his eyesight was beginning to dull, and, as his vision descended into blackness, he felt a strong arm around his waist pulling him upwards. As his senses finally began to desert him, he was still aware of Brulet's voice, nearby.

'Now, now, Professor, you're not getting away that easily. We've got far too much to discuss.'

Chapter 51

The plump nurse once again rapped a knuckle against his hospital room door whilst balancing a plastic dinner tray on her other palm. Behind her, a long white corridor extended a hundred metres back to the cafeteria she had just fetched it from. It was her fifth such delivery of the morning, and her knees were already aching at the thought of a tough day ahead.

Rapping harder this time, she pushed her way through the door to find her patient sitting up in bed and wearing earphones, as he watched the television fixed to the opposite wall. Letting the door slam shut behind her, she placed the plastic tray on the raised table in front of him. 'You spend far too much time watching television, Professor. It's not good for you. Now come on eat up.'

Harker sighed grudgingly, slipped off the headphones, and stared down at the metal plate cover. 'Let me guess, its rubber steak again?' He forced a smile; he had been in this hospital for over a month, and, four times a week, it was the same thing.

'You better make it quick because you've got a visitor on the way. He should be arriving in a few minutes.'

Harker gave up a groan. 'Dean Lercher strikes again.'

The nurse carefully tucked in his blankets and made her way back to the door. 'I wasn't given a name, but it could be. Enjoy,' she said sympathetically with a wink before leaving to continue her rounds.

Doggie had been a constant visitor to his bedside since being admitted to the hospital. At first, it was a comfort to have his friend keep him company, discussing their amazing adventure as the dean referred to it, but, after a month, they had both run out of things to say, so they just kept rehashing the same old conversations over and over. To say it was becoming tedious was a complete understatement.

Harker pushed the unappetising plateful to one side and reached for the remote control, turning up the volume and focusing his attention once again on the Sky News report he had been following.

'And so closes the latest chapter of the Vatican scandal that has rocked the Catholic Church to its core. Authorities are still at a loss to explain the events leading up to the shooting of Cardinal Giuseppe Rocca inside St Peter's Cathedral a little over a month ago. The reason for Cardinal Vincenzo's abduction and Cardinal Rocca's connection with a string of murders is still shrouded in secrecy as Church leaders in the upper echelons of the Vatican continue to remain tight-lipped about the whole affair. What's even more worrying still to millions of devout Catholics is the disappearance of Pope Adrian VII himself soon after the shooting. Despite efforts by both law-enforcement and religious officials alike, the ex-Pope has yet to be found and still casts an ominous shadow over the inauguration of Cardinal Salvatore Vincenzo as supreme pontiff more than two weeks ago. Pope Gregory XVII, as he is now known, was formally president of the Vatican's Governorate, which oversees all the Church's finances and state security. After being abducted by Cardinal Rocca, his strength and leadership in recent weeks ensured he was a favoured candidate for the papacy and many have since welcomed his liberal thinking as an important means of bringing many back into the Catholic fold by promising reform. It is for this reason Cardinal Vincenzo took the same name as Pope Gregory VII, who was famed for purifying the Church during the eleventh century after its clergy had fallen into disrepute. But, with the previous Pope's disappearance still a mystery and the investigation into Cardinal Rocca's dealings yielding few results, many are expecting a difficult road ahead for the Catholic Church. In connected news, the policeman who initially linked Cardinal Rocca to these crimes and was himself there on night of the shooting has once again made a general plea for anyone to come forward with information as to the identity of a suspect who committed suicide in a Rome jail on the same night.'

The report flicked to a clip of Superintendent Perone, surrounded by Dictaphones and gruffly waving his finger. 'No matter what it takes, the police will identify this dead boy and trace his involvement with Cardinal Rocca.' Behind him, Detective Angelo Barbosa watched on silently as his boss continued to stress his point.

'Because no one is above the law. Not even a cardinal.'

Harker pressed the mute button, deciding he had heard enough. After being dropped off almost half-dead at the entrance of the Ospedale Santo Spirito, just a mile from Vatican City, he had fallen into a coma and had stayed that way for over week. After finally waking up, the doctors had informed him that if the blade had penetrated an inch to the left; it would have pierced his heart and killed him instantly.

'You're lucky to be alive, Mr Harker. It seems someone up there is keeping an eye on you.' The truth of the comment had not even registered with Harker whose thoughts had been, and still were, wholly preoccupied with the safety of Maria Genova and her child, if it had survived. *Were they OK and where were they now?* Those were questions he could not voice out loud, even to Doggie.

Once he was safely on the mend, Superintendent Perone and his assistant had paid him a visit, but nothing had come of it. Since the arrest of Drazia Heldon by the British authorities, many of the murders Harker had been originally accused of were now attributed to the Magi hit man. The giant brute had been confronted on his way out of the museum, shooting at a policeman whilst attempting his getaway, and had been finally wrestled to the ground by no less than ten uniformed police. There were still been many unanswered questions, but the superintendent had been persuaded that Harker had not been directly involved. He also mentioned the heat he had been getting from the top brass to leave the Cambridge professor out of his investigation: a parting gift from Brulet and a testament to the Templars' power around the globe. In fact, the only authority that had interviewed Harker, apart from Perone, had been the FAA regarding the downed jet in Lake Bracciano. Doggie had diverted most of the attention for that one, and the crash was judged to be an unavoidable accident. They even went so far as to hail Harker a hero for bringing the aircraft down without loss of life. No one was even aware of the death of John Caster, as his body had mysteriously disappeared from the wreck, and the pilot's body, when recovered, had been recorded as having suffered a heart attack that set off the series of events leading to the crash.

The Templar organisation, it seemed, had not kept itself off the radar for hundreds of years just by chance, and something Brulet told him back at the villa had proved it. 'The Magi and Templars are unified in one cause and one cause only—to keep their respective existences hidden from the rest of the world.'

That was clearly the truth, for even Genges' body had disappeared mysteriously from the Teutonic cemetery, and no trace of blood had been found anywhere. To cap it all off, when the authorities had subsequently searched the Academy of Sciences, the secret entrance behind the portrait of Isaac Newton had been filled in with cement. Even though the police were keen to excavate it, the Church had refused and that had been that. Harker had not even mentioned to anyone the underground Magi headquarters, so, at first, he was puzzled as to how the authorities came to know of its existence, but after hearing on the news that a cardinal priest had also survived a shooting on the same night Cardinal Rocca had died, it all made sense. Father Reed's military training had served him well, and he had managed to make it out of the necropolis and into the open before the Vatican police found him. His survival was one piece of news that Harker had welcomed wholeheartedly.

Superintendent Perone had tried to question him about the underground den, but he had kept his mouth firmly shut, and after the Church had closed ranks around Father Reed, the story had disappeared. Harker's own silence, unfortunately, had not been emulated by Doggie, and he had only just managed to convince his old friend to keep quiet about the two organisations, much to the Dean's frustration. 'How can we keep it quiet, Alex? The people of the world deserve to know. Two secretive organisations fighting a war in the shadows for the direction of Christianity for well over a millennium, my God man, how can we not say something?'

Harker had to illuminate the dean on the danger to his life, not from him but at the hands of the same shadowy organisations he threatened to expose. Doggie had eventually agreed to keep quiet but not without a caveat. 'I won't say a thing, but I want your word that you'll keep me in the loop for the future. If you discover anything new, I want your word that you'll tell me.'

Harker had agreed, even though the promise was a lie in itself. If Doggie were to discover the full extent of the Magi's plans regarding the Christ child, he would never have been able to stay silent, whatever the danger, and there was no way Harker wanted Doggie's welfare on his conscience.

He took a long sip from his box of juice and mulled over the fate of the young Maria Genova. He remembered seeing blood on her dress just shortly before losing consciousness. Did it signify a miscarriage? Had the child been lost? After over a month with no further word from Brulet, it was a question that would have to remain unanswered, at least for now.

He felt his stomach spasm at the thought of knowing so much and yet so little. It would be difficult to simply go back to the world of archaeology which now appeared somewhat inconsequential to him. But he was reassured by a single thought. Imagine how much else there might be waiting to be discovered?

A sharp knock on the door distracted him from such thoughts.

'Come in, Doggie. I've been expecting you,' Harker called out, though dreading the same old thread of conversation that now awaited him.

The door swung open, and a tall man in a black suit and trilby hat quietly entered the room.

'Professor Alex Harker?'

The sight of the man in front of him and his startling green eyes almost made Harker drop his juice box. His visitor was of a formidable size, and Harker was already reacting to the alarm bells sounding off in his head. Trying to remain as nonchalant as possible, he scanned his table tray for any suitable weapon but saw only the plastic cutlery. He grabbed the knife and pointed it at the stranger. It was merely a symbolic gesture since the blunt utensil could barely penetrate his steak, let alone a man's chest. Harker suddenly felt like a complete berk.

'Yes, I'm Alex Harker. What do you want?'

The man removed his hat to reveal the familiar-looking silver-coloured hair that immediately put Harker at ease. Surely, this man was a Templar.

The visitor placed the trilby to his chest and offered a courteous bow. 'I come to you with an invitation from an old friend of mine—and a new friend of yours. There is a car waiting downstairs to take you to a meeting with him.' The messenger hesitated for a moment as he scrutinised the patient. 'If you have not sufficiently recovered from your wounds, I have been instructed to arrange a more suitable time.'

The man had hardly finished his sentence before Harker was hopping out of bed, on to his feet and heading for the wardrobe. 'No, I'm ready to go.' He reached in and pulled out a shirt and trousers. 'How long will it take to get there?'

'I'm sorry, but I can't tell you that.'

Harker hurriedly pulled on a pair of socks. 'OK, well can you tell me where we're going?'

The Templar once again shook his head. 'Sorry, Professor, I can't do that either.'

Harker stripped to his waist, threw on a white shirt, and then began to undo the button on his green hospital trousers, stopping just short of revealing his modesty. 'Well, how about giving me some privacy. Can you do that?'

The hefty Templar smiled. 'That, I can do.'

Chapter 52

The smooth buzz of the Mercedes Benz's engine calmed Harker's frenzied thoughts as the vehicle made its way through the narrow streets. It was the first time in a month that he had even been outside the hospital, and the experience was making him feel light-headed and dizzy. On the streets outside, Rome's residents were going about their daily business, and he realised how much he had missed the routine of daily life. The car slowed to let a couple of priests make their way to mass, followed by four youngsters dressed in the white robes of choirboys. It was sights like this he had missed during the past month, the vibrancy of a city and its people.

As the Benz sped up again, it suddenly dawned on Harker that this was a Sunday, confirming that he had totally lost track of the days whilst recovering from his injuries. He glanced at his watch, which read 11 a.m. All over Rome, people would be making their way to mass in one of the nine hundred Catholic churches spread across the city, and the idea of all that activity created a warm feeling in his chest after a month of complete boredom.

The car turned left along an avenue crowded with such people, and he wondered if they had any idea of the battles taking place all around them—battles for their very faith and beliefs. If they could be made privy to the ongoing war between the Magi and the Templars, and how Jesus Christ had almost walked the earth for a second time, how would the Catholic world . . . no, the Christian world take it?

The Mercedes pulled up at the end of a side street, and his guide opened the door and ushered him out on to the pavement. Harker took a moment to gaze up at the building in front of him. He recognised it immediately as the church of San Benedetto, one of the smallest in Rome, tucked away just off a main road. He had visited it many years ago with Archie, and both had been impressed by the majestic sculptures that adorned the interior and exterior of such a seemingly small, insignificant edifice.

'This way, Professor,' the Templar beckoned, and Harker followed his escort through the imposing entrance doors and into the church itself, where ten people occupied the two tiny pews as a grey-haired priest took his position in front of the altar.

'It's just down here,' the Templar whispered, pointing out a set of steep, narrow steps leading down to a lower level. 'I'll be waiting up here to take you back to the hospital.' He noticed his guest's look of uncertainty and once again pointed downwards. 'Please, you're expected.'

Harker cautiously descended the steps. At the bottom, he found an open doorway, where a voice he knew all too well called out to him. 'In here, Professor.'

Harker entered to find himself in a room bigger than the church upstairs and he was immediately greeted by the familiar sight of Brulet wearing his pair of chic aviation sunglasses that glinted in the light as he marched over and shook Harker by the hand. 'Well, you definitely look much better now than when last we met.'

Harker let go of the handshake and lifted his shirt to reveal the fresh bandages strapped across his chest. 'I even have a souvenir to remember you by.'

The Grand Master gave deep laugh. 'Quite so, and what a souvenir it's going to be! Please take a seat.'

Harker sat himself down on the simple wooden chair opposite Brulet, wincing at the pain of his healing wound. The souvenir was still pretty raw.

'Well, Alex, with your help, we've landed a major blow on the Magi, but be under no illusions that they're not out of it by a long shot. There are plenty of other family members seeking to fill the empty positions Genges and his brothers have left behind. I can assure you that John Wilcox will be already planning his next move, but, thanks to you, we now know who he is, and that means he won't be able to slip by so easily without being noticed. It also helps to have purged the mole from our own organisation, whose help to the Magi cause is well and truly over.' Brulet gave a satisfied smile.

'You mean Lusic?'

'Yes, and believe me when I tell you that his days of spying are at an end. To cross your own brothers in arms deserves the worst punishment imaginable, and that nasty little traitor cost the lives of many Knights' good men who died because of his lust for power. He, unfortunately, escaped in all the confusion, but we'll find him. After all, the world is a small place when you're on the run.'

His answer was unsettling, and it reminded Harker how little he knew about the man sitting opposite him. 'You're not going to kill him, are you?'

Brulet looked genuinely offended. 'We are not common murderers, Alex. The Templars believe in fairness, justice, and the truth above all else. We leave the grotesqueries of human nature to the Magi. But when one of our own betrays us in the way that Lusic has done, then it must be treated as an exception, and there are worse things on this earth than just death.' Brulet's eyes narrowed cunningly at the thought before he changed the subject. 'Well, what a world you now find yourself in and what a story lies behind it. It's a shame you can never tell anyone.' He winked, and, for a moment, Harker had a horrible feeling he was about to be executed on the spot. But Brulet noticed the stiffening of his body and reached over to tap him reassuringly on the shoulder. 'My dear, Professor, the Knights

Templars do not reward their friends with violence. And you have proved yourself to be a very trustworthy ally even if you have spoken about us to your friend Dean Lercher.'

Harker froze again. *Was there anything Brulet didn't know?*

'No matter, because without proof, it is just hearsay. But . . .' The Grand Templar raised a white finger to his lips. 'That's where it ends. The truths you have learnt must stay a secret. Understand?'

'I understand, but . . .' He could hardly bring himself to ask the question. 'There's one thing I need to know. Did the mother and child survive?'

Brulet stood up and pushed open a door just to the right of where they were sitting. 'Why don't you see for yourself?'

Harker pulled himself out of the chair, ignoring the ever-throbbing pain in his chest, and made his way over to the doorway. There, in a comfortable-looking armchair, sat Maria Genova in a flowing white dress. In her arms, she cuddled a baby with wispy black hair and olive-toned skin.

'She doesn't remember anything much and we have decided to leave it that way for the moment. In time, we will explain to her what really happened during her stay at the Vatican and how she managed to end up in our care but suffice to say she has no memory of you.' Brulet gripped his shoulder tightly. 'But I promise you, in time, she will.'

Maria Genova looked up at the pair of them and smiled as the baby in her arms continued sleeping peacefully. Harker struggled to contain the feeling of overwhelming love aroused by the sight in front of him that he had to bite his cheek to stop himself from gasping. 'Is he, different?'

Brulet shrugged his shoulders. 'It's too early to say, but we will find out in due course. The important thing is that he is allowed to grow up and decide for himself. If it is meant to be, then it is meant to be. His *brother* preached that all people should be free to live their lives in peace, and I will offer this little one nothing less.'

As Harker watched the young mother embracing her child, their eyes locked, and, for a moment, he thought he saw a spark of recognition flicker in the young Italian girl's dark, brown pupils. She tilted her head to one side as if trying to figure out why the younger man in front of her looked so familiar. Then the spark was gone.

'Yes,' Brulet continued, 'give it time, and she may remember. And, if not, I'm sure you will be happy to pop in from time to time to help jog her memory.'

It took a second for Harker to register what the Templar had just said. 'Pop in?' He had assumed this would be the last time he ever encountered the Templars. 'You mean I can come back? But you told me that only Templars may know your world.'

'Yes, well, I'm sure we can think of something. Follow me.'

Brulet gently closed the door behind them and calmly made his way down the adjacent passageway, heading deeper into the chapel's basement, until they arrived at a bronze door adorned with many different symbols, most of which Harker recognised, but some he did not. They included the Christian cross, the Jewish Star of David, and the Islamic crescent moon, the eight-spoked wheel symbolising Buddhism, the yin and yang of Chinese Taoism—in fact, symbols representing almost every major religion in the world. In the very centre, surrounded by the other religious icons, sat two larger symbols: the Maltese cross of the Knights Hospitaller and the iconic emblem of the Knights Templars.

'What is this place?' Harker asked.

Brulet reached out and rested his hand on the time-darkened metal handle. 'This, friend, is a sacred place. One of only four existing in the world: this one here, one in London, one in Jerusalem, and one in the United States.' An odd look flickered through Brulet's eyes, a conflicting mixture of peacefulness, confidence, and sheer aggression. It was such a strange expression that Harker felt his stomach frisson with excitement.

'It is here that Knights of the Order are initiated under the watchful eyes of God, and it is here you will find your destiny.' Brulet pushed open the door to reveal a modest domed chapel half as big as the one above. The walls were covered with images of saints and prophets, running along both sides of the room, whilst at the far end stood a magnificent white marble altar bearing a variety of religious statues. But what really caught Harker's attention was not the artistic riches but the eight men equipped with shiny silver breastplates and swords who lined the aisle—each one, staring at him without emotion.

Brulet took Harker by the arm and guided him towards the altar, the Knights saying nothing, only following the new arrival with their eyes. They were of all different ethnicities—Asian, Chinese, Arab, European, African, and Japanese—all stood there and watched him silently.

Brulet stopped before the altar, situated directly below a mosaic unlike any Harker had seen before. It looked like a Roman design but instead of being composed of ceramic tiles, they were made of gold, silver, and bronze. Together they made up a map of the world with the countries in bronze, the seas in silver, and all the capital cities indicated by thick decorative golden wedges. It was one of the most impressive pieces of craftsmanship he had ever seen and was still admiring it as Brulet finally began to speak. 'Leaders of the Templar Nation, you have been summoned here on this day to witness the induction of a new member to our Order. So say I.'

'And so say we,' the other Templars replied in unison.

'The man who stands before us has shown himself to be worthy of the code that binds us, showing namely courage, respect, honesty, and integrity. But more than that, he has revealed himself to possess one of the most important traits of all—a protector of the needy. And it is these values that have guided the Knights Templars for almost a thousand years, and it is these same qualities that will safeguard the people of the world during the next thousand. And so now I ask that you, the high council of the Knights Templars, do bestow upon this worthy candidate the right to join with us and defend the faith that reveres one God above all men.'

'Harker heard the unsheathing of swords behind him, and the eight Templars then surrounded him, resting the tips of their silver sword blades upon his shoulder in turn.'

'Now kneel.' Brulet gently pushed Harker down on to one knee before drawing his own sword and tapping him lightly on each shoulder and finally on the top of his head.

'Do you, Alex Harker, swear to protect the weak and defend, by your actions, the incorruptible word of God and all it stands for?'

'Yes, I do.' Harker was surprised at how easily the words emerged from his mouth, but it felt right to him, and he spoke it without hesitation, much to the satisfaction of Brulet.

'Then let it be known throughout the Order that from this day onwards, you shall be known as Knight Alexander, defender of the faith and protector of the weak. Now rise, Sir Alexander, and greet your new brothers.'

The Templars sheathed their swords and waited for their newest member to rise to his feet. Harker could feel beads of sweat forming on his forehead, even though the room was noticeably cold, and he was finding it difficult to focus on any thoughts at all. Once back on his feet, the high council of Templars began to embrace him in turn, each with broad smiles on their faces. Once that was done, they silently made their way out of the chapel, leaving Harker and Brulet alone.

'Well, good knight, welcome to the Order.'

The mental fog that had overcome him just minutes earlier cleared and Harker's mind was suddenly screaming with questions.

'Don't you think you should have warned me first?'

'I'm sorry, Alex, but no potential member is ever told beforehand. It must be decided upon in the moment. It is like falling in love—you know it's right or not right, but either way in your heart, your gut, you just know. It has been done like this for centuries, I hope you were not too taken aback.'

'Taken aback? Yes, you could say that. I just wish you'd given me time to think about it. I'm an ex-Catholic priest, and I'm not sure how this will sit with my conscience.' Harker was starting to feel like he just got mugged.

'Professor, your induction into the Order was decided upon by me personally, and as such your membership will be treated as a special case. I am not expecting you to become involved in any actions undertaken by the Templars. Not unless you want to. Your task is to do one thing and one thing only—to protect the truths you have learnt during these past few days. Outside of that, you may be as involved or as uninvolved as you want, but there's something you must know. You will always have a friend in the Templars, and if you ever need our help, then all you need do is ask.'

Brulet pulled out a business card from his trouser pocket and passed it over. It was blank except for a single telephone number. 'Simply call this number, leave a message, and after that just wait. We will find you.'

The unsettling feeling in Harker's stomach began to subside, and he let out a tight-lipped laugh. 'If anyone had ever told me I would become a Templar, I'd have had them committed.'

'And if you do ever tell anyone, I'll have *you* committed,' Brulet replied jokingly but meaning it. The Grand Templar gestured towards the exit, and the two Knights made their way out of the chapel, stopping briefly at the doorway.

'I had no idea how far and wide the Templars organisation extended.' Harker pointed to the door itself, covered with symbols.

'Religions are devised by man and for man, but there is one constant running throughout that binds all faiths—one god, the same God. It is only how we pray to him that distinguishes us from each other, and that is the Lord God we Templars serve, nothing more, nothing less.'

The point was simple but struck a chord with Harker. After all, he had lost faith in men, some men, but never in God—and he could live with that.

'So what now?'

'There's a car already waiting to take you back to the hospital. As for me, I have a certain matter to attend to.' As usual with Brulet, the answer was cryptic, but there were still a few things Harker needed to know before they parted ways because there was no telling how long it might be before Brulet would make another appearance.

'What are you going to do to Lusic?'

Brulet laughed out loud. 'I'm afraid some things are above your right to know, Alex, but if it troubles your conscience that much, then I will let you know when we do finally catch up with him.'

Harker nodded uncertainly. 'And what about Maria and the child?'

Brulet smiled knowingly as if he had been waiting for that question to arise. 'As I said, they will both get a chance to live a normal life. We will relocate them somewhere safe and then keep a watchful eye on them.'

Harker still felt concerned by the answer as Brulet could tell. If anyone ever learnt the truth, then every crazy under the sun would be after her.

'Professor, relax. Believe me when I say she will be totally safe. Now go back to the hospital and rest and then get yourself back to the UK and your students ASAP.'

Harker gave his most confident smile and nodded. His gut told him that this whole thing was too important to be over, and, so far, Brulet had been on the money about everything. *Damn,* he thought, *is this man ever wrong?*

Chapter 53

Harker dropped his leather satchel on to the thick Persian floor rug before falling face down on to the bed with a heavy groan. *What a day!* He'd taught four lessons, had to reprimand six students for shoddy work, and supervised an examination as a favour to a flu-ridden professor. All in all, he was absolutely shattered. To make matters worse, he was being forced into attending a black-tie exhibition on Neolithic artefacts later that evening, which Doggie had sprung on him just minutes before packing up for the day.

'Come on, Alex, my dates backed out, and you know this Neolithic stuff isn't my thing. C'mon, do me a favour,' his friend had begged. 'I'm sure there will be a few attractive fillies for you to engage with.'

Harker had burst into laughter. *Attractive women at a Neolithic artefacts exhibition?* That was a joke. It was far more likely to be full of bearded old men in tweed jackets, all smoking pipes. Of course, he had agreed eventually, though reluctantly.

'Having good friends is overrated,' he now grumbled into the duvet. 'Bloody overrated.'

Since getting back from Italy a week ago, he was struggling to get himself back into the swing of things. So much had happened in such a short time, and now everything seemed . . . well, a bit mundane. He didn't miss fighting off attacks on his life; that was for sure, but he just felt left out of the loop, and it was frustrating. Several times, he had to stop himself from calling the number Brulet had given him. Common sense had prevailed in the end because after all, what message could he have left anyway? 'Oh, hi there. I've just called to see what your secretive organisation has been up to lately. Discovered any fresh plots for world domination?'

That would have gone down like a lead balloon with his new Templar brothers.

He hauled himself off the bed and stepped over to the large picture window overlooking Midsummer Common and the enticing skyline of Cambridge beyond it. Down below, bathed in the yellow hue of street lights, the road was still full of life. A city never sleeps—people walking dogs, a couple arguing, and a cyclist cursing the white van that had nearly clipped him. If only these people knew of the shadow world that operated around them without their knowledge and if they did get to know, would they be protesting in the streets or would it be just another headline that simply faded from people's minds within a few months as newer, more exciting news stories filled their short-term memories? Harker shook his head at the thought. No, it was too big for that, and it would have created an outcry if not mayhem in the Western world whilst here he was with full knowledge and no one he could tell.

On the side table behind him, his iPhone pinged to signal the arrival of a new message, and he reluctantly picked it up. It was probably Doggie expecting a lift to his crappy exhibition. Harker pressed the messages button, and a PDF file attached to a short note popped up with no details of the sender. It read simply: 'Translated for you. Enjoy and then destroy. SB.'

He double-tapped the file, and the first of fifty pages appeared on the small LCD screen, bearing a single title: 'The Testament of Jesus of Nazareth'.

Harker almost dropped the phone in surprise, and he immediately reached for the landline.

'Doggie, it's Alex. I'm sorry but something much more important has come up. I'm going to have to take a rain check. Sorry, mate, I owe you one.'

'Oh, great, thanks a lot, you bastard.' Harker hung up before his friend had time to finish. The resentful dean would be a total pain in the arse tomorrow, but he'd survive, and this text his mobile was now displaying was far too intriguing to leave for even a second.

Harker sank back into his brown leather armchair and began to devour every word appearing on the screen.

'Yeah baby,' he shouted at the top of his voice. 'I'm back in the loop.'

Chapter 54

Maria Genova tossed back her thick curly black hair and let the cool breeze sweep over her. It felt good to finally be outside after so many months being stuck indoors even if she didn't remember much of it. What had Mr Brulet called it? Retrograde amnesia? It was something to do with being under the anaesthetic for too long during the birth of her son. The fact was she couldn't even remember who the father was, let alone the occasion of getting pregnant. If it had not been for that Catholic care organisation headed by Mr Brulet himself, she dreaded to think what her situation would now be. She had never encountered what she considered to be an albino before, and the sight of him had initially struck fear into her, but she had eventually come to recognise that he had only her best interests at heart. The Christian organisation had provided her with a lifeline, and, until her memory came back fully, she was happy to stay in its care.

Maria gazed lovingly down at the sleeping baby in her arms, snugly wrapped in a thick woollen blanket. Oddly, for the moment anyway, all her troubles seemed irrelevant. Her newborn was healthy, and the bond of love she felt for him was growing stronger day by day, so for the time being any questions could wait. She gazed out across the still waters of Lake Okeechobee and sighed happily. 'What a beautiful view!'

She had arrived in Florida just a few months earlier, but her grasp of English was already impressive, and she now found herself conversing regularly with her escorts in their native tongue. On her arrival, she had been escorted immediately to a somewhat isolated log cabin in Belle Glade, less than half a mile from this wonderfully scenic spot overlooking the lake which, according to the brochure, was the largest freshwater lake in the state.

The shoreline was dotted with keen fishermen and couples enjoying a leisurely afternoon stroll. Maria could not imagine a more peaceful place on earth. Of course, she could not really remember anywhere else, due to the amnesia, but she bet that if she could, this view would remain amongst her favourites. Overhead, the blue sky was starting to turn grey, and she felt a speck of rain on her arm. Within seconds, it would be pouring, which was typical of the Florida weather as she had discovered.

The escort provided by Mr Brulet had gone to pick up some groceries from the local shop and would be back in a few minutes, so she hurried over to the tree line, covering the child as best she could. There she found herself huddling next to another woman seeking refuge under the same tree.

'Weather here's like nothing I've come across before,' the woman remarked. 'Not like back home, that's for sure.'

Maria nodded courteously before returning her attention to the child and wiping a few droplets from his forehead. The other woman peered curiously at the child. 'Oh, isn't that sweet? How old is he?'

'Two months.' Maria said proudly.

The woman's lips curled in delight. 'They're so cute at that age. You really need to treasure these early days because they'll be gone so quickly.'

Maria finished mopping the baby's brow and held him up for the woman to get a better look.

'Oh, he's just so precious. May I hold him?'

Maria hesitated for just a moment before reconsidering. 'Of course.'

The woman took the child in her arms and gently rocked him back and forth. 'What a special little man he is, and so beautiful! Oh, how rude! Let me introduce myself.' She offered her hand. 'My name's Claire . . . Claire Dwyer.'

The End

Acknowledgments

I would like to give a special thanks to my editor, Peter Lavery, for the generosity of his time and taking a shot on an unknown. I will always be grateful.

My thanks to Mandy O'Reilly for her keen grammar skills and continuing support throughout the writing of this book.

I thank Liam O'Rafferty of Red Rocket Graphic design for the bookcover.

And just as importantly to Mum, Dad, Tamsyn, and Alex.

26581975R00231

Made in the USA
Lexington, KY
23 December 2018